CELESTINA'S HOUSE

CELESTINA'S HOUSE

Clarissa Trinidad Gonzalez

RARE
MACHINES

Publisher: Meghan Macdonald | Acquiring editors: Julia Kim & Kwame Scott Fraser | Editor: Julia Kim
Cover images: figure: Yuliya Kashirina/adobestock.com; lizard: OGri/istock.com; flowers: Phairojn Fugtongyoo/shutterstock.com; background texture: Vincent Burkhead/unsplash.com

Library and Archives Canada Cataloguing in Publication

Title: Celestina's house / Clarissa Trinidad Gonzalez.
Names: Gonzalez, Clarissa Trinidad, author.
Identifiers: Canadiana (print) 20240310330 | Canadiana (ebook) 20240310365 | ISBN 9781459754003 (softcover) | ISBN 9781459754010 (PDF) | ISBN 9781459754027 (EPUB)
Subjects: LCGFT: Novels.
Classification: LCC PS8613.O57 C45 2024 | DDC C813/.6—dc23

We acknowledge the support of the Canada Council for the Arts and the Ontario Arts Council for our publishing program. We also acknowledge the financial support of the Government of Ontario, through the Ontario Book Publishing Tax Credit and Ontario Creates, and the Government of Canada.

Care has been taken to trace the ownership of copyright material used in this book. The author and the publisher welcome any information enabling them to rectify any references or credits in subsequent editions.

The publisher is not responsible for websites or their content unless they are owned by the publisher.

Printed and bound in Canada.

Rare Machines, an imprint of Dundurn Press
1382 Queen Street East
Toronto, Ontario, Canada M4L 1C9
dundurn.com, @dundurnpress

To my parents,
who always enjoyed a good story.
I think you'll like this one ...

Prologue

Ora Pro Nobis

The old crone lit a candle as she cast her mind across the Malate district, past the neon signs and girlie bars, to Remedios Circle, and finally to the grand house with the dragon gates. A *Hail Mary* came to her lips, as it had countless times before. A prayer for the house and its perturbed spirits.

In the shadow of the Nuestra Señora de los Remedios Church, the ancient woman sat, minding a stall filled with medallions, religious figurines, and candles.

Years ago, a young woman named Celestina had come by and bought a candle. "Please pray for my Great-Aunt Selena, and for my house," she had said. Every Wednesday she returned, until the day she left the country with a broken heart. Only heaven knew when, or if, she would be back. Still, the crone prayed — for Celestina, for the ghostly Selena, and for all the restless souls that walked the district.

After the prayers, the old woman crossed the churchyard and walked to Remedios Street, which was dotted with lurid signs announcing, "Happy Hour" and "Friendly Hostesses." In her mind,

Malate was still a village of genteel mansions, as it was before the war that forever changed the world.

The woman's eyes were cloudy now, but no matter. For endless time, she had witnessed earthquakes, typhoons, revolutions, and invasions as waves of conquerors had marched these streets and claimed Las Islas Filipinas as their own. After an eternity inhabiting these islands, she no longer needed eyes to see.

As she reached the wide lane that led to the dragon gates, the air carried a faint cry to her ear. The house had been vacant for years, but as the street people knew, in the depths of night, when the bars were dark, a sad kundiman ballad could be heard coming from the house, playing on an out-of-tune piano. The place was cursed, shadowed by tragedy and death. The old woman had once thought the young Celestina would break her family's chain of misfortune and live happily with her Mestiso. Perhaps she still could.

The crone uttered a short Latin prayer for Celestina's house, then started back to her stall for another long day of redeeming souls.

*

The dragons' glass eyes glowed as the setting sun blazed over Manila Bay. At half past five, trucks and trailers rolled into the lane where the grand house stood, bearing weather-beaten men with pickaxes and sledgehammers. The foreman was on a call with their client, the owner.

"I heard this joint is haunted. Is that true?" asked the man with an axe.

The men lit cigarettes and gaped uneasily at the creatures that guarded the gates.

"I don't know, but look at that dragon," the sledgehammer man said, pointing to the clawed feet that had broken free from their iron frames.

"That's just rust," a man holding a battered crowbar assured himself.

At six o'clock, a silver late-model Hummer quietly arrived and stopped at the edge of the work site. The foreman approached the Hummer and waited for his client to emerge. When the door opened and the man stepped out, he was well over six feet tall, with the broad shoulders and chest of a leading man from an old film noir. The man smiled as he took off his aviators. His complexion was like polished bronze, but his superbly chiselled face announced him as a genuine mestiso.

"Hello," the Mestiso said as he extended his hand.

"Pleased to meet you, señor," the foreman replied, trying not to stare.

The Mestiso had greenish eyes and almost blond hair — rare even among those with the blood of Kastilas and Amerikanos in their veins.

"My men are ready," the foreman said.

"I need some time," the Mestiso replied as he walked past the phalanx of trucks.

So many years ago, he had stood thunderstruck outside those very gates after he had followed a young woman home. With its serpentine roof and great puddle-shaped windows, the house looked like a many-eyed chimera that had seen much wonder and tragedy in its time.

The iron creaked with life as the Mestiso entered the gates. He stopped briefly by the broken fountain, from which thick vines had sprouted. Voracious weeds had long swallowed the cobblestones that led to the entrance hall. Inside, he walked past the wrought-iron and glass elevator, and ran up the winding stairs to the mezzanine apartment and entered. The wall of mirrors rekindled in him the memory of a long-ago dance he had shared with Celestina. Pressed against her supple body, he had guided her into a dip, lower and lower, until her hair grazed the mahogany floors and her scent filled his breath. He wanted to linger in this perfect memory, but the foreman was anxious to get started.

Reluctantly, the Mestiso continued his ascent to the third-floor apartment, which still had crates holding forgotten remnants of their former life. But those could wait. He pressed on to the atico apartment, where he had lived with Celestina in contented exile. His hands caressed the carved double doors as he entered their former domain. The great room smelled almost as it had during their life together, albeit faintly — the garlic, limes, and saffron of their cooking; the leather and paper of her books; and the jasmine from her skin that clung to him after they made love.

He made his way to the kitchen, where he spotted something painfully familiar: a long wooden stool fitted with a serrated circular blade. Almost nobody in the city would recognize this artifact now. Only people who had lived during the time of fresh coconuts would know to straddle the stool's long back, grate the white flesh against the blade, and squeeze the rich, fragrant cream from the shredded meat. For a moment, he was a young man again, full of fire, watching his lover work, fully aware of the erotic movement of her breasts.

He left the kitchen and made his way to the upper level of the atico but could not bring himself to enter their old bedroom. Too many memories. He had long meant to divest himself of this property. But how could he possibly hand this over to a stranger? This was not just a building; it was a vessel holding the life and love he had shared with Celestina.

As he descended the mahogany steps back to the great room of the atico, he felt a breeze, soft as a whisper, caress him. The small hairs on his nape bristled. It was the ghostly Selena, humming a tragic kundiman in his ear.

When the Mestiso finally emerged from the house, the district's darkening sky was awash with neon lights. He nodded silently to the foreman before walking back to his Hummer and driving away.

"Let's go!" the foreman shouted to his crew.

At his word, the salvage team advanced on the building with their hand tools and gas-powered chainsaws. Oblivious to the beauty they were dismantling, these hard men saw only metal, wood, and glass. First to come off were the dragon gates, carved doors, and puddle-shaped windows. Next came the chandeliers, pillars, decorative ironwork, and hardwood floorboards.

The foreman marched in followed by a few men bearing wooden ramps and heavy-duty hand trucks. Straight to the third-floor apartment they went, gathering crates and boxes from the Mestiso's old life. A picture frame tumbled out of an overfilled box. The foreman picked it up and wiped off the dust. A sad-eyed flower girl looked at him from the steps of a church. The frame felt heavy for its size. He could tell it was real silver. His wife would like this, he thought as he discarded the picture and slipped the silver frame into his jacket pocket. The wealthy Mestiso would never miss it.

On his way out, the foreman saw his two strongest men carrying a carved pillar from the atico apartment. Out of the corner of his eye, he caught a glimpse of something glowing, like two pieces of coal in the dark wood of the pillar. That something, whatever it might be, disappeared before his eyes, making his blood run cold. He instinctively reached for the Virgin Mary pendant around his neck, imploring it for protection.

Hours later, the loaded trucks drove away in darkness with their precious cargo. At the Manila Pier, the Mestiso waited in a hired ship destined for his private island.

At the work site, the demolition crew was ready with their sledgehammers and wrecking ball. Hour after hour, in the bluish glow of electric lanterns, the building stood defiant. Until finally, the wrecking ball with cruel precision found the spot that would bring the structure to its knees.

The ghostly Selena screeched as the house came down around her.

Outside the Remedios church, the old woman blew out her candles. *One less link in Celestina's chain of malas,* she thought, locking up her stall and casting her mind across Manila Bay.

Somewhere in the harbour, in the dimly lit belly of his ship, the Mestiso sat in the cargo hold surrounded by the gates and doors and pillars, weeping over the bones of Celestina's house.

1

Malas, Swerte, Mana

Celestina was barely five years old when she got her first lesson on the concept of *malas*. She was not allowed to have a pet since dogs and cats made the house smell and shed hair all over the furniture. Her father did indulge her request for a "pet cactus" from an itinerant plant vendor who made the rounds in their neighbourhood. It was a Bullwinkle cactus, a comically funny figure to the child's eye, with a body that looked like it had been flattened with a rolling pin. It had two small branches that stuck out like ears and two longer ones that suggested outstretched arms ready to hug. Unlike the other cacti in the vendor's cart, this one had only the slightest hint of spikiness.

She named it Gumby, after the cartoon character she liked. Thereafter, it took its place on her bookshelf, beside a mermaid doll and her drawing of a creature that looked like a horse crossed with a dragon. Gumby's residency lasted until the eagle eyes of Stella, Celestina's mother, spotted it on the bookshelf.

"What is that?"

"That's Gumby," Celestina replied brightly.

"Well, Gumby is a cactus. We do not keep cacti in the house. It's *malas*."

Little Celestina had heard the word countless times before. It meant something bad, although she did not know exactly why or how. She immediately mounted a valiant defence of her pet. "Gumby is a good cactus. He only has baby spikes. He can't hurt anyone."

Stella sat down so she was eye to eye with little Celestina. "If you keep a cactus, you won't find a husband. You'll become a spinster. We don't want that."

"What's a *splinster*?" little Celestina asked.

"A *spinster*," Stella corrected, "is an older lady who never married. A matandang dalaga. They're the ones who grow old alone."

"Oh. Are the nuns in school spinsters?"

"No, my dear. They're married to Christ."

"Is Manang Rio a spinster?" the child asked as her mind turned to their very own housekeeper.

"Yes, she's a spinster."

"Is she going to be okay?"

"I think so. She's lucky because she's with us. Otherwise, who will care for her when she can no longer care for herself?"

And so, Stella removed Gumby the Cactus from the shelf and consigned it to the outer edges of the garden, where its thorns would serve as a deterrent against *malas* and other manner of evil. Following her, little Celestina looked at the high walls that surrounded their house, with their sharp wrought-iron spikes styled as fleurs-de-lys. She had serious doubts that Gumby's baby thorns were up to the lofty job Stella had foisted upon it.

After a week on guard duty, Gumby the Cactus fell prey to a hungry monitor lizard. The bayawak, according to Manang Rio, was the size of a guitar. It devoured the cactus in one gulp before disappearing into one of the storm drains. Little Celestina, mercifully, did not witness Gumby's grisly end, although she did see the pot bearing the cactus stump, which was still juicy. Henceforth, the giant lizard would make appearances in nightmares whenever she was troubled.

That was Celestina's first lesson in *malas*, and it would not be her last. Over the years, she learned that cracked mirrors, chipped dishes, and dead clocks were verboten in their house for they invited poverty and death. It did not stop there. By Stella's decree, the toilet lid must never, ever, be left up. To do so would be to flush your money down the sewer. Her husband regarded her beliefs with exasperation and often "forgot" to put the toilet lid down. They had no shortage of issues to fight about, but this gesture of civil disobedience was always a dependable middle finger to Stella's house rules.

There was another more benevolent but no less demanding force Stella often tried to summon: *swerte*. It was credited for the rise of Sebastien Sytanco, Stella's father and the patriarch of the clan. Every aspiring entrepreneur in the country had heard about his story — the young man who went from managing a dusty shoe store to owning luxury shopping centres in every major city on the archipelago. *Swerte* was embodied in the logo emblazoned on his establishments, his initials styled as upward-moving dragons forming the ultra-auspicious number eight.

We need to attract *swerte*, Celestina often heard. *Swerte*, she would learn, were things or actions that invited wealth, abundance, happiness, and long life. It was the reason the Sytanco family wore life-affirming red during weddings and birthdays. And it was why her grandfather kept aquariums with arowana fish, their scales round and shiny as gold coins. *Swerte*'s domain stretched from the noble to the absurd, judging from her mother's laughing Buddha with conspicuous man breasts.

The byzantine logic fascinated and amused Celestina to no end. She had not realized it then, but her mother's belief system was a masterwork of syncretism — Chinese feng shui with a Filipino

Spanish vocabulary and a touch of indigenous animism thrown in. At their core, the Sytanco family members were still Chinese — even with their Hispanicized names and Catholicism, their fluency in the local dialects, and their philanthropy in local causes. Their identity bound them and gave them strength. But it also assured they would remain the Intsik even after generations in the former Asian colony of the Spanish empire.

*

Celestina was twelve when she learned about *mana. Mana* was the word her mother used for their family traditions and heirlooms, for genetic qualities or quirks inherited from a parent or ancestor, and for the money and property that naturally passed down from parents to children. Since her Lolo Sebastien was a wealthy man, her mother should have been rich as well. But clearly, she was not. After folding eight pillowcases and three sheets with Manang Rio, Celestina blurted out the question that had been squirming on her tongue since she was six years old.

"Manang," she asked their housekeeper, who was busy with her ironing, "why aren't we in a big house in Olympia Heights like Lolo and the other Sytancos? Why do we live in Misericordia?"

"Perhaps you should ask your mama," Manang replied as she swiped the flat iron on a banana leaf to scent the linens.

"I can't," Celestina replied, conjuring an image of her proud mother, stylishly dressed by a talented costurera and adorned in real diamonds and jade.

Rio Orosa said nothing as she placed another starched sheet on the ironing board. She had served in the Sytanco mansion since she was eighteen. Over the years, the servants had come to regard her as a big sister due to her common sense and take-charge manner. They called her *Manang*, an honorific that was now permanently attached to her name.

CELESTINA'S HOUSE · 11

Many of the servants still wondered why she had been re-assigned to the modest house in Misericordia Valley. Truth was, she liked her current assignment much better than the Sytanco mansion. Stella and her daughter had always felt like a real family to her. For that reason, she decided she owed Celestina the truth.

"Your mother was disinherited," Manang finally said. "Your lolo cut her off."

"What? But why?" Celestina asked.

"It's true, my child. Your mother disobeyed. That's why she had to buy this house on her own. And so, she'll have no *mana* when your lolo passes away."

The young girl stopped folding and looked at Manang with indignation. "No *mana*?"

"That's right. No money for her."

"That's cruel."

"She was supposed to marry a rich boy. It was arranged. But she ran off with your papang. She made your lolo lose face. Oh, he was angry like Diyos Ama during the great flood. For days, the big house shook with his voice."

The words went into Celestina's ear and into her uncomprehending brain. She could certainly picture her grandfather unleashing fury and flood waters upon anyone who disobeyed him. But try as she might, she could not imagine her parents as young and madly in love. They could barely stand each other, and when they did talk, they ended up arguing about toilet lids, money, and her father's late nights.

"Good thing your lola is around to help your mama," Manang Rio continued. "Even then, she struggles and *malas* follows her like a dark anino."

Manang Rio's revelation stayed with Celestina long after they put away the sheets. Now she understood why her mother so feared *malas* and so fervently courted *swerte*, and why they lived in the valley called Misericordia — mercy — below the lofty Olympia Heights.

2

Of Love and Caterpillars

Celestina's *malas* began before she was born, in an act of rebellion, in a place that had no tolerance for outlaws, political or romantic. It was the sixties going into the seventies. Ferdinand Marcos had just won a second term — a victory made possible by the millions taken from the nation's treasury and, some whisper, supernatural assistance. People were starting to see the true man ruling in the false Camelot. In streets and on campuses, students and intellectuals protested the rising tide of lawlessness, the lavishness of the Marcos family's lifestyle, and a military budget that was rapidly overtaking the budget for schools and universities.

Amidst this turmoil, the Lyceo Loyola University stood serenely on its eighty-five-hectare campus, a verdant sanctuary overlooking a valley of shoemakers. Teachers sternly reminded students to use words, not Molotov cocktails. Those who took part in violent protest would be automatically expelled, with no chance for appeal. Change would come, but at a rather more leisurely pace, in a school that echoed with the surnames of former presidents, generals, and captains of industry.

*

The school year started with a buzz of excitement as Antonio Errantes parked his 1968 Mustang in one of the spots reserved for professors. The car was a dark metallic green with a blackened chrome trim and grille to match. He stepped out in suede desert boots, khaki chinos, a fitted navy crewneck, and a midnight-blue Harrington jacket with a distinctive tartan lining. As he walked into Faber Hall, students asked each other, "Who is that?" Too old to be a college boy, but not the kind of teacher they were used to seeing. Until recently, their professors had been retired statesmen or priests in starched barong tagalog shirts. Those who were not clerics were academics so devoted that they might as well have been monastics. Antonio was the rare treat: the recent winner of the country's highest literary honour and a good-looking man still in the fullness of life.

On Antonio's first day, the Chair of the Humanities Department asked him to do a reading from *Siquijor*, his landmark novel about the powerful pagan forces living under the skin of their Catholic nation. Antonio was a little nervous. He had previously done a well-received reading at the state university, his alma mater. But that was a democratic institution that produced a more radical breed of leaders and thinkers. Students from the state university considered Lyceo Loyola a bastion of reactionary politics and elitism.

Antonio's natural confidence took over as soon as he entered the auditorium. He looked around and saw what seemed to be a stable of thoroughbreds — tall, athletic youths with well-chiselled features, glossy hair, and perfect teeth. He was a gifted speaker and was certain he could conquer this audience by the end of his reading.

Antonio noticed her just as the Chair finished his glowing introduction. She sat near the podium so she would not miss anything in the lecture. Even in that auditorium full of blue-bloods, she stood out — a petite but exquisitely formed creature with the glass-like skin of upper-class Chinese girls. He regarded her with his well-honed eye for beauty, trying to spot a flaw that would make her more human. He looked at the creases of her neck, the crook of her elbows, and the tips of her unvarnished fingernails. Every millimetre of her pearly skin was unblemished and clean, and that purity stirred him in ways other women never could.

Antonio was not the only one who felt the spasms of love that day. Years before his body was ravaged by his vices, he was a rakish figure who looked like he could ride a black steed or command a frigate in the high seas. And then there was his voice, which flowed like a river of sweet, dark chocolate. Minutes into the reading, the girl abandoned her note-taking and followed his velvet baritone into the mysteries of Siquijor Island. That girl, he would later find out, was Stella Sytanco — the only daughter of the Twin Dragons emporia mogul.

Like Stella, the other students followed Antonio into the dark heart of the enchanted island. They held their breaths as the patriarch of the tale began to whisper his diabolical plans to the four-hundred-year-old balete tree. For once, the students were not looking at the clock, waiting to catch up with friends. In fact, they were a little disappointed when the bell rang as they were all dying to know how far the patriarch would go to satisfy his bloodlust.

The students filed out quietly, wondering if the administration had somehow made a mistake. Nobody was supposed to enjoy required reading. The girl was still in her seat, seemingly lost in a dream. She smiled shyly at Antonio before quickly joining her friends. As the sound of footsteps receded into the hall, he sat in the empty room feeling as if he had received a visitation from a celestial creature previously unseen by mortals. From that moment on, he would have no peace.

He was certainly not the first teacher to be attracted to a student. Such affairs happened all the time and quite openly at the state university. But this was the Lyceo, the most Catolico cerrado of schools in that still very Catholic nation. It had been made abundantly clear to him that professors were not allowed to date or become intimate with their students, even if the student was over the age of consent. Although the sexual revolution was well underway, it would have to wait at the university's gates for another decade. He had not thought the policy was worth challenging at the time of his hiring, but that was before he laid eyes on the peerless Stella.

As he ate a solitary bachelor dinner back in his apartment, Antonio thought, to hell with the university and its fossilized policies. He did not get to where he was by being obedient. Long ago, he had decided that he did not like the path laid out for the men in his family. So, he made his own.

He was the first in his family of military men and seafarers to embrace the life of the mind and acquire the trappings of culture. His father was a ship captain who commanded large vessels laden with metal ores destined for Japan. He had expected his sons to follow in his footsteps. He was a brusque man with no time for the softer things in life. For years, the captain openly scoffed at Antonio's chosen vocation. Writers were weak and effeminate, his father had always said. Baklâ. Antonio had taken it with a laugh and a quip, until the day he finally had had enough. His siblings would forever remember the day Antonio replied — with a punch that floored the strapping captain for a full ten-count.

As he lay in bed that night, burning with love and lust, Stella appeared in his fantasies to soothe his lonely flesh and spirit. He did what he had to but felt no better afterward. A man wanted what he wanted, and no gatekeeper was going to stand in his way.

The morning, however, brought more sober thoughts as he drank his strong coffee and got ready for work. *Wait until you have tenure before you start breaking rules,* he told himself. *Get friendly with her but wait until she graduates to make your move.*

He drove to the university with a renewed resolve to immerse himself in work. After his first class, he headed for the Rare Books Library, situated in a quiet corner of the leafy campus. He thought it might be a good spot to get some writing done between classes. But as fate would have it, he found her working at the lending desk.

For days, he struggled to write in the library. Eventually, he gave up, knowing it was almost impossible to produce a coherent sentence in her presence. Still, he went back to Rare Books, day after day, submitting himself to the exquisite torture of wanting the untouchable Stella.

✵

Around the school, students were suffering another kind of torment. The campus butterflies had had a bumper crop of babies that year. They hatched in the flower beds and spilled onto the benches where students liked to study. They dropped from trees and onto the hair and shoulders of unsuspecting students. As the caterpillars grew fat, they started shedding insect hair.

Students broke out in red itchy rashes on their limbs, necks, and eyelids. They rushed to the clinic for relief and soon used up the year's supply of calamine lotion and allergy pills. The intensity of the itching made the students feverish and sleepless at night. Concerned parents called, fearful that their children had contracted a virulent strain of pox. Public health officials were summoned to find the cause of the outbreak. They ruled out measles and chicken pox before turning their attention to the caterpillars.

The administration acted swiftly, bringing in agriculture-grade insecticides to deal with the caterpillar problem. Classes were suspended for three days until the fumes cleared. There would be no butterflies or any other pollinators that year. The mango trees remained barren and the flowering santan bushes bare. It would be two years before a butterfly was seen on campus again.

Antonio was back in Rare Books the day classes resumed. At closing time, Stella locked up the library, walked up to him, and gently held his hand as if she had been doing it forever. Neither of them said anything at first. Finally, he spoke and said, "I love you. I was going to wait until you graduated to tell you, but you obviously already know."

"Father wants me to wed his friend's son," Stella said. "We're getting married after graduation. I never thought about questioning my father's plan. Then you came and woke up my heart."

"My father tried to arrange a life for me too," Antonio said. "I told him I'd sooner die than live a life that's not for me."

"I wish I could say that to my father. I don't even know who I am or what's right for me," Stella said. "All my life I've obeyed the rules and tried to honour our family. I don't know anything else."

"Do you love this young man, Stella?"

"Oh, Antonio. I don't know."

"Be honest with yourself. This is the rest of your life. You've got to know."

"We get along, but there's no fire! It's like hanging out with a cousin."

"Life is too short to spend with someone you don't love."

For Stella, the obedient, responsible daughter, this fearless, larger-than-life man was exhilarating. For the rest of the year, they carried on as outlaws of love, working out iron-clad alibis for their covert dates. They coupled furtively in the archives of the Rare Books Library, parked in a grassy field at the far edge of the campus, and made love in his apartment. They loved each other until they could no longer bear to be apart. And when that time came, they made a fateful trip to City Hall and then presented themselves to Stella's mother — as husband and wife.

For Teresita, Stella's mother, there was no good way to break this to her husband Sebastien. She tried her best to be the mediator between her husband and her daughter, but the news hit him like an atomic bomb. The mansion thundered with the sound of Sebastien Sytanco's voice. "Bring me that hijo de puta so I can kill him myself!" Terrified servants scurried for cover, while Teresita packed up Stella's things to spare her the full force of Sebastien's wrath.

When Sebastien's rage finally burned out, he locked himself in his study to assess the damage. He thought he knew his daughter, the girl who was unfailingly studious, modest, and respectful to her elders. But how little he understood the young woman who so carelessly walked away from an advantageous marriage. And for what? For that fortune-hunting lech Antonio Errantes?

From the day his daughter was born, Sebastien had carefully made provisions for her future so she would never have to experience the hardships he had endured. He even found a suitable husband for her: a serious and honourable young man whose father happened to own the largest chocolate company in the country. Now, his hopes and plans for his daughter were laid to waste, and for the rest of time, he would have to bow his head in shame before his friend, the father of Stella's betrothed.

When Sebastien finally came out of his study, it was with a hardened heart and a revised will. He divided his estate between his wife and his other two children, believing that with no *mana*, Antonio would soon leave his daughter, and Stella would return home properly contrite. It was a miscalculation on Sebastien's part, as Antonio stood by Stella, and Stella got a job in an investment bank catering to Chinese clients.

But Sebastien's influence was as wide as his anger was deep. Antonio was not invited back to the Lyceo's faculty the following year. Neither did he manage to find another position at any other university. And that was a problem because despite their precautions, Antonio and Stella had conceived a child.

3

A Birth and a Death

The months leading up to the baby's birth were difficult. Antonio remained out of work, and Stella soon became too big to be on her feet for any length of time. Seeing this, Teresita Sytanco dispatched one of her most trusted maids to Stella's house to take over the housekeeping duties. Stella was pleasantly surprised to receive Manang Rio, the woman who used to feed and dress her before school.

Manang was different from the other servants in the Sytanco mansion. While the others had grown plump from sloth and constant snacking, Manang stayed as slim and nimble as the tikling birds that waded in the rice fields of her home province. Nobody had to prod her; she did her work, and she did it quickly, with purpose. Best of all, she kept to herself and disdained idle chatter and gossip.

"Manang, I'm so glad you're here," Stella said. "I have a wicked craving for your Chicken Tinola."

Manang Rio had no husband or children to call her own. She was thrilled that Stella was about to have a child. They were going to be a family.

*

During the last weeks of Stella's pregnancy, it became clear to her doctor that a normal delivery would not be advisable, given the size of the baby and Stella's petite frame. Teresita once again stepped in and put her daughter in the city's best maternity hospital. The almost ten-pound baby girl was delivered via Caesarean section. Stella was still convalescing from the surgery when the nurse came into the room, so she handed the baby to the father.

Antonio received the bundle nervously, with Grandmother Teresita reminding him to support the baby's neck. Carefully, he loosened the swaddle so he could see the baby's face. He used to think newborn babies were ugly and gnome-like. He had always shrunk back whenever he saw their cone-shaped heads and swollen features, which he understood were due to their passage through the birth canal. He was a little surprised to see his baby's perfectly shaped head and well-defined features.

She looked at him, seemingly knowing, with Stella's catlike eyes. Antonio recognized himself in her sturdy frame and around the edges of her cherubic face. There he was — in her arched eyebrows and reddish-brown wisps of hair that framed her face. Until now, he thought no one on earth could compare to his wife. This child, part cherub and part imp, was clearly more than the sum of their genetic contributions. Antonio felt a surge of joy as he covered her face with kisses. She smelled like a sweet and gentle ocean.

The baby regarded the fuzzy figure in whose arms she lay. She recognized that deep voice and felt safe in the cradle of those strong arms. So began the close bond between father and daughter.

Later, just as dusk began to shadow the hospital grounds, the exhausted new father went for a short walk. It had been a scorching day, and he could still feel the heat radiating from the cobblestones and stone benches. He had not gotten far when a hot, electrically charged wind swept over him. He fell to the ground softly, as a leaf would. Conscious but unable to move or speak, Antonio was caught in a mysterious whirlwind of joyful singing voices. After a moment of panic, a feeling of serenity and blessedness descended upon him. Closing his eyes, he let go of his fear and opened himself to the unseen singers. He did not know how long he had lain on the ground, but it was long enough to watch the fading light turn from coal red to an inky blue-black.

As the wind died down, the voices faded into the evening. Finally, Antonio was able to get up and brush himself off. He sat down on a bench for a long time, wondering what had just happened. Whose voices were those and for what did they rejoice? Were they heralding the arrival of a new life or the death of an old one? He did not know. He did know that his baby was a little piece of heaven in the purgatory that was currently his life. And that was why he named her Celestina.

*

Little Celestina spoke her first word before she was five months old, when most babies were still babbling. It was a clearly articulated "Papa," often followed by a gesture toward one of Antonio's personal effects — his slippers or his reading glasses. Her second word followed soon after that. It was "boo" for book, underlined by a finger pointed toward her ever-growing book collection. She started walking at nine-and-a-half months, much to the surprise of Stella and Manang Rio. Stella would always remember the day little Celestina pulled herself up on the coffee table and toddled toward the bookshelf.

Thereafter, Celestina used her newly learned skill to get the books she wanted and deliver them to Antonio for a reading. It went on like this for the next few months. Her appetite for stories was voracious, and by the time her first birthday rolled by, they had gone through her entire story collection several times over. So Antonio began making up his own stories, with characters from Philippine myths and legends, to keep his daughter entertained. He introduced her to diwata, spirits in the form of enchanting women who guarded forests and rivers. He told her stories of tree-dwelling giants called kapres. Later, when she came to her period of "Whys," he made up short tales to answer the million and one questions she threw at him. Why are atis fruits lumpy? Why do coconut shells have faces? Why do fireflies carry light in their tails? Why is the sea salty? Why do tears taste like the sea? This collection of tales would later become *The Book of Whys*, Antonio's only children's book.

For the first two years of her life, Celestina's world revolved around Antonio's company and Manang Rio's care. Stella, who had gone back to work after Celestina's first birthday, became something of a beautiful but distant presence in her daughter's life.

Antonio eventually found work again — through the sudden passing of an old school friend, the graphic novelist known as Chukchak. Antonio, upon the invitation of the departed's family, gave a speech where he reminisced about their friendly rivalry. He told the mourners the origin of the unusual nickname. "It was the sound of the red *X* from his editorial pen," he said. "The twin stakes to the heart of literary stinkers. He never minced words, never hesitated to call out bad ideas. We're better writers and artists because of those chukchaks."

Chukchak's family, friends, and colleagues cried and laughed as they celebrated the man's life and career. After the funeral, the publisher of New Legends Comics offered Antonio the departed man's job. It was quite unlike the academic career Antonio had imagined for himself, but after two years of domesticity, he was eager for an audience beyond a demanding toddler.

The charismatic Antonio proved to be a natural for the job as head of story development for New Legends' serialized graphic novels. Story after bestselling story sprang from his fertile mind. Young writers and artists surrounded him, called him "The Maestro," and vied to learn from a master of tropical gothic. Women, especially, were drawn to his magnetism and roguish looks. Film executives flocked to the publishing house in search of blockbuster material for the movie-hungry Filipino public. The Maestro's picture routinely appeared in the issues. There he was, a handsome cad with a slyly arched eyebrow, inviting you to the underbelly of paradise.

The hours at work routinely bled into late dinners with colleagues and drinks in clubs, bankrolled by movie executives who wanted to make sure their goose kept laying golden eggs. At first, Antonio reluctantly took part in this office culture. But as the months rolled by, he began to take to the fiery discourses fuelled by liquor and shabu, and to the cunning showgirls who knew their way through a man's desires.

Little Celestina would often be asleep by the time he got home. Night after night, she asked for the big man, the one who had been the centre of her universe. Manang Rio and Stella took turns reading to her, but neither of them could compare to the master storyteller. And in her dreams, Celestina would play the stories again. This time in his voice.

4

Ambos Mundos

Sometime in her fifteenth year, Celestina grew five inches, seemingly overnight, lost her baby fat, and acquired the supple, curvaceous figure of a young Brigitte Bardot. The transformation happened too quickly for her to notice. Her mirror showed the same wide-eyed gaze and open smile she had worn since she was a little girl. A child's face perched on a woman's body. To the beasts inside men, this combination of innocence and allure proved irresistible. She realized that men looked at her now, though she did not understand why. She never thought herself to be a beauty, especially compared to her Sytanco cousins who had porcelain doll faces and ballerina bodies, no matter how much chocolate they ate. What she did know was something in men's crooked smiles and sidelong glances made her feel like a hunted animal.

Antonio noticed the changes as well, one Saturday, over a late family breakfast. He wondered when his baby turned into this fresh-faced vixen. Time seemed to be hurtling down life's freeway at blistering speed. The years were flying by. Where had he been? Lost in work, in his mind's adventures? Lumbering through the perpetual hangovers that followed his late nights? He felt rotten, as he should, and told himself he would do better, for the sake of his daughter. Impulsively, he asked, "Would you like to work with me this summer? It'll be fun. You can watch us make stories, and we can spend some time together."

A surprised Stella protested, saying, "I told you she'll be working with me at the firm. I've already arranged it."

"Your office? That'll be a bloody bore for her," he quipped. "You'll be there supervising her every move."

"I want her to learn marketable skills."

"Yeah. How to stroke rich people's money."

"And what would she learn from you? How to pull an all-nighter?"

"You don't know how creative people work because there's no art in your soul."

The exchange grew increasingly irate, spiralling into an argument that had nothing to do with Celestina or the summer job. It was a sadly familiar pattern, and Celestina was bloody sick of it. She slammed her hand on the dining table and said, "Why don't you ask me? It's only my life!"

Her parents stopped arguing, surprised at their daughter's unfamiliar boldness.

"I want to work with Papang," she said firmly. "No offence, Mama, but his office seems more fun than yours."

Stella ceded victory to Antonio that day, telling herself perhaps it was for the best. Her heart had long given up on him as a husband. Whatever affection she used to feel for him had been snuffed out by his casual infidelities and reckless spending. He did care for their daughter, that much she could see. And she believed he had it in him to be the father Celestina deserved.

*

Celestina thought she was prepared for her first day at her summer job. She had practised typing on her mother's Olivetti typewriter, and she had studied the storylines and characters of New Legends' graphic novellas. Her father had given her lessons in concept development, storyboarding, and the art of the pitch. She had even watched Tagalog movies so she could become conversant with the colloquial dialogue used in her father's popular serials.

That morning, she put on a dark purple blazer with shoulder pads, gold buttons, and a nipped-in waist. She paired it with black stirrup leggings and suede ankle boots. The mirror showed her a confident, fashionable woman who looked much older than her fifteen years. "Bring it on," she told the woman in the mirror. With her leatherbound agenda and tote bag in hand, she went downstairs to join her father in the car.

At the office, her father was quickly pulled into an impromptu meeting with the publisher and a movie producer. She had barely settled into her desk before two young men from the editorial team introduced themselves and offered to show her the lay of the land. They were exceedingly polite, if somewhat awkward. Almost all the writers and graphic artists were male, and most of the other staff were stern, elderly women with family ties to the owner. It was rare to see a young girl in the office, let alone a pretty one. Little wonder the place was called "Boy's Town." The flow of work slowed down considerably as the self-appointed tour guides presented her to the different departments. Young men left their desks to introduce themselves and show off their work. The bolder ones dusted off their English conversational skills, knowing that the Maestro's daughter was a colegiala.

Celestina was relieved when her tour was finally over, and she returned to her desk. She wished her father would hurry up and finish his meeting. It had been thoroughly unnerving to have so many eyes trained on her. At around half past eleven, an illustrator from the art department found his way to her desk. With a shy smile, he laid down his offering — an armful of prized music tapes from his collection.

"Tell me which ones you like. I'll make you a mixtape," he said.

Neither one of them saw Antonio come in, but suddenly there he was, with his arm around his daughter, telling her admirer, "You're punching above your weight class."

The young man quietly slinked away while Antonio perused the tapes. Mostly European synthpop featuring pretty boys wearing too much eyeliner.

"Thank goodness, you're back," she told her father.

"Are the guys bothering you?"

"A little … I know they're just trying to be nice. It's just a bit much."

"Let's go for lunch," he said.

With that, Antonio whisked his daughter away to the formerly elegant Santa Cruz district.

*

Celestina clung to her father's arm as they navigated the river of people flowing from all directions. She felt as if she might get crushed if she dared slow down.

"Hold on to your purse," he whispered as they walked past turn-of-the-century houses converted into dormitories. "This is not your rich lolo's town."

Tall and built like a battleship, Antonio sliced through the crowds as if they were water, giving Celestina room to breathe. The humidity made her feel like a siopao in a steam basket. He hailed a pedicab painted with a smiling Santo Niño in full red velvet regalia and told the driver to go to a street that was unfamiliar to a sheltered girl like Celestina. After a noisy, diesel-fuelled ride full of death-defying manoeuvres, they stopped in front of Ambos Mundos, a restaurant that had been in business before the archipelago was even a country. Celestina froze as she saw the enormous black creature lounging by the entrance. To her eyes, it looked like the Hound of Hades, reborn as a bristly hippopotamus. "This is Liempo," Antonio said with a chuckle. "He's a potbellied pig. Isn't he cute? The owner keeps him to bring in *swerte*."

Liempo was obese, even by pig standards, sporting a belly that sagged with the weight of his pampered life.

"I'm afraid he'll charge at me, Papang."

"Charge? Just look at him. He's much too fat and happy," Antonio said as he caressed one of the pig's innumerable jowls.

The manager came out to greet Antonio before turning to Celestina. He recognized the Chinese features of her face and greeted her in the Hokkien dialect that many of the local Chinese spoke. "Lee ho bwoh?"

She returned his greeting brightly with "Ho, kam siah." After exchanging pleasantries and a warm handshake, Celestina quickly added that Liempo was "Ko tsui," like a giant puppy.

Heads turned as the manager led them past the downstairs cantina filled with students and blue-collar men. Celestina had trained herself to stand tall and look straight ahead to avoid making eye contact. Antonio met the men's stares with amusement. He knew they were looking at his daughter. *Keep dreaming, guys*, he thought.

They went up a flight of stairs leading to an air-conditioned dining room. The manager gave them the centre table and signalled a waiter to bring in some icy drinks. The noise dropped perceptively as people stopped to examine the young beauty with the famous gothic Maestro. Celestina sat down quickly, grateful for this cool sanctuary from the heat. Dabbing her forehead with a hanky, she turned her attention to the thirteen-page menu. Like their country, the selection was a long-simmering cultural cocido — with continental European dishes like bouillabaisse, six kinds of paellas with local produce, Chinese dishes bearing Spanish names, and regional dishes featuring ingredients such as cow's blood and minced beef lungs sautéed in the holy trinity of garlic, onions, and tomatoes. A meeting of both worlds, east and west, true to the restaurant's name. A waiter arrived with an icy San Miguel beer and a cold, milky black jelly drink. Celestina felt lightheaded from the excitement of the morning. The swirl of conversations and aromas in the dining room did nothing to soothe her nerves. "It's too much choice. I can't decide," she said as she continued to examine the menu.

Antonio held her hand and chose two dishes he thought she would like. As the waiter walked off with their order, Antonio playfully slid his beer toward her, saying, "Here, have a drink. I think you deserve it."

She hesitated for a moment before picking it up to take a delicate sip. It was bitter on her tongue but smooth going down. She took another drink, a bigger one this time, pausing for a minute or two, as she felt the tension lifting from her shoulders.

"Not a word to your mother," Antonio said with a conspiratorial smile. "If this gets out, you'll be spending your summer with her, counting rich people's money."

She shook her head emphatically, her cheeks charmingly flushed. "I promise. I like being with you. Seeing you build your dark worlds."

"My dark worlds? Really? Why is that?"

"When I read your stories, they feel real. More real than this world, sometimes. There are moments when I feel like this is all just a facade. The real stuff is what's beyond the stage lights." She stopped as she realized she had already said too much. "Sorry, I'm babbling. Forget it," she said as she took another drink.

Antonio immediately picked up on the troubled thoughts beneath her offhand remark. "Celestina, look at me," he said.

"Yes, Papang?"

"I've visited the darkest corners of the human mind. Nothing you say will be strange to me. Now tell me what's going on."

"I was in class one day, and I had this moment. The teacher turned into a ventriloquist's dummy before my eyes and my classmates became clay figures, like Gumby. Suddenly, I thought, this is not a real teacher. It's just a block of wood regurgitating words. And the kids were just cartoons acting out someone's script. I told cousins Gidget and Mikee. They said it was creepy and I was weird. Am I weird, Papang?"

Antonio had to pause to take in his daughter's words. "I know that moment, Celestina. Because we are the same. And most people are not like us. They're content to go along with the show. Not me. I've heard the song of angels, and I've listened to the whispers of devils. I'm not afraid to go behind the curtain. To take control of the story."

"You did that with Mama, didn't you? That's why I'm here."

"Yes."

"Do you regret it?"

"No. Why should I? I got the better end of the bargain," he said with a loving caress on her cheek. "I know your mother regrets it. It's obvious she misses her world."

Celestina felt a deep sadness as her father spoke. She drank a little more to take her mind off the matter. She had finished half the bottle of San Miguel by the time the food arrived. Antonio leaned forward and said, "That's enough drinking for now, young lady."

"Yes, sir," she replied with a playful kiss.

By the time the Paella Ambos, Tortang Alimango, and crispy pata were finished, all the morning's anxieties had left her spirit. With bellies full and heads giddy with drink, father and daughter said goodbye to the overfed, happy pig of Ambos Mundos. Giggling, they walked back to the street holding hands and hailed a pedicab back to the New Legends building.

"Thanks for lunch, Papang. It was fun," Celestina said as they walked back to her father's office.

The midafternoon sun streamed through the dusty blinds and rested on Celestina's radiant face. Antonio paused to admire the young woman born from the collision of his gritty world and Stella's rarified realm. Life had yet to take Celestina's sparkling laugh or dim her spirit. He wished he could keep her forever. He could not, of course. All he could do was bask in her sunshine for the time they had together. He must not waste a moment.

5

Building a Monster

Antonio sat in his darkened office and closed his eyes. He had asked not to be disturbed for the next hour, even in the event of a fire or coup d'état. By now his staff was used to his eccentricities. He did not lock his door, nor did he have to. They knew his temper and sharp tongue only too well and dared not breach his sanctum. His staff liked to joke that the old Maestro needed his siesta. But Antonio had a different destination — a place that lies just before slumber.

He sat still in his chair even as his consciousness hovered around the office, an unseen watcher. He could see his daughter, looking very fetching in tight, high-waisted jeans and a Duran Duran T-shirt. She was in the art department, observing the penciller sketching thumbnails from the approved storyline. The other boys were distracted, he could tell, stealing glances at the nicely formed posterior that swelled from her tiny waist. "Touch her and you'll be singing soprano in a church choir," he whispered in the boys' ears.

The inker glanced over his shoulder, and the colourist looked around uneasily.

"What's the matter?" Celestina asked.

"This place is haunted. We're sure of it," the inker said with a nervous laugh. "We always feel like we're being watched."

Their voices faded as Antonio untied himself from time and space. He felt himself falling into a warm ocean, plunging past schools of wildly coloured fish, down to the depths of the seaweed forest, down to where marine creatures carried their own light. He fell through decades and centuries in minutes, sinking until he hit the powder-soft ocean floor. There he lay in the graveyard of sunken warships, treasure-laden galleons, fallen civilizations, and fearsome creatures that now lived only in nightmares. He dug his fingers into the rich sediment. This was the soil to which all things returned, and from which all creations were born. People often asked him where and how he got his story ideas. He always told them the stories were already there, hidden like pearls, in the ocean of our collective unconscious. The trick was being able to dive down long enough to gather them.

He stayed there for a long while, exploring the magnificent skeleton of a two-headed sea serpent. He examined its fangs, which were sharp and hooked. He thought of all the people who were content to live their entire lives in the shallows. *Poor unfortunate fools*, he thought. Their souls craved beauty and mystery, but they were terrified of what they might encounter in the depths. Too afraid of dying to be fully alive.

Suddenly, he saw a flash of silver from the corner of his eye. He stood still and waited for the water to stir again. He heard a gurgle of bubbles and followed the sound, all the way to the sea serpent's dorsal fin. There it was — a fishlike creature propelled by gossamer silver wings. It had a lithe body reminiscent of a young woman, and a bifurcated tail that moved in alternating fashion, like a pair of legs. He moved slowly, so as not to frighten it, inching closer until the two of them were eye to eye. The creature had blue-green orbs for eyes, a little bump that suggested a nose, and a small mouth curved into what looked like a smile. He offered his hand in greeting and said, "hello." The creature touched his hand with a silvery fin and opened its mouth into an O.

"Hola, Papang," it spoke in his daughter's voice. "Are you okay in there?"

Back in the surface world, Antonio opened his eyes and saw the halo around his daughter's silhouette by the opened door.

"I'm so sorry to disturb you. I was worried," she said.

"Come in, Celestina. Shut the door but keep the lights off."

"Did I wake you?"

"No, cariño. I wasn't asleep. Just letting my mind wander. It's part of my creative process."

Celestina felt her words catching in her throat. She could make out her father's outline in his chair, but his voice was coming from another place, much deeper.

"I'll leave you be, Papang."

"Stay," Antonio commanded as he clicked on his desk lamp.

Celestina stepped back in fright as she saw her father's face. He had always been a good-looking man, but his features had coarsened over the years due to his heavy drinking and late nights. At that moment, he looked downright haggard, and his eyes were red, as if he had been swimming.

"I'm working on our next serial. You're going to help me build a monster."

Celestina reluctantly sat down and grabbed a yellow pad. She tried not to look into his eyes or betray her discomfort.

"What did you have in mind?" she said, trying to inject lightness into her voice. "Mutant beast? Flesh-eating ghoul? Malevolent nature spirit?"

"Forget those. I'm interested in the most dangerous creature that ever lived. The only one that can end life on earth as we know it."

"Are you talking about humans?"

"Yes. A man."

"Women can be monsters too."

"Of course. I've built many lady monsters. But a man is already halfway there," he said.

Antonio's voice seemed to resonate all around her even as he sat still behind his desk. Celestina, the girl who never carried a sweater and always sought out air-conditioning, felt a damp chill deep in her bones. She wrapped her arms around herself and summoned a bowl of hot wonton soup in her thoughts.

"What does our monster look like?" Antonio continued. "Should he have a birthmark, a disfigurement?"

Celestina thought for a minute before answering, "No. He's beautiful and radiant. Blessed in every way. The monster is inside. Like the maggot in a shiny apple. That's a lot more terrifying to me than a deformed face."

Antonio stood up and walked in the shadows as his thoughts churned. He could see his daughter breathing faster as she conjured her handsome monster into being. There was nothing like a dangerous man to get a woman's heart racing. He tried not to stare at the woman blossoming before him. He loved women, and he enjoyed the games they played, but they were most beguiling when they were on the cusp of maturity, not yet aware of the power they wielded over men. He understood why men risked jail sentences and madness to taste this delectable fruit.

Celestina hugged herself tighter as she felt his eyes all over her.

"Tell me, my dear," he asked. "How does he present himself to the world? What's his profession?"

"He's an artist. A sculptor, perhaps. Maybe he likes to sculpt angels as a sign of his lofty aspirations. He goes to church and tries to live a virtuous life."

"I like where you're going with this," he said, as he stood close to her. "Let's look at his motivation. What does your monster want in his heart?"

Celestina bit her lip, as she sometimes did when she was working out a problem. "He wants to bring something pure and perfect into the world ... to capture a piece of heaven."

"Very good, my dear. You've planted the seeds of his destruction. Now, we make bad things happen."

She jumped slightly as she felt him caress her shoulders. His hands felt feverish against her cold skin.

"Think of his motivation as a coin," he said. "One side is shiny, and the other is black. His aspiration for perfection is the shiny side. The blackened side is his pathology — the abnormality that would make him monstrous."

"He's lonely because no real woman is as perfect as his creations," she replied. "He can't fall in love, but he can no longer bear the loneliness."

Antonio's mind hurtled between his time at the Lyceo with Stella and the monster he was now creating with his daughter. "Keep going. Push him until he goes over that line to the dark side, and he can no longer return."

"How about this? He resorts to dark spells to summon a heavenly creature. Then he woos her and steals her from God's Kingdom."

A tear fell from his eye as he remembered the day he eloped with Stella. It was another lifetime ago. And Sebastien Sytanco was still punishing him for it. So what? Antonio shrugged. Generalissimo Intsik Beho can hate me to hell and back. I got an angel and a lovely daughter out of the ordeal. I still won.

Then why are you crying, Antonio? asked a voice inside him.

Antonio planted a gentle kiss on his daughter's head and said, "Thank you, cariño. I think he's going to be a beautiful monster. Now we put it aside to let the idea bloom."

"Yes, Papang. Is there anything else before I go?"

"That's all for now. I'll see you after work. We'll have dinner at Papagayo. Do you still like to dance?"

"Yes," she said too quickly, eager to leave his office. Celestina fairly bolted for the exit, nearly tripping on a box of previous issues on her way out. Her ears were filled with the sound of her own heartbeats as she shut the door behind her. This was a side of her father she had always sensed but never seen, until now. She did not care for it and went for a walk to put it out of her mind.

In his office, Antonio turned off his lamp and sat in the darkness, savouring the clean scent Celestina had left in her wake. He let the scent take his mind to places it should not go. Unknown to him, his frequent travels to the depths had been changing him, and not for the better.

*

Celestina read her cousins' letters with a tinge of envy. It was sweet of them to send her pictures, as she could not join them in California. There was a picture of Mikee and Gidget at Universal Studios, each holding an ice cream cone five scoops high. There was Gidget in the palm of King Kong's furry hand. And there was Mikee standing shoulder to maw with the killer shark from *Jaws*. There were more pictures, this time on Rodeo Drive, with the girls carrying shopping bags full of loot. The last shot showed them with giddy smiles as they posed with the debonair actor from their favourite nighttime soap opera.

Celestina had never been to America, and she bristled at her cousins' letters, which were peppered with hyperbolic descriptions of all the amazing things they had seen, eaten, and experienced "in the States." *The steaks here are the size of café tables, and prawns are as large as Batman's boomerangs*, they wrote. *They have every ice cream flavour you can imagine, with peanut butter cups and Skor bars smooshed in, if you ask. There are six- and eight-lane highways, where the cars can go a hundred miles per hour. As for the guys, California boys are tall and chiseled like movie stars. So gwapo!*

"I wish Mama had let me go with them," Celestina said. "I'm missing out on all the fun."

"You know your mother was concerned about our money situation this year. Anyway, I think Europe is more your style," Antonio said, trying to cheer up his daughter. "Maybe you can work here part-time during the year, and we can save up for a trip next summer."

Antonio took her shopping to lift her spirits. For the next few weeks, father and daughter renewed their bond with frequent trips to malls and ice cream shops. During those times, Antonio relaxed into his charming old self and got to know the young woman who was like him in so many ways. She laughed at the same things, picked up on the same absurdities, and shared his fascination with life's mysteries.

So clever and such a knockout, Antonio thought as he took her into shop after shop. Celestina acquired a kittenish wardrobe of skin-baring sundresses, capri pants, and form-fitting knit tops, all with Antonio's approval.

After work, he took her out to Latin dance clubs where couples drank cocktails with names like Paloma or Caipirinha and showed off their salsa moves. Tall and womanly, young Celestina easily passed for eighteen and never had anyone question her age. She knew how to move to music, thanks to years of dance lessons. Although she had been told she was not slim enough for professional ballet, her natural allure commanded an audience everywhere they went. When people asked about the girl on his arm, Antonio introduced her simply as, "My date, Celestina."

Celestina understood the game and was happy to play along. She felt proud to be squired around by a man of style and stature. They lived this enjoyable fiction, unbeknownst to Stella.

It was harmless fun, Antonio told himself. Just an old father basking in the glory of youth. But the relentless pace of work, late nights, and heavy drinking began to take their toll on Antonio's judgement. As did the street drugs he dabbled in when Celestina was not looking. He liked feeling her body, so fragrant and ripe, close to his. At first, he was ashamed of his feelings. But the longer they lived in this fiction, the more real it seemed.

She made ever more frequent appearances in his fantasies. He began drawing her, Vargas-style, in his private sketchbooks. Over time, the fantasies became more vivid, and the memory of the child he once held in his arms faded. As a young man, he had told himself that no taboo was strong enough to keep him from the woman he loved. Fifteen years later, he would hear these words again, whispering like Eden's snake, deep within his deranged heart.

6

Monsters' Night

It was the night of the premiere, the highlight of Celestina's summer. *Mariposa of the Moon* was one of her father's most popular serials, and now it was on the big screen. Celestina and her father would be seated in the VIP section, along with the producer, director, and stars. For the first time that summer, she was not envious of her cousins vacationing in the States.

Celestina had done her hair in an au courant shag, à la Sheena Easton. Once she was satisfied, she took to a three-way mirror to review her look. She had been practising all week to get it just so. She wanted to look like those Patrick Nagel girls on the walls of her father's office. She had coloured her dark auburn hair jet black for the occasion. Her porcelain-hued face stood in sharp contrast to her inky hair and cherry-red lipstick. She had a special outfit ready, hand-picked by her father. It looked impossibly small on the hanger. It was not a dress she would have chosen for herself, but he convinced her it was appropriately glamorous for the occasion. She took off her kimono and very carefully put on her Wolford hose from Europe. They were expensive but they made her legs look flawless and glossy, like Barbie doll limbs. She then shimmied into the form-fitting black dress styled like an old-fashioned corset. As much as she pulled the hem down, the dress barely made it to the midpoint of her thighs. Finally, she stepped into a pair of patent leather stilettos. They were wickedly uncomfortable, but she had to admit they made her look statuesque and sleek like those girls in music videos. She wondered if she could really pull it off, but it was too late for a change of outfit. She put on a pair of large lightning-bolt earrings, grabbed her purse, and made her way downstairs where her mother was waiting to take her picture.

Stella's smile turned into a look of quiet horror as she watched this MTV tart coming down the stairs. Manang Rio came in from the kitchen and supplied the words the speechless Stella could not. "Diyos mio, Celestina! Is that your dress or your underwear?"

Manang Rio's protestations were cut short by Antonio's footsteps. He announced his arrival downstairs with a happy tune and a trail of expensive cologne. He went straight to his daughter, took a long appraising look, and let out a slow wolf whistle.

"They should put your picture on a bomb and drop it on the Great Makoy," Antonio quipped.

"I don't get it," Celestina said.

"Better that you don't."

"Marcos," Manang Rio whispered.

Stella pulled her husband aside and said, as calmly as she could muster, "She can't go out like that!"

Antonio rolled his eyes and said, "You're too uptight, Stella. Relax and let her enjoy her beauty and youth." Without waiting for Stella's reply, he turned to Celestina and said, "Get in the car. We don't want to be late."

Stella noticed that her husband had grown his hair out and sported day-old stubble like those Miami cops on TV. He was dressed in a tuxedo, sans bowtie, opting to accessorize with a silk scarf adorned with skull prints. He also wore playfully mismatched earrings — a thick gold hoop in one ear and a diamond stud in the other.

"Are those my earrings?" Stella asked.

"I'll return them after the premiere," he said as he gave her a quick kiss. "Ciao, baby!"

Stella and Manang Rio stood by the front door and watched the pair drive away in Antonio's black-and-bronze Chevy Camaro. He had bought the car without consulting Stella, and she was still mad about it. They could have put that money to better use. Stella wondered if she had made a mistake in letting Celestina work with her husband. He had too many bad habits their daughter could pick up. Still, both Antonio and Celestina seemed much happier these days. Perhaps Stella had grown too uptight for her own good. Whose fault was that? Somebody had to be the grown-up in their marriage. It was never him.

She started a flurry of tidying up — picking up magazines, books, and half-empty Pringles tube cans — to distract herself from her angry thoughts. In her rush, she bumped into the pot of her prized jade plant. She had been carefully cultivating each shoot into a treelike form, and after five years, she finally had a miniature jade forest. The pot shattered into several jagged pieces and the little trees scattered all over her dining room floor.

Stella sat down to have a good cry while Manang Rio swept up the broken pieces. Stella's self-pity was cut short by a phone call. "It's Czarina," Manang Rio said, Stella's cousin from Cebu. Stella had never been so glad to be interrupted. She choked back her tears, cleared her throat, and ran to the phone to give her best impression of cheerfulness. Stella listened gratefully as her cousin chattered on. "I miss you so much, cuz," Czarina said. "It's been ages since we've talked."

By the end of the conversation, Stella realized she needed a break from the city, from work, from the house, and from the whole misbegotten life she had chosen.

*

Celestina had a moment of panic as she prepared to disembark from their car and walk the red carpet. She had lived most of her days in a modest school uniform. She had no idea how to move in that revealing dress. She tugged at her father's hand and said, "Papang, how do I get out of this car without giving everyone a free show?"

"Are you going to deny the boys a glimpse of paradise?" Antonio teased.

"That's not funny, Papang," Celestina said anxiously.

"I'm just having fun. Hang in there," he assured her. "I'll talk you through it."

Antonio got out first and opened the door for her. "Take your time. Make them wait," he said as he took her hand. "Now, knees and ankles together, swing your legs around, slide out slowly. Good. Now we stand and smile for the cameras."

He pulled her closer to him as the photographers took their places. Not knowing what else to do, she put her hand on her hip and struck a modelish pose. Their picture would appear in the next day's entertainment section — a striking young vixen and a roguish older man, captioned as "The Maestro and his Muse."

Cameras followed them as they walked hand in hand to the theatre. Inside, the lobby buzzed with excitement as industry people from the publishing and movie worlds mingled and waited for the arrival of the stars of the evening. Antonio proudly introduced Celestina to the movie's director and to the film executive who produced the movie. She was left alone to chat with them as Antonio got pulled into conversations with old friends and well-wishers. The two men were polite enough, but she could tell they were appraising her as if she were a sports car they were looking to buy.

The director was the younger and hipper of the pair. He introduced himself by his professional name, Pilak, which meant silver in Tagalog. He mentioned the films he had directed.

"I'm sorry. I haven't had a chance to see your films," Celestina admitted.

The girls at her school did not watch Tagalog movies. They were considered baduy, fit only for maids, blue-collar men, and the lower classes. She asked him instead what he considered most challenging about his job. He laughed and without a moment's hesitation replied, "Those damnable love scenes."

"I don't need to know why," she giggled bashfully.

Pilak kept talking as if he did not hear her. "I'm so sick of haggling with actresses. Negotiating for every millimetre of exposure. They think I'm doing it for my own gratification. I tell them there are easier ways to get off."

The film executive, widely known as Tito Roz, smiled and looked on as Celestina chatted with the director. She took care to regularly nod in Tito Roz's direction. Even the shy and quiet ones have something to bring to the conversation, the nuns at school taught her. She had seen him in occasional TV interviews and in the gossip magazines Manang Rio liked to read. He did not fit her stereotype of film executives. She always pictured them as cigar-smoking, glad-handing fat cats. She thought the Tito honorific was apt, as Roz seemed more like the quiet uncle who worked in the accounting department. She was about to thank him for supporting her father's work, when he asked, "Are you under contract with anyone?"

Celestina then realized that Tito Roz had made a mistake.

"I'm not an actress," she explained. "I'm a production assistant at New Legends publishing."

"I see. You're too pretty to be behind the scenes. Call me if you ever want to do a screen test," he said, handing her his business card.

Antonio came back just as the usher was showing the VIPs to their seats. Once they were seated, Celestina put her head on his shoulder to quiet her mind. The flash of cameras, the admiring looks, and Antonio's evident pride in her was a heady brew. Celestina always felt like a big, ungainly water buffalo beside her cousins, the ethereal nymphs. But on that seemingly magical evening, in the arms of this dashing man, she understood how it felt to be a desirable woman.

*

Tito Roz smiled as the last scene of *Mariposa of the Moon* faded and the credits rolled. An electric shiver washed over him as the audience applauded. He knew he had another hit. He had no time for cineastes and other snobs who looked down on trashy serialized novellas. To him, it was like buying a profitable turnkey operation. By the time the serial was done, he had a built-in audience of fans ready to pay all over again to see the movie adaptation. Besides, he really liked Antonio Errantes. Despite his literary pedigree, Antonio had no qualms about working on screen adaptations of his serials. There is no such thing as highbrow and lowbrow, Antonio had told him when they first met. A good story is a good story.

Tito Roz watched as the theatre emptied and the guests made their way to the exits. They were going to the after-party he had arranged for the cast, crew, and story team. He believed in rewarding good people in a properly grand manner. It kept the *swerte* coming in. He could see Antonio and his date taking their time. Needless to say, the girl was not Antonio's wife. Everybody knew he was married to Sebastien Sytanco's daughter. It was not unusual for a successful middle-aged man to have a querida. All men had needs, and they were not always met in the marital bed. Ultimately, thought Tito Roz, it was not for him to judge Antonio or what he chose to do with another consenting adult.

Outside the theatre, the producer could see Antonio and his date waiting for the valet to deliver his Camaro. The girl gazed at Antonio with obvious admiration. Tito Roz could see Antonio drinking in her attention. Men needed that, almost as much as they needed food. She seemed like a nice girl, well spoken and well mannered. Tito Roz hoped she would not be cruelly discarded when she was no longer at the peak of her youth and attractiveness. Perhaps she would take him up on his screen test offer. If she were smart, which she seemed to be, she would take advantage of her youth before it faded. The valet soon came around with the Camaro. Antonio inspected it to make sure there was no damage. Satisfied, he took out a crisp bill and handed it to the young man. Tito Roz watched as the girl got in the car and took control of the radio. The Camaro roared off down the boulevard, leaving the faint chorus of "More to Lose" by Seona Dancing in its wake.

*

The club was filled with industry insiders and glitterati dancing to the Birmingham DJ's party mixes. Tito Roz slipped in almost unnoticed. That was the way he liked it. He had no use for the showbiz drama and intrigue. That was for the fans. To him, it was a business, pure and simple.

He patrolled the party room discreetly to see if everything was in order. The leading lady was holding court in the VIP area. She was a third-generation actress, born into showbiz royalty. Like the character she played in the movie, she suffered from a generational curse. Spoiled rotten and emotionally fragile, she had been using street drugs to cope. Her mother and her grandmother before her both abused alcohol and died before their time.

Tito Roz watched the leading lady's friends to make sure nobody was slipping her shabu. He had already spent good money sending her to rehab. She had better not backslide if she wanted to continue having a career.

The leading man preferred to hang out behind the bar and chat with the production crew and wait staff. Tito Roz "discovered" him three years ago, an X-ray technician at a medical laboratory. Regular guys who became famous had one advantage over those born into showbiz royalty: They were equipped for life after fame.

Tito Roz quickly nodded and smiled at assorted second unit and assistant directors as he made his way to the smaller private area. He stood quietly behind the curtain while Antonio and the girl slow-danced to a fast song. There were two empty wineglasses, an open bottle of champagne, and a large, half-smoked joint on the table by the chaise longue. She was clearly tipsy and a bit high, with heavy-lidded eyes and a silly half smile. Antonio leaned close and whispered in her ear. Her lovely, sparkling laugh rang clear through the moody music. Transfixed by the sight and sound of her, he stopped dancing and led the girl back to the table. He poured her another drink while his hand rested on her leg. Swaying to the music, she sipped her champagne while he fondled her knee and stroked her thigh. Through her tipsy haze, she brushed away his hand. With an amused shrug, he took a long drag on his joint before leaning in, hand in her hair, to give her a slow, smoky kiss. Her body stiffened and struggled before going limp under his.

Bass notes filled the room like a monster's heartbeat as Tito Roz walked away. He already knew how the scene would play out. In the end, she would surrender because his hunger was much stronger than her fight.

Oh, women and their games. She should have known that Antonio Errantes was not a man she could toy with. No doubt, she got something from him — nice clothes, fancy dinners, a foot in the door. Now he was taking his part of the deal — like those ancient deities who gave bountiful harvests in exchange for the blood of maidens. Would he call them monsters? Tito Roz refused to judge. It all depended on what you prayed for and what you were willing to lay down on the altar.

*

Early in the morning, while it was still dark, Antonio Errantes woke up in his guest room still dressed in most of his party clothes. He had done something horrific, and he only hoped he had done it in his nightmares. Stumbling out of bed, he staggered out the door, careful not to make too much noise lest he wake up Stella in the master bedroom.

A sliver of light from Celestina's room illuminated the dark hall. Softly, he opened her door. She lay in bed like a broken doll, arms and legs splayed. She turned and looked at him with a wordless "Why?" in her eyes. He knew then it had not been a nightmare. He sat next to her in bed and crumpled into a heap of sobs. "I'm a monster," he wept, over and over.

When he finally stopped sobbing, he looked at her with wild eyes and said, "I love you. I don't care if I go to hell for it."

She let him crawl to her, to comfort himself in her arms. The monster had been unleashed, and the only way to escape from it would be to run away or to die. Soundlessly, she wept, for herself and for the father she had lost.

7

Unspeakable

Thelmo the driver checked his watch as he drove the old Mercedes-Benz sedan into the modest subdivision in Misericordia Valley. He was a former lieutenant in the army, but now he worked for Sebastien Sytanco's family. Affluent Chinese families were prime targets of kidnappers, so Thelmo's main job was to get the three Sytanco granddaughters safely to school and back to their homes or after-school activities. He was licensed to carry a firearm, and he was trained in arnis so he could fight with sticks, should it come to that.

It was his first day back on the job after the girls' two-month summer vacation, and he was fifteen minutes behind schedule. A fender-bender had backed up traffic on the main road. In the backseat, Mikee and the slightly younger Gidget had been talking non-stop since they left Olympia Heights. They could not wait to tell their cousin Celestina all about their adventures. The girls switched between Hokkien and Colegiala English, the English-Tagalog patois of private-school girls.

The driver did not speak any of those languages, but he caught enough of the conversation to know that the girls took full advantage of their freedoms in the States. Such things would never happen under his watch, of course. Beyond that, he had simply learned not to care. He tuned out and turned his focus back on the road and the rainfall. He thought it was ridiculous that the Philippine school year started during the rainy season. Already, he could feel the tires cutting through two inches of rainfall. He hoped the waters would not rise any more.

Sebastien Sytanco did not waste money on the latest models of fancy cars, so Thelmo was driving a Mercedes-Benz that likely came out the year Gidget Sytanco was born. But even a tank of a car like that was powerless against deadly flash floods.

The other granddaughter named Celestina was already outside the gate waiting for him. She was the last one to get picked up, as she was the only one who did not live in the large Sytanco compound in Olympia Heights. Celestina was, by all accounts, the "poor" granddaughter — the child of the famously disinherited Stella. But Sebastien decided that putting Celestina in the carpool was better than paying a big, fat ransom to some small-time thugs. Beside her was Manang Rio, holding an umbrella the size of a small hut. Manang walked beside Celestina until she was safely inside the car. She greeted her cousins shyly. So much had changed in the past months; she no longer felt like the same person.

"We missed you, Celle," Mikee said. "We felt bad you couldn't come."

"We got you a present," Gidget said. "This is Whiskers."

Celestina found herself holding a luxuriantly furred stuffed rabbit. Its head was tilted just so, and there seemed to be a kind soul behind the glass eyes.

"He's made of mink," Gidget said, stroking the rabbit's soft belly. "We couldn't resist."

"Thank you. He's adorable," Celestina said with as much enthusiasm as she could muster.

It was not at all unusual for high school or even college girls in this part of the world to own stuffed toys. A year ago, Celestina would have smothered the mink rabbit with hugs and kisses, but now, she felt incredibly old.

Still high from their glorious summer, Gidget and Mikee failed to notice their cousin's listless demeanour. They lost no time launching into stories.

"Mikee met someone," Gidget teased.

Celestina smiled graciously as Mikee whipped out snapshots of herself and Rhys, the young half-Chinese guy she met on the beach. He lived next to their aunt's house in Malibu with his British father, who directed documentaries.

"He's gorgeous," Celestina said.

"We kissed," Mikee swooned. "It was so, so wonderful. I felt like I was filled with butterflies, and I was going to float away."

"Wow. That must have been some kiss," Celestina replied.

"Have you ever been kissed, Celestina?"

"Yes," she said after a couple of beats. "By Papang." Celestina quickly looked away and pressed Whiskers to her chest. But no matter, Mikee was too giddy to notice.

"She doesn't mean a daddy kiss, silly girl," Gidget laughed. "She means on the lips. With tongue. By a guy."

"No, not by a guy. Just Papang," Celestina heard herself say.

"Tell her more, Mikee," Gidget said. "She needs the juicy details."

"Rhys and I made out a little bit. He let me touch his … you know. I was too scared to do anything else. But I saw *it*."

Celestina felt her breath coming in short, shallow bursts as Mikee's words ricocheted inside her head. Celestina could not recall what was said after that. All she remembered was a sharp spasm in her belly followed by the taste of acid in her mouth. "Stop the car!" Celestina ordered.

Thelmo the driver saw Celestina's chalk-white face in his rear-view mirror. He pulled over quickly and managed to get Celestina out of the car, seconds before she got violently ill on the side of the road. He put on his hazard lights, gave Celestina a sip of water, and waited for her stomach to settle. He was relieved the rain had slowed down to a drizzle, but they were most certainly going to be late for morning prayers and the flag ceremony.

"Go on," Celestina said. "I need some air. I'll walk."

"You know I can't let you do that, Miss Celestina," the driver said, not unkindly. "I'll take you home after I drop off your cousins."

"No, I'd rather go to school," she replied firmly. She did not want to have to explain herself to her mother and Manang Rio.

Back in the car, Celestina gratefully accepted his suggestion to have her sit in front. Her cousins sat quietly in the back seat, wondering what had just happened. They were supposed to feel bad that Celestina got sick by the road. In truth, they felt annoyed because she ruined their fun.

Celestina realized she could no longer be part of this sisterhood of cousins. No longer could she bare her heart to them. That heart was now filled with unspeakable secrets. After several tense minutes, they arrived at the gates of Colegio de la Inmaculada Concepcion. Gidget and Mikee got out and walked into the gates hand in hand. Celestina did not try to keep up with them. She would have to find her own path from there on.

*

Stella had been gone for only a week, but Manang Rio could not shake the feeling that their household was on the brink of a catastrophe. At four o'clock, just as she was gathering the last of the sheets on the clothesline, Celestina came back from school. Even through the uniform, Manang could tell that the girl's waistline was thicker and there was a hint of a bump on her usually flat tummy. All at once, it struck Manang. She had not seen blood on the girl's underpants since school started.

Manang Rio crossed herself as she realized the horror of Celestina's situation. How could this have happened? She and Stella guarded that girl like a sacred treasure. There were no boys at her exclusive school, not even a male teacher or janitor. The neighbourhood youth never even got close to her. They only ever saw her through the window of the family car or being dropped off by her carpool. Who was the man responsible for this?

She had been meaning to talk to Celestina, but the girl was as silent as a ghost lately. Manang tried to think of a plan as she gathered the dried laundry. One of the sheets had been stained by a bird dropping. Ruined after all her washing and sun bleaching. "Punyetang ibon," she cursed the errant bird. She angrily threw the sheet back into the laundry sink and stomped into the house with her basket of linens. Celestina was the closest thing she had to a daughter. No mother wants to see her daughter become a disgrasyada.

Manang Rio marched upstairs and knocked on Celestina's door. "I'm here with your clean laundry," she said.

Celestina opened the door, then quickly buried her head back in her homework. As Manang began stripping the bed, the stale smell of Antonio's cologne filled the room. A short, sharp breath escaped Manang's lips as she realized the odour was all over Celestina's bedsheets. How long has this been going on, she wondered? How could she not have seen it? Manang Rio always felt something was not right with the way Antonio looked at his daughter. She cursed herself for not listening to her instincts.

"Celestina, are you going to tell me, or do I need to say it?"

Without a word, Celestina stood up and laid the housekeeper's hands on her belly.

Manang Rio held Celestina as the tears came. "I'll call your mother in Cebu. She's the only one he's scared of. Until she gets home, you say nothing to him, understand?"

Celestina nodded tearfully, grateful that the secret had been extracted from her.

"Now gather your things," Manang said. "You sleep in the kubo with me."

That night and for the next few nights, Celestina would sleep soundly in the small cottage in the corner of the garden, where Manang stayed after her workday was done.

Antonio's car rolled into carport at ten-thirty, just as Manang Rio was reading from her Hiligaynon dialect prayer book. She could see him turning on the lights in the house. Minutes later, she heard his voice thundering at her door.

"Where did you take her, bruha?"

Manang Rio walked to the window, slid the panel open, and calmly faced Antonio. His eyes gleamed like a wild animal's and his breath reeked of the cheap gin colloquially known as Marca Demonyo.

"She is hurting and in need of a mother's love. I'm taking care of her," she said.

Antonio uttered a Chavacano curse and stormed out of the gate, back into the night.

"Demonyo," she muttered under her breath.

*

"Stella, your daughter needs you. Come home as soon as you can," Manang had said in a brief, cryptic phone message left on Czarina's answering machine early that day. Prior to that call, Stella was having nightmares — visions of Celestina being stalked by an unseen animal. The dreams put a dark cloud over Stella's otherwise pleasant vacation. Her cousin Czarina blamed the nightmares on the state of Stella's marriage.

"You need a better husband," Czarina said when she drove Stella to the airport to catch an early plane back to Manila. "You take care of your family, but no one's taking care of you."

Czarina's words and Manang's phone call were still echoing in Stella's mind as she put down her bags and handed Manang a box of Torta Mamón Cebuana — egg yolk–rich cupcakes flavoured with star anise. On any other day, Manang would have received the gift with delight and made tea for everyone. Today, she took it without a word and put aside Stella's bags before asking her to sit down.

"Tell me the bad news," Stella said.

"Celestina is *with child*. Two months, maybe three."

After a long, stunned silence Stella spoke. "I don't understand. She's a good girl. She's not even interested in boys yet. How could this happen?"

Manang Rio shook her head and blurted out, "You want to know how? Why don't you ask your demon of a husband? He can tell you exactly how it happened!"

To her dying day, Stella would vividly remember how she felt after hearing those words. A great fireball rose inside her, consuming the joy and hope she so carefully tended in her heart. In a blind rage, she grabbed one of her golf clubs, marched into Antonio's study, and smashed all his expensive whisky bottles. When she was done with them, she unleashed her wrath on his awards, his big screen television, and the art on his wall. Then, with her bare hands, she tore into his books, magazines, story drafts, and drawings. She found his favourite Wayfarers, threw them on the floor, and crushed them under her heel. When it was over, the room was a wasteland of broken glass and ripped paper. And Stella was nothing but embers and ash.

She sat in his chair, oblivious to the bleeding cut on her hand. Manang pressed a clean tea towel on Stella's wound before picking up pieces of broken glass.

"Leave it, Manang. I want him to see what he's done."

"Do not lose your head over this, Stella. Your daughter needs you to be strong."

Stella said nothing more. She had no more anger, hate, or any other feelings for the man she once loved. All she had left was a stark picture of what he had become. Strangely, her head had never been so clear, and her heart was dead calm.

*

The three women gathered in Manang Rio's hut after a quiet early dinner. Antonio would not be home until later. Celestina sat still with downcast eyes as her mother laid out their plan.

"I'll tell your principal you'll be living with me in Cebu for the rest of the year. I'll arrange for you to stay at the Heart of Mary Villa with the Good Shepherd Sisters. You'll have a tutor, and the Sisters will take care of you until the baby comes. After that, I'll take you and the baby home. We'll tell people we adopted an orphan from Cebu."

"I can't have the baby," Celestina said. "Every day with it would be a reminder of what happened. I can't do it."

"Abortion is a mortal sin, as you know. It's also illegal," her mother said sternly.

"It's not illegal in Hong Kong or Taiwan. I know someone's cousin who had it done at a hospital in Hong Kong."

"Put that thought out of your mind," Stella replied. "We cannot add any more *malas* to this house."

"She's too young to be a mother," Manang spoke up. "And you, you're too busy to raise another child. Why not leave it with the nuns so it can go to a nice family?"

"Please, Manang, it's not your place to speak on family matters."

Manang fell silent. She had given her adult life in service to Sebastien Sytanco and his family. The elder Sytancos always said the helpers were family. Honeyed words, of course, but it was nice to hear them. Stella's remark was a sobering reminder that blood, and only blood, mattered to the Sytancos.

"I hate this child," Celestina said. "I will hate it every day of its life."

"We will work through this. The child is a Sytanco," Stella replied. "It will be raised here with us and be given a proper education. As for Antonio, he'll have to go."

Both Celestina and Manang understood that Stella had laid down the law, and there was no changing her mind. They watched her walk back to the house to wait for Antonio. Manang turned off the lamp so Celestina could rest. Celestina tried to sleep, but evil whispers in her head taunted her. *You let it happen.* Manang felt Celestina's restlessness from the other side of the room.

"Would you like another pillow?" Manang asked.

"No, thank you."

"Would you like to talk?"

"Yes, Manang. Tell the driver I'm not feeling well. I'm going to Quiapo tomorrow."

The elder woman sat up and turned on the light again. "Listen to me, anak. Quiapo is a snake pit. They take one look at that pretty, light-skinned face of yours, and next thing you know, you're kidnapped and sold to a rich Arabo. I won't let you go there."

"I'll risk it. I must see an herbalista. Their potions must work. They've been there forever. I've heard many stories."

"Many fakes, my child. If you don't do it right, the child will be born damaged, then you have a bigger problem. You must know where to go."

Celestina picked up on the subtle hint buried in the maid's words. "You know where to go, don't you, Manang?"

The older woman replied with a silence that echoed through the night.

"Who was the father, Manang?"

"Nobody you know."

"Take me to Quiapo. Take me to your herbalista."

"Go to sleep. You're not thinking straight."

"Take me or I'll find another way. I'll fling myself down the stairs. I'll even do it with a wire hanger. Don't think I won't."

"That's enough! You are not killing yourself over this."

"I'd rather die than have his child. I know it's going to be a monster like him. I have nightmares about it," Celestina sobbed.

Manang Rio took the weeping girl into her arms and let out a weary sigh. She was faced with an impossible choice. Stella would curse her if she helped, but the girl might just kill herself if she did not.

"You stubborn like your mother! Go to sleep. We must get there before the sun gets too high up in the sky."

*

That evening, Antonio came home at around half past eight. The house was eerily quiet. There were no sounds of Manang Rio putting away the dishes in the kitchen, or Celestina watching her MTV. He was surprised to see Stella's luggage by the door, where Manang had left it that afternoon. Stella was not expected to come back until the following week. He called out to her but got no reply. The double doors of his study had been flung open. Perhaps Manang had been cleaning. He walked in to find the wreckage of his personal treasures and did not need to ask who or why. It was over for him.

Antonio cleared the debris from the couch and sat down with his head in his hands. He did not hear his wife walk in.

"Congratulations," a familiar voice said. "You're going to be a father. Or is it a grandfather?"

He looked up and found Stella standing amidst the pile of torn books and papers, dressed in a pure white cutwork camisole and matching crisp pyjamas.

"I'm sorry, Stella. I don't know myself anymore. I seem to be possessed by something. It makes me do regrettable, monstrous things."

"I want you to leave, Antonio. Before you hurt anyone else."

"Where would I go? This is my home. My family."

"Your family is no more, Antonio. You've broken us."

"I need help, Stella. I need you."

"I can't help you anymore, Antonio. I can barely save myself or my daughter."

"I'll do anything to make this right."

"Goodbye, Antonio," she said as she took off her wedding ring. "I want you to have this. Maybe it will remind you of what you destroyed."

As she walked away, Antonio remembered when a young Stella favoured him with a smile, and it seemed as if he had been given a benediction. *What have you done, Antonio? What have you done?*

8

Quiapo

Celestina and Manang Rio's trip to Quiapo began at the jeepney stop by the wet market where residents of Misericordia Valley bought fresh fish and meat. It was only the third time Celestina had taken public transit in her life. She momentarily forgot about her grim errand as she stared at the fantastically decorated bodies of passing jeepneys. There were miniature chrome steeds perched on the hoods, Day-Glo pastoral scenes with majestic water buffalos, and airbrushed depictions of the Virgin Mary in all her glory. Soon the ride bound for Quiapo arrived at their stop. A painting of Jesus crowned with thorns graced the door on the driver's side. Celestina's eyes were drawn to the vividly painted blood on his forehead. *Forgive me, Lord*, she said in silent prayer.

The ride would take Celestina and Manang Rio from their comfortable, middle-class home to the guts of a sprawling, chaotic metropolis. They held on as their vehicle careened from street corner to street corner. There was no waiting until the next stop as passengers boarded and disembarked anytime and anywhere they pleased.

When traffic slowed to a crawl, Celestina distracted herself with the jeepney's decorations. The driver's compartment had a brightly lit altar featuring a crucifix, a garland of everlasting flowers, and a small statue of the Virgin Mary. On the passenger side, decals of pin-up girls mingled shamelessly with passages from the Book of Psalms.

An hour after they left Misericordia Valley, they arrived in front of Quiapo Church — known to millions of devotees as the home of the Black Nazarene, a reputedly miraculous statue of Christ carved out of blackened wood. In the shadow of the great church was a bazaar where one could buy bootleg videos, amulets, and herbal cures for everything that ailed human flesh. Manang guided Celestina through the thicket of hawkers and fortune-telling stalls. Celestina felt drained by the heat and nauseated by the stench of garbage and diesel fumes.

A legless vendor dressed in a dirt-streaked T-shirt wheeled over to Celestina and Manang in his makeshift wooden trolley. "How about you buy a medallion, pretty girl? Blessed by a priest already, very holy," he said with a smile.

Celestina was overcome with pity. Her grandfather's pets led better lives than this poor wretched man, yet he carried on with admirable enterprise and spirit. She bought a medallion and told him to keep the change. She was about to commit a sin worthy of excommunication. Perhaps the medallion might buy her a scrap of mercy when it was her time to be judged.

Manang pulled her along, mindful that other vendors and beggars might soon swarm them. The woman and the girl walked until they came to a row of stalls bearing garapons of mysterious herbs and barks. Displayed prominently were flasks of potions euphemistically marked "pamparegla" — remedies for delayed periods. The herb and potion vendors did brisk business, year after year, quietly selling their brews in the dark laneways around the imposing Baroque-style church.

Manang Rio looked around until she spotted a familiar character among the rows of sunbeaten faces — an old woman puffing on a brown Alhambra cigarillo. "That's her," Manang said. They approached the stall and Manang spoke to the old woman in the Hiligaynon dialect. There was a flash of recognition in the old woman's eyes followed by a smile revealing teeth stained from decades of smoking unfiltered tobacco. Celestina was shocked to see that the old vendor had the lit end of the Alhambra inside her mouth.

"How long has your regla been delayed?" the vendor asked between puffs.

"More than two months," Celestina said.

"Good thing you came to me now. You wait any longer, and the pamparegla might not work anymore."

The old woman handed her a bag of herbal capsules and six flasks of grape-coloured liquid marked with crudely printed labels. "Drink a third of the liquid from one of the flasks, three times a day before meals. Follow with these capsules. Do that for six days. No sour food or cold drinks. After that, your period will return."

Celestina could hear a priest's voice booming from the loudspeaker of the Quiapo Church. It spoke of the Lamb of God who took away the sins of the world. She held on to the priest's words while another, more sinister, voice whispered to her, *There's no mercy for the likes of you.*

*

On the seventh day, Celestina woke up with the taste of mud and pickling lime in her mouth. It was, she realized, the bitter herbs bubbling up from within. She got up and forced herself to eat some breakfast before telling her mother, "I'm not well. I want to stay home today."

Stella felt her daughter's forehead and gave her a hug before leaving for work. "I'll tell Manang to make you some Chicken

Tinola with lots of ginger," she smiled. Celestina choked back her tears and nodded.

Celestina's cramps started soon after her mother left. She decided to go back to bed, but on the way upstairs, a sudden gush of blood sent her running to the bathroom. She sat on the toilet and watched the water turn redder and redder.

"Help me!" Celestina yelled out as she felt increasing waves of pain. Hearing this, Manang ran upstairs. It was happening. It was time. She found Celestina crying, legs and body twisted in anguish.

"Use your breath to help your body push."

Celestina did as she was told. The minutes stretched out, suspended in agony. A large clot passed, and then another. The pain subsided, and time snapped back to its old form. Celestina instinctively looked down at the contents in the bowl.

"No need to look. It's just blood," Manang said.

"You know that's not true, Manang," Celestina said as she caught a glimpse of pink amidst the red. It was encased in a bubble and was reminiscent of a mouse.

Manang did not reply. She quickly flushed the toilet and helped Celestina into the shower. Strong, rough hands washed Celestina as warm water gently sprayed on her head. She remembered being dried with a soft towel that smelled of bleach, then being led down the hall to her room.

"Take these two Cortal tablets to help with the pain," Manang said as she poured a glass of water for Celestina. "I'll be downstairs making soup."

Celestina swallowed the pills with a full glass of water before collapsing on her bed. She watched without emotion as the vague, faceless figure of Manang disappeared behind the door. Her back felt clammy against the plastic liner laid on top of her bed. She turned and lay on her side, only to have her bedside crucifix reproach her. Ashamed, she turned away and buried herself deep in the quilt. She could pray for forgiveness, but she did not deserve it. This was, after all, what she wanted.

An hour passed, and the bleeding started again. This was how it was going to be for the next few days, Manang told her. She cried out as sharp stabs of pain rose from her womb. In her torment, she prayed for release, even if it came in the form of death.

*

The warm, gingery aroma of Chicken Tinola greeted Stella as she opened the door. For a moment, she forgot about the maelstrom her family was caught in. Chicken Tinola was the magical soup that got you on your feet when you were laid down with illness. Maybe the soup will help heal whatever ailed their household.

Stella called out for her daughter, but Manang Rio said, "She's resting." Stella helped herself to the tinola, filling her bowl with succulent dark meat, chili leaves, and fragrant broth made with young native hens. Manang declined Stella's invitation to join her, saying, "I had some of the sopas earlier. I'm not very hungry."

Stella quickly finished her solitary meal then went to the kitchen to find Celestina's favourite bowl. She filled it with a good helping of broth, chicken thighs, and green papaya. She carried the tray upstairs and softly opened Celestina's door, so as not to startle her. Celestina looked pale, and her face was dotted with beads of sweat. Stella set down the tray and touched Celestina's forehead. She was running a fever. Her lips were moving, but Stella could not make out what she was saying. Stella rushed to the bathroom to get a wet washcloth.

"Celestina," Stella said as she dabbed cool water on her daughter's face. "I brought you some soup."

Celestina stirred and opened her eyes. Her gaze, usually sparkling and mischievous, was glassy. She looked at her mother but did not seem to see her.

With rising panic, Stella said, "Talk to me, child."

Celestina smiled and said, "Great-Auntie Selena came by for a visit." With that, she closed her eyes and promptly fell back into a delirious sleep.

A shiver went through Stella when she heard the name. Selena Sytanco was the older half-sister of her father Sebastien. Neither Stella nor Celestina had ever met her. Selena died during the Second World War, a quarter of a century before Celestina was born.

Stella ran to the phone to call their family doctor. Just as she was about to dial the number, she heard a soft knock. Manang came in and said, "Celestina miscarried this afternoon."

After a taut silence, Stella replied, "You helped her do it, didn't you?"

"She was going to do it, whether you liked it or not. Better she does it right than kill herself trying."

A slap landed across Manang's face, sharp as whiplash.

"Who do you think you are, making life-or-death decisions for my daughter? This is my family. You're just a housekeeper," Stella hissed. "Now get the hell out of my sight. Before I get you arrested."

The chastened maid left her duties and stayed in her kubo for the rest of the evening. Stella phoned Doctora Lim, their long-time physician and her mother's friend. They could count on her to be discreet.

Doctora Lim came soon after, followed by a quiet ambulance, so as not to draw attention from the neighbours. Stella recounted, without emotion, the chain of events that led to the emergency. The doctora listened with the composure of one who had seen and heard it all before.

"We have to take her in to make sure she doesn't go into septic shock," she said. "Likely, there's some excess tissue or part of the placenta that wasn't expelled."

Celestina was carried out on a stretcher, put in the ambulance, and driven to the doctora's private clinic. For the next few hours after her operation, the girl drifted in and out of delirium, now and then conversing with an unseen visitor.

Stella sat numbly as Celestina edged dangerously close to the "other side." She tried to pray, but her entreaties were drowned out by sinister voices inside her head. *What did you expect, Stella? Danger has always been part of your husband's charm. You knew, you had always known there was a beast inside that dazzling man.* On and on the voices went.

Stella remembered how Celestina used to light up whenever Antonio was around. How she primped and preened for him in her cute little sundresses and youthful beauty. And who could compete with that? *What were you thinking, Celestina, when you answered his invitation? Did you think you might replace me in his affections?*

Doctora Lim's calm voice interrupted Stella's dark thoughts. "The worst is over. She'll pull through. There might be some uterine scarring. You understand what that means, right?"

"Yes, I understand," Stella said in a voice she barely recognized.

"Go home. You're tired. I'll ask my chauffeur to drive you."

A bone-weary Stella sat back in the doctora's BMW and let the night scenes of the city wash over her. A street urchin tapped on Stella's window as they waited for the light between Quezon City and San Juan. The driver shooed him away so he would not smudge the glass. Stella barely registered the street kid. She felt guilty for blaming her daughter. Celestina was just a child, despite appearances. By the time the light turned green, Stella had surrendered to the blessed forgetfulness of sleep.

9

Silent House

Celestina opened her eyes suddenly as her back hit the hard mattress. Her spine still held the memory of falling from a great height. She did not recognize the room, with walls the colour of old bones. The distinctive smell of disinfectant and iodine told her she was in a clinic or hospital.

She remembered taking a long drive with a lady visitor who looked a bit like her mother. They drove along a boulevard by the sea, lined with palm trees. Celestina was certain it was Roxas Boulevard, but without the tall buildings. There was a lovely young lady riding a tawny horse on the promenade by the shore. After a long while, they reached a lane with a strange shimmering tower. Instantly, they were inside, in a great room full of elegantly dressed people. They seemed to know Celestina and welcomed her like family. She felt pleased until she saw herself in a mirror, dressed in a white silk blouse — and a blood-stained skirt.

"It doesn't matter," the lady said, undoing her scarf to reveal a bloody gash. "We're family."

Celestina walked through the tower's chambers, listening to fascinating conversations in languages she had never learned but somehow understood. She could have stayed longer, perhaps forever, but the lady said, "It's not your time. You have to go back."

Suddenly, the people and conversations were gone, and Celestina was inside a glass room. "I don't want to go back," she said to the lady. "I want to die. I deserve to die."

The lady's next words were lost as the sliding doors of the room closed. And the room started falling, dropping at an ever-increasing speed.

Celestina sat up to clear the vertigo from her head. She suddenly understood the long chain of *malas* that had led her to the bone-white room in which she was now confined. As she looked around the strange room, she caught a glimpse of herself in the mirrored tray on the nightstand, and saw the eyes of a feral animal. Soon after, Doctora Lim, her nurse, and Stella walked into the room. The doctora was pleased to see her patient up, if not about.

"How are you feeling, Celestina?"

"Like I've been pulled apart and stitched back together," she replied, looking past the doctora to her mother.

"We knew you'd come through. Sytanco women are fighters."

Celestina barely registered the doctora's determinedly upbeat words. More than anything, she wanted her mother to just hold her for a while, to tell her that everything was going to be fine, and they were going to be a family again.

"Mama ..." she called out.

Stella reached out to touch Celestina's cheek, noticing the newly prominent cheekbones and unfamiliar hardness on her daughter's face. It was a dispassionate touch, more curious than loving. And the coolness of it wounded Celestina more deeply than a slap.

"I'm taking you home after Doctora Lim examines you," Stella said. "I'll be waiting outside."

Celestina nodded, swallowing her unspoken plea. She knew that her mother had changed, and whatever ties kept them together were now severed.

After the examination, Celestina got dressed, with the help of the nurse, and allowed herself to be led to their car, where Stella was waiting. It was a slow drive home to Misericordia, and the silence between them made the journey seem even longer.

Perhaps, thought Celestina, it would have been better if she had died. Then all the *malas* would have gone to the grave with her. The jagged edges of their family tragedy would have been smoothed out by the tides of time, and she would have been just a happy memory. Celestina's morbid ruminations continued even as they entered the Misericordia Village gates. It was not long before she saw "the house with the high walls," as their neighbours called the Sytanco-Errantes residence. Towering walls were a common feature in the properties of Chinese families. They served to deter thieves and shielded the family from the prying eyes of neighbours. Looking at their walls, she thought, *This is a house built for secrets.*

Stella honked two times — a quick tap for the first one and a longer lean-in for the second one. After a short wait, the gates swung open to let them in. Manang Rio was waiting for them.

"I missed you, anak," Manang said as she took Celestina in her arms. It was the hug Celestina had wanted from her mother.

Stella whisked her away to her room for the prescribed bedrest. As they walked past the mirror in the vestibule, Stella noticed how much her daughter resembled her estranged husband. Tall and well-built like Antonio, Celestina carried herself with the same defiance. She certainly had a Sytanco face, but the expressions were all his, down to the way her eyes drilled into you if your argument was weak.

Upstairs, a freshly made bed was waiting for Celestina.

"I replaced your old mattress," Stella said. "I hope you'll find this one comfortable."

"Thank you, Mama."

"Is there anything else you need?"

"Yes, Mama. I need to know ..."

"What is it that you want to know?"

"I need to know if you can still love me after all this."

"We're family, and we'll stick together," Stella replied with the merest smile. "That's all that matters. Now get some rest."

Celestina watched as Stella closed the bedroom door. A tear rolled down her cheek. Right then, she realized she had come back, but she had not come home. She curled up in bed, closed her eyes, and dreamed of the bayawak that ate her cactus. Once again, the giant lizard was running back to its lair, with its next meal in its muscular jaws. This time, the victim was not a plant. It was a baby, with the umbilical cord still attached.

10

Feral Children

The shy young man first noticed her in the town of Dolores, at the start of his climb to the peak of Mount Banahaw. It was a place considered holy by Semana Santa pilgrims, Rizalistas, UFO watchers, and other souls in search of enlightenment. With a full busload of climbers, the mountaineering club was more like an invasion than a pilgrimage.

But even in that sea of backpacks and bodies, she stood out, a striking figure with a piercing gaze. She was tall for a young woman, carried herself well, and had the telltale features of a Chinese mestisa, which his eyes found especially pleasing. She did not chatter or chit-chat as so many women were inclined to do. She stayed at the edges, observing the proceedings with a vaguely amused expression. Most intriguing of all, she carried within her a pure blue flame, strong and constant. It was a quality she shared with his mother.

The young man himself did not talk much, as he had little in common with his classmates. The state university was a sprawling metropolis compared to the remote seaside village where he was raised. He had read such classics as *Twenty Thousand Leagues Under the Sea*, but had no idea what *The Love Boat* was, since his television access was limited to whatever happened to be playing on the old TV at the town carinderia. As keen as his mind was and as hard as he worked, he feared he would always be socially stunted. Perhaps it was wishful thinking, but the young man sensed he and the quiet young woman could have some wonderful conversations.

Sadly, he found it hard to keep up with her or with anyone else for that matter. His lungs and legs were not accustomed to the challenging terrain. With his heavy backpack, he felt like Christ on the way to his own crucifixion. He soldiered on until they reached the Kristalino Falls where they would camp for the night, amidst the giant ferns and the sound of roaring water. He barely managed to wash up and eat before his exhausted body gave in to sleep.

*

The young man began the day wishing he had not woken up. So deep was his fatigue that he asked the pack leader to go on without him. "I'll find my own way back," he said.

"We leave no one behind," the pack leader replied. "If you quit, we all quit with you."

Unwilling to face the humiliation of derailing forty-nine other people, the young man told himself he would reach the peak through sheer mind over body.

The next hours were a blur of cuts and scratches from low-lying branches and scrub near the top of the mountain. The young man's knees buckled as soon as he reached a clearing at the peak. Lying face down on the soft grass, he spotted tiny flowers that looked like edelweiss. He realized he had left behind the humidity and lushness of the lower slopes for a different climate. The peak was its own country — a land of rocks and clouds, and of hardy plants that would not have been out of place in the Alps. The light, unfiltered by a forest canopy, was almost too much for his eyes — eyes that always saw too much. He closed them for a moment.

There was much laughter and many cameras clicking. Hearing this, the young man managed to get to his feet and walk to the lookout. He pointed his vintage Leica, a gift from his professor, toward the glistening lakes and verdant coconut groves of Quezon Province. His photography session was soon interrupted by a tap on his shoulder. It was the young woman.

"You look like you know how to take a good picture," she said, holding out her small camera. "Could you take a shot of me by the caldera?"

Standing at the edge of the lookout, she raised her arms to claim the sky and the land beneath it.

Few people remembered that Mount Banahaw was a volcano. The caldera was formed during its last eruption in the 1700s — a reminder of the less benevolent side of the holy mountain.

"Thanks. Could you take one more of me by that ledge?"

Before he could say anything, she had made her way up and over to the edge of a rock formation. He could feel his hand shaking as she stood on the narrow ledge.

"You'd better get down, miss," he implored. "That looks dangerous."

"Take the picture already!"

Fingertips tingling, he snapped three quick shots, all the while praying she would not lose her balance. Once certain he had taken a decent picture, he called out, "I have your pictures. You can come down now."

Nimble and unafraid, she walked across the ledge, down the rock formation, and back to the young man. "Thank you," she said, retrieving her camera.

He was about to introduce himself, but she had already rejoined her designated group in setting up camp.

The day's buoyant mood carried the mountaineers into the evening's bonfire festivities. Flasks of potent coconut flower spirits and local rum were passed around after the fireside supper. Eric, a veteran of seven climbs, regaled the novice climbers with tales of his adventures. The mountaineer spoke of a miniature sea teeming with fat crabs in the heart of one seaside mountain. He also recounted a terrifying encounter with a winged female ghoul in Mount San Cristobal — Banahaw's evil twin. He took off his shirt to display a ragged scar that ran down the length of his torso — a souvenir from his Cristobal adventure, or so he claimed.

The young woman's eyes followed the scar from his chest down to his tight abdomen. Eric had a wiry body that went well with his long, wolfish face and spiky mane of straight black hair. He was not particularly handsome, but there was no question about his charisma. Like a fire dancer, he spun and twirled his stories like so many torches.

Elsewhere, people had started to form groups and couples. The designated party masters brought out mixtapes, while another one hooked up his Walkman to small but powerful speakers. Several mountaineers played along with small bongos, indigenous percussions, food tubs, and other makeshift instruments. The thumping music called the mountaineers around the bonfire. First came the women. They were laughing, shaking their hips, their inhibitions loosened by the alcohol that freely flowed around the camp. The guys soon followed, well-built youth who strutted their stuff like game cocks.

The quiet young man scanned the crowd for the girl. He wanted to ask her to dance, or at least talk. He found her sharing a flask of liquor with Gloria, another veteran. Gloria drank her share and the girl polished off the rest in one long quaff. The blue flame within her swelled into a red sun.

The young woman walked toward the bonfire and eased herself into the gyrating chain of bodies. Round and round the mountaineers went, a hypnotic blur of hair and arms and hips.

Eric the storyteller soon found himself beside the girl. She turned her head just enough to catch his eye. Her cheeks were flushed, and her full lips parted in a wordless hello. His eyes followed the beads of sweat from her smooth neck to the creamy skin just above her breasts. He felt the sharp stab of desire as he watched the drumbeats move through her firm, shapely body.

The bacchanalia continued until the dancers exhausted themselves. Many had paired off. Joints were offered and lit, and the pungent scent of ganja flavoured the mountain air. After several tokes, Eric and the girl started kissing and before long they had disappeared into his large tent.

Inside, Eric turned on a small lamp so he could see his prize. He had never been with a light-skinned girl before. They were too grand to give themselves to regular guys. He quickly slipped off her tank top and unhooked her bra. His head was buzzing with the good weed and at the sight of the glorious, American-style tits before him.

She let Eric take off the rest of her clothes and lay back, wishing for a night to make her forget about all the other nights.

"By the way," Eric asked casually, "what's your name?"

"Celestina," the young woman replied as she impatiently helped him out of his clothes.

Outside, the quiet young man watched as the lewd silhouettes acted out the timeless dance of man and woman. He looked away when the action got too intense. To his eyes, it was like watching someone getting gored by a bull. He thought wistfully about the young woman in the tent, reproaching himself for being too shy. He would have loved to hang out with her, maybe even see a movie. *Oh well*, he thought to himself, *maybe in another life*. He bid the lovers and the stars goodnight and crawled, alone, into his tent. Surrendering to tiredness and too many libations, the young man, Vergilio, let his mind wander back to his hometown and the oft-told story of the day of his birth.

*

It was fifteen minutes after high noon when night came to the coastal village of Barrio Guadalupe. The untimely darkness sent chickens, goats, and pigs back to their pens to sleep. Moths and bats took flight, while the feral dogs of the village looked to the sky and howled. Superstitious folk gathered in the church and waited for the Four Horsemen of the Apocalypse to appear.

"Repent," the old priest told the villagers. "The end is upon us."

One after the other, people confessed their sins out loud. Village drunkards, petty thieves, gamblers, gossips, and voyeurs all fell on their knees and begged for mercy. The Philippine Sea churned restlessly, as if waiting for the word to unleash its power. But the hours passed, and no Horsemen came. No one was more disappointed than the old priest when daylight came back hours later.

In the excitement of waiting for the Rapture, nobody noticed the absence of two women — the schoolteacher and the midwife. As dawn broke for the second time that day, roosters crowed and birds chirped. A cry was heard from the schoolteacher's house, and the two women emerged with a newborn baby. The boy was named Vergilio, after his late father, who had died at sea a few months before his son was born.

No one could know for sure if the timing of his birth had anything to do with Vergilio Luz's heightened powers of perception. But from the time he could see, he knew people were like lamps, vessels for a mysterious fire.

He learned to tell a person's character from the kind of light they carried. Old people carried gentle red embers, while babies were bright yellow fireballs like freshly hatched suns. The village tattlers had tongues of flame that flared like grease fires in the presence of intrigue. He learned to keep his distance because he knew that the flames would singe him. But people like his mother carried a strong and constant blue flame that saw him through the dark days of his childhood.

On the day Vergilio turned ten, the old priest died. His successor came soon after to preside over the funeral rites. Padre Noche walked slowly, carefully surveying the people in his parish. It was hard to tell whether he was a well-preserved old man or a prematurely aged young man. His hair was almost all grey, but one could see that he had the delicately muscled build of a boy on the cusp of manhood. His face would not have been out of place in a boys' choir, with its elfin nose and narrow jaw, but his complexion was the colour of cold ashes.

In his eulogy, Padre Noche called the body "a prison for the spirit." He declared, "Death is a release from earthly suffering." As he spoke, Padre Noche's eyes closed, and his mouth formed a blissful smile, as if he were already anticipating that release.

A deep, bone-chilling cold enveloped the young Vergilio. The boy's mind struggled to understand this odd priest and his apparent desire to enter death's embrace. Instinctively, Vergilio's eyes fell on the area between Padre Noche's heart and solar plexus. The boy then realized he was looking at a vessel like no other. A lamp with no light.

*

It was the morning after the big bonfire dance, and only the keenest of the early birds were awake. As soon as the young man's eyes popped open, he sensed it. *She's in danger.* He scrambled out of his sleeping bag and grabbed his boots. The camper in the next tent was splashing water on his face. Another was brewing strong Batangas coffee.

A few tents away, Vergilio spotted the storyteller and the young woman from the night before. The sun had yet to cast its full light, but the lovers were clearly not having a good morning-after. Vergilio could see that the storyteller's inner light crackled dangerously, sending off sparks like an exposed livewire in a rainstorm. He grabbed the young woman by the shoulders, perhaps more roughly than he intended.

"We were having a great time last night," he yelled. "What the hell changed?"

"Last night was last night. Right now, I need to be alone."

"You're a stuck-up little bitch. Just like all the other mestisas."

Without thinking, Vergilio picked up a large stone and slowly approached the couple. "That's enough," he said, feeling the adrenalin rushing into his blood, and the blood pumping into his muscles.

Surprised and grateful for the reinforcement, the young woman moved close to the quiet young man, shoulder to shoulder in a gesture of solidarity. Then she spoke in a low voice full of steel. "Listen up," she said to the storyteller. "You had your fun, and I had mine. I owe you nothing."

The storyteller threw a dirty look at the young man before stomping off.

Vergilio stood shaking, his breath making steam in the cold mountain air. He felt the young woman's hand on his, gently releasing his grip on the rock. "You can drop that now," she smiled.

"You shouldn't sleep with strangers," he blurted out. "You never know. You could get someone with a nasty temper, like that one. Or a real sicko."

"That would be just my luck."

The girl felt a sudden fondness for this well-meaning young man who looked eerily like the actor Robert Downey Jr. by way of Bollywood. He spoke English with a soft but discernible Visayan accent, something the snob in her immediately noticed. She found it endearing to hear that accent coming from Robert Downey Jr. Impulsively, she threw her arms around the young man and said, "Thank you for saving my stupid ass."

So began the friendship between the eighteen-year-old Celestina and Vergilio Luz, the young man she would thereafter call Verg. They continued their conversation as they descended from the mountain and slowly let each other into their innermost thoughts. During the long bus ride home, they sat together, asking each other about their dreams and nightmares.

"I have nightmares about flunking out and going back to Barrio Guadalupe to plant kamote," Verg said. "I love my mother, but that place is nothing but ignorance and darkness."

"I have many nightmares," Celestina said as her eyelids began to grow heavy. "But I only have one dream. More than anything, I want … a home."

"Don't you already have one?"

"I live in my mother's house. It's not a home. Not anymore."

"Is she cruel to you?"

"Not exactly. But her heart has gone cold."

To Verg, it was a startling revelation, made even more poignant by the casual way she divulged it. He wanted to hear her story, but her inner light was fading into a small blue flicker. Her body was weary, as was her spirit. He offered his shoulder as a pillow for her head, and gently stroked her hair as the bus rumbled along the pockmarked highway. "Sleep," he whispered. "I'll wake you up before we reach your stop in Manila."

She looked into his eyes and saw there was no lust or other hidden agenda in his offer. A feeling of peace washed over her. It had been a long time since she felt safe with a man.

*

The city was well into its night shift by the time the chartered bus from Mount Banahaw approached the terminal. Verg looked at the girl resting on his shoulder and whispered, "Wake up. We're in Pasay."

"In a minute. Let me just finish this ..."

Verg let her stay in her reverie, and on his shoulder, a little longer. Until today, he thought he was doomed to spend his university years friendless. Now, he had shared secrets with this cool, smart, and possibly mad English lit major from the Universidad de la Elitista, as his classmates called her school. Maybe their friendship would only last the length of that bus ride, but he wanted to savour their connection for as long as he could. Discarding his customary timidity, he said, "It's getting late, Celestina. Let me take you home."

"I don't want to go there," she replied.

"Oh ... What do you want to do?"

"I want to eat sisig. I've never had it, you know. My mother said it's fit only for riff-raff and lasenggos. *As if,*" she rolled her eyes. "I could name a dozen Chinese dishes scarier than minced pig cheeks."

"I know a place that serves great sisig," Verg replied. "It's a beer garden. So be prepared to be ogled by lasenggos."

"I'm not afraid. I know you'll defend my honour," she smiled.

"But who's going to defend *my* honour?"

"After the sisig, I want to get a tattoo," she added with a conspiratorial look. "We should both get one."

"I don't know about that ..."

"The design revealed itself to me while I was sleeping. It'll be so cool. I'll draw it for you."

"I'm going to regret this," Verg chuckled helplessly.

As the bus pulled into its spot, they strapped on their backpacks and got ready for their next adventure, as friends and fellow wanderers.

11

The House with the Dragon Gates

On the day of her graduation from university, Celestina received two gifts from her grandfather — a modest trust fund and the title to a property called the Twin Dragons Tower. No one was more surprised at the unexpected benevolence than Celestina. As the daughter of the disinherited Stella, Celestina had not expected to receive *mana* or anything of significant value from her grandfather. Perhaps this was one of his occasional bouts of generosity, she thought.

"It's a Peacetime building. One of the few that survived the war. Quite striking," Stella said.

Celestina sensed the unspoken in her mother's cheerful pitch. All day long, she waited for the rest of the story to unwind. It would be much later when Celestina would find out why she was chosen to inherit the property commonly known as the House with the Dragon Gates.

❋

Rocky the superintendent waited impatiently by the wrought-iron gates. Mrs. Teresita Sytanco and the other guests were arriving soon. He had been looking forward to meeting the daughter and granddaughter of Ma'am Teresita. There was an important matter to discuss. It would be nice to have real people to talk to. He missed being around the living.

The Twin Dragons Tower had been vacant for almost a year. The last tenant, an antiques dealer who had rented the entrance hall, left after an incident involving an ivory statue, a flying object, and a lawsuit.

Rocky wondered if Mrs. Sytanco's daughter and granddaughter had been informed of the incident. He had noticed odd things and heard disturbing sounds in the house before. But this was the first time he'd witnessed such a dramatic incident with his own eyes. It had happened while he was helping in the antiques shop. The customer involved was a newly rich man who fancied himself a collector. The antiques dealer found the man unbearable — a pretentious amateur who asked too many uninformed questions. The man had asked why an ivory Virgin Mary statue, supposedly from the Spanish era, looked suspiciously like a Chinese girl. The shop owner, bristling at the insinuation he was selling fake goods, told the client to go back to his Philippine history books. Many of the ivory carvers from that era were artisans from China. The statue's features, therefore, reflected the artisan's ideal of beauty. The man, offended at the suggestion he was ignorant, sniffed and said he did not really care for the Intsik Virgin Marys. Finally, the antiques dealer lost his composure and said, "Please get out of my store and don't ever come back. We don't want your business."

The men had no idea what happened next. The antiques dealer saw a flash of gold swooping toward the man. He thought it might be an errant bird that had entered the hall while the doors were open. Then he heard a dull clunk, followed by what sounded like a bell tolling in the showroom. He found his customer face down on the floor, clutching his bleeding head. Beside him was a golden arinola, rumoured to be the very object at the centre of a long-ago presidential scandal.

Rocky remembered how the shop owner had turned to him with a look of horror.

"Did you do this?" he asked.

"No, sir," Rocky replied, still in shock. "The chamber pot launched itself."

The alleged presidential chamber pot had weathered the impact with only a slight dent. The customer was not so lucky. Rocky quickly attended to the man's wound, while the antiques dealer called an ambulance. He prayed that the man would not expire in his shop; that would be big *malas*.

Once fully recovered, the man hired a nasty lawyer and charged the shop owner with personal injury arising from neglect. The battered customer eventually accepted a considerable settlement in exchange for dropping his charges. After this incident, the antiques dealer closed shop and moved to faraway Coron Island in Palawan.

"This place is nothing but *malas*," he had said as he loaded the last crate into his truck.

Rocky paced around the driveway as he mentally rehearsed his spiel. He would thank the Sytancos for their generosity. After all, they let him stay in the furnished flat for free and made sure he was well supplied with food and other necessities. But he thought he deserved a raise after ten years of service. After all, he was the only superintendent who had the intestinal fortitude to stay at that job. Not too many people could put up with midnight piano performances, asphyxiating nightmares, and now, flying chamber pots. Perhaps he was just a nobody to the Sytancos, but for now and for the foreseeable future, he was the only nobody they got.

❈

Celestina would always remember the first time she visited the Twin Dragons Tower. Her grandmother Teresita came over to Misericordia Valley in a chauffeured minivan, accompanied by a maid from the Sytanco mansion. Stella then bid Manang Rio and Celestina to pile into the van.

"Do I really have to go?" Celestina whispered to Stella.

"Yes, you do. Show some gratitude," Stella reminded her sharply.

Celestina reluctantly took her seat by her grandmother and mother as the driver set off for the Malate district. With the city's epic traffic jams, the drive felt as long as the Acapulco-Manila galleon crossings of the Spanish Era. She amused herself by listening to the helpers' commentary as their vehicle passed various historical landmarks. Celestina learned that the Imperial Japanese Army had torched a venerable women's college while students and nuns were locked inside. "My cousin works there as a janitor," Teresita's maid said to Manang Rio. "He swears you can still hear the screams when the building's empty."

As they crossed Lambingan Bridge, Manang Rio talked about dozens of children who reportedly went missing during its construction. "No bridge can be built without blood sacrifice. Ask any construction worker," Manang Rio stage-whispered to her seatmate.

The blood-soaked one-upmanship went on for the next hour until the minivan reached Roxas Boulevard and slowed to a crawl. The midday heat radiating from asphalt and concrete pierced the veil of their air conditioning, making the rest of the ride unbearable. Celestina felt like jumping out of their vehicle and walking the rest of the way. At least she had a chance of catching a breeze outside. By the time their car turned the corner by the Aristocrat Restaurant, Celestina felt wilted and cranky. Teresita noticed, with great distaste, a handful of girlie bars near Remedios Circle. From there, it was a short distance to a private lane, and to the dragon gates that guarded the building and its grounds. Something about the view felt familiar to Celestina.

"Have we been here before, Mama?" she asked.

"No. Maybe you remember it from family stories," Stella replied as Rocky, the superintendent, opened the gates for the minivan.

They parked beside an ancient white Lincoln Continental the size of a small boat. Celestina followed her mother out of the vehicle, then helped her grandmother get out.

"Thank you, my dear," Teresita said, as she gripped her granddaughter's arm. "My knees don't work the way they used to."

Once she was steady on her feet, Teresita took Celestina by the hand and led her to a spot where she could see the property at its best vantage. "Here it is. What do you think?"

Celestina stared at the odd structure before her. "Could someone tell me what I'm looking at?" she asked. She had always thought of buildings as a series of stacked concrete boxes. Whatever this structure was, it was not a box. It was more like a creature out of a dark fairy tale — seemingly made of fondant and candied fruit, with a dragon's spikes as a hat. Its lower half was partially clad in ivy, looking as if it had sprung out of the earth from a giant magical seed.

"This was your Great-Aunt Selena's home and music school. It's quite the miracle it survived the war," her grandmother explained. "So many buildings were bombed during the Liberation."

"It's like a vision from another realm," Celestina said.

"Selena was … eccentric," Teresita explained. "She was an admirer of the Catalan architect Antoni Gaudí. One of his followers designed this building."

Celestina had only a vague idea of who Gaudí was. A rich classmate once described the architect of the Sagrada Família as "high on God and shrooms." This memory brought a smirk to her face, which she quickly tried to hide.

"What's so funny?" her mother asked in her voice of ice and steel.

"Nothing," she replied. "But I want some of whatever those Catalans are smoking."

This potential flashpoint was defused as Rocky welcomed Teresita Sytanco and Stella in his songlike Ilonggo accent. Teresita introduced her granddaughter as the new owner of the Twin Dragons Tower. Rocky shook Celestina's hand respectfully, despite his discomfort. She was an unsettling sight to him with her black-rimmed eyes, dark purple lipstick, and flowing black dress. He could not decide whether she was in mourning, in costume, or into witchcraft. Perhaps it was a strange moda picked up by the youth these days. No matter, she was now his boss. His carefully rehearsed spiel would have to wait.

In the superintendent's flat, he served them tea and steamed siopao buns from a nearby dim sum restaurant. Duly refreshed and revived, they proceeded to stroll the grounds. There was a dormant fountain at the centre of the garden. Conceived as a highly decorative space of sculptural palm trees, the garden now hosted Rocky's crop of bitter melon, tomatoes, and summer squash.

At the back of the house was a small swimming pool, long dry and covered with large wooden boards. Celestina's black dress soaked up every joule of heat from the sun. She looked around for shade and was drawn to a kalachuchi tree in full bloom. She wished for the slightest hint of breeze to provide relief. Instead, she heard a faint murmur in the air. "Ai shiteiru yo," a distant man's voice whispered. She then felt a breath on the nape of her neck, warm and full of human desire. "Ai shiteiru yo," a woman's voice, much closer, whispered back. Celestina turned around to see the face behind the woman's voice, but the breath had faded into the afternoon heat.

"Hello?" she called out. "Who are you?" She waited for a response, but all she heard was her mother calling. It was time to see the rest of the house.

✻

She doesn't remember, but Celestina and I have met before — that day her spirit almost gave up on earthly life. She entered my realm with her tear-streaked face and a bloodstained skirt. I let her stay for a while.

"I want to die," Celestina said. But it wasn't her time, so I sent her back — to the body that was pale and broken. "We're Sytancos," I told her. "We're fighters." And I watched over her until the spark of life returned and her body found the will to live again. I knew then we were kindred spirits, and we were going to meet again.

*

Rocky and the five women crammed themselves into the wrought-iron and glass elevator. He slammed the inner door shut and pressed the button for the mezzanine. The antiquated contraption shot up with a jerk before shuddering to an abrupt stop. Peering through the elevator's glass walls, Celestina could see the entrance hall below with its chandelier and a small lounge area. Soon the door opened to a spacious apartment featuring a wall of mirrors, which were cracked in a few places.

"These have to be replaced," Stella said to Rocky. "It's *malas*."

Celestina left her mother and grandmother to discuss the apartment's feng shui while she admired its free-flowing design. It was hard to believe that such an open-concept space was built in the late twenties.

"Selena used to rent this space to the Marion Harper Academy of Dance," Teresita said, closing her eyes to see a fond memory. "All the daughters of the buena familias went to her school for ballet and ballroom dancing."

As she looked around, Celestina noticed a shiny black reception desk of a more recent vintage. It was decorated with gaudy marble panels and fitted with a brass plate that spelled out the name of the last tenant — "The Bombshells." Sidling up to Rocky, Celestina asked, "Who are the Bombshells?"

"The Japayukis, Miss," he replied in a near-whisper. "They used to train here."

Celestina had heard about Japayukis. They were the girls who went to Japan to entertain businessmen in nightclubs. The name carried intimations of easy virtue and prostitution.

"Where are they now?" she asked.

"The girls don't want to come here anymore."

Celestina saw Rocky's eyes meet her grandmother's. There was something they were not telling her. Her mother took her hand and said, "Let's take a look at the conservatory."

Rocky and the party of women walked back to the elevator. As Celestina stepped in, she remembered a room with clear walls from a half-forgotten dream.

*

The door opened to a spacious but dusty apartment distinguished by high ceilings and large, puddle-shaped windows. The sunlight filtering through the frosted glass gave the space a cool, shady feeling.

Stella spotted the grand piano as soon as the elevator opened. She sat down and started picking out a tune. It took a while for her fingers to regain their musical memory, but soon she was playing a halting but recognizable "Clair de Lune."

Taking her granddaughter aside, Teresita said, "This is where your Great-Aunt Selena used to hold music lessons. She was a tough teacher, I'm told. Vases and candelabra would fly whenever a student got sloppy with their technique."

Teresita's anecdote brought a little smile to Celestina's face. Over the years, this was how Celestina got to know her great-aunt, through elder relatives' stories, especially the ones that spilled out when everyone was full of wine and nostalgia. The elders always ended up talking about the glories of the Philippines' idyllic Peacetime, followed by the hardships of the Japanese Time during the Second World War. Now and again, Selena's name would come up. She was one of two children from her great-grandfather's first marriage. Her beauty was like the rarest of opals, they said, with a fire to match. She had her pick of suitors, but she never married. She died during the Japanese Time. Celestina never asked how. To her and her cousins, the war was not real. It was just another dusty tale.

Despite knowing little about her great-aunt, the conservatory looked and felt familiar. The main room had curves where regular rooms had corners. Celestina found her way to a smaller room that once served as her great-aunt's office. Beside an old office desk was a dusty trunk filled with yellowing pages of sheet music, ledgers, and souvenir programs. Among the papers was a woodcut of a potted orchid perched on a windowsill. It was done mostly in black and white, to highlight the lush beauty of the flower, with its blue, almost violet petals. Celestina recognized the distinctive puddle-shaped window in the background. It was the very window before which she was standing. She wondered about the artist whose name, in Japanese characters, was printed at the bottom of the woodcut. Etched under the Japanese characters were the numbers "1944" — the year before the country was liberated by Allied Forces. Who had painstakingly captured this orchid's fleeting beauty during the time of war?

She took the woodcut and prepared to rejoin her grandmother and mother. Suddenly, she was eager to see the rest of the building.

*

He came into my house as the enemy. One day, late in the morning, Captain Fushido and his men rattled the gates of the Twin

Dragons Tower. With their guns and bayonets, they shoved past my groundskeeper, Ramon, and marched into the conservatory where I was giving piano lessons to a rapidly dwindling number of students.

"I'm looking for Mrs. Adelina Corpuz," the captain said in flawless, British-inflected English.

The captain was a tall and elegant-looking man, quite unlike those bowlegged foot soldiers who terrorized people with their casual brutality. Adelina's husband was a spy working for the Americans, the captain said. It was important that I tell him everything I knew, for my own sake. I had not seen Adelina in almost six months, and I knew her husband only in passing.

"She told me she was going back to her province in Tarlac," I said. "Her grandmother owns a hacienda there. She said she would write me as soon as she could so I can visit. I haven't heard from her."

"Is that all you're going to tell me, Miss Sytanco?"

"I'm afraid that's all I know."

"You will tell me when you hear from her, won't you?"

"Yes, sir," I nodded even as I contemplated ways to get a warning message to Adelina.

The captain met my eyes and smiled coldly. "I wouldn't try to warn her if I were you, Miss Sytanco," he added. "I don't want to have to charge two people with treason."

The captain walked around the conservatory looking at instruments and examining the glass case containing my collection of musical memorabilia. His men stood there, firearms in hand, as my few remaining students huddled in a corner, hoping that their numbers would provide them a measure of safety. He stopped by my piano and leafed through the music sheets in my piano bench until he found a piece that caught his fancy.

"Do you like Chopin, Miss Sytanco?" he asked.

"Yes, of course," I said.

He commanded me to play and handed me the sheet music to "Nocturne in C-Sharp Minor."

"That won't be necessary," I told him. "I know it by heart."

So, I played, certain it was to be the last piece I ever performed. He listened with great attention and thanked me with applause in the form of five precise claps. I should have been relieved by the applause, but I was too afraid to feel anything. I had played very mechanically, but he liked my performance well enough to ask for an encore.

"Do you sing, Miss Sytanco?"

"Yes," I said in a pinched voice.

"I would like to hear a Tagalog song."

In my nervousness, I forgot nearly all the Tagalog songs in my repertoire. I sang "Nasaan Ka Irog," a kundiman about longing and heartbreak. It was the only one I could remember. I saw the ice melt from the captain's eyes. I didn't realize he was also fluent in Tagalog. At the end of the song, he uttered a quick "thank you" and left abruptly with his men in tow.

Henceforth, the captain would come every Friday after my students left for the day. He would ask me to play the piano for him and sing a Tagalog or English song. In appreciation, he gave me potted orchids and Japanese prints called ukiyo-e, which he sketched, engraved, and printed himself. This was the captain I came to know — a warrior with the soul of an artist.

People in the district saw a vastly different man — a skillful and often cruel interrogator who could read your thoughts from the twitch of an eye or the way you scratched your nose. He told me that music gave his soul small moments of beauty and humanity. I was happy to have met someone who understood that music and art mattered, no matter how ugly life had become. Though our countries were at war, our souls slowly fell into a deep friendship.

*

The wrought-iron door of the elevator slid open to the top floor apartment where Selena Sytanco once lived. Teresita called it the "atico," a quaint-sounding name to someone like Celestina, who was used to the more modern term "penthouse." Celestina's eyes were immediately drawn to the soaring ceiling, pool-sized windows of frosted glass, and hand-carved double doors.

The other women made their way through the once-majestic space, now piled high with old furniture, successive generations of audio and video equipment, books, and trunks filled with documents and photographs. Manang Rio stopped to look at an ornately carved wooden post by the stairs. Something about it had caught her peripheral vision — two glowing dots, like embers on dark wood. Looking more closely, she was certain she saw two lizard-like eyes and a mouth on a fat face. Gingerly, she touched the wood. It felt warm, and she could swear she could feel it rising and falling as if it had breath.

"Ma'am Teresita, you have to look at this," she called out. "I think there's *malas* in this post."

Teresita Sytanco quickly glanced in Manang's direction, saying, "It's not blocking anything. We could get a feng shui expert in here sometime. He can tell us what to do to improve the flow of *swerte*."

Manang Rio was about to reply when Stella asked her to make a list of things that could be sold, donated to charity, or given away to those who had served the family for a long time. Little did the Sytancos know that Manang had looked into the eyes of an ancient and malevolent creature, whose kind has visited people's nightmares for centuries.

Meanwhile, Celestina was busy doing her own mental inventory. Even through the clutter, she could pick out the pieces that belonged to her Great-Aunt Selena. There was a victrola, an Art Nouveau–style sofa upholstered in copper green and gold damask, a table with mother-of-pearl inlay, and an escritoire with carved dragon feet. Celestina made a beeline for the escritoire. A puff of dust tickled her nose as she turned the key to release the hinged desktop. Letters, bills, and her aunt's monogrammed stationery sat, sepia-toned and brittle, in the compartments above the graduated drawers. The glass bookcase above the drawers held a set of classics ranging from *Meditations of Marcus Aurelius* to *The Picture of Dorian Gray*. She noted two volumes that showed visible signs of wear: an English translation of *The Pillow Book of Sei Shonagon* and *A Wreath of Cloud*, one of the volumes from Arthur Waley's translation of *The Tale of Genji*. Tucked in with the books were two other small woodcuts. One was a print of a gold-and-red koi fish, and the other was a cup of tea on a table in a shady veranda.

"Rocky, is there a veranda in this apartment?" Celestina asked.

"Yes, miss. By the dining room," he said, gesturing to the western part of the apartment. "Follow me."

Celestina's skin tingled with a sense of foreboding. As sure as she knew the secrets of her own heart, she was certain something dark was about to come to light.

*

As our bond blossomed into something more than friendship, the captain's visits became more frequent. He liked to sit by the koi pond on my veranda to make sketches of my fish. One day, he asked me for the fishes' names. It never occurred to me to give them names. He sat with me while I christened them: Quicksilver, Phoenix, Goldleaf, Sunset, Jade.

As the war dragged on, commodities became scarce. I told him I would have to replace the koi with common carp to supplement my household's food supply. We had already dug up part of the garden to plant sweet potatoes. A wistful sadness washed over his otherwise impassive features.

"Our bodies need food, yes," he said. "But our spirits need something more."

The next day, his men came bearing gifts of vegetables, live chickens, and sacks of rice. The gifts came every month, and I accepted them so I could feed those who stayed on to help run my house. I had to be discreet about my friendship with Captain Fushido, lest I incur the wrath of my neighbours. I had not thought about how my household staff might feel about our friendship. I had not heard the stories from the streets or battlefronts. I had not witnessed the atrocities they had seen. I should have known better. I'd lived my life boldly, with no apologies. How sad that it should end with so many regrets.

*

The superintendent showed Celestina to the dining room and opened the creaky French doors leading to the veranda. The roof was cracked and in need of repair. The space had since been overrun with ferns and spider plants, but she could see that it was the same table and view captured in the woodcut. Beyond the sitting area was the dry pond that was once alive with jewel-coloured fish. Her grandfather had koi ponds in his mansion and his shopping malls, for good fortune and abundance. Below the balcony was the blooming kalachuchi tree she had admired earlier. She inhaled deeply as the sweet, gingery fragrance of the flowers rose to the balcony. Suddenly, she felt a sadness, sharp and deep as a knife wound. She did not hear the sound of slippered feet approaching the veranda.

"Ma'am Teresita wants to speak to you, Miss Celestina," Rocky said.

As she turned around, he saw the calligraphy of tears and kohl on her cheeks. Without knowing why, he felt terribly sorry for this girl in mourning dress. Kindly, he offered his kerchief for her tears. "Thank you. Tell her I'll be there shortly."

Celestina took out a compact and cleaned her face as best she could. Drawing herself tall, she walked back past the dry pond, past the sitting area, to the French doors that led to the dining room. There, just above the right doorknob, was a brownish stain, roughly the shape of a large leaf. Perhaps mud or an imprint of decayed foliage, she thought. Higher up, on the left door, was an almost identical stain. She stopped cold as she slowly recognized it was a hand, drawn in dried blood. A grisly farewell. A ghostly message from the past to her. Shaking, she placed her palm over the stain. It was smaller than her hand, but they fit together like two nesting dolls.

*

The first time he confessed his love to me was also the last time I saw him. The kalachuchi tree was in full bloom and its perfume scented the afternoon air. He whispered to me, "Ai shiteiru yo." I whispered it back and we kissed, even though we both knew it was madness.

After that, he told me with tears in his eyes, "Forgive me, Selena. But I must harden my heart again. I cannot fight a war with this love inside me."

We kissed again before we said goodbye, for the last time. I was devastated to my core. I spent the rest of the day sitting by the koi pond watching the fish we had named together. I didn't hear the footsteps, didn't see Ramon, my groundskeeper, standing behind me with the well-sharpened knife he used to cut the necks of live chickens.

His hand felt rough and heavy as he held me down by my shoulder. I barely felt the knife's blade slice into my neck, but I felt the warmth of my blood as it flowed down my blouse. He called me "Jap's whore" and "traitor."

I clutched my neck to try to stop the bleeding as I stumbled back into the dining room to get help. It was already too late. With my last few breaths, I cursed him and his descendants. "May *malas* rain on you like chamber pots full of piss."

For a long time, I hated Ramon. I realize now I did not see the war through his eyes or hear the stories he heard — of young men tortured and young women forced into service as "comfort women" for Japanese soldiers. I only wish I had lived to see the end of the war. Perhaps the Captain and I would have had a chance once all the bombs and guns were put away.

*

Teresita and Stella waited for Celestina to join them in the study. Celestina entered, hoping nobody would notice she had been crying.

"You called for me, Gwa-ma?" she asked.

Teresita called Celestina to their huddle. "Yes. This building is in a much better shape than I thought," she began. "We can find a buyer for this place. Developers will have no problem converting it into condos or lofts."

Celestina listened with confusion to the proposition. She had not thought about what to do with the property that now belonged to her.

"We'll invest the proceeds in some dividend stocks," Stella added. "It'll be a good addition to your trust fund."

The words buzzed in Celestina's ears like so many flies. As sensible as the plan sounded, she did not like being railroaded into someone else's idea. It was her life, and she was bloody well going to have a say on how it was lived. In a firm, low voice, she finally said, "I don't want to sell. I'm going to live here."

Teresita and Stella looked at each other, reluctant to explain the house's troubled history to Celestina.

"Trust me, Celestina," Stella said. "This is not a good place for you."

"If not here, then where, Mama? There's no place for me in your house."

"That's not true, Celestina," Stella said with a cracked voice.

"It is, Mama," Celestina replied. "I'm tired of not belonging. I need a place where I feel at home."

Seeing her plan going awry, Teresita stepped in. "Celestina, my dear. You cannot live in this house. Your Great-Aunt Selena was murdered here by her groundskeeper. Do you understand? This place is haunted and full of *malas*. That's why none of the tenants stay."

"You don't have to tell me, Gwa-ma. Why else would Gwa-kong give this to me? Give the *malas* to the disinherited granddaughter. It's quite clever now that I think about it."

"That's enough, Celestina! Apologize to your Gwa-ma at once!" Stella admonished.

"Let her speak her mind, Stella."

Turning to her granddaughter, Teresita said, "It's not like that at all, my child, although I can see why you think that. I want you to have a nest egg. I don't want you to struggle any more than you must. But I should have consulted you about our plans. I forget you're no longer a child."

"The reasons don't matter, Gwa-ma. I like this place, and I want to live here," Celestina said.

"Are you sure, my child?"

"Perhaps this is where I belong. In the world of ghosts," Celestina replied with a wry smile.

Neither Stella nor Teresita could sway Celestina from her decision. As they piled back into the van and drove away, Celestina felt a tingle rising from the soles of her feet to her temples. In her mind's eye, she was standing on the edge of a seaside cliff. There may be jagged rocks beneath the waves, but she would rather jump than go back.

12

The New Lady of the House

The church bells rang at dusk, calling the faithful to the Nuestra Señora de los Remedios parish. It was the day's last mass. Outside the Baroque-style church, the crone sat in her stall, surrounded by lit candles and echoes of prayers. The lolas remembered her from the Sundays of their childhood. *She was already old when we were still in pigtails*, they would say to their grandchildren.

Generations of faithful had visited the crone's stall to buy candles in the hope she could bring their prayers to Our Lady of Remedies. Barren couples came to ask for children. Rich and poor alike came to plead for the healing of a sick loved one. After the war, the crone saw more and more desperately lonely people. They came to her to ask for a soulmate, someone to rescue them from their solitude.

These were not the only souls who came to her. There were also those who no longer travelled with their bodies. She lit candles for them, too, and prayed for their release.

Today, a dirt-streaked boy carrying sampaguita garlands approached her with a message. "There's a new lady in the dragon gates house," he said. "Selena's grandniece. She has been to the land of the dead, but she made it back." The boy would know, as the land of the dead was where he resided ever since that unstopping jeepney ended his earthly existence.

The crone thanked the ghostly street urchin and offered a prayer for him. She had known Selena, the erstwhile lady of the house, back when rich people lived and played by the bay. That was before the war. The city changed after that. The wealthy no longer came. Now the promenade belonged to everyone — street children who sold garlands, vagrants, and ladies of the night. Sadly, Selena never left. She was trapped in regret, clinging to a life that had been taken from her.

Casting her mind across the church plaza, past the bars and restaurants, the old woman offered a prayer for Selena's grandniece.

"May God and the Holy Mother give you strength to face the ghosts and demons that haunt your house."

The crone felt weary. It had been a long day. Too much misery, suffering, and death. Too many ghosts. Time to let in a new life.

13

Breaking Walls

It was a beautiful evening, much like other evenings at La Sulipeña. Crystal chandeliers sparkled above marble floors. Mahogany furniture gleamed with polish and care. Every table was adorned with voluptuous peonies and set with richly embroidered linens, gold-rimmed china, and cut crystal. For those used to a more modern aesthetic, it was almost too lavish. But for La Sulipeña's diners, it was just perfect.

That night, a prominent clan was gathered at the centre table. The guests included a large party of Filipino Americans from Boston who had flown in to celebrate their matriarch's eightieth birthday. The extended family had long been divided along political lines, but tonight, they came to a rare consensus. Everyone agreed that the Beef Wellington à la criolla and lemongrass suckling lechon were the most delectable dishes ever to grace their feasts.

The dinner was far from over. The birthday cake, desserts, and after-dinner drinks were about to arrive. A low hush fell over the dining room as two stately waiters emerged from the kitchen with gleaming, laden trolleys. The first waiter served the tartaletas de mangga, a small egg-yolk custard called Tocino de Cielo, and café fuerte. A few paces behind, the second waiter proudly presented the St. Germain birthday cake decorated with crystallized violets.

The after-dinner treats were almost eclipsed by the appearance of a princely mestiso seemingly sculpted by a Baroque master's chisel. The man had a powerful build, with broad shoulders and a deep chest, yet he moved like a dancer across the gleaming marble floors. His perfect profile was punctuated by long-lashed eyes and lips that were just a bit too ripe for a man. But for all his beauty, it was his smile that truly electrified a room.

He looked laid back but elegant in an Armani suit as he greeted the members of the prominent clan. The matrons blushed and giggled like teenaged girls as he favoured each one of them with a warm hug. "You look ravishing this evening," he whispered to one. "You smell like a rose garden," he told another. The honeyed words flowed naturally from his tongue, like nectar from ripe fruit. Some men were born warriors, and some were born lovers. He had not the slightest doubt which one he was. Since childhood, he loved the feel of women's soft bosoms and the warm scent of their skin. He was not a conceited man, by any means, but he knew ladies appreciated what he brought to the party.

He greeted the men like old friends and asked how they enjoyed their meal. It had been a good quarter-century since the visitors from Boston had dined on real alta cucina Filipina. He would have chatted with the men longer, but he was more impatient than usual tonight. Once the cake was sliced and served, he quietly slipped away.

At the waiting area, he quickly nodded to diners and waiters, stopping to tell the hostess to replace the too-fragrant lilies by the entrance with more subtle roses or camellias. His stomach felt like a bubbling caldero by the time his chauffeur arrived. It hardly mattered that, earlier in the evening, he had polished off a dish of Lobster Visayas and a medium-rare porterhouse with a side of artichokes sautéed in garlic and olive oil. His stomach demanded something else.

"Where to, sir?" Fidel asked as the Mestiso settled in the backseat of the Mercedes-Benz.

"I don't know, but I'm dying for a balut."

"I know a place in Malate," Fidel said with a sympathetic look.

His boss had been doing a lot of roaming lately. It usually happened in the middle of the week when the restaurant was not too busy. The Mestiso would get restless and invent an errand to slip away. He would then ask to go to the pier or a night market to try a dish he had heard about from one of the waiters or cooks.

How sad, Fidel thought. This man could afford to have steak and champagne every night, yet he hankered for street food. Fidel himself did not care for rich people's food. All he needed was a simple dish of salted fish and hot rice with charred tomatoes to be a happy diner. But it was not his place to question another man's cravings. Rich or poor, he understood all men were slaves to their hunger.

The car sailed noiselessly past the queen palm trees and gates of the restored colonial mansion that was La Sulipeña. On the cobblestoned street, it slowed down as it waited to pass the horse-drawn kalesas. Fidel cursed the kutcheros under his breath. "Sorry, sir," he said, realizing that his invective was well heard inside their air-conditioned cocoon. "Kalesas just don't belong in the city."

"Intramuros is not the city, Fidel. It's a museum. A living museum."

As the road widened toward the exit, Fidel passed the horse-drawn carriages and sped toward the puerto that would lead them to Bonifacio Drive, into the real city. There were no horses outside the walls of Intramuros, save for the chrome steeds that graced the hoods of the jeepneys.

The Mestiso did not mind the other vehicles and their chaotic driving too much. He was not behind the wheel tonight. He could just sit back and watch the show. He had met tourists from all over the world in his restaurant. Skip the historical tours, he wanted to tell them. Riding a jeepney was the authentic cultural experience.

He barely noticed the Rizal Monument, the monolith marking the final resting place of the country's national hero. His stomach rumbled louder as Bonifacio Drive turned into the palm trees of Roxas Boulevard, which ran parallel to Manila Bay's promenade. Here and there, he saw lovers silhouetted against the moonlit bay. The neon sign of the forever-popular Aristocrat restaurant was their cue to turn. They had arrived in Malate. The takeout window of the restaurant had, as always, a long line of office workers, night shift nurses, and partygoers waiting to order fried chicken or pancit.

Fidel drove around Remedios Circle and found a spot on a quiet side street. "I'll wait here, sir."

"No. Go home to your family. I'll take it from here."

"There might be muggers, sir."

"I'm sure the mugger and I can work out something. Goodnight, Fidel."

The Mestiso got out of the car and made sure Fidel drove away. Then he looked around the plaza and made his way to the vendor with the most customers. He waited his turn then asked the man for four duck eggs. The man fished out the warm eggs from his basket and placed them in a paper bag, along with packets of sea salt.

"I put an extra one in there, gwapito. You need to *keep it up*, eh! Make us some mestiso babies," the vendor said with a sly smile.

Catching the vendor's drift, the Mestiso smiled and met the man's gaze with a cocked eyebrow. His girlfriend, Ysabel, and his other ladies could attest that *keeping it up* had never been a problem. Still, he happily accepted the extra egg and handed the vendor three large bills, saying, "Keep the change."

The vendor knew what he was talking about when he touted the infamous duck eggs as an aphrodisiac and a fertility booster.

No researcher had ever done formal studies to validate this, but the proof was there, in the teeming city of millions, serviced by an army of vendors selling balut at every bus stop, street corner, and plaza.

The Mestiso took one of the eggs and sharply rapped the small end on his Omega watch. With a neatly groomed finger, he cleared the bits of eggshell to make a small opening. A tingle of anticipation coursed through his body as he brought the egg to his lips. The first sip of warm amniotic soup quickly gave way to a long, thirsty slurp. It was like a pot of long-simmered broth, boiled down into this eggshell copita. Pure umami. He quickly ripped away the rest of the eggshell to reveal a large, butter-coloured yolk nestled yin-yang style with a small, rubbery albumen. He opened the packet of sea salt and sprinkled it on the yolk before taking a bite. A symphony of oysters, queso fresca, and white truffles danced on his tongue. The second bite brought him to the duckling curled up in the heart of the egg. It was smaller than a one-peso coin, devoid of bones, beak, or feathers. More essence than flesh, it melted in his mouth and slid down his gullet to become food for his sinews.

The Mestiso sat on a bench and ate the other balut eggs as he watched the district's denizens pass by. Street urchins, bar musicians, and the occasional baklâ streetwalker doing a note-perfect performance of a good-time girl. Above him, swarms of flying ants circled the streetlight in search of mates. There he was, worlds away from his gated communities and country clubs, but strangely content. In that grimy plaza in Malate, he was not a celebrity restaurateur or the son of Salvador and Isabel San Miguel. He was just a man sitting elbow to elbow with other hungry men.

The Mestiso smiled as he swallowed the last tasty morsel. For the first time in that long day, his belly felt truly satisfied. Sitting back, he began heartily breathing in the second-hand smoke from the stevedore beside him. Noticing this, the man tapped out a Marlboro from its pack and said, "Cigarette, Joe?"

"It's Jo-ma," he replied as he took the proffered cigarette. "Salamat."

"Sorry, boss," the stevedore said. "I thought you were Amerikano. You don't look Filipino at all."

"Don't I?" he laughed. "Maybe you just have to look closer."

Josémaria San Miguel was used to this by now. At Cornell, his classmates used to call him "that Spanish guy with a Hawaiian grandmother." In Europe, people would speak to him in Italiano or Español. Regardless of how he looked, he felt Filipino in his heart and to his very core.

Josémaria and the stevedore started a conversation about boxing and politics. Others joined, and soon they were talking in that earthy way men spoke when there were no women in the room. With the balut sitting nicely in his belly and the laughter of men in his ears, Josémaria spent the rest of the night savouring life in the world outside his walls.

*

Verg waited in the car while Celestina ran back to the kitchen to grab the wine coolers. "Hurry back," he had said, hoping Mrs. Errantes would not come out to chat. Celestina's mother gave him the creeps. She looked like a woman carved out of marble — outwardly lustrous, but dark and devoid of fire inside.

He eyed the picnic basket longingly. Celestina had packed it with crusty bread, Edam cheese, Chinese ham, and strawberries from Baguio City. He was about to reach out for the baguette when Celestina came back with the wine coolers. She quickly tossed the drinks in the backseat and started the car for the long trip to Malate. Manang Rio opened the gates for them. Stella came out just as the car was driving off.

"Is that young man her nobyo?" Stella asked as her daughter sped away. "They're always together, but not a word to me about him or his family."

"No, he's not her nobyo. They're playmates. Just two children gallivanting."

"I don't understand young people these days," Stella said. "They act like they know everything about the world, yet they behave like twelve-year-old savages. Can't even have a simple conversation with me. No manners whatsoever."

Manang said nothing. She was just a housemaid, after all. She did not have the right words, but she understood in her heart. Celestina may have graduated from university, but she was not ready to grow up. Perhaps she wanted to recapture a childhood that had been taken from her. Quietly, Manang cheered on the young woman she had come to love as a daughter.

*

The serpentine roof shone brightly under the early afternoon sun. "There it is! My very own haunted castle," Celestina said as their car approached the dragon gates.

Rocky was expecting them. He opened the gates and waved them into the driveway leading up to the carport. A wide-eyed Verg took off his Wayfarers and stared at the fantastical structure they were driving toward. Its curvaceous body gave it a humanoid appearance. He almost expected the "castle" to start walking.

"Come, I want you to see the apartments," Celestina said. They boarded the elevator to Selena Sytanco's old music conservatory. She had instructed Rocky to keep all windows and doors open in the apartments to let out the mustiness and bring in light.

Verg put his sunglasses back on as Celestina showed him the place. Even with the assorted furniture from previous tenants, the place felt cavernous. He felt disoriented, unaccustomed as he was to spaciousness after a lifetime of living in cramped quarters. Now here was a place big enough for the life he had imagined.

"What do you think, Verg?"

"I could get lost here. You wouldn't find me for days."

"You'll have lots of room for your equipment. And all the stuff you love to pick up on our trips. We have commercial and residential zoning. You can set up that studio you've always wanted."

"Are you offering me this apartment?"

"Yes, I am."

"Sorry ... I'll have to pass."

"Just like that? May I ask why?"

"Whatever the rent is, I can't afford it."

"I'll give you a deal," Celestina responded brightly. "You can have it for the princely sum of pay-what-you-can every month."

"Well, I don't feel right taking advantage of your generosity," he said.

Celestina shook her head. "You know I always wanted my own place, right? Well, here it is, by the grace of God and my grandfather. But it wouldn't be a real home without you."

"Oh, Celestina. I couldn't ..."

"C'mon. Look at those high ceilings and this open space, and this light. Wouldn't you want to wake up to this every day?"

"It's absolutely amazing, but —"

"You know you want it," she whispered as she softly laid her hand on his chest.

Verg's heart skipped a beat and resumed at allegro vivace tempo. He was not used to this side of Celestina. For four years, they had been two overgrown children going off on adventures. Now, here he was, helpless in the face of her unsheathed femininity.

"Give me six months," Verg finally said. "Just until the work starts coming in. Then charge me whatever the market price is."

"You got a deal!" she said before releasing his heart from her touch.

Verg could see that her usually small, constant blue inner light had grown into something like a crackling yellow bonfire — inviting but also potentially dangerous.

"Can we eat now?" Verg said, feeling quite spent from their negotiation about the apartment.

"There's a veranda upstairs," she said. Let's go."

The two friends spent the rest of the afternoon picnicking on the veranda where Selena Sytanco once sat with her Japanese captain. Sometime after their third wine cooler, Verg heard a wistful melody playing on a faraway piano. His eyes darted to search for the source.

"Rachmaninoff. 'Rhapsody on a Theme of Paganini,'" Celestina said. "You hear it too, don't you?"

"Is that …?"

"Yes. Great-Auntie Selena. She's welcoming us to her home."

*

Celestina, I know you can hear me when your mind is quiet. Savour every moment of your time on earth. Surround yourself with life's finer things and fascinating people. Take a lover. Put on your best dress and listen to a performance of Mahler's Resurrection Symphony. Even with all its pain, life is still better than death. Death is nothing but echoes and eternal longing.

14

A Sweet Life

Josémaria was born into sweetness. His mother, Isabel Pellicer, was a mestisa from the province of Pampanga, and the matriarch of a two-hundred-year-old hacienda and sugar refinery. From her father, she inherited vast tracts of sugar cane land and a lineage that went back to the middle son of a Castilian marqués who made the voyage to Spain's Far East colony to seek his fortune.

Isabel had the lean, angular features of her Castilian ancestor, which gave her a slightly masculine appearance. Still, she carried herself with élan, and people considered her a great beauty despite her beak-like nose and longish face. She never lacked for admirers or suitors. By the age of twenty-one, she received three serious offers of marriage from well-born young men. But Isabel's heart took its sweet time. At a relatively late age of twenty-six, Isabel finally accepted an offer of marriage from the dashing Salvador San Miguel.

Salvador was a man of good looks, great charm, and grand ideas. Salvador had come into his looks from his mother, an interior designer who once represented Louisiana in the Miss America pageant. From his father, he inherited several office and apartment buildings, and an uncanny instinct for spotting the next frontier. Early in his career, Salvador transformed one of the city's most polluted industrial wastelands into a landscape of gleaming skyscrapers. This achievement made his reputation as a visionary developer.

Isabel and Salvador expeditiously produced two handsome, healthy boys within the first few years of marriage. Rafael, the first son, was a serene baby who slept through the night and cried only when he was hungry. In time, he became a darker, masculine incarnation of his French-American grandmother, with the same finely wrought features, regal bearing, and unshakeable poise. He shared his father's temperament and grew into the same interests, clearly the natural heir to Salvador's empire.

Josémaria, the second son, was even more special. He came into the world at a robust twelve pounds, blessed with a beatific smile and a halo of golden-brown curls worthy of a Renaissance painting. His sparkling eyes were the colour of fine amber, and his limbs were strong, with rolls of pleasing baby fat. Even jaded doctors sighed when they saw the charming new arrival. The nurses who changed his diaper giggled and whispered, "Oh, the ladies will surely love this one."

Over the years, that baby became an Apollonian youth — tall, with exquisitely modelled features reminiscent of archangels in religious art. In contrast to his slim, patrician brother, Josémaria had a superbly masculine body, with a broad chest and back, and well-muscled limbs. He might have come off as a lumbering giant if not for the improbable lightness in his step and equine grace of his movements.

This young man grew up in a stately twelve-room mansion in Cameron's Court, an old-money gated community established shortly after the American rule of the Philippine Islands ended in 1946. The "village," as the residents called it, was just two and a half square kilometres, but it had its own nineteenth-century

Franciscan church; an Episcopalian cathedral for the diplomats and expatriates; chic restaurants; stores selling truffles and other gourmet goods from Europe; and a country club with fifteen tennis courts, three swimming pools, and two polo fields. Apart from the years Josémaria had spent at Cornell University, this immaculately groomed gated community, shaded by majestic acacia trees, had been his world for most of his life.

Like his older brother before him, Josémaria took a position at his father's firm. But he soon realized that skyscrapers left him cold, and he had no interest in the minutiae of real estate development. His heart lay elsewhere — in the deeply embedded traditions of his mother's family. He flirted with the idea of opening a village pasteleria featuring traditional pastries and elaborate fiesta dishes still served at his maternal grandparents' hacienda. This idea went the way of a summer fling the day he attended a friend's wedding in the historic district of Intramuros.

*

Early in the morning, before the sun got too hot, Josémaria got into his Maserati Coupé and set off for his friend's wedding. Outside the gates of the tree-lined village, a diesel-powered mega-city roared. The Maserati merged into the river of cars and buses, joining the weekend traffic headed for the cooler climes of Tagaytay and the nearby beaches of Batangas. He popped a Roxy Music tape into his stereo to make the commute more bearable. With any luck, he should make it to Intramuros before the *Avalon* album was over.

The final, instrumental piece called "Tara" was playing by the time he approached the historic Intramuros gates. Centuries ago, it was the Spanish Empire's military and political base in Asia. Now it was an obligatory stop for tourists and a photogenic backdrop for grand weddings. This was only the third time in his life that Josémaria had been to the walled city — the first was when he served as a ring bearer for his Tiya Elvira's wedding, and the second was when his family was invited to the archbishop's birthday dinner.

Finding parking on the narrow cobblestoned streets was its own little adventure. Josémaria's search brought him to a side street he had never seen before. There stood the ruins of a colonial-style mansion — once home to the owner of Perfumeria Prado, the colony's largest manufacturer of perfumes and soaps. The mansion was bombed and razed during the Second World War, like numerous other buildings in Intramuros. No family or next of kin ever stepped forward to claim it after the war. So, it waited for decades, through typhoons and tropical heat. The ruins had seen the country's postwar prosperity and lived through the dictatorship of thieves. Now here it stood before him, inviting him to explore.

The sound of horses' hooves filled Josémaria's ears as he entered the mansion grounds. Was it the horse-drawn kalesas of the current day's tourist trade or was it the echo of carriages from the past? The formerly grand rooms were now home to exuberant bougainvillea that had grown over and around the mansion's crumbling walls. Occasionally, a detail would catch his eye — a fragment of a window panel with pearl-like capiz shells instead of glass, or hand-painted encaustic tiles on a stair landing. Outside, where the garden used to be, was an old but still fruitful tamarind tree. Though he was a young man, he had always felt a strong affinity for places and objects with history. *Once there was beauty, laughter, and life in this place,* he thought as he walked through the roofless rooms.

The tolling of the cathedral's bells broke through his reverie. It was time to head over to the wedding. His finely embroidered barong tagalog rustled as he made his way off the grounds. To the birds that lived in the tamarind tree, this creature — in lily-white pineapple silk — might have been a visiting angel.

At the gate, he turned around to look at the abandoned mansion one last time. A gust of wind blew a cinder into his eye. It was an infinitesimal speck from one of the crumbling walls. The beautiful ruins had taken residence in him, like a grain of sand in an oyster.

*

The haunting fallen mansion in Intramuros stayed with Josémaria long after his friend's wedding, stirring in him an intense, almost painful longing for the lost beauty of the past. For the next several nights, half-remembered memories rose from the depths of his mind and appeared in his dreams.

On the first night, he recalled his tenth birthday party at his grandparents' house, with the Lengua Financiera and hand-churned mantecado ice cream he loved so much. He saw the thick, creamy buffalo milk and deep-orange egg yolks they used for the base. He felt the thrill of his silver spoon clinking against the crystal sundae bowl as he scooped the golden-yellow delight into his mouth. In his sleep, he sighed as the taste of custard cream, butterscotch, and lime zest danced on his tongue. And he knew that no gourmet ice cream on earth could ever compare.

The next night, he relived summers spent with his cousins at the hacienda, where they ate ripe guavas right off the trees, rode horses, and eavesdropped on kitchen gossip. He remembered stealing the chicharon, still hot from the oil, that the kusinera had prepared for the helpers.

On the third night, he revisited the Decembers of his youth, with the sound of mellifluous voices singing carols and the smell of pineapple and demerara sugar caramelizing on the Christmas ham.

The dreams continued for weeks, dredging up long-forgotten sense memories that shaped his childhood. His recollections were so enthralling that his present life paled in comparison. At merienda time, he was disappointed that the country club served arroz caldo without Spanish saffron. That would not have happened in his grandparents' house. Later, at the lobby café of a grand old hotel, he stared irately at the halo-halo iced dessert that came with chipped ice instead of feathery snowflakes of hand-shaved ice. Why bother doing something if you are not prepared to do it with care?

Outside, he looked at the modern city, with its ugly concrete boxes and glass-and-steel sentinels. It made him pine for the time-less grace of old buildings. During quiet moments, his thoughts inevitably drifted back to the burned-out abandoned estate in-side the old city. And in his heart grew a longing — that he may capture his cherished culinary and sense memories into one lumi-nous pearl, so they would not be lost in time's relentless tides. For months, this wish grew and took shape until he could no longer hold it. One day, in a torrent of words, he told his mother about his vision for the ruins in Intramuros.

"I see a place to celebrate life's landmark moments. We'll serve the paellas, the lechons, the bisteccas of one's dreams. People will tell their grandchildren about our dishes. The place will be grand but welcoming, like the home of an old friend."

"Like your Tiyo Rico's home," Isabel said with a knowing smile. "An old, genteel friend with exquisite taste in art and cui-sine. And a pantry full of jamon serrano and gourmet conserva."

"Exactly. I wish people understood me the way you do, Mama."

"I believe you can make it happen," she said. "Now, write it up and make a good business case for your father."

And that was what Josémaria did. It took some effort to get his father to warm up to the idea. For all his reputation as a vi-sionary, Salvador was a pragmatic man who liked stone, steel, and other solid things. Filipinos loved to eat, so food had always been a profitable business, but Salvador had serious questions about the business model his romantic, often flighty son was proposing. For instance, why offer an ambience that invited people to linger over a cup of coffee? Why bother with the care and love involved in old-world dishes when most people cannot tell the difference between risotto à la Milanesa and Royco rice soup?

"Not everyone is like you, Papa," Josémaria said gravely. "People need beauty and romance in their lives,"

"Oh, I understand romance," Salvador replied with a smile. "But remember, the honey doesn't last if the money doesn't come in. A restaurant is a business, Josémaria, not a game you can drop when the thrill is gone. The shareholders will want a return on their investment. And the staff will be counting on you to feed their families. You can't be a dilletante."

"With all due respect, Papa. I will build unforgettable memories the way you build your skyscrapers," Josémaria promised. "I guarantee the memories will last longer than many buildings."

In the end, Salvador had to relent because, for the first time, he saw purpose and passion in his younger son's eyes.

With his father's words of warning constantly at the forefront of his mind, Josémaria acquired the ruined estate and set out to fulfill his vision. First, workers came in to clear the land of shrubs, debris, and rocks. Once that was done, more men came with trucks to install sewers and lay down pipes. In the weeks that followed, armed security guards were posted at the construction site to watch over the large deliveries of limestone, marble, and hardwood. Architects and artisans were brought in to give life to the materials. Loads of black soil were laid down and royal palms were planted on the spacious grounds. Two years after his fateful encounter with the ruins, La Sulipeña rose. It was his homage to the imperial cuisine and hospitality of his mother's ancestors in Sulipan, Pampanga.

Built on the fertile banks of the Rio Grande, the town of Sulipan once prospered from rice and sugar cash crops. Its grand houses regularly welcomed senators, military leaders, foreign dignitaries, and European archdukes as guests. From that world rose a Creole cuisine, rooted in the land but thoroughly fluent in the great culinary traditions of Europe. Sulipan's days of grandeur were long gone, but Josémaria wanted its spirit to live on, as alta cucina Filipina.

Diners flocked to La Sulipeña despite its inconvenient location. They came for the food, stayed for the ambience, and lingered for a glimpse of its impossibly handsome owner. Within its walls, people fell in love, got engaged, and celebrated weddings and anniversaries. From the unbearable longing that grew in his heart, Josémaria had created a space where life was beautiful, if only for a few hours.

15

New Souls for an Old House

For the next few months, roofers, electricians, plumbers, paint-
ers, and carpenters worked to prepare the Twin Dragons apartments for its new residents. Celestina had already set up some
furniture — a bamboo living-room set built by a local artisan and
hand-finished with black lacquer. With help from Manang Rio,
she made fitted cushions with fabric bought in Divisoria. The bold
fan coral design went surprisingly well with her great-aunt's jade
damask loveseat and a four-panel Chinese screen depicting jewel-
coloured koi. Celestina could not wait to move in and start her life,
in a house of her own.

On the last week of the restoration, Celestina sat down to write
an ad for the mezzanine apartment. She thought about how and
when to best disclose the previous owner's continued presence.
There was no good way to sell spectral appearances and occasional
flying objects unless she planned to open a haunted castle carnival.
She decided her best chance for success would be to select tenants acceptable to both her and Great-Aunt Selena. So, she wrote,
"Wanted: Tenant for a well-designed, spacious, freshly painted

atelier space in the heart of bohemian Malate. Minutes away from Manila Bay, restaurants, and art galleries. One bedroom plus an office or den. Cozy galley kitchen with working vintage gas stove and fridge. One bathroom with shower and clawfoot bathtub. Large main room fitted with wall-to-wall mirrors. Suitable for creative professionals, yoga and fitness studio, or dance school. Serious inquiries only. Rental rate and other conditions to be discussed with suitable candidates."

She looked it over and added, "No Japayukis or strippers, please."

Later in the afternoon, she set up a makeshift buffet table in the garden and served pancit canton, Aristocrat fried chicken, and large glasses of calamansi limeade for the contractors, as well as the maids who had helped with the cleanup. Now and then, she glanced at her watch and looked toward the gate. Verg was supposed to come by with his furniture and equipment. He was late. She decided to set aside a plate of food before the workers finished off everything on the table. The men were on their second helping when a little blue econobox rattled into the lane and parked close to the gates. It was Verg.

Celestina ran toward the gates to meet her friend. "Hey, cute Datsun. They don't make them anymore, you know."

"Rojo's aunt wanted to donate it to charity. He figured I'm a good one," Verg smiled.

"Is he adopting you?" Celestina asked with a touch of envy. "Tell him we come as a package."

"Nah. We're too old and gnarly to be adopted. They always want the little babies."

"Oh, well ... let's get you moved in."

"Grab a box."

"Are these all your worldly possessions?" she asked as she peered into the back seat.

"There's some darkroom equipment and lights in the trunk. Rojo and I will take care of them."

As he spoke, a red Jeep Wrangler rumbled into the lane and parked behind Verg's jalopy. A stocky man dressed in a fringed buckskin jacket jumped out from the driver's seat. With him was a slim middle-aged woman dressed in Converse sneakers, white jeans, and a chambray shirt. She wore her hair in a chic pixie crop and walked with the easy, confident strides of a tomboy. Celestina had only met her twice, but she recognized Rojo's wife, Lille.

"We're helping Verg move in," Rojo said. "He's told us so much about your house. We just had to see it."

Celestina had come to know Rojo over the course of her friendship with Verg. He and his wife had no children. They did, however, take Verg under their wing, giving him an education far beyond his Commercial Arts degree.

"I'll give you a tour later," Celestina said to her guests. "Let's go help him."

Rojo and Lille each picked up a box, while Celestina carried a rolled-up straw mat and four pillows to the elevator. It took only a handful of trips to move Verg's scant possessions to Selena Sytanco's former conservatory.

Celestina then led her visitors on a tour of the building. She began with the mezzanine apartment and ended up back in the garden where they had started. By the time they were done, Lille was smiling and squeezing Rojo's hand. Without further formalities, Rojo said, "We'd like to rent the mezzanine apartment."

"There's something you need to know," Celestina said.

"Yes, we know about your great-aunt," Lille replied. "I think she'll like us."

"Are you selling your home in Tagaytay Hills and moving back to the city?" Celestina asked.

The couple eyed each other, quietly picking up the thread of their long-running conversation.

"No. We're not selling it," Rojo said. "We just need a pied-à-terre, closer to work."

"Yeah ... he likes seeing Taal Lake every day. Me, I'm just not ready to give up the city."

"I'd be thrilled to have you," Celestina said.

The day ended with handshakes and more glasses of calamansi limeade, this time spiked with white rum. That evening, Celestina tore up the advertisement she was about to run in the classifieds. She had a feeling Great-Aunt Selena would get along very well with the building's new tenants. *Swerte* was finally coming around to her side.

As the four housemates sat in the garden relaxing, Verg was pleased to see that they all had the same warm orange glow. Each person like firewood burning for a cozy communal hearth.

✻

Two days before Celestina was expected to move, Manang Rio announced she wished to be reassigned to Celestina's house. "It's a big place. She's going to need help with cleaning, cooking, and the other che che bureche of running a household. Besides, I need a change."

Celestina looked to her mother, then turned to Manang saying, "You're always welcome in my home."

"Well, I guess I'm officially an empty nester," Stella shrugged before thanking Manang for her service. Stella then excused herself to go upstairs, ostensibly to prepare a cheque to recognize the housekeeper's loyalty. She stopped by her daughter's room, which was now bare except for the bed that Celestina declined to take with her. Standing by the doorway, Stella waited for the tears that were not to come. She felt herself floating up and up, until she was looking down on her forlorn figure and hollowed-out existence.

✻

Celestina's life as a young bohemian in Manila started auspiciously with a lucky find in the vast flea market of Bambang. There, in one of the segunda mano stores, she unearthed an Yves Saint Laurent tuxedo jacket from the late sixties. It was a striking piece, double breasted with a peaked satin lapel. It fitted her curves more closely than intended, so she could not wear it with a blouse. Still, she could spot a gem, even when it was covered with a thick layer of dust and other things she would rather not think about. She grabbed the jacket and walked nonchalantly to the vendor, hoping he would not withhold it to sell to collectors.

With the lucky find safely stowed in her shopping bag, she went to the next store. An hour of digging yielded an oxblood-red leather jacket, a skirt with tulle roses, a shredded tank top with a dirty stencil of a daggered heart, and a pair of upholstery brocade jeans with eyelets down the sides. She moved to a pile of dresses where she found a finely crafted size-two sheath in golden yellow shantung silk. It had one bare shoulder and one origami sleeve, and it was just her mother's size. She thought about buying it, but there was really no point. Her mother regarded vintage clothing as carriers of bedbugs and *malas*, particularly if it belonged to someone who had passed away. Reluctantly, she left the dress in the pile for other people to fight over.

Celestina was about to call it a day when her eye caught the distinctive silk stripe on a trouser leg. Discreetly, she extracted the garment from a pile of undistinguished gabardine pants. It was an Yves Saint Laurent tuxedo pant — the bottom half of the jacket she had found in the first store. After inspecting it for signs of wear, she gave it a good shake and quickly paid. With her very own Le Smoking suit in the bag, Celestina headed around the corner to break for lunch. Never mind if her mother believed that second-hand clothing was *malas*. Celestina left the bazaar feeling like a relic hunter recovering long-lost treasures.

*

Celestina first turned up at Bar Iguana the night it was paying tribute to the Lizard King. Dressed in her heart-and-dagger tank top and upholstery brocade jeans, she walked in with her friends, the makeshift family from the Dragon Gates house. Eyes followed them as they made their way to a table near the stage. The people in the bar knew Lille and Rojo, and the young man they had taken under their wing. But tonight, all eyes were on the young woman, so insouciantly alluring with her messy tumble of auburn waves, cherry-red smile, and vintage finery.

A waiter came by to take their drink orders. A Red Horse beer for Rojo, an Aperol spritz for Lille, and two glasses of the sweet but very lethal Weng Weng for Verg and Celestina. She chattered excitedly with Verg in anticipation of the band. The drinks had just arrived when the keyboard player's electric piano started playing the haunting sound of raindrops. Celestina took a long sip before letting her feet take her to the dance floor. At the bar, washed-out hippie women smiled as Celestina moved her body to "Riders on the Storm." *Oh, how glorious it was to be young and beautiful,* the women thought. The men were watching her too. Weary in their middle age, they suddenly felt the invigorating rush of desire. Celestina acknowledged nothing except the music.

After a few songs, Celestina took a break and sat down with her friends at their table. An older man came by and clapped a friendly hand on Rojo's shoulder. The man wore a custom-made nappa leather jacket, and his long, shiny hair was slicked back in a neat ponytail. In a faint Italian accent, he chatted with Rojo, hoping for an invitation to sit at their table beside the charming young woman. No such invitation was extended, so the man introduced himself. Celestina obliged him with a smile and a handshake before turning her eyes and ears back to the stage. Determined, he slipped her a business card with a whispered invitation to call him for lunch. She nodded vaguely, but her mind was already in "The Severed Garden." Other men sent drinks her way, which she cheerfully accepted until Rojo said to her, "That's enough for now."

A waiter came over with grilled squid and pork sisig. Their table was humming with the voices of people who had known Rojo when he was a young man. Stories of memorable road trips on motorcycles flowed between sips of beer. For Celestina, this scene was everything that had been missing from her old life at her mother's house.

Verg was the first to call it a night. He left during the break, pleading an early meeting and other work obligations. His head was reeling from the bourbon, brandy, and rum combination of the Weng Weng, which was local slang for well and truly hammered. Walking home, he could feel his inner light sputtering while Celestina's was still burning bright. Lille and Rojo stayed for three more songs, then called for the bill as the singer caught his breath after "Break On Through."

"Oh, c'mon," Celestina protested. "The night's young."

"Yes, but we're oldies, my dear," he said.

Alone now, her table littered with drinks sent by admirers, she lingered until she heard the arabesque-sounding guitar of "The End" and the singer crooning a poignant goodbye to a love and to life.

She finished her last drink as the band members took their final bows. Walking home, she felt a sudden melancholy darkening her upbeat mood. She picked up her pace and was soon entering the pedestrian gates of her house.

The music stayed with her as she brushed her teeth and washed off her makeup. Suddenly, she felt very weary. She fell asleep as soon as she clicked off her bedside lamp.

During the deepest part of her sleep, the arabesque guitar started playing again as a familiar scene appeared. A small child was having a picnic with her doll, unaware that a giant lizard was watching. With its tongue flicking, it moved stealthily toward its prey. She tried to warn the girl, but the monster had already snatched her and disappeared into its lair.

Celestina woke up, crying as if her heart had been ripped out.

✲

The midmorning sun flooded the room as Manang Rio parted the curtains. Celestina clung to her pillow, waving away an offer of garlic fried rice and eggs malasado.

"Just a cup of tea, please," she said, as she pulled the sheets over her face. "I work better on an empty stomach."

Minutes later, Manang arrived with the tea — a strong reddish-brown brew, slightly oversteeped, prepared with a splash of creamy Bear Brand milk, the way Celestina had taken it since her teens. She drank her tea in bed while glancing at the headlines in the newspaper. Once the caffeine had kicked her awake, Celestina put on a pair of sarong pants and a T-shirt with an image of the buffalo-like wild tamaraw. She walked downstairs to the office space she had carved out near the veranda and sat down at her great-aunt's desk. She wrote through the morning and the lunch hour, drafting the outline of a travel essay based on a fondly remembered Mountain Province trek with Verg. Once she was happy with her draft, she set it aside so she could look at it with fresh eyes the following day.

She stopped to cobble together a quick meal at around two o'clock. Beef tapa and a bit of leftover rice sautéed with garlic, served with a fried egg on top.

Meanwhile, Manang was in the plaza returning from the market. She stopped at a kiosk for a tamarind drink. Cold, sharp, and bracingly sour, there was no better way to fight the midafternoon heat.

"How's your senyorita?" asked the vendor. "I haven't seen much of her."

"Oh, she's in the house, writing stories," Manang replied. *Takes after her father*, she thought with a touch of regret. *Mana sa Papa.*

Later in the afternoon, while Manang was getting dinner ready, Celestina moved to the garden with her poetry notebook and her second cup of tea, this time dosed with a splash of brandy. She needed the potent spirit, she told herself, to relax so inspiration would come, and the words would flow. In truth, she drank because she was in pain, hurting from a wound that had never healed, an injury inflicted on her body and soul.

When she felt tired, she went back to her room to take a nap until dinner was ready, and the night began all over again.

*

One Tuesday night, Rojo came up the elevator with an invitation. "There's a poetry reading at the Bravo Café," he said. "Lille's friend is hosting it. Come out with us."

Celestina agreed because she enjoyed listening to Rojo's stories and the café served good sangria. That evening, she clapped for the poets who came up to read. It was not easy to bare one's soul to a room full of strangers. Rojo, clearly unimpressed, remarked on the shallow talent pool and the stream-of-consciousness ramblings that passed for poetry.

"I think it's time we heard a new voice," he said.

"I don't think so," Celestina said, catching his drift. "I might just shrivel up from embarrassment."

"It's mortifying, sure. But if you can bring up one little pearl of wisdom from the abyss, it would be well worth it. Don't you think?"

Rojo poured everyone another round of sangria and said nothing more about the matter. Celestina sat quietly until she finished her drink, then excused herself to go home early.

The week passed, with Celestina mostly keeping to herself in the garden of the Twin Dragons Tower. She went back to the café the next Tuesday, wearing a necklace she had fashioned out of amulets and religious medallions purchased from a nearby church. She asked the bartender to make her a potent cocktail with calamansi lime juice and a ninety-proof liquor distilled from the sap of coconut flowers. She called the drink Sisa, after the famous madwoman in Philippine literature. Duly fortified, she strode to the microphone clutching her poetry journal.

"This is 'A Prayer for an Angel in Limbo,'" she said, her voice cutting through the murmurs of the friendly crowd.

To my unchristened one
who never drew an earthly breath
whose cry never bruised the midnight air
who never knew this mother's care

Your body sleeps
in blood and mud and piss
Just another drop
in that watery abyss
Your heart knows no hate
but you live outside of grace
You're innocent
but by the sin of Adam and Eve
you're stained

Have mercy on her
whose only sin was to be born
Give me her share of humanity's stain
What's another year in hell for me?
Just a tick in eternity

Give her wings
so she can fly
from limbo's shadowy realm
And let me see her one last time
before she enters Heaven's Gates.

The hush of suspended breaths filled the café as Celestina finished reading. Somewhere in the back, a young woman was crying. She bolted for the door, leaving her young man behind. He went after her, prompting the waiter to chase him down to settle the bill.

Rojo was the first to stand up and applaud Celestina. Lille joined him, followed by Verg, who saw Celestina's light flickering wildly. One by one, the people in the audience burst into genuine applause. Surprised, Celestina bowed shyly and fled from the stage. She ran out, across Remedios Circle to the edge of the wide lane where the Twin Dragons Tower stood. A weathered bench caught her just as her breath ran out and knees gave in. Just a few feet away from her was the couple from the café.

"I can't do it. I can't do it," the young woman cried.

Malate was full of human drama. This was just another night, Celestina thought as she watched the woman crying her heart out. She felt a warm, rough hand on her shoulder. "Are you okay?" Rojo asked as Lille and Verg sat down beside Celestina.

"I don't know," she said. "I just dragged strangers down my personal abyss. I have no idea if I came up with any pearls."

Across the bench where they were seated, the young woman from the café had stopped crying. The young man put his arm around her and whispered something that made her smile. Then the two of them left, hand in hand.

"You did, Celestina," Rojo said as he cast his eyes toward the couple. "I know you did."

Celestina followed Rojo's glance, and in a leap of intuition, understood. A tear ran down her cheek as they watched the couple walking away together. For once, she felt she had set something right in the world.

*

Before long, Celestina acquired a small but devoted following for her poetry readings. Every Tuesday, they showed up — first, the old hippies still in search of enlightenment, then pale youth marked with ink and scars. They came to read from notebooks filled with pain. After that, they waited for Celestina to take them to her darkest midnights.

When the readings were over, they thanked her, clutching her hand like drowning souls. They told her their stories of wasted chances, missed soulmates, and grinding loneliness. She said little, mostly she listened. And they left looking a little less broken.

People recognized her last name and fondly recalled her father's stories. She reminisced with them before duplicitously saying, "May God rest his soul," and moving on to another topic.

With the poetry readings, a happier, more self-assured Celestina emerged offstage. Manang Rio watched with cautious hope. For years, she had lived with that other creature — the angry, brooding girl in Misericordia Village, holed up in her room with its black curtains, vampire books, and drawings of childlike tiyanak monsters, believed to be earthbound souls of aborted babies.

This emergent Celestina smiled and mingled with people, though not the rich friends Stella would have wanted for her. None of that mattered to Manang. For years, she had prayed for Celestina's healing, and now, it seemed God was starting to listen.

16

Terra Incognita

Celestina was not the only one who blossomed during that heady first year at the Twin Dragons Tower. Word had spread about the talented photographer in residence. Selena's former conservatory now hummed with the constant flow of clients. First to knock were the owners of neighbouring restaurants, then the creative people from advertising agencies and publishing. With them came the models — sleek, leggy creatures with pouty smiles and hungry eyes. Gradually, Verg shed his downcast posture and erased the last vestige of his Visayan accent. He now carried himself tall, proudly bearing that Hollywood resemblance, along with his own bristling intelligence.

The changes did not go unnoticed. Manang Rio could see that Celestina was beginning to desire something more than friendship with the young photographer. She took extra care with her appearance and showered her friend with attention. She brought him food when he was too caught up in his work to stop for lunch. In the evenings, she showed up at his door with a charming smile and yet another invitation to a "can't miss" event. To her disappointment, his work kept him busy well after business hours.

"Manang," she finally said one day. "How do I make him see me? You know, as a woman?"

Manang took Celestina's hand and gently said, "He isn't ready to be a man. You'll scare him with your attentions."

Dejected, Celestina started going out alone. But everywhere she went, she saw couples. Inside the Insomnia Bar, fashionable pairs made out to the hot, swinging jazz of a local band. At the plaza rotunda, they sat on benches while they rested their ears from the loud music of the clubs. Celestina could tell who had been together for a long time. They did not talk much; they did not need to. They touched constantly — hands seeking kneecaps and thighs in easy intimacy.

Looking at happy couples made Celestina feel desperately alone. Her soul longed for a deep bond, and her body ached for a man's touch. This desire was a source of deep shame because it was awakened by someone who had no right to her body. As much as she fought it, the hunger was stronger than her resolve.

It happened during a concert by the shores of Manila Bay. Celestina found herself sharing a moment with a tall, blue-eyed stranger. The evening breeze carried the heat of the equatorial sun. He pressed a cold beer against her bare back and whispered in her ear while the band played a salsa rock tune. She turned around and, with a naughty smile, took a swig from his cool drink before turning back to watch the band. She closed her eyes and moved to the unabashedly sexual rhythm of the music.

"You're driving me crazy," he whispered hoarsely as his hands followed the swivel of her hips. He was mad about these islands, especially the women. They were so much sexier than other Asian girls. They had soul, and their bodies seemed to carry some secret Latin music.

They continued their dance in his room at a nearby hotel. For all the urgency of their coupling, there was no real intimacy.

He made love to his island fantasy, and she imagined a soulmate with whom she could share herself, both body and soul. This brief encounter was not love, but it silenced the howling loneliness of the night.

*

Celestina should have been thrilled. She had been waiting anxiously for weeks. Now here it was, her travel essay about Batad, sleekly laid out on thick, glossy paper in *Mabuhay*, the in-flight magazine of Philippine Airlines. It was accompanied by Verg's photographs of Batad's rice terraces in all their golden, harvest time glory.

It was only a year and a half earlier when she and Verg had walked the narrow path to that isolated village in the highlands of faraway Ifugao Province. It seemed so long ago. She smiled wistfully as she revisited the memory.

How Verg had grumbled when the minibus let them off miles away from their destination. She had "forgotten" to mention that the only way to the village was through a footpath in the woods. They had rented a bamboo resthouse for a week. There were no showers, so they had to bathe with rainwater collected in a jar. In the mornings, the owner had brought them a gamey meat stew and laffa. Verg was puzzled by the appearance of Israeli flatbread in a village without televisions or electric power. The owner had learned the recipe from Israeli backpackers who had stayed with their family the previous year. Luckily, Verg forgot to ask about the stew. Nobody had to tell Celestina what it was. From its flavour alone, she could tell it was not beef, pork, or even goat. It was a highland delicacy: dog meat.

She leafed through the magazine article while finishing her strong black tea. She missed her best friend, her fellow wanderer. He was too busy to have adventures with her now. Soon, she would be nothing but an old friend, good only for reunions. He would probably forget about her and get it on with one of the models who regularly turned up at his apartment. It hardly mattered, she told herself. She was used to being alone now. She put one copy of the magazine on her bookshelf and slipped another one into an envelope for Verg. After breakfast, she walked downstairs and slid the envelope under his door.

She spent the rest of the morning overseeing the restoration of the fountain and koi pond at the behest of Lola Teresita. "Let *swerte* flow into your house like water," her grandma had said. Indeed, Celestina was grateful that good luck had been visiting her lately. Perhaps the renovations could convince *swerte* to linger a bit longer, maybe even stay for good.

*

Late in the afternoon, Verg showed up at Celestina's apartment with a bottle of sparkling wine. She could tell by the label that it was the real thing from the Champagne region of France, and not some cheap bubbly from California. "What's the occasion?" she asked.

"Just a thank-you. For everything. This place has been nothing but *swerte* for me."

"There's a method to my madness," she replied with a secret smile.

"You're right on that one. By the way, what are you doing tonight?" he asked.

"I was going to check out the night market by the Folk Arts Theatre," she replied.

"I have a better idea."

"I'm listening," Celestina said with interest.

"Dinner at La Sulipeña," Verg smiled triumphantly.

"Oh. That's fancy. Did you inherit a small fortune?"

"Not quite. I cashed the cheque for the coffee-table book."

"The one about Philippine haute couture in the sixties and seventies?"

"Yes."

"Good enough. Yes, I'd love to have dinner," she replied, her light sparkling brightly, which pleased Verg.

"Super! Don't forget to chill the champagne. See you at seven. I got to run," he said as he hurried to the elevator.

As she turned to put away the champagne, she wondered if Verg had just asked her out on a proper date.

*

It was twenty minutes to seven o'clock. Celestina had just finished painting her lips in a rich, satiny red. She walked back from her full-length mirror to check her silhouette. She had decided to wear a backless halter made from light wool suiting. It was styled somewhat like a man's vest, and it went well with a pair of elegantly tailored pinstriped pants. Both pieces bore the name of a now-forgotten Parisian label, Françoise. She put on a pair of midnight blue stiletto pumps and struck a vampy pose before the mirror. Admittedly, she wanted to look as good, if not better, than the models who routinely showed up at Verg's studio.

She had both pieces tailored so they would fit her figure perfectly. The top was a little snug around the bust now. She undid the top button and told herself that after tonight, she would cut back drastically on her rice and dumpling intake. Satisfied, she grabbed her purse and made her way downstairs. She went to the kitchen to fetch the champagne, which had been chilling in a vintage silver bucket full of ice. In the great room, she put on Astrud Gilberto and waited for Verg. It occurred to her that she was twenty-two years old and had never been on a proper date. Worse still, she knew plenty about sex but practically nothing about love.

Verg came up the elevator sharply dressed in a light-grey herringbone jacket, smoky mauve shirt, dark denim jeans, and two-tone wingtips. His thick black hair had been styled into an artfully careless pompadour. Celestina stared shamelessly at the handsome stranger before her.

"Wow. Did Robert Downey Jr. raid Gatsby's closet?" she quipped.

"Yes, he did and thank you. You're not bad yourself," Verg replied. His eyes lingered on her strong shoulders and the bit of side breast displayed by the deep halter cut. Her light now looked like a miniature but luminous moon shining for him.

"Should I cover up the tattoo?" she asked, suddenly conscious of the souvenir from one of their youthful capers.

"Hell, no. Give the society girls something to talk about."

He walked to the bar where the champagne was chilling. Deftly, he uncorked the bottle and poured the drink into champagne flutes. With the fine bubbles tickling their palates, they reminisced about past adventures and made a toast to future ones.

Manang Rio came downstairs to wish them a nice time on their "date." Celestina shot her a dagger-filled look, but Verg simply laughed along.

"Don't worry, Manang. I'll get her back to you by midnight."

He took Celestina's hand, the way he did in the old days, and they half-scampered toward the elevator, laughing all the way down to Celestina's car.

✻

Celestina's heart beat a little faster as they approached the gloriously restored pre-war villa that housed the legendary restaurant. A valet met them at the driveway and helped Celestina out of the car. Sensing his friend's nervousness, Verg put his arm around her shoulder in a protective gesture.

At the reception area, they were greeted by a statuesque morena hostess with a sleek chignon. After checking their names, she asked them to follow her into the dining room. She had the distinctive queenly walk of someone trained on the beauty pageant circuit. Perhaps she had never made it to the international pageants because she was too slim and her features did not fit the classical mould. But the restaurant owner knew exactly what he was doing when he asked her to walk up and down the restaurant during her interview.

The dining room echoed with the effervescent laughter of "the Fireflies." It was the name Celestina gave to those who lit up the night in clubs, cafés, and restaurants. The Fireflies stopped gossiping when they saw the statuesque gatekeeper with the attractive arrivals. Celestina summoned her mother's hauteur and strode into the luxurious dining room with the air of a young queen. Her eyes took in all the sumptuous details laid out for the guests — high ceilings dripping with crystal and capiz chandeliers, marble floors white as moonlight, walls dressed in gilt mirrors, and a striking fresco of a plantation owner's home by the Rio Grande de la Pampanga.

The hostess led Celestina and Verg to their table, set with gold-rimmed china and table linens edged with intricate openwork designs, calado style. The crisp smell of the starched linens mingled with the perfume of camellias casually arranged in a sparkling Waterford vase. Celestina traced the calado embroidery of her napkin with a lacquered fingernail. This was not her grandfather's kind of luxury. This was an invitation to a gracious life from a gentler time.

They were soon joined by their host, who introduced himself as Manuel. He was an amiable man, at ease with everyone from visiting ambassadors and celebrities to the boy who washed pots in the kitchen. He was quite happy to answer questions and talk about the more unfamiliar and esoteric Sulipeña dishes. Celestina took an immediate liking to him. His generosity of spirit was apparent in his willingness to guide two clueless novices through an unforgettable dinner. The two young people perused their menus with a mixture of excitement and panic. Eventually, they surrendered themselves to Manuel's recommendations.

From the first bite of their poached quail-egg tartlets, they felt their mood lighten. They abandoned their customary dark humour and settled into a flirtatious exchange that grew bolder with each dish. With the ambient laughter and happy clink of goblets and silverware, Celestina began to feel like one of the Fireflies. To Verg's perceptive eyes, Celestina looked positively incandescent.

The dinner continued with a course of baked pear and wild spinach salad with roasted pili nuts and native cheese. With the arrival of the main course, featuring pork roast with delicately crisp skin, made from the San Miguels' own heritage breed of pigs, the two friends wondered if true happiness was genuinely within their grasp. By the time the dinner plates were cleared, they were looking at each other with lovers' eyes.

They were momentarily distracted by a sudden hush in the room. A tall, good-looking mestiso had emerged from the kitchen. He stopped to chat with a waiter, oblivious to the eyes on him. The statuesque hostess sashayed in, bearing a midnight blue blazer. She helped him into the garment, and he thanked her with a smile that could melt stone. Now dressed for dinner, the man sauntered over to the big table where his old friends were waiting.

"That's Josémaria San Miguel, the owner," Verg said, quite aware that the handsome Mestiso had caught Celestina's eye. Even in that room lit up with crystal chandeliers and candles, Verg could see that the Mestiso was radiant, like a small sun that people revolved around like planets.

"I thought he'd be much older," Celestina replied with surprise. She had not expected La Sulipeña's Old World elegance to come from a man in his early thirties.

"I hear he loves the ladies and the ladies love him back," Verg said breezily.

"Oh, I don't doubt it," she replied.

"Dare you to smile at him. You might get a date. Or at least free champagne," Verg said half-jokingly.

"I don't really care for society playboys," Celestina declared as she turned her attention back to her friend. "I prefer tortured artists."

At that moment, Verg saw a flash, a strident flare cutting across Celestina's otherwise luminous presence. She was remembering the other tortured artist in her life. She slapped away the thought as soon as it appeared. *Not on this lovely night.*

Manuel came to their table to introduce the evening's special dessert — the playfully named tibok-tibok. It was an exquisitely simple pudding, made with fragrant heritage rice and creamy water buffalo milk. Celestina and Verg listened distractedly as their host described the origin of the Sulipeña blancmange's name.

"It's cooked over a slow fire. And it's ready when the mixture pulses like a beating heart," he explained with flourish.

Manuel served up two desserts, plated with aromatic banana leaves and topped with coconut curds. Another waiter brought in civet coffee, brewed strong and taken with cream and muscovado sugar. Verg and Celestina ate quietly, with the host's words whispering in their ears. *Like a beating heart.* They politely declined an offer of the house's special mango liqueur, eager as they were to be alone.

After settling the bill, the two walked out silently, hand in hand, ready to cross into the unexplored terrain of love.

*

Celestina entered Verg's sparsely furnished room and sat on a weathered bench, a piece rescued from an old barber shop whose owner had since retired. She was familiar with his space, so she no longer found it odd to see a bedroom so obviously missing a bed. He had spent his childhood sleeping on a banig mat on the floor. Mattresses scared him, especially the soft ones. They made him feel as if he were sinking in the sea, as his fisherman father had died.

She watched him unroll the handwoven straw mat and put out extra pillows for her.

"Here you go," he said awkwardly. "I can get more pillows if you need them."

"It's not as if we'll be doing a lot of sleeping," she replied. There was a peal of amusement in her voice.

She waited for Verg to approach her with a caress or at least a word of desire. Sadly, the delicious chemistry they felt at La Sulipeña had vanished. Now it was up to her. She decided to make the first move, knowing her friend was inexperienced in matters of love. She walked across the mat and deftly unbuttoned his shirt.

"Kiss me," she whispered as she explored his smooth muscles with her hands.

"Okay," Verg replied timidly. He decided to start with soft kisses, but she clearly had other ideas. After following her lead, he let his instincts take over. She seemed to like what he was doing, so he figured he was on the right track. In truth, she was the only woman for whom he felt anything resembling desire.

She guided his hands to her buttons and then her breasts. They were perfect, as he imagined they would be. Firm, and delicately pointed. She slipped off her pants and arranged herself on the mat so he could see her body to its best advantage. Her body was fuller than it had been during their trekking days, but it still had the requisite curves in exactly the right places. In all her magnificent nakedness and the white-hot radiance of her light, it was her smile that pricked his heart. It was open and expectant, like earth to rain.

He shed the rest of his clothes and lay beside her. Celestina noted with disappointment that he was still soft. She had never had this problem with lovers before. She reached between his thighs to help him along. After several futile strokes, it became clear that he needed more help. She slinked down and tried to rouse him with her mouth. He pulled back, visibly mortified. "I'm sorry," he said. "I can't do this."

"I don't understand," a stunned Celestina replied.

"I didn't understand either, until this moment. Now I know. I can't. I never have. And I probably never will. I'm sorry."

Celestina stood up and quickly threw on her clothes. Somewhere, she thought, the spirits of *malas* were laughing at her. "Great performance at the restaurant," she said. "You really had me."

Verg watched sadly as his friend walked out of his bedroom, her light all but extinguished. Back at La Sulipeña, he was a young man on the brink of love. Here, he was just a boy haunted by a grey figure from his past. He got up from the straw mat and stood in front of the full-length mirror, regarding his nude, smoothly muscled body and well-wrought features with dispassionate eyes. His mind went back to all the models he practically had to fight off during work, and how he never felt anything for them. Then he thought about his friend, the one woman who fascinated him and made his heart beat a little faster. *Sorry, Celestina. But I am, for all intents and purposes, a eunuch. A beautiful eunuch.*

Upstairs, in the atico apartment, Celestina knocked at the door of Manang Rio's room. Manang took one look at Celestina's face and knew that things had not gone well. She took Celestina in her arms, as she had done many times before, and said, "You know, some boys just get older. They never grow up."

Celestina fell asleep in Manang's room that night, certain that God was punishing her. Somewhere in the shadows, another soul was weeping. Selena Sytanco had high hopes for this match. She had hoped her unfortunate death would not bring *malas* upon the house and its occupants. Now she mourned, as her grandniece would, for a sad, stillborn love.

17

Forever, Boy

The boy woke up to the smell of bleach and tincture of iodine in the air. He looked around the unfamiliar room, from the water stains on the ceiling to the ancient iron bed on which he lay. Stretching out his cramped arm, he realized he was attached to an intravenous drip. Through the fog of illness, he tried to piece together the events that had led him to this room. He had a clear recollection of being hauled to Enteng the Barber's house by two well-muscled uncles.

"You're the only boy in the village who's not tuli. You need to get it done so you can become a real man," his uncle had told him.

A real man. Years later, the boy would recall those words and laugh until he cried.

*

The boy and his uncles were greeted by Enteng, who functioned as the village manunuli when he was not busy cutting hair. He led them to the backyard, where chickens roamed scratching for worms. The boy nearly fainted at the thought of what awaited him in the hands of Enteng, but one of the uncles quickly revived the boy with a slap.

The old barber plucked guava leaves from a nearby tree and handed them to the boy. "Chew," he ordered.

The boy chewed as best he could but gagged as he attempted to swallow the bitter-tasting leaves. One of his uncles caught him before he choked.

"Gago! Don't you know anything? Don't swallow! Just chew."

The manunuli beckoned him to a spot under a tree. There was a smooth wooden stump sitting low to the ground with just enough of a cutting surface for a child's penis.

"Pull down your shorts and kneel," the old man ordered.

One of the uncles came and held down the boy while the old man positioned him on the cutting block. The cutting surface was coloured dark brown by dozens of previous customers. "Don't flinch or the manunuli might cut off your titi," one uncle said.

The boy had imagined the procedure would go quickly, if not painlessly. In fact, it took the manunuli three excruciating blows to sever the foreskin. The boy was then asked to spit the chewed-up leaves on the cut, to help with the healing. He could not imagine how this could possibly be good for a cut but nevertheless did as he was told. As he was dismally bad at spitting and all such manly pursuits, most of the slimy pulp landed on the stump instead of his titi.

He spent the next few days wearing a skirt so as not to disturb the wound. When he dared peek, he saw that the tip of his penis looked like a deformed overripe tomato. He was told to expect this. But as the week went by, it became apparent that the wound was not healing. He fell into a delirious fever, which did not respond to either Vicks VapoRub, aspirin, or concoctions prescribed by the village herbolario. The nearest doctor was hours away by bus.

In desperation, his mother called the only other person in the village with medical training — Padre Noche. She remembered from his sermons that he had studied to be a doctor before he was called to the priesthood. If a man of God and science could not help her son, then who could?

*

Padre Noche listened, once again, as the boy's mother tearfully recounted her son's state.

"His tuli is not healing. He's burning with fever. This morning, I heard him talking to my late husband. I'm scared his father has come to take him."

The priest smiled patiently despite his frustration with the stubborn village traditions and superstitions that refused to disappear.

"Mrs. Luz," the priest said with a weary smile. "Only one Father can decide when it's our time. Your son is delirious with fever from his infection."

"Please help him, Padre!"

"I'm taking him back to the rectory so I can properly care for him. He needs antibiotics. After that, I'll need to monitor his condition," he said to the boy's mother.

It was an order, not a request, and the mother would not have dreamed of questioning it. She hurried to pack a small bag with her son's clothes. Then she ran to the neighbour's house to enlist a young man to carry her son to the priest's Jeep.

"I'll call you when his condition improves. Right now, pray for him and get some rest," the priest said.

The young man offered to go with the priest to help move the boy into the rectory. They did not have far to go, but the narrow roads presented an abundance of obstacles, from stray animals to an impromptu basketball game. During the drive, the priest had time to reflect on the villagers' misguided notions about manhood and the traditional tuli. He wanted to be angry, but he learned long ago that emotions only led to bad decisions and suffering. He had known the boy's mother as the English teacher in the town school run by the Franciscan order. She was a good teacher, by all accounts, smart and patient with those who did not have the inclination for the subject. He could not fathom why she had allowed the tuli to be inflicted on her son.

When they finally reached the rectory, the young man carried the boy into a room that had been scrubbed and disinfected with bleach by a church volunteer. The priest thanked the young man and proceeded to wash his hands to examine the boy. He could only hope it was not too late, and the boy would make a full recovery.

*

The boy drifted in and out of nightmarish sleep for two days as his body fought off the infection and worked through the trauma of the botched circumcision. The priest entered the room just as the boy was coming out of his feverish state.

"You're in my home," Padre Noche said to ease the boy's confusion. "Your mother told me there were complications with your tuli. She asked me to help."

The boy recoiled at the sound of Padre Noche's voice. He stayed silent, hoping the priest would go away. Before the boy knew it, the priest was standing beside his bed. Padre Noche's expressionless, unlined face reminded the boy of an embalmed and retouched corpse ready for casket viewing.

From earliest childhood, the boy had known that people's bodies held a mysterious inner fire, and that fire was both light and life. This priest had no more fire than the alabaster saints in the church.

"I want to go home," the boy said.

"You will. You're not out of the woods yet, but I think you'll recover soon, God willing. Pray with me."

Padre Noche proceeded to utter a healing prayer, closing his eyes as he laid hands on the boy's genitals.

The boy gasped as the priest pressed against him through the thin sheet. His hands felt icy, so cold that the boy felt they might burn him. "Don't touch me," the boy heard himself screaming. "Leave me alone."

His screams were lost, heard only by the insects and ghosts in the rectory. He could only watch in horror as this lightless vessel stood over him, uttering verses in some unearthly tongue. As Padre Noche came to the end of his strange prayer, the boy thought he felt the heat of fever leaving his body. He tried to get out of bed, but the priest said, "Not yet. You need your rest." The boy felt "no" rising to his lips as a small voice inside urged him to run. Sensing this, the priest moved his face close to the boy's and slowly stroked his hair. One by one, the thoughts were snuffed out like church candles at the end of the day. The last thing the boy remembered was the faint smell of smoke.

The next morning, the boy woke up and got out of the iron bed. His throat was parched and his belly was empty, but he no longer suffered from fever and pain. He slunk out of the rectory and took the alleys back to the village to his mother's house.

His mother was grateful to have her son back. Thereafter, she and their relatives showered Padre Noche with gifts from their kitchens, fish ponds, and farms.

The boy never told his mother about the darkness he saw when he had looked at Padre Noche. Nor did he tell her what had happened at the rectory. He did not see the point. Why should he disturb her peace with something she could never hope to understand? Death had already taken her husband, much too early. Let her enjoy this one small victory. It was a wise and merciful thing to do.

*

Over the next few years, the kids in the village began to change. They grew taller, and their scrawny frames began to fill out. No longer children, they were now binatilyos and dalagitas. The boy saw his fellow binatilyos changing inside and out — their fires burning hotter and brighter as their physiques changed. They looked at the dalagitas' bodies and felt desire. Boys and girls paired up and fell in love. They went a little crazy and carried on as if they were in some kind of divine trance.

The boy spent his free time alone, drawing in his sketchpad and reading books or the serialized graphic novellas he picked up at the corner store. He was a castaway, stranded on the isle of childhood. His old friends assured him that someday he would find someone and fall in love. But the only feeling that burned in him was his wish to escape the village.

Absorbed in the vivid worlds unfolding in his mind, the boy scarcely noticed that he, too, had changed. His body had grown strong but remained smooth, with none of the unruly hairiness that plagued other young men. His complexion was flawless, interrupted only by the merest shadow of a moustache. With long-lashed, haunted eyes and delicately chiselled bones, his face had a soulful beauty no other man could approach. But through all the changes in his body, the boy never felt the yearning that so transformed his friends. Instead, he looked at his books and out to sea, longing for a different life, with people who had inquisitive minds and ambitions.

When he turned sixteen, he won a scholarship to the state university in Manila. He had heard scary things about the city — about cutthroat thieves who would lop off your finger to steal a ring — but he nevertheless packed his belongings and boarded a ship to the national capital. He was housed in one of the student residences in the university. To a young man from a small seaside village, the sprawling campus seemed like a city unto itself, with its cafés and pubs, art cinema, repertory theatre, and an athletic centre with a multi-lane pool. The dormitories were veritable Babels, with students from different islands of the archipelago, plus hundreds more from other Pacific islands, East Asian neighbours, and the Middle East.

While other lads partied and hung out with girls, the young man haunted the libraries and great lecture halls, devouring immense amounts of information to feed his hungry mind. The librarians came to know him as a monk-like figure who spent hours poring over books, studying the works of Monet, Van Gogh, and Hiroshige. In his second year, one of his professors found him fast asleep on a book of Margaret Bourke-White's photographs. Moved, the professor gave him an old Leica and found him a part-time job photographing artifacts at the national museum. So began his informal education with the artist known as Rojo.

The young man's beauty was evident even during his university days. Strangers, especially girls, often stopped him on the street to remark on his resemblance to a certain Hollywood movie star. In truth, the movie star would have looked like a rougher, slightly thuggish relation next to the young man. Women desired him, yet he looked at them and felt nothing.

It would take years for him to realize that something was taken from him that day in the rectory. And that he would never know desire or enjoy the touch of a woman because an essential part of him had been robbed of its fire.

18

Old Demons, New Ghost

Celestina and Verg's friendship would never be the same after that ill-fated night. Gone was the playful banter and innocent joy they took in each other's company. But in their stillborn love, they found comfort in sharing a bed after a bad day or a bad dream. It was enough for him, but not for her. More and more she stayed out late, finding release in the arms of strange men.

It did not take long for Manang Rio to notice Celestina's overnight outings. Once, she had second-guessed herself, but never again. This time, she blurted out without hesitation, "You won't find love in places where people go to drink away their problems. Go to church. Do charity work with your lola. Maybe you'll meet a decent man there."

Taken aback by Manang Rio's boldness, Celestina reverted to her Sytanco imperiousness to hide her shame.

"What I do at night is my business. You're not my mother. Stop trying to be," she replied.

The words shot out of her mouth like poison darts. Celestina realized, too late, the cruelty of what she had just said.

"Am I not a mother to you?" Manang replied. "I have cradled you. Held you when you were broken. You think you're so strong now, but you're still not whole. Why do you think I stay when I could have a peaceful life in my province?"

"That will do, Manang," Celestina said icily.

Later that day, she offered an apology.

"I'm sorry. Lord knows, you've been like a mother to me, Manang. But I am what life has made me. You're better off not knowing some of the things I do."

And those would be her last words to Manang Rio.

*

Celestina woke up early the next day to make breakfast for Manang Rio — ginger tea, crispy danggit, and egg on garlic rice. It was the decent thing to do after the regrettable things she had said. She brought the tray to the older woman's bedroom, set it down on the table near the terrace, and happily approached the bed. Manang had kept up her old habit of sleeping with a mosquito net, even though the windows were all screened.

"Are you sleeping in?" she teased. "C'mon. Gising na!"

Expecting to see a peacefully slumbering Manang, she lifted the mosquitero and saw her face — eyes open, mouth frozen in a silent scream. Unable to accept what was before her eyes, Celestina pleaded with the unresponsive woman.

"Wake up, Manang. I made breakfast. Eat before it gets cold."

Meanwhile, in the apartment below, Verg stirred on his straw mat. His body clung to the last precious minutes of sleep, but somehow, his eyes opened. He sensed something was wrong. He got up and hurried to the elevator without stopping to put on his robe. The muffled sound of a woman's voice met him as the door slid open to her apartment. It was coming from the upper level, where the bedrooms were. Celestina was not usually up that early, he thought. Following his ears, he ran up the short flight of stairs. From the hallway, the sound of crying was unmistakable. He turned left at Manang Rio's room, where the sobs were coming from. There, he found Celestina babbling an incoherent litany beside the old woman's body, which was now absent of light.

After a moment of shock, Verg gently covered Manang with a sheet and said a silent prayer for her soul. He then took Celestina into his arms and held her until she calmed down. He tried to stay composed as he figured out what to do.

"I'm going to call emergency services," he said, unsure about the next course of action.

"No!" she replied. "Call my mother first."

Even from the depths of her grief, she had not forgotten her family's instinctive mistrust of public officials.

Verg picked up the old-fashioned rotary phone and dialed a number his fingertips remembered well. He heard himself saying, "Hello, Mrs. Errantes. I'm sorry ... but ... Manang Rio passed away in her sleep last night ... No, ma'am, it doesn't look like she passed peacefully."

After he hung up, he sat down with Celestina, who was now curled up in a corner wrapped in Manang's shawl.

"Your mother will be here soon. Go to your room and lie down. I'll make you some tea."

Celestina nodded weakly and squeezed his hand before stumbling out of the departed's chamber. She had a bad feeling more *malas* was on the way.

*

Stella arrived later in the morning with a city coroner known to her family. Verg showed the coroner to the bedroom where Manang Rio still lay, while Stella spoke with her daughter.

"I can speak to the coroner if you don't feel up to it," she said.

"I'm fine, Mama. I can take her questions."

By now, Celestina had calmed down, with the help of some tea and generous swigs of plum brandy. They went upstairs to join Verg and the coroner who was inspecting the room for signs of forced entry. The coroner could find no such evidence, but Verg could see something he had never seen before — a mysterious glow hovering in a corner of the room. It was Manang — no question about it. She may have died, but she had not left.

The coroner walked to the bed and pulled down the sheet to examine the body more closely. There were no bruises, ligature marks, or any other signs of foul play that she could see. She was drawn to the expression on the dead woman's face — the look of horror in the still-open eyes and the mouth that was frozen in midscream. She turned to Celestina and asked, "What time did you discover the death?"

"I came in before seven-thirty in the morning. I thought it would be nice to make her breakfast for a change."

"What was her state when you discovered her?"

"I found her looking just like this," Celestina said. "I couldn't believe it at first. I kept saying to her, 'Wake up!' But she was already —"

"In rigor mortis?"

"Yes."

"Did she have any ongoing health issues?"

Celestina shook her head. "I've never seen her sick. We made her go to the doctor every year, anyway. Her doctor said she's one of the healthiest seniors he's ever seen. No high blood pressure, no heart disease, no diabetes. She walks to market every other day. And she had no vices."

"Did you hear anything during the night?"

"No … but she told me she had bad dreams sometimes."

"I see."

The coroner thanked Celestina and arranged to have the body taken to the morgue for a postmortem examination.

Stella made the funeral arrangements while they waited for the coroner's report. The coroner called two days later with her ruling on the probable cause of death — Sudden Unexplained Nocturnal Death Syndrome. Most people called it by its local colloquial name — Bangungot.

*

The death of Manang Rio hit Celestina with unexpected force. For two weeks, she woke up in a grey fog, turned on the television, and watched the images flit by before diving back under the covers to wait for the spasms of sorrow to beset her once again.

After drifting off to a fitful nap, she would wake up with a dull headache well after noon and go downstairs to find something to eat — usually a bowl of soupy Beef Pochero or Chicken Tinola from Lille. Celestina's thoughts would inevitably turn to her last conversations with Manang. *Why do you think I stay when I could have a peaceful life in my province?* It had never occurred to Celestina that the old woman stayed because of love. *Why would you devote your life to a selfish little brat like me, Manang?*

*

It was another day at the house with the dragon gates. Bright daylight poured into the master bedroom of the atico apartment, prompting Celestina to open her eyes. She must have forgotten to draw the curtains the night before, she thought. She sat up and reached for the mug of strong black tea on her nightstand. It was in her favourite handmade pottery mug, served at the perfect temperature with just a splash of creamy Bear Brand milk and no more. She took several sips and looked around her room. For the first time since the death of Manang Rio, the fog had lifted, and her mind was clear. Her first thought was, *I did not make this tea.* It could not have been Lille, Verg, or any other member of the household. Only one person knew how Celestina took her morning drink, or which mugs she preferred. As she finished her drink, she said, "You can stop making me tsaa, Manang. It's time for you to rest now."

The armchair across the room creaked ever so slightly, its cane-work seat groaning under an unseen weight.

"Please, Manang. I don't need any more ghosts in my life. Let me mourn you in peace."

With an insolent click, the reading lamp beside the armchair came to life. Celestina threw off the covers from the bed and put on her robe, muttering to herself. In death, as in life, Manang was as stubborn as the proverbial mule.

*

It wasn't my time to die. Not yet. I promised myself I would watch over Celestina until she was strong enough to look after herself. These islands are dangerous for young women, especially the pretty ones. Lots of monsters; some of them are even human. Once a monster snatched her innocence, under our very own roof. I'll never forgive myself for failing to protect her. He's been put away in a home for mental cases, I was told. It was better than he deserved. From now on, I'll trust my gut. Maybe I'm not educated or clever like Stella, but I have a mother's instincts.

From the first day, I had a bad feeling about the Twin Dragons Tower. I told Ma'am Teresita there was *malas* in that post by the stairs. I saw it looking at me — a fat face with two lizard eyes hiding in the wood. Ma'am Teresita looked at me like I was crazy. For all their talk about being "family," in the end, I was nothing more than their superstitious housekeeper from the bundok.

Of course, I was right. I saw it again during my first night at the apartment. I had just turned off the lights to retire for the evening. I had to pass that post, of course, on the way upstairs. I couldn't help but glance at it as I held the handrail for balance. I ran upstairs quickly and clung to my blessed crucifix for protection.

In the weeks that followed, I felt its presence constantly. It was there, lurking, like a cunning old rat. Sometimes, in a darkened room, I would catch a glimpse of fiery yellow eyes. Clearly, something was watching me.

One night, I half woke up, gasping for breath. Through the fog of my sleep, I saw it — a dark, ugly she-demon sitting on my chest. She laughed as she ground her big, fat ass into me. I knew right away it was a Bangungot.

As a child, my mother taught me to wiggle my toes whenever a Bangungot visited. This movement wakes you up so you can break the she-demon's hold on you, my mother said. So, I wiggled my toes until life returned to the rest of my limbs. Quickly, I turned on my bedside lamp. A dark, shapeless form rose from my bed and whooshed through the air before disappearing into my wall with a loud bump. That was the first close encounter I had with the Bangungot, and it wouldn't be the last.

The she-demon finally got me one night. I was deep in a dream I've been having since Celestina was born. In it, I was carrying a swaddled baby while walking down a muddy road. I felt danger, but I couldn't run. I kept sinking until I was waist-deep in mud. It was at that moment when the Bangungot struck. She slipped into my bed and wrapped me in her enormously fat limbs. I felt my lungs slowly collapsing as I struggled to free myself from her suffocating embrace.

I remember trying to wiggle my toes, but I was paralyzed. By morning, I was cold and lifeless, my face frozen in midscream. I'm not sure why this she-demon picked me, out of all the residents. Bangungots were supposed to favour men, so it doesn't seem fair.

But my job here is not done. As I said, these islands are full of monsters. And even though it was a Bangungot that claimed my life, I know the human monsters out there are, by far, the most dangerous ones.

19

The Grown-Ups in the House

It was the last Saturday of the month, almost three weeks since Manang Rio had passed away. Celestina remained in her self-imposed exile in the atico apartment. Rojo was now genuinely worried. He should be back home in the cool hills of Tagaytay, but he could not in good conscience leave the grieving girl alone. He decided to stay and work on *Pasaheros*, the painting he had started before the whole household was turned upside down over Manang Rio's death. Every day, his wife, Lille, went to the atico apartment to check on Celestina and brought comforting Pochero or Chicken Tinola. Grief had to take its course, but he suspected that Celestina might be in the grips of something deeper and more insidious.

Her now-reclusive father was a heavy drinker rumoured to be suffering from melancholia and paranoid delusions. It would be a shame if she went down that same road. She had beauty, youth, and a keen mind, but he could see that she drank too much. She was obviously carrying a lot of emotional baggage, so he was glad she had found a poetic outlet for it. When she comes out of mourning, he might also suggest to her to find a day job so she could get out of her head and out of the house occasionally.

Rojo had seen too many lives eaten away by depression and the pharmacological crutches people used to self-medicate. He himself had no need for such crutches. He had his wife, his art, and his family of students and friends. He also had the confessional, a vastly underrated tool for maintaining one's sanity. It was free, and it came with no side effects. He recommended it to anyone who would listen. Sure, religion was no longer fashionable in his circle, but as an artist, he knew better than to cut himself loose from a source of boundless inspiration. There would be no Sagrada Família, *Pietà*, or the *Ecstasy of Saint Teresa* without belief in the divine, he always told his students. The so-called anarchists and rebels could go on exhibiting used condoms on stained bedsheets, but they should stop calling it art.

He and his wife had been plotting to take "the kids" to a spiritual retreat. His heart went out to Verg and Celestina because they were both so lost underneath their youthful swagger. Neither had a father in the picture, and both were distant from their families. They were just crying out for gentle guidance in a world with too many bad choices. He and Lille were not able to have kids, but over the years they had met many young people who needed parenting. In his own mysterious way, God had given him a chance to be a father, or at least a cool uncle.

As the clock ticked closer to noon, he looked in the fridge for the previous night's roast pork. Perhaps he could coax Celestina out of her mourning with a grilled Cubano sandwich. He was pleasantly surprised when she emerged from the elevator, dressed in street clothes, carrying a purse and a sheaf of papers in one arm. She handed him the papers and said, "Rojo, you seem to know a lot of important people. Could you put in a good word for me?"

"I'll see what I can do," he replied.

"I appreciate it," she said. "And please thank Lille for the delicious food. She was a lifesaver."

"I'll tell her. Are you feeling better?"

"Well, I couldn't possibly feel any worse than I did. So, yes, I'm feeling better," she smiled.

Celestina paused to look at his painting of a baroquely painted jeepney in front of Our Lady of Remedies Church. Her eyes scanned the spectral passengers boarding the vehicle. She pointed to a tall, thin figure dressed in a floral shift, much like the one Manang liked to wear for Sunday mass.

"Is that Manang?"

"Yes. I added her. I wanted her to have a ride."

"That's nice of you. I think she's planning to stick around for a while, though," she sighed as she headed for the front door.

The sun was shining, but it was not too hot. From the window, Rojo could see that she was walking toward the gates, and there was a little spring in her step. She scanned the state of the grounds and had a chat with Rocky. Nodding, she opened her purse and handed him a thick envelope. His face broke into a wide smile, and he said something that looked like "Salamat!" She waved goodbye and headed out to the street.

Enjoy your day, young one, Rojo smiled. *Don't hurry back.*

*

After weeks of absence, Celestina returned to Bravo Café the next Tuesday, had her usual drink, and went onstage to read her poem called "The Mourning After." Following her reading, she quickly gathered her purse and portfolio to avoid lengthy conversations with well-wishers. A lean man with silver-streaked temples approached her.

"I really enjoyed your reading," he said.

"Thank you," she replied with the merest smile. She was used to older men approaching her with less-than-honourable intentions, so she headed straight for the door without giving him another look.

The man easily matched her pace without breaking his serene expression. "Rojo told me about you," he continued.

"Oh. I'm sorry, I didn't realize you were a friend," she said.

"I'm Anton. I'm the editor-in-chief and publisher of *Coup*. We launched it five months ago. Do you have time to talk?"

"I have some time."

"There's a place near the boulevard that makes the best tuna kilawin. We can talk there."

He led her to Platitos, a small, sleek tapas canteen cleverly built in the space between a vintage apartment hotel and a travel shop specializing in Corregidor Island boat tours. The server brought them young coconuts filled with their own sweet water. The yellowfin tuna came impeccably fresh and gently "cooked" in lime juice and tossed with paper-thin slices of shallots and long green chili. Pork belly cubes, rendered until crisp, were sprinkled on top for textural contrast. Ceviche-type dishes were not served in the Sytanco-Errantes household. Her mother was afraid of catching parasites from uncooked food, and for years, Celestina made this fear her own. Nonetheless, she could feel her palate tingling before she even tasted the dish. Hunger won over fear in the end. She dove in with gusto, wondering if this was the way humans were always meant to eat.

"I like your travel writing very much," Anton said. "I saw the article you wrote in *Mabuhay* magazine about that remote village by the Rice Terraces. I also like the one in *Woman Today* about Mount Banahaw."

"You remembered me from those two pieces?" she asked in disbelief.

"Your last name caught my eye," Anton said.

"Oh."

"But it was your stories that reminded me why I stay in this crazy country."

"Thank you. I don't travel much these days. I manage the Twin Dragons Tower. It has a couple of apartments and a million things that need fixing. But I do have a few ideas I'd like to pitch."

"You can pitch them when you start. I have an opening for an arts and culture editor, if you're interested. My current one took a job in Singapore. Says she's had it with this country."

It took a minute for Celestina to realize Anton had just handed her a lifeline back to sanity. They shook hands and parted after the meal.

On the way home, she passed Remedios Circle. As always, the cafés, bars, and music halls were alive with predatory nighthawks, brooding owls, light-chasing moths, and all the souls who worshipped the night. Celestina walked on. She no longer wanted to be part of that nocturnal world of escapism and forgetting.

*

Celestina's new job flung her amidst the privileged as she covered the season's movie premieres, theatrical performances, and concerts. She had grown up around rich people, so this did not faze her. In fact, she had made an art form out of living on the fringes. But she had not counted on the anguish she would feel after seeing the Fireflies.

Night after night, she found herself surrounded by them — dazzling young things who flocked to the city's cultural and social events. She watched them from the edges of their world as they bantered and played. Parties vied for their sparkling presence. And men forgot their troubles and became like boys again.

At home, Celestina would ask herself, how was it that life never weighed on the Fireflies' souls or dimmed their sparkle? Their images tormented her even in the daylight hours as she struggled with the demands of her job. She could not help but compare herself to them. There they were, creatures of laughter and light;

and here she was, all silence, shadows, and lead. If she no longer belonged to the nocturnal world of forgetting, and she did not belong with the Fireflies, where did she belong?

*

"I'm not the right person for this job," Celestina told Anton one morning as she handed in her resignation letter. "I was content enough with my life until I took this job. And now … I don't know."

Anton listened, not just to what Celestina was saying but also to the things she had left unsaid. After a long pause, he spoke. "I believe you're the right person for the job. But not as the wounded poet."

"Well, that's what I am. Are you not accepting my resignation?" she asked, puzzled.

"No, I'm not," Anton replied. "You can't just leave me in the lurch. Word would get around and you'll never get another job."

"I don't know how I can keep doing this, Anton."

"I would advise you to do what every person who has a job does."

"What would that be?"

"Look within you and find the part that can best negotiate this terrain. She's in there, I promise you," he said firmly.

Celestina stood chastened and speechless as her planned exit from *Coup* magazine was thwarted by Anton's well-chosen words.

"Now, if you would excuse me," Anton said as he took a phone call. "I have to speak to an old friend."

Celestina brought Anton's words back to her desk as she mulled over her next steps. It sounded like valuable advice if she could figure out how the hell to actually put it into action.

At lunchtime, she decided to take a drive to the Baclaran flea market to lift her mood. After a quick meal of charcoal-grilled pork skewers at one of the food carts, she set off for her favourite sellers to see their new stock. Deftly navigating the maze of stalls, she found the Punjabi woman with green eyes. The woman greeted her jovially before proffering a cropped blouse embroidered with tiny mirrors. "I've been saving this for you," the vendor said.

Celestina hesitated, knowing that her abdomen was no longer as tight as it used to be. She bought the blouse anyway, as a gesture of goodwill, and added a pair of softly billowing silk pantaloons before bidding the Punjabi woman a warm goodbye.

Two stalls over, a former starlet puffed on a cigarette while re-arranging an assortment of vintage clothes and accessories. A pair of large oval sunglasses with jade-green frames caught Celestina's eye. The faded beauty held up a large hand mirror as her customer tried on the sunglasses. On anyone else, they would have looked cartoonish. But on Celestina, the result was larger-than-life, glamourous, and just slightly off-kilter. "You look like an old-time movie star," the woman remarked with just a pinch of flattery.

Yes, a movie star, Celestina thought gleefully — for a female remake of *The Fly*. She decided she liked the way the glasses looked on her and wore them back to the office. Anton, who was coming back from a lunch meeting, joined her on the elevator ride. "I see there's good treasure hunting in Baclaran today," Anton remarked. "You should wear those glasses for your editor's photo."

Two months into her job, Celestina debuted her column, cheekily dubbed "On the Fly." She combined reviews with liberal lashings of dark humour and mordant social commentary. It was her way of telling readers that, although she moved with the Fireflies, she was her very own kind of creature.

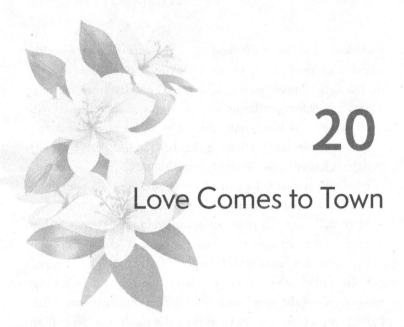

20

Love Comes to Town

Love finally stopped by Celestina's house the night she met Johnny. He came to the stage of The Hideout folk house to perform with his Ibanez guitar, his two-stringed kudyapi, and his flute. She was there to cover the show for her next column. Let's show the other side of the city for a change, she told Anton. The real city, not the shiny oases we usually feature. Now here she was, deep in the university belt downtown, inside the place where many historic protests of the seventies had been hatched.

The Hideout's glory days had been during the martial law years of the Marcos dictatorship. The audience had changed considerably in the past two decades. Only the faded posters of Bob Dylan and the folk rock band Asin served as reminders of the place's radical past. That night, office workers met with drinking buddies and relaxed to the ballads of "The James Taylor of Mindanao," as the management billed Johnny's act.

Celestina stood alone by the bar with her notebook, pen, and penlight, listening as Johnny launched into a soulful version of "Fire and Rain." His voice was good, though not as powerful as the ones recording companies preferred. But she liked the intimacy of his vocals and the way he unwound the words to tell the story. The popular local singers were all voice, no heart.

Johnny looked to his audience as he came to the end of the song, gratefully acknowledging their applause. "There you go, .guys," he said into the microphone. "Your golden oldie. Now, how about we listen to a bit of original music?"

Audibly disappointed, the mostly male crowd shouted half-drunk requests for "Handy Man" and "Don't Let Me Be Lonely Tonight."

"Sorry guys. I'm a musician, not a jukebox," Johnny said with his professional smile. He ignored the hoots and defiantly introduced his song. "Ladies and Gentlemen, this is 'Davao Still Life.'"

Without familiar riffs or choruses to hang on to, the men soon drifted back to their beer-fuelled banter. By now, Johnny was used to the 101 humiliations of the struggling musician. Since he had decided to embrace this life, producers repeatedly told him that his voice was good but not great. He was too short, they said, and too dark-skinned. He was not bad to look at, but he was not pop-star material. Besides, his themes were too "heavy." He should write more love songs and ballads — songs that played well on the radio and in karaoke bars. He often wondered how much of him had withered inside from the casual cruelties of audiences, promoters, and producers. Yet here he was again, presenting his soul's work to drunken strangers.

Celestina looked around at the disinterested audience, immersed in their boozy camaraderie. She felt like slapping every last drunken one of them. Angrily, she muttered, "Would it kill you to listen to an original song?" She took a drink of her cerveza negra and turned her attention back onstage.

As Johnny sang, the garishly lit stage with its time-worn posters gave way to the honey-coloured light of a perfect Mindanao day. Celestina found herself walking past vendors offering dragon fruit and extravagantly plumed birds in bamboo cages. Johnny's voice momentarily faded as a chorus of dialects rose in time to the music. Her ears caught a snippet of a conversation in Chavacano — the Philippine Spanish Creole of her father's family. There was music in its syllables, so unlike the Hokkien she heard at her mother's family gatherings. She wanted to stop and eavesdrop on the sounds that used to bring her so much joy, but they were soon drowned out by the increasingly feverish pace of Johnny's strumming.

"Slow down," she whispered. Then he paused and held it for two breaths, before tearing into his strings with two thunderous chords. One chord, one explosion. The fragment of Chavacano was lost in a deafening blast.

"Bomba! Bomba!" With his voice and guitar, Johnny painted anguished cries piercing the air as bombs rained nails, ball bearings, and razor blades onto marketgoers. Caught up in the scene Johnny had created, Celestina heard a child crying. She turned around to look for the child, but one final blast sent her hurtling back to the folk house.

Celestina leaned against the bar, trying to regain her composure as the song wound down. Her boot touched something hard and slippery — a fragment from the bottle of beer she was drinking. She picked up the shards and apologized to the bartender. She realized she could barely hear herself or the music through the ringing in her ears.

Johnny finished to scant applause. It was then that he noticed her, tall and shapely, standing in the shadows by the bar. "Come on up, miss," he said into the microphone. "Plenty of seats here."

The entire room turned to stare at her. The bartender, noticing her confusion, escorted her to the empty table by the stage. Johnny stared, breath suspended, as she took her seat just paces away from him. There was something otherworldly, even dangerous, in the cast of her eyes, but he could not look away. He would not have been surprised if she'd had fangs hidden under that delectable pout.

Johnny had planned to do a song about the endangered Philippine eagle but decided to switch to "Haplos." It meant "caress" and was the closest thing in his repertoire of original music to a romantic ballad. He lifted his flute from its stand and started to play an extended introduction, evoking the birdsongs of Mindanao. The gentle notes calmed the ringing in her ears, and the words carried her to the first dawn where she was Mother Earth and he the sky. Celestina wanted to stay there as the sky's breath warmed her skin and flowers cloaked her nakedness.

The men in the bar briefly interrupted their conversations to applaud the last fading notes of Johnny's flute. He could hear them ordering another round of drinks, but he no longer cared. He bowed to her, his audience of one. Her cheeks were flushed, and her lips parted, as if anticipating a kiss. He tried in vain not to stare at the hint of cleavage escaping her T-shirt. She admonished him with a sharply cocked eyebrow, though the curve of her lips did betray a hint of laughter.

Johnny spent the rest of the night working to impress his new muse. He showed off his skill with the acoustic guitar and the kud-yapi, an Indigenous two-stringed boat lute from his birthplace. He could tell that he had piqued her interest. She had probably never met a guy from Mindanao. These bourgeois Manileños would fly to Hong Kong or Singapore for a long weekend, but never once set foot in Mindanao.

Mindanao was known to many Manila people only through headlines, though it was home to paradisiacal beaches, virgin forests, and the majestic Philippine eagle. They read about bombings in public places, Communist insurgents collecting "tax money" from villagers, and separatists kidnapping too-intrepid tourists for ransom money. Sometimes, these ransom demands were quietly met, and prisoners were released. Other times, the papers would report a severed head turning up in some small town or another. The culprits were almost never caught because Mindanao was considered its own land, a place where the laws of Manila did not apply. Manileños often wondered why reckless foreigners risked captivity to experience Mindanao. Johnny understood why. Beyond its incomparable beauty, Mindanao had a fierce soul that resisted assimilation. And that drove the seekers mad.

Celestina stayed until the very last song, much longer than she had planned. She had heard performances of kudyapis and other tribal instruments during her travels. But this man was not a musical anthropologist playing ancestral songs. He was an entirely contemporary troubadour, as Bob Dylan, Carole King, and Leonard Cohen were. After the show, she approached him and said, "You write great songs, but you're playing to the wrong crowd. Don't cast your pearls before swine."

The lady was right, of course. But as he stood before her he thought, *This long-faded folk house does not seem like such a bad place for me.* She handed him a business card and introduced herself as the arts and culture editor of the magazine *Coup*. She wanted to sit down and interview him.

Johnny nodded and mumbled a barely audible "Yes, sure," as he stared at the business card of Celestina Sytanco Errantes. *You've been flattered into muteness,* he reproached himself. *Where are the words that flow so eloquently from your poet's heart?*

Celestina sensed his nervousness. She switched from English to Tagalog and asked the waiter to bring Johnny whatever he wanted.

"Salamat," he said gratefully. With the adrenalin from his performance wearing off, he could no longer ignore his empty belly. He ordered a large bowl of Kalderetang Kambing and rice with some bird's eye chilies on the side.

The waiter soon came back with the kaldereta and two bottles of cerveza negra. Celestina drank her beer as she watched Johnny crush the chilies into the stew. Mindanao's food leaned toward the fiery spices of Java and Sumatra. To him, the food in Manila tasted like meat doused in tomato syrup. He was thankful that the kaldereta was palatable if a bit timid. He ate quickly until not a grain of rice was left.

Celestina glanced at the clean plate in front of Johnny's much-too-lanky frame. She realized he was a lot smaller than he looked onstage — a good three inches shorter than she was. His hair was styled in some manner of moptop, three decades after the Beatles had abandoned it, and the eagle on his T-shirt was a mere ghost after going through one too many washes. Now, her admiration began to turn into something akin to pity, but she quickly brushed away these feelings. She had a job to do and questions to ask.

"That song 'Davao Still Life' was raw and powerful. Tell me, what made you write it?"

Johnny smiled despite the painful psychic wound she had opened. It was rather novel to hear his song called "Deau-vow Stihl Layf" instead of "Dabaw Istel Layp," as most local speakers would say it. She had the telltale colegiala accent — the accent of girls who went to exclusive schools for the rich and burgis. Caught between his pain and her charms, he stammered and stumbled through the tragic event.

"I was there," he heard himself saying. "I was having lunch in the Davao Public Market with a friend. That's where all the *Davao Sun* reporters ate. I went down to the bodega to use the washroom. I was on the stairs when the bomb exploded. I was thrown down the steps and landed on the concrete floor. I dislocated my shoulder and suffered a concussion."

"And your friend?"

With a long swig from his beer, Johnny said, "I had to trip over bodies to get to him. I remember picking out nails and razors from his face before they took him away in an ambulance. He died two days later in the hospital."

"I'm so sorry. I didn't mean to dredge up a painful memory," she said.

"That's okay. Anyway, I was a mess for a couple of years. Every sound sent me ducking for cover — car horns, motorcycles, a fork dropping on the floor. And especially thunder. I was like a cowardly dog who hid and whimpered during electrical storms. It's still hard for me to talk about it."

"And how did you go from that to writing music?" Celestina wondered.

"I needed a way to make peace with sound again. So, I dusted off my guitar and started playing the pieces I had learned from my parents. Then the new songs started to come. The words and melodies wrote themselves inside my head. They were formed before my hands even knew how to play them. It was painful. I felt …"

"Frustrated?"

"Swollen. Like a dam about to burst open. I had to learn quickly so I wouldn't go crazy. That's how it was. Still is."

"I sense regret. Do you regret becoming a musician, Johnny?"

He thought about his old life, before the incident at the Davao City Market, when music was no more than a pleasurable hobby. Now there was no going back, and he could not stop the music any more than he could bottle Mindanao's Maria Cristina Falls.

"I understand if you don't want to answer it."

"Do I regret it? Sure. All the time," he smiled bitterly. "I often think about going back to my job at the *Davao Sun* or even an advertising agency. I fantasize about settling down, getting a car, buying a house, and all that. I probably will when all this shit finally grinds me down."

"That would be a shame," Celestina said earnestly. "I'm speaking selfishly because I would really miss your music."

"Thanks. That means a lot, coming from a lady like you."

She flagged the waiter and asked for another beer. Johnny's keen ears noted how she pronounced it "ther-ve-tha," as the

Kastilas would, rather than the more streetwise "ser-be-sa." He should really hate this slumming colegiala, he thought. She represented everything his leftist professors taught him to detest. But damn, she was hot, and no amount of indoctrination could make him think otherwise.

Celestina dropped her eyes to take a long drink from her beer. It was thrilling to be desired, of course, especially when one's heart was suffering from a drought. In fact, she did not mind Johnny's unrelenting gaze.

"May I ask you something?" he said.

"Yes?"

"That's a great tattoo you have there," he said pointing at the four-branched pinwheel inked on her arm, right where a military person would display rank. "Did you pick it out from a catalogue of tribal tattoos?"

"Nooo," she said with a dagger look aimed his way. "It came to me in a dream, after I climbed Mount Banahaw. I sketched it on a discarded Marlboro wrapper. Then I had it done in a tattoo shop in Pasay, right after I got off the bus. Is that authentic enough for you?"

"Okay. I'll shut up now," he said, feeling like the world's biggest jerk.

"It surprises you because of how I look and speak. Ask an honest question. Maybe you'll learn something," she replied, trying not to sound too irritated.

"Sorry. Obviously, it meant enough for you to etch it on your skin. I'm curious about its meaning."

"I did it on a whim, but a professor later told me it was a symbol for journeys. The four branches here represent north, south, east, and west. This circumflex here is a roof, a symbol of home. Dreams speak to us. We just need to learn their language."

"I get it. Life's a journey. On the way to our spiritual home. I like that. I wish you a good one," he said.

"Thank you. I hope it turns out well. Sometimes I feel as if I'm just wandering with no direction or destination."

"I have another question, Celestina."

"Your last one," she said. "I'm interviewing you, remember?"

"Do you have a boyfriend?"

"Oh my. You're pretty smooth after a couple of beers," she said, not entirely surprised. What kind of Filipino man would he be if he did not try?

"You didn't answer my question," he pressed.

After a moment's hesitation, she shook her head and said, "No, I don't have a boyfriend. I seem to be *malas* in that field."

He smiled and said, "The men in this city are fools."

"Thank you … I think," she replied. Seeing that the mood was turning light and amiable, she quickly asked his permission to take some photos.

After a few shots and several more swigs of beer, Johnny picked up his lute and sang "Puki Puki" — an unabashedly ribald ditty about a salty eggplant dish named for the most female part of a woman's anatomy.

"I see you're not limited to sociopolitical commentary," Celestina quipped. She was rather enjoying this unexpected side of the soulful troubadour.

With the friendly banter flowing, Johnny could feel their professional rapport blossoming into a genuine human connection. The moment was interrupted by the night manager's arrival to announce closing time. He handed Johnny his cheque and thanked him for the show. He also gave Johnny a coupon for free beers and Pika Pika for two.

Celestina likewise wrapped up her interview and offered him a ride home. It was the least she could do to show her appreciation.

Johnny smiled as he weaved through chairs and tables on their way out. Free beer and half an hour more with her. It must be his lucky night.

*

Celestina's little black Honda stopped at a street dominated by a tall, whitewashed wall. The wall had been there long before Johnny had settled in Manila. Only long-time residents remembered that the wall was part of Imelda Marcos's beautification campaign for Manila in the seventies. Since she could not eradicate the slums, she built walls and hid them. Somebody had already spray-painted "No Futur" on the recent paint job.

"Good night and thanks for the interview," she said. "Give me your address, and our intern will send you a copy."

Without thinking, Johnny leaned across and planted a tender, almost reverent, kiss on her lips.

"Stay with me," he said. "I don't want to be by myself anymore."

It was not the first time Celestina had heard that plea. Men, for all their bluster and bravado, were terrified of being alone. Another man, much older than this one, once told her the same thing. Why do these men think she could rescue them? How could she when she could barely find her own way out of the wilderness?

"You have to go now, Johnny. Let's not make this awkward."

By now, he could no longer hear the straining voice of reason. His hand moved to caress the silky skin on her nape and shoulders, strumming unrelentingly until he found the chord of her desire. He kissed her again, this time with all his hunger. And she replied in her loneliness. When the moment came for them to be alone, she followed him into the hidden world behind the whitewashed walls.

The smell of rot hit her as she looked at the great warren of shanties and cinder block dwellings around her. Somewhere in that maze was half a decrepit house that Johnny shared with two other men from the provinces. Johnny's friends were still up drinking with some neighbourhood men. They sat shirtless around a rusted table on a patch of compacted earth. The table was covered with empty beer and gin bottles. The men elbowed each other as they spotted Johnny walking down the dirt path with what looked like a real live high-class mestisa. They greeted their friend effusively, hoping for an introduction.

Deeply embarrassed, Johnny acknowledged them with the merest nod before quickly disappearing into the house. "Sorry," he said, now painfully aware of the squalor into which he had dragged her. "You know I'm not like them." He desperately wanted to show that though he lived in a shantytown, he was no istambay street corner bum.

"I know you're not," she said. "Let's not talk anymore."

They went to the bedroom he shared with his two friends and bolted the door. He undressed her slowly, as if unveiling a rare artifact. Even in that dingy room, Celestina looked majestic. He took his time, flicking his tongue around her nipples and stroking her thighs. As much as Johnny wanted to, he felt almost ashamed to enter her.

Sensing his hesitation, she said, "Do it before I change my mind."

"Yes, ma'am," he quipped as he playfully cupped her breasts. He could feel her lust breathing like a wild animal in the room. Outside the room's thin walls, the neighbourhood men continued their camaraderie over cheap liquor and beer, stopping only occasionally to eavesdrop on the lovers. In the room, the slum had ceased to exist. Johnny was gone, lost in her sighs.

Soon, the rain began to fall on the patchwork shanties in the slum. The unseasonable rainstorm quickly turned the dirt roads into mud and sent mini-waterfalls down flimsy roofs and walls. The drinking party took refuge inside the house, which by now was filled with sounds of pleasure. The men tittered knowingly but otherwise remained silent to let Johnny enjoy his lucky night. As the rain showed no signs of stopping, each man commandeered a corner and tried to sleep.

Behind the locked door, the lovers clung to each other, bodies desperately seeking release from the pain of solitude, of frustration, of loss.

"I love you," Johnny cried out as he finished.

Celestina's body went limp as she let out a soft, low moan. She tried to ignore the endearment uttered by this stranger in this room that smelled like sweat and cigarettes. Love wasn't the reason she was there, and she knew it. She had been introduced to the physical pleasures of sex before she was ready. But she never forgot and continued to crave them even as they brought her to strange beds in low places.

"I said, I love you."

"Sure you do," she said, tousling his hair.

"I mean it."

"Don't, Johnny. It's not going to end well."

"I understand you better than you think," he replied. "Your spirit hungers for a great love. But you're much too proud to accept a humble man's offering."

Celestina fell momentarily silent before saying, "It isn't my spirit that hungers."

Unfazed, he replied, "I can satisfy you in every way you need. Just give me a chance."

Celestina thought about throwing on her clothes and leaving, but she could feel sleep coming for her. "Maybe," she said before closing her eyes. "Let's talk in the morning."

Johnny stroked her cheek tenderly. "Maybe" was an outside possibility, but at least it was not a "no." So far, it was the best thing Manila had thrown his way.

*

At daybreak, while most of the slum dwellers were still snoring in their cots, the lovers picked up their fallen clothes, tiptoed around the sleeping men, and walked through the muddy paths back to her car.

"Think about what I said," Johnny implored. "I'll call you after I come back from my gig in Angeles City."

"Goodbye, Johnny. Thank you. It was really nice," Celestina said as she gave him a parting kiss. Johnny played music like Orpheus himself, but what good was an Orpheus who lived in a fetid slum? A teardrop swelled in the corner of her eye as she got into her car. She glanced at Johnny and the whitewashed wall before driving away.

Part of Celestina wished her mother was around to be properly mortified by her latest escapade. As she came to a stoplight, she realized something. After spending her teens defying her mother, she was now weighing Johnny on her mother's coldly pragmatic scale. She was her mother's daughter after all.

Inside the walled slum, Johnny reflected on the enigmatic woman who had shared the night with him. How blithely she had spoken of her body's hunger. He was not accustomed to women like her. Men were the ones expected to compartmentalize sex. He himself did not. He loved and cherished every woman with whom he had been intimate. Celestina was only the third. That was not a lot for a Filipino man of thirty years. *Celestina, we would be so good together*, he thought. *I would love you with everything I have.* He lingered on the wonderful thought, knowing full well that pursuing her would be certain heartbreak. *Leave the night to the night*, he told himself. But his heart had other plans.

*

Not long after her bittersweet encounter with Johnny, a package arrived at Celestina's desk. Inside was a slim hand-bound book with cryptic writings on the left-hand pages and Tagalog verses on the right ones. The note from Johnny said, *I've had this for a long time. It's a collection of pre-Hispanic poetry. I want you to have them. With love, Johnny.*

Celestina leafed through the book, lovingly examining the mysterious glyphs on the left-hand pages, as well as the Tagalog translations. Two poems caught her attention: one about friendship, and the other about love. As she lingered on the words, she remembered her doomed love with Verg. How wonderful it would be to have the comfort of friendship with the life-affirming fire of passion. She wished she could feel that fire with Johnny, who seemed so painfully ordinary outside of his music. Still, she was pleased with his offering and her heart began to open up to the possibility of friendship.

She was still working when, at half past five, the security desk announced a visitor. It was Johnny.

"Hello," Johnny smiled shyly, quite unsure what kind of welcome he would receive.

"It's good to see you. Thank you for the book," Celestina said. "I really liked the poems about love and friendship."

Emboldened by her welcome, he worked up enough courage to ask, "Would you like to take a stroll with me? Watch the sun set? If you're not doing anything, that is."

"Why not?" she replied. It occurred to her that although she worked near Manila Bay, she always managed to miss the famous sunset that was the subject of countless paintings and postcards.

They walked together along the bay, chatting about Johnny's campus show in Angeles City until the magic hour arrived. He'd had a good show, he told her, and he got the students excited and on their feet with his original songs. Timidly, he held her hand as they watched the explosion of orange, pink, and cobalt fade into black. After sundown, they dined together at By the Bay, a small and very casual eatery by Manila Bay known for its grilled seafood dishes. They spent the rest of the evening visiting Celestina's regular haunts in Remedios Circle in Malate. She acquainted him with all the cafés, galleries, and music bars that sought out brave voices beyond the mainstream. She made it a point to introduce him to Corazon, the proprietor of Bravo Café.

At the Penguin Café, professors and pundits of all stripes mingled with foreign journalists on Asia-Pacific postings. Next door at Insomnia Bar, designers and models partied with slumming socialites and diplomats, while statuesque drag queens performed cabaret revues. At the patio tables, filmmakers, artists, and writers plotted alcohol-fuelled projects over Pika Pika and glasses of cheap red wine. Over at the Cienfuegos Gallery, a flutist from the Cordillera region performed against the backdrop of Rojo's latest exhibit.

Johnny struggled to take in the names and heady mix of personalities around him.

"How do you like my little neighbourhood so far, Johnny?"

"It's interesting, but not what I'm used to," he said cautiously. "But why do you call it your neighbourhood?"

"Because I live here. Why else?"

"I thought women like you lived in Cameron's Court or Olympia Heights."

"Did you think I was rich?" Celestina laughed as they perused the papier-mâché passengers in one of Rojo's installations. "Sorry to disappoint you, but I'm not an heiress. Just someone who writes for a living."

"Where exactly do you live? Maybe I can visit sometime."

"Walk me home. I live right around the corner."

Celestina led him to the gallery's back door, which opened to the leafy, half-hidden cul-de-sac where the Twin Dragons Tower stood.

Johnny blinked as the building came into view. To his eyes, it looked like a fever-induced apparition, both sublime and grotesque. He thought it odd to have such a grand place so near the red-light district.

"This property belonged to my Lolo Sebastien's half-sister, Great-Aunt Selena," she explained. "Back when this neighbourhood was a respectable district. My grandfather gave me the place as a graduation gift."

"That's quite the graduation gift. I was happy to get a gold watch," was all he could say. All week long, he had longed to kiss her and hold her, but now he felt truly out of her league.

"My mother fell out of my grandfather's favour. This place and some pocket change is all I'm going to get of the family fortune. Just so you know," she said pointedly.

"I see."

"I can introduce you to my cousins if it's a rich girl you really want. See if you can work your charm on them."

He stood close to her and gripped her shoulders with unexpected force. "No!" he said. "I don't want your rich cousins. I don't want anybody else. I want you."

The gesture thrilled her but also scared her. She brushed his hands away and said, "I think we best say good night now. Thanks again for the book."

Quickly, she unlocked the pedestrian gate and went inside. Johnny watched as she disappeared into the shadows of the garden. He took one last look at her Twin Dragons Tower before starting his journey back to his walled slum. The iron dragons seemed to be sneering at him. Still, more than anything, he wanted to be with her inside those gates.

*

Johnny's life started to improve after he met Celestina. He stopped taking the countless little indignities people loved to throw his way. He stood taller and spoke up. People started listening to what he had to say. He started refusing offers from glorified beer gardens and other dives. He even found a decent hairstylist to style his hair instead of having his friend butcher it. The most important change had taken place inside him — in his heart and in his guts.

Meeting Celestina was the best thing that had ever happened to him in Manila. If he could win her love, his years of striving and dislocation would mean something.

Following the concert in Angeles City, he was offered another concert, this time in a music hall near the Saint Louis University in Baguio, the summer capital of the Philippines. It was a six-hour bus trip from Manila to the Cordillera region, but he was not about to complain. His audiences were there — in the colleges and universities where passions and ideals still burned bright.

By the time his bus arrived in Baguio City, copies of *Coup* had hit the newsstands. He saw the magazine at the bus station, next to the lottery tickets and bags of chicharon. There he was, "The New Orpheus," sitting back, strumming his ornate two-stringed instrument in a silent ballad. It was the photo taken by Celestina just before they had left The Hideout folk house. He remembered the moment well. He was relaxed and happily smitten. There was a shadow of mischief, even flirtatiousness, in his otherwise earnest face. It was the first photo of himself he really liked.

The promoters lost no time in turning the cover photo into posters and T-shirts. Johnny shared the bill with two other performers, but it was he who entranced the audience with his poetry, fire, and unexpected humour. With arms outstretched, the audience sang with him about the day Bathala, the pre-Hispanic deity, sent down a mighty bird to survey his creation. And with his final encore, they wept to his apocalyptic ballad about the last tree on earth. For the first time in years, he felt the lyrics he had once written with so much passion. Throughout that concert, Celestina's words rang in his ears. *Don't cast your pearls before swine. Find your audience.*

After the Baguio show, Johnny went back to his hotel feeling as if he had made wonderful, passionate love to the world. He had found his audience. Utterly spent and blissfully empty, he fell asleep in his clothes.

*

Three days after his concert in Baguio City, a feverish and tired Johnny showed up outside the Twin Dragons Tower. Rocky opened the gates and escorted him to Celestina's apartment. A surprised Celestina welcomed him warmly. Her hair was still wet from her shower. He could see a sprinkling of freckles where the sun had touched her face. In his eyes, she was perfect, just like this.

"Congratulations," she murmured as he came up to kiss her cheek. "I heard it was a great concert."

"You didn't tell me I would be on the cover," he quipped. "I could have worn something nicer,"

"It wasn't up to me. Anton makes the cover decisions."

"Thank you for believing in me," he said sincerely. "I owe it to you."

"You don't owe me anything. It's your work. You simply found your audience."

"You should have been there."

"Maybe next time. You look a little ill," she said as she felt his warm forehead. "Are you okay?"

"I never felt better," he replied.

She saw that something had changed. There was fire in his eyes.

"I have a gift for you," he continued. With that, he slipped off the batik jacket he had been wearing over his T-shirt and proudly displayed the new tattoos adorning his arms.

She recognized the pre-Hispanic letters right away from the book he gave her. They were lines from the poems of love and friendship, painstakingly etched using thorns and soot.

"I made a special trip to a tattoo artist in Kalinga for this," he said. "I showed her a photocopy of the poems you liked."

Gently, very gently, Celestina ran her fingers over his still-tender skin. The words seemed to come alive under her fingertips, whispering of passion, devotion, and shared hopes and aspirations.

"I don't own anything of value, nor do I expect to inherit much," he said. "All I can give you is my friendship, love, and whatever else life hasn't taken from me."

It was a grand gesture she could not refuse. She let him hold her, wrapped in the indelible promise etched on his arms. She told herself that they would be happy together as friends and lovers in her haunted house.

21

Rigodon

After several weeks together, Celestina could no longer bear the thought of Johnny going back to his walled slum. "Your spirit is too fine for that wretched place. Stay here with me," she told him.

And so, Johnny left the hidden slum and moved his possessions into Celestina's apartment. Since she had become used to the strangeness of life at the Twin Dragons Tower, she neglected to tell him about the quirks of the residents, beginning with herself. There was the matter of her preferred sleeping arrangement. Johnny was a little surprised when, upon arrival, Celestina showed him to his own quarters in Manang Rio's old room. The space looked like the European apartments in his imagination, down to the wrought-iron chandeliers, four-poster bed, and French doors that opened to a leafy balcony. It was almost as big as the entire square footage of his old hovel. He should have been thrilled, but what he really wanted was to share a bed with her.

"I don't want you to feel fenced in," she explained when she saw the disappointment in his eyes. "You need your space. As do

I. My door will be open if you want to visit," she added with a sweetly naughty smile that took some of the sting out of their arrangement.

Manang Rio was not at all pleased to see a strange man in her room. She made it less than pleasant for him by making the room cold and pulling off his blankets in the middle of the night. After several days of this, Johnny finally spoke up, and Celestina realized what was happening.

"It's Manang Rio," she said. "I'm sorry. I should have properly introduced you to her."

Celestina took Johnny's hand and walked him to the corner where the family altar was ensconced. Before he could ask any questions, she lit two sticks of incense and gave one to him.

"Manang Rio, you wanted me to find a good man," she said with a bow of her head. "Well, here he is. This is Johnny, my nobyo. Treat him well. For me."

She then turned to him and said, "Go on. Introduce yourself."

"You can't be serious," he replied.

"It's a bit like praying," she said in response to his incredulous look.

"Manang Rio," he began. "I'm a musician from Mindanao. My intentions are entirely honourable. I hope you can learn to like me because I love Celestina very much."

Celestina bowed her head and placed the incense on the stand. He followed suit. "Manang has been with my family since I was a baby," Celestina explained to him. "She helped raise me. She's my other mother. Six months ago, she passed away."

"Shouldn't she be sumalangit by now?" He felt ridiculous even asking. He believed in the afterlife but introducing himself to an overprotective yaya who had been dead for half a year strained his sanity.

"I guess she feels she has unfinished business, so she's hanging around."

Manang Rio was much more amenable to Johnny after that, although she continued to play the occasional prank on him, just to show that she was still watching.

Johnny learned to live with his novel situation, in his quarters across the hall from Celestina. He did not need too much personal space, but he understood her need for periods of solitude. Deep down, however, he felt that something was missing. He wanted more intimacy than the average "conjugal visit." He longed for the unguarded conversations that happened when the soul was most open — in the late hours, in a shared bed.

Then there was the matter of Selena Sytanco, the imperious former Lady of the Manor. Selena made herself known to Johnny through her very particular taste in music. He noticed the CD player jammed every time he tried to play any music on the rock spectrum. His attempt to rehearse an electric version of "Davao Still Life" in the kitchen was met with extreme disapproval — expressed with a bottle of pungent Clavio Patis hurled in his direction. Fortunately, the bottle only grazed Johnny's temple, but the kitchen stank of fermented fish sauce for weeks.

"My great-aunt is not used to rock music," Celestina explained nonchalantly. "I always use headphones when I listen to U2."

Johnny slowly got used to the quirks of Celestina's unseen family members. Compared to where he had been the year before, this was paradise. Or so he told himself. He had a job at a local radio station, he was getting better gigs, and he was living with the woman of his dreams.

Navigating the human terrain of Celestina's kingdom was much trickier for Johnny. At first, he was intimidated by Rojo, but the painter and Lille welcomed him and helped nurture his gifts, as they had done for many young creative souls over the years.

Verg was another matter. Celestina hoped that the two men in her life would become friends, but Verg coldly rejected Johnny's attempts at friendship. Verg's aloofness had Johnny wondering if there was something romantic between Celestina and the young photographer. Johnny's suspicions were further stoked when, one night, he went to visit Celestina's room with amorous intentions. He was surprised to find her deep in conversation with Verg. Neither one was wearing very much, just skivvies. Verg was a good-looking guy — tall, slim, and smoothly muscled with a striking facial resemblance to that actor in *Less Than Zero*. Johnny noticed, for the first time, that Verg and Celestina had nearly identical "journey" tattoos.

"Excuse me," he said, feeling rather stupid for saying so.

"What do you want?" Verg said with a withering look at Johnny and the flame burning strongly within him.

"C'mon in, Johnny," Celestina said. "Verg, we'll talk in the morning."

Verg reluctantly took his leave with nary a glance in Johnny's direction.

Confused, Johnny sat down and asked, "I'm not sure what I just saw. Perhaps you need to lay out some things for me."

"That," she replied with a gentle kiss on his cheek, "was two friends talking. Nothing more."

Johnny shook his head and laughed. "I'm having a hard time believing the 'nothing more' part. Do all your friends have free access to your bedroom?"

"He's been there for me since I was a lost teen. So yes, I'm here for Verg whenever he needs to talk."

"Suddenly, I don't feel very special," Johnny replied as he got up to leave.

He headed back to his room and shut the door, feeling as though he was in a foreign land where he understood neither the language nor the customs. He questioned the wisdom of his heart and the woman it had chosen for him. Who was this princess who freely gave him her body but always held back her heart? What was this strange little kingdom of hers with ghostly family members who did not realize that they were dead? And who was this Verg and why did he have special access to her? He had questions but no answers. Minutes later, he heard her knock.

"Come in."

"There's no need to be jealous," she assured him as she slipped into his bed. "You alone make my soul dance."

His anger dissolved in her honeyed words and lips. Setting aside his reservations, he told himself that their love would prevail over the increasingly apparent differences between them.

*

Verg watched from his window as Celestina waited for Johnny by the carport. Rocky approached her with a list of cleaning ladies with good references. She then gave Rocky her list of chores and errands for the day before throwing her briefcase in the backseat of the car. Johnny finally came down with his guitar case and two tiffin containers. Verg listened to the dance of Celestina's and Johnny's voices from his window.

"Leftover pork adobo with hard-boiled eggs and steamed rice," Johnny said.

Celestina seemed pleased, even though she usually saved her appetite for the evening. "Did you put any greens in the baon?" she asked.

"Nope," he replied. "The water spinach looked a little mushy."

"You always put too much rice in my lunch," she chided. "I'm trying to lose weight."

"Don't," he said. "You're perfect the way you are."

"Sweet talker!" she laughed.

It was no secret that Verg disliked Celestina's Orpheus of the Slums. But Verg had to admit she seemed happier these days. She smiled more, and her flame did a little dance every time Johnny uttered one of his corny endearments. Still, she could have done much better, with her looks, intelligence, and pedigree. During one of their late-night talks, Celestina admitted to Verg that she was not in love with Johnny. But he was good to her, she said, and she would learn to love him, in time.

Verg watched the car pull away until it finally disappeared past Remedios Circle. *Goodbye, my haunted Celle*, a voice in him said. He and Celestina had been drifting apart for a while now. Johnny was just the kicker. Celestina had embraced womanhood and love, with all its uncertainties. Good for her. So where did that leave him? Verg wondered. Desired by women but unable to fully function as a man? Her presence, a constant reminder of what he could never become. Once again, a thought came to him, a thought that had become a frequent visitor since that ill-fated night after their La Sulipeña dinner. *It's time to leave Celestina's house.*

✣

The taxi stopped under the neon sign of a club called Octopussy. Josémaria gave the driver a generous tip before walking over to a portable food stall where a young man was fanning the charcoal fire of his grill.

Josémaria hungrily perused the selection of deliciously charred pork skewers, golden brown chicken feet, and chili-flecked chicken entrails. His finely tuned nose picked up the soy sauce, pineapple juice, and calamansi in the marinade as the treats sizzled on the flame.

"Barbeque, Adidas, or IUD, sir?" the vendor asked cheerfully.

"Three sticks of IUD, please."

"Good choice, sir," the vendor said as he handed Josémaria a paper plate with the grilled serpentine chicken guts.

After his snack, Josémaria walked around the Ermita district, passing establishments with names like the G-Spot and Pussycat Gang until he came to a crowded club called the Wanchai Wench.

He sat down at the bar, ordered a local beer, and watched two dancers onstage doing a rather unconvincing girl-on-girl number. With his amber eyes and sun-kissed brown hair, he might just be another white man ogling slim brown girls. A bar girl approached him to offer her company, which he politely declined. The truth was the whole district made him sad. The girls of Ermita were not the slick, sexually confident showgirls in the financial district clubs. They were desperate girls from the slums or the countryside, a little too young or too old, and too unsophisticated to be erotic. Except to the red-faced white men who routinely washed up on Philippine shores.

He had overheard the men's stories often enough. Deadbeat fathers and former high-flyers on the run for tax evasion or fraud. Old men trapped in their youthful adventures, sunburned and alcohol-soaked, fugitives from respectable life.

As sad as the Ermita district was, Josémaria went back because it helped to relieve the numbness that afflicted him in his quiet moments. Sometimes, his wanderings would reward him with a tiny moment of beauty. A new face, not yet hardened by the district's life. A genuinely tender moment between two dancers, off to the side of the stage just before their show. In his gut, he was searching for that unnameable something — that mythical ingredient that would banish flatness and impart flavour and fragrance to his life. As a boy, he used to marvel at how one pandan leaf in the rice pot could infuse the grains with notes of vanilla and toasted nuts. He wished the pandan's magical qualities could extend to all aspects of life.

After the show, Josémaria paid for his drink and left the club. It was a clear and cool Tuesday, much too nice to spend in the company of drifters and deserters. He hailed a cab and asked the driver to take him to Malate.

After a short ride, Josémaria got off at Remedios Circle and followed his ears to Bravo Café. The place had a respectable crowd for a Tuesday, mostly young creative types and a few artists and writers Josémaria vaguely recognized. There was a musician on-stage. Silky-haired and tattooed, the man strummed an exotic-looking lute shaped like a lizard and decorated with feathers at the headstock. The song began with fluttering strums evoking a dragonfly's wings and gradually transformed into the menacing whirr of a military helicopter.

The singer, he realized, was Johnny Dalisay. Josémaria had seen him performing his political and environmental folk songs on television. He remembered dismissing the singer as a coffee-house activist, a nice college kid with the requisite radical politics. Josémaria soon realized that the song was clearly personal, about a boyhood lost to never-ending military campaigns against the insurgents their conflicted country had given birth to.

Josémaria found an empty banquette and settled in for the show. A waiter soon came with a menu and a saucer of roasted peanuts.

"Just a shot of mezcal, please," Josémaria said. "With a platito of sea salt mixed with minced siling labuyo, and a wedge of lime or dalandan, if you have it."

As Johnny finished his song, he thanked the audience and proceeded to introduce Celestina, a local poet reading from her just released chapbook. Josémaria's heart sank, disappointed there would be no more music. He had just ordered a drink, and it would be a shame if he had to leave so soon. Then he saw her walking toward the stage to join Johnny. She was a mestisa, but more Chinese than Spanish, quite unlike Josémaria's girlfriend, Ysabel, whose mother was a Puerto Rican beauty queen. With her firm, curvaceous figure and defiant gaze, the poet reminded Josémaria of Tamara de Lempicka's Art Deco sirens. Celestina was dressed simply in dark vintage jeans and a black tank top, confidently accessorized with a collar made of amulets and religious medallions. She also had a pinwheel-shaped tattoo on her arm. A goth girl, he thought, or whatever they call themselves these days.

Onstage, she introduced her poem, "The Wandering Soul (Lagalag)." It was, she explained, a wanderer's invocation or provocation of the forces of life. Johnny plucked electric heartbeats from his guitar as she started to speak.

> Take the softness of my sheltered feet.
> Wound them with jagged mountain paths.
> Colour your rubies with my bloodied soles
> and put them in crowns to adorn your kings.
> Set loose your mocking winds, strip away my vanity.
> In the harsh light of your sun, melt my illusions.

She paused as Johnny's guitar played out a raspy hum, much like an electric cicada. On his banquette, Josémaria sat completely still as the poet spoke to the depths of his heart.

> Carve me with your waves and crush me
> between your tectonic plates.
> Stoke your furnace with my sins.
> Burn away my brittleness.
> Christen me with fire.
> Make me ... unbreakable.

A triumphant scream rose from Johnny's guitar as Celestina ended her recitation. The air in the café vibrated with the harmonic feedback. But it was her voice, her words, that were reverberating inside Josémaria.

For the first time in his life, he understood why the wandering flame burned with such intensity in him. He lived in sweetness, far from poverty and suffering. But his spirit craved adventure, even danger, and the invigorating sting of real life.

The waiter arrived with the mezcal and all its fixings. Josémaria took a sip of his smoky drink and prepared to introduce himself to this poetess of dark tales. But before he could make a move, Johnny pulled her into his arms for a hungry kiss.

You lucky S.O.B., Josémaria thought. Musicians never seemed to have trouble attracting the ladies. Regardless of looks, hygiene, or income, one could always count on a musician to turn up with a leggy model or a leather-and-lace–clad beauty. It was not often that Josémaria envied another man, but at that moment, he allowed himself to do just that.

The couple walked out, hand in hand, stopping to chat with friends and well-wishers along the way. Josémaria quickly ate the dalandan sour orange with the sea salt and finished the rest of the mezcal. He then left a large bill on the table for the waiter before setting out to catch up with the couple. He followed them as discreetly as he could — out of the café, across the plaza filled with party people and night vendors — to a leafy lane dominated by the shapely silhouette of a most unusual building. So, this was where she lived, he thought as he came closer to the property. The building stood there with its huge windows staring back at him like sad, haunted eyes. He could see the undulating lines of the roof by the light of the streetlamps. The tiles glistened like the plates of a sleeping dragon, reminiscent of that Gaudí house he had visited so many years ago in Barcelona.

The spacious grounds were fronted by imposing iron gates decorated with S-shaped dragons. The couple entered through a smaller pedestrian gate and disappeared into the shadows of the garden. Josémaria noted that the side gate bore the number 8, even though there were no other houses on the lane. Below the number was a small metal plate with the name "Twin Dragons Tower." He knew the Chinese Filipinos considered dragons and the number 8 auspicious, but it was odd to see such a grand piece of real estate in Malate these days. All the affluent Chinese families had settled in their own gated communities and rarely, if ever, came to this part of the city. Likely, the house was built during Peacetime, that golden era his grandparents often spoke about.

Who was she, this enchanting young woman who lived in the house with the dragon gates? All he had was her first name and the memory of her haunting words. He stood there like a lovesick schoolboy wondering why he did not at least say hello to her. After a while, he came to his senses and told himself she was already spoken for. And so was he. He walked back to his car to start the long drive back to his parents' mansion, in their gated world of Cameron's Court.

22

Crossing Borders

It was the afternoon before the night that changed Johnny's life. He was going to play at Migs's club at eight o'clock. "Bring your A-game," Migs reminded Johnny. "An old mate from Manchester is in town. He might drop by. He knows everyone in the music business. Who knows …?"

"You got it, Migs!" Johnny said without hesitation. Migs Michener owned the club, as well as the only record label to take a chance on Johnny's music. So, Johnny was eternally grateful to the crazy Jewish half-Brit, half-Filipino impresario.

Still, practice and perspiration went only so far. Every artist needed inspiration. Right now, Johnny's inspiration was on a call with her grandmother. They were talking about renovating the covered veranda. He waited half an hour until she put down the phone and plopped onto a chair.

"That took the wind out me," she sighed.

Johnny smiled knowingly and walked over to rub her shoulders.

"Come watch me tonight," he said as his fingers unknotted her muscles. "Get out of the house. Spend some time in the land of the living."

"I don't know. You'll be onstage most of the time. I'll be alone."

Undaunted, he kissed her shoulders and said, "Please. I could use a little help from my muse tonight."

"Muse?" she giggled. "Can I wear a flowing tunic and carry a flute?"

Johnny had been nothing if not patient and solicitous with her. How could she refuse this simple request?

That evening, after a simple dinner of rice and leftover pork kalderobo, they drove to the other side of the metropolis, to Quezon City, named after the president who had famously said, "I would rather have a government run like hell by Filipinos than a government run like heaven by Americans." He certainly got his wish, Celestina thought, as they dodged an unmarked excavation large enough to swallow her small car.

Celestina knew the location of the club well even though there was nothing to announce its presence on the street. No neon lights, no doorman, not even a name on a shingle. The club operated on the second floor of a building meant for notary public offices and the like. Only the steady stream of youth, dressed according to their musical tribes, pointed the way to the venue. The door to the club was marked with a stencilled silhouette of the owner's head, with its distinctive halo of spiky hair. There was no official name, but everyone called it Migs's place.

Johnny escorted Celestina to a table near the stage, where Migs joined them. Soon the club was filled beyond capacity, with people spilling into the hallways and stairwells. The charged hum of the crowd filled the air as the people waited for the music. Johnny had certainly come a long way from that waifish figure in The Hideout folk house, Celestina thought. No longer did he have to implore a tipsy audience for a few minutes of their attention. Tonight, he was a musical shaman to those in search of meaning.

He paused to acknowledge his lady's presence before singing "Haplos." Many years ago, he had written the song as a ballad about earth and sky. Now, it had taken on another life as a love song and was played on radio stations everywhere. As he sang, a fire stirred in Celestina's heart. He wore his silky hair past his shoulders now, brushing against a handwoven vest, which he wore without a shirt. She noticed that he had put on some muscle now that he was eating well and exercising. Though still a slim man, his presence filled the stage like a full orchestra. Her eyes lingered on his lean, heavily tattooed arms as he played the guitar. She had always loved the music, but this was the first time she felt love for the man. By the end of the song, whatever part of her she was holding back had broken free.

He looked in her direction and touched his lips and chest in a gesture that needed no words.

I love you, too, Johnny, she thought. And it frightened her. She turned to make conversation with Migs, but he seemed to have slipped off. She looked around and saw him in a huddle with a group of foreigners. The man in the porkpie hat looked remarkably familiar. Where had she seen him before?

During the break, Migs pulled Johnny into the huddle. The foreigners seemed very eager to meet Johnny. The men soon disappeared behind the stage. "Thanks a lot," Celestina muttered. As she predicted, she would spend the entire evening alone in the noisy crowd. Migs finally re-emerged just before the second half of the show started and sat down beside Celestina.

"What was that about, Migs?"

"You'll see," he smiled.

Johnny came out singing the intro to "Haunted," a dark ballad inspired by the Twin Dragons Tower. She liked this stripped-down, almost acoustic version; it let the pathos in Johnny's voice shine through. Soon, he was joined on stage by the man in the porkpie hat. The crowd erupted as the foreigner sang the first lines of the verse in his unmistakable lilt. It was Orwell Linley, the frontman of the iconic Orwell's Tales, singing in a tiny, unmarked club in Quezon City. Celestina whipped out her small camera and manoeuvred herself as close to the stage as possible. The two voices played so well together — one as intimate as a lover's whisper, and the other a call to arms. Celestina could feel her skin tingling. By the time Orwell and Johnny got to the chorus, the room was aglow with the flames of a hundred Zippo lighters. The roaring applause at the end of the song said it all. Johnny was right where he was meant to be.

※

Celestina waited in the car, lightheaded from the excitement of the performance. What a night. Johnny was still at the club discussing business. She took out her pad and wrote down some notes for the story she was going to pitch to Anton. After twenty minutes, Johnny came out of the club, flushed and out of breath. He quickly put the two guitar cases in the trunk and got into the front seat.

"Sorry," he said. "Migs ambushed me."

"Why didn't you tell me Orwell was going to show up tonight?"

"I didn't know. Migs told me an old friend from Manchester was in town, that's all."

She nodded and leaned in, murmuring sweetly, "You were amazing. A fucking force of nature."

Johnny chuckled nervously as he felt her hand sliding up his thigh. He had been crazy in love with her from the beginning, but he was never sure about her feelings. She was affectionate enough and receptive to his advances, but in all the months they had been together she never once made the first move. Now here she was declaring, in no uncertain terms, that she wanted him. As his mind slowly went white, all he could remember was her sweet voice urging him on, growing hoarse with lust. When they were done, he lay there on her skin, somewhere on the border of love and madness.

❋

In the weeks that followed, Celestina and Johnny loved each other with a heat that surprised even their closest friends. During that time, they were often late for work. They slipped out of parties to be alone and stayed in bed all weekend until hunger compelled them to venture out. It was no secret that Johnny had been deeply in love with Celestina from the very beginning. But those who were aware of her more temperate feelings were bewildered to see the two of them entering a rather belated honeymoon period.

It was during this time that Johnny received a phone call from Orwell Linley.

"We want you to join our No Borders tour. It's time the world heard your music."

Orwell could make a roll call of cities sound like a siren song. In his mind, Johnny saw himself walking along grand boulevards lined with gilded statues, perfectly sculpted trees, and palatial buildings. Then his heart reminded him of the woman who was waiting for him at home. And suddenly, it was not an easy choice.

"I'll have to think it over," Johnny said. "It's a lot to process."

"This is your ride, Johnny," Migs later urged him. "You've got to get on board."

Not long ago, Johnny would have travelled anywhere on God's earth to perform with the likes of Orwell. Now he was tired of wandering. Why did *swerte* have such lousy timing?

❋

After two days of being unusually quiet, he finally told Celestina about the phone call.

"That's wonderful news. How long are you touring?"

"Two years," he replied flatly.

After a pause, she said, "It will go by very quickly for you."

"Will you come with me? It'll be a great adventure."

"I have a job and other responsibilities here. I can fly out for a visit. Meet you in one of the cities."

"It won't be the same."

"Things aren't meant to remain the same, Johnny. The universe is handing you a gift," she said. "Just take it."

He lived with the thought for the next few days until he could no longer delay the inevitable. Migs was calling him every day, reminding him that this was a once-in-a-lifetime opportunity that would open countless doors.

A week and a day after Orwell's phone call, he went home to Celestina to tell her he was joining the world tour. Instead, an impulsive proposal slipped out. "Let's elope. I know a judge who can do it right now. I don't need to do this world tour. I can keep doing music here. I'll help Migs produce music for other artists. I'll do movie scores and ads. We don't have to be apart. We can start a family right away."

Celestina went quiet as she realized all that Johnny was willing to give up for her. In desperation, she replied, "Two years is not a long time. We can talk about marriage when you come back."

"No," he replied, eyes wild. "I waited a long time for you to love me. I'm not losing you now. Marry me."

He waited for her to melt, to throw her arms around him and utter an enthusiastic "yes." Instead, she looked at him with an expression bordering on contempt, and replied, "For an intelligent man, you're incredibly stupid."

"Celestina, how can you say that?" Johnny said, confused at his beloved's harsh response.

"Can't you see? Do I have to spell it out? I'm damaged. Believe me, I'm not worth giving up your dream for."

He watched sadly as her bedroom door closed. For days, he tried to talk to her in the hopes that she would change her mind. It soon became clear that she would never again open her heart to him.

Over the next month, friends, fans, and industry colleagues celebrated his imminent triumph. But he did not feel like a winner at all. Not when he had to look at Celestina's locked door, night after night.

As his departure date approached, he received a package from Celestina's tailor containing a crisp dress shirt, a proper suit, a well-cut winter coat, and two scarves — one in silk and the other in fine wool. The coat was an exact copy of the overpriced Armani piece he had once admired in a shop window. "Stay warm," the note said.

And when the day came, Celestina delivered a sombre Johnny to the international airport where Migs was waiting. Taking her hands in his, Migs said, "Thank you."

Then she turned to Johnny to say, "Bon voyage. Take care of yourself," before bidding him a tearless goodbye.

The tears would come later, after Johnny and Migs had disappeared into the sea of departing travellers. She had done the right thing for Johnny. So why did it hurt so damn much?

23

A White Night

It had been a few months since Josémaria last saw her. Now there she was, just a few steps ahead of him, in the grand lobby of the Cultural Center of the Philippines, where one of the theatres was staging Bizet's opera *Carmen*. There was plenty of skin and toned bodies on display, but she stood out in a Le Smoking suit accessorized with ruby-red lips and slicked-back hair. A fan-shaped gold peineta in her hair acknowledged the evening's Spanish theme. She paused to look at paintings and installations before turning left at the wine bar. The bar was serving Spanish libations, to complement the opera showing that night. Perusing the selections, she asked for a Tinto de Verano.

From her peripheral vision, Celestina caught sight of the tall man in white on the other end of the bar. He was watching her. Men had been looking at her since she was fifteen. It used to make her feel like a hunted animal. Now, she was nobody's prey.

Soon the man was walking toward her, ignoring ladies who were flashing inviting smiles.

"Hello, Celestina," he said softly as he sidled up beside her. "So, you left your tattooed musician at home tonight. Lucky for me."

Celestina recognized him from that ill-fated evening with Verg at La Sulipeña. She never imagined someone like Josémaria San Miguel would even know who she was or who she had dated. He was obviously interested, but her heart was still too raw.

"He and I are no longer together," she said plainly.

"Oh, I'm sorry to hear that. You two looked very much in love."

"He is where he needs to be. Where he's meant to be," she said, realizing she had already said too much. "Life goes on."

"Yes, it does. By the way, I'm Josémaria. I heard your poetry reading at the Bravo Café," he said. "Your poem about wanderers really spoke to me."

"I'm pleased to hear that," she replied. "The café holds readings every Tuesday. Drop by again and check out the other poets," she added as she finished her drink and started to walk away.

Undaunted, he kept pace with her as she made her way to a new art installation.

"You'll have to excuse me if I'm not very sociable," she said. "I'm here for work."

"Oh? What do you do, Celestina?"

"I'm the arts and culture editor of *Coup* magazine. I'm doing a review of this opera."

"Hmm ... You know, I'm an arts patron. Why don't you interview me? Ask me anything. We have fifteen or so minutes before the opera starts. Or we can always schedule a longer one for later."

"Thank you. But I don't do puff pieces for society figures."

"Society? You make it sound as if all I do is attend galas. I could have an easy life, you know, but I choose to work. The restaurant business isn't what you would call leisurely."

"It's nice that you have the choice. Most people don't have that luxury."

"We can only play the hand we've been dealt. I've been given a good one, and I've done my best to use it well."

"I'm sure you have, Mr. San Miguel."

"Have you even been to La Sulipeña?"

"Yes, I have."

"What do you think of it?"

"The food was sublime, and everything was perfect ..." She shrugged.

"Go on," he said. "I can take constructive criticism."

"You serve wonderful food ... and a beautiful illusion," she replied, her mind going back to Verg and the fancy dinner that ended in humiliation and tears.

"An illusion, you say?"

"Yes. Of a world long gone. Or perhaps one that never was. A comforting fantasy that we cling to."

"How easily you dismiss what you don't understand."

"I'm sorry you don't like my opinion. But you asked, and I answered."

"That 'illusion,' as you called it, is hospitality. It's the royal treatment we Filipinos give our guests, and all the subtle touches that make the experience an unforgettable memory."

"Sure, there's an art to hospitality. No argument there. But my beat is arts and culture, and I'm here to do a review of this opera," she said, hoping to end the conversation and get on with her evening quietly.

"You don't get it, do you? You think this building we're in is the sum our culture? This Brutalist-style construction brought to us by Imelda? This middlebrow production of *Carmen*?"

"Our culture is the sum of our aspirations and endeavours," she replied. "We may not have unlimited resources, but we have talent and heart to spare."

"That much is true, but here's my point," he said. "If you want to understand the soul of our people, don't look to cover versions of

European operas. Look to our kitchens and all the amazing ways we use the bounty of our land. Think about the special ways we or-chestrate flavours or pamper our guests. I've been to the finest res-taurants and hotels in Europe and America. I can tell you that we more than hold our own among the best in the world. Hospitality is our true art. Not this building or this show."

Josémaria paused to catch his breath before adding, "Enjoy your opera, Miss Arts and Culture. See you around."

The truth of his words sank in as she watched him walk away. Realizing her error in judgement, she called out and said, "You're right."

He stopped and turned to her in surprise.

"I apologize ... I misjudged you," she continued. "I should transcribe your speech and give it to the next arrogant brat who takes this job."

At least she recognizes a good argument, he thought. Ysabel would disagree with him without bothering to understand the substance of his assertions. It was never about getting to the truth of the matter with her. It was about the bragging rights that came with winning.

"It's quite fine. I'm used to being misunderstood," he replied. "Besides, I can never stay mad at a woman. Especially one as good-looking as you. I'm weak that way."

As the two declared their truce, the chimes rang announcing the start of the opera. The elegant patrons lingered with their drinks and conversations. Under their big-city skin, they still moved to island time. Josémaria took this as his opportunity to extend his invitation.

"Would you be my guest tonight, Celestina? There's plenty of room in my family's opera box."

"Yes, as long as you don't expect any favours, professional or otherwise."

"No favours. Just the chance to get to know you. Shall we?"

He offered his arm to her with a flourish she remembered well from another man in another time. She stared and hesitated for a minute.

"What's the matter?" he asked. "Is there a ghost standing behind me?"

"You reminded me of someone when you did that," she replied as she took his arm.

"Old boyfriend?"

"No. My father."

"I can live with that. Do I know him?"

"Possibly. He used to write those serialized graphic novellas in the komiks."

"Antonio Errantes?!"

"My, you have a good memory."

"Well, that certainly explains a lot," he said with a look of amusement.

"It does, doesn't it?" she said wryly as they climbed the stairs leading to the opera box.

The usher greeted Josémaria warmly and escorted them to their seats. She was hoping he would drop the subject, but he continued with evident interest.

"I used to steal those komiks from the servants' quarters of our house. It wasn't *Playboy*, but the illustrations were close enough."

"Naughty boy," she said.

"I was drawn in by the girls, but it was the tales that ultimately got to me. Your father was a hell of a storyteller. I remember the one about the man who lured an angel through magic and then abducted her. That one scarred me for life," he said, only somewhat jokingly.

"I know what that's like," she said with a sad, brave smile.

"Was he not a good father?" he asked with concern.

"Regrettably, he was not. But he was true to his style. Epic, even in failure ... Shall we talk about something else?"

Celestina was relieved when the lights went down and ended the conversation. Josémaria tried to watch the opera but was distracted by the tantalizing bit of silky skin revealed by her low-cut jacket.

Toward the end of Act Two, as the loyal soldier abandoned his respectable life to win the untameable Roma woman's love, Celestina remembered the day she cut Johnny loose. Tears slid down her cheeks as she thought, *Stupid man. Can't you see? She's not worth it.*

"Are you okay?" Josémaria asked as he noticed her sniffling.

"Just allergies," Celestina said as she quietly vowed not to expose herself further.

He cupped her chin and looked deep into her eyes. "I think I understand," he said, dabbing her tears with his handkerchief.

His eyes were golden and unexpectedly soft when he was not posturing, she thought.

He signalled the steward for two glasses of wine while the other patrons below them rose for intermission. As they waited for their drinks, he put his hand on hers, and suddenly, she did not feel so very alone.

*

The curtains came down and the applause faded, but one couple remained seated. They had not spoken until that night, yet they were no longer strangers, and any attempt at formality was now moot. Josémaria turned to Celestina and said, "It's a lovely night for a stroll."

She took his arm as if she had been doing so forever, and they joined the other theatregoers in their leisurely exodus. Outside, the breeze from the bay carried away the city heat. Scarcely were they out of the travertine edifice's shadow when a scruffy urchin approached them and offered him sampaguita garlands for his "girlfriend." He talked to the boy and asked about his parents.

"My father is gone," the boy said. "My mother is sick. My big brother and I sell garlands at night and newspapers by day. We don't go to school anymore."

It was a familiar but sad story that Josémaria had heard many times on his wanderings. The garlands were flowers for altars, not lovers, but Josémaria bought them anyway. He gave the boy two purple hundred-peso banknotes for two simple garlands and told him to keep the change. The urchin looked at the bills, certain the Mestiso had made a mistake. Quickly, the boy dashed away before the error was discovered.

"I think you would look lovely wearing these. May I?" Josémaria asked as he held up the garlands.

"Yes," she replied as she leaned forward to receive the garlands. "I adore these flowers. May I ask how much you gave that boy?"

"Too much and not enough," he said sadly. "My family has a foundation for street kids. This is for me. It makes me feel better."

"It could be the act of kindness that changes his life. You never know."

They strolled toward the seawall and gazed at the ships docking at Manila Bay. Now and then, they would see young lovers embracing or hustlers going about their nightly business. Behind them stood the distinctive silhouette of the Cultural Center, with its deep concave cantilevers on the sides. His arm felt reassuring and strong, the way her father's arms used to feel before he betrayed her.

"Would you care to join me for a snack?" he asked delicately, reluctant to end their night. "I know a great seafood place, just around the corner."

It was a glimpse into his secret wandering life. Not an invitation he had ever extended to any woman. Certainly not one he would even think of offering Ysabel.

"Are you talking about By the Bay?" she looked with astonishment.

"I am. Is that so surprising?"

"For you? Yes," she said. "How does someone like you end up at a seaside eatery? Or at a Malate café listening to an obscure poet?"

"I wander," he confessed. "After we close the restaurant, I go to all the places I hear about from the waiters and cooks. Sometimes, I just roam around the city, wherever my feet take me, and watch the night people. The street children, the vendors, the ladies of the evening."

"Does anyone know?"

"Just my chauffeur. My girlfriend only cares about things that concern her."

"Girlfriend, huh?"

"Yes … Ysabel Duarte," he smiled with a touch of regret.

"I saw her at a gala fundraiser once," Celestina said. "She really knows how to light up a room."

"She certainly does," he replied.

"You have a stunning girlfriend and a charmed life. Why do you do wander, Josémaria?" Celestina asked.

"Because … I need something more to feel alive. As incredibly ungrateful as it sounds, that's the truth."

"I appreciate your openness. You're nothing like the man I imagined you to be," she smiled.

"I'm glad I redeemed myself in your eyes. Would you join me for some seafood, then?"

"I have a review to write. Perhaps another time," she said. "You can walk me to my car."

So, they walked together, enjoying the warmth of each other's bodies amidst the cool breeze. As she unlocked her car, he handed her his business card.

"I know you're still getting over your musician," he said. "But maybe you can call me sometime. Just to talk, as friends. I think we have a great connection."

"Maybe I will. It was lovely talking with you."

He gave her a warm hug and a kiss on the cheek, just milli-metres shy of her lips. He caught a whiff of brine, much like the scent of those little towns where women harvested salt from the sea. At first, he thought it was the salty breeze from the nearby bay. Then he realized that it was her — her hair and skin smelled of salt. Of tears. And he saw in his mind's eye there was a great sadness in her, and he longed to understand why.

"Goodnight, Celestina," he said, reluctant to let her go.

The moon above cast its light on the handsome Mestiso in white and the fetching young woman in Le Smoking. Around them, waves, wind, and vagabond spirits all knew neither Celestina nor Josémaria would sleep well that night.

24

Despedidas

Celestina often thought about Josémaria in the days that followed. There was his magnificent physicality — his tomcat purr of a voice, his powerful body, and the old-fashioned gestures that flowed so naturally from him. There was also the covert invitation in his smile, which hinted at a more dangerous side. But most surprising of all was his unexpected compassion. She remembered the way he talked to the boy who sold them the garlands. And the way he talked to her during their brief time together. She could tell he listened, and he felt her pain.

Every so often, she would see his business card while rummaging through her overstuffed purse. She always told herself that she would call him whenever she had a quiet moment at work. That, of course, never happened. Between life, her job, and the responsibility of overseeing her property, she felt about as flat as day-old champagne. Why call if she had no effervescence to offer?

After a few weeks, she decided that Josémaria belonged to another world, out of her reach. To desire him would be to set herself up for disappointment. Far better to consign their encounter to memory than to expose it to the harsh realities of life. Thereafter, she would remember that night whenever she needed a sweet, momentary escape from the quotidian aspects of her existence.

*

It was a Sunday afternoon in the city. As with other Sundays, traffic moved from churches to the sprawling shopping malls across the metropolis. These malls were the modern-day paseos and public squares, where women showed off their latest outfits, friends bonded over gossip and shopping, and families dined on everything from Mongolian grill to Viennese pastries. Today, much of the traffic was flowing to the improved and expanded Twin Dragons MegaPlaza. Tens of thousands of people would walk through that megamall that Sunday. Somewhere in this sea of shoppers were Celestina and her mother, Stella, the erstwhile heiress to the Twin Dragons fortune.

They had agreed to meet at the Ferragamo store, on the sixth level where the nicest shops were located. After browsing, they walked the air-conditioned indoor boulevard and made their way to a stylish Hong Kong–style tea house whimsically named Tsaa-Cha. They ordered steam baskets filled with four-treasure chicken rolls and pork shumai topped with crab roe. Celestina was thankful for the steady arrival of food, which rendered conversation minimal.

Stella made the announcement just as the dessert cart arrived. "I'm moving to Canada," she said after an hour of circling around the subject.

Lost in her thoughts about reviving her boarded-up swimming pool, Celestina looked up momentarily before diving into the steam basket bearing the mango pudding. She was wondering when her mother would get around to making this long-hinted-at move. Continually hearing about the North American branch of the Sytanco clan, with their free health care and visa-free access to the United States, was getting on her nerves.

"Thanks for the heads-up," Celestina said with barely concealed sarcasm.

"I gave it a lot of thought. Sometimes, you must grab the wheel to take charge of your own *swerte*."

"I agree, Mama. It's your life to live the way you see fit. When do you plan to go?"

"I'll be leaving in four months. After I put all my affairs in order. I'm finalizing the sale of our house in Misericordia Valley. I'll give you a cheque for your share of the proceeds."

"Oh, okay, thanks … Where in Canada will you live? I hear that the winters there are brutal."

"I'll be staying at my cousin's place in Markham, by Toronto, while I get set up."

"It's a good thing we have relatives everywhere," Celestina said. Toronto was in the same time zone as New York, but she had no idea where Markham was.

"Perhaps you could visit me from time to time," Stella suggested. "You might like it."

"Sure, I wouldn't mind, as long as we go to Manhattan," Celestina said flatly.

Mother and daughter finished their tea in silence. At the next table, an extended family sang a full-throated "Happy Birthday" to an elderly man smiling a golden-toothed smile. Celestina could feel part of her being slowly moving up and away from her body, floating past the diners on the tea room's second level, up to where gilded bird cages hung as light fixtures. Looking down, she saw their silent table amidst a cavernous space full of noisy, happy families.

Somewhere in the rush of servers and busboys, a tray of dishes was dropped. The resulting crash ricocheted from wall to wall, gathering strength until it hit the ceiling with the force of thunder.

The noise sent the absent part of Celestina diving back to their table where her mother was perusing the bill.

They parted ways at the parking lot, by Celestina's car, with Stella awkwardly hugging her stone-faced daughter. Celestina did not reciprocate as she thought the gesture was born of guilt, not affection.

A weary Stella said, "This angry young woman act is getting old, you know. I've tried every which way to heal this family. What else would you have me do? Just tell me!"

"Do whatever makes you happy, Mama. Don't worry about me."

With that, Celestina got into her car and drove away from her mother and out of the gleaming mini-city that belonged to her grandfather but would never pass on to her. She felt neither sadness nor joy, for this was just another one of life's endless farewells.

*

The last time Celestina saw this many Sytancos together was on her grandfather's seventieth birthday. Everyone had come to Ninoy Aquino International Airport to give Stella a proper send-off. They all felt a little sorry for her, the adored baby of Sebastien Sytanco. Sebastien was conspicuously missing. That was not surprising considering his pride, which Stella notoriously had bruised more than two decades before.

Celestina's grandmother was going on the plane as well, to visit their North American relatives and to help Stella get settled. One of Celestina's uncles shouted, "Family picture time!" through the buzz of Hokkien, English, and airport announcements. Celestina tried to disappear into the crowd of relatives, but the uncle found her and plunked her in the centre of the shot, between Stella and the matriarch, Teresita. Both Celestina's mother and grandmother looked formidably polished and seemingly ready for a state visit in their Max Mara suits and Louis Vuitton luggage. The elder

Sytancos rarely donned casual clothes, and especially not when travelling. They needed to look wealthy, respectable, and cultured. God forbid those foreign customs officials mistake them for domestic workers or tourists looking to overstay their visas. After several posed shots, Stella and Celestina exchanged awkward farewells, each acutely aware of their conflicted feelings.

"I hope you visit me," Stella said once again. "Who knows, you may like Canada."

Celestina gave her mother a perfunctory hug before watching her disappear into the departure gates. At least you still have Lola, Celestina thought. I have no one. She quietly slipped away from the gaggle of Sytancos and headed for the exit. All around her, families welcomed fathers and siblings and mothers coming back from contract jobs overseas. There, amidst the happy reunions, Celestina's solitude felt like a deep, open wound.

*

There was a fiesta at the Twin Dragons Tower. The entrance hall had been dressed up with wildly coloured kiping — rice wafers moulded from kabal leaves. There was a stall set up with steaming hot rice cakes topped with sugar, coconut, white cheese, and salted egg. There was another stall offering garlicky Pancit Habhab noodles playfully served in paper cones. Beside these two larger stalls were smaller ones offering cool drinks with tapioca pearls and seagrass jelly cubes. Lille had even hired a sorbetero with his "dirty ice cream" cart full of ube, queso, and tsokolate flavours.

Upstairs, the mezzanine apartment was already humming with friends and friends-of-friends. A large table was covered with an island-style feast featuring spicy pork satays, slivers of green mango with shrimp paste, impeccably crisp shrimp and cabbage fritters, and grilled Chicken Inasal, golden and redolent with lemongrass. At the centre of all this preparation was Verg. This was his despedida, his grand send-off, as he had taken a position as an art director in Dubai.

In the kitchen, Celestina hugged her old friend. "Write, if you occasionally remember me," she said. "At least send pictures."

"I couldn't forget you even if I tried," he smiled. "I'll miss our late-night talks."

The two friends held hands and laughed about old times. In the living room, more guests were arriving. Lille's voice cut clear through the reggae music and loud chatter as she greeted the guests.

"It sounds like New Year's Eve out there," Verg remarked.

"I know. We'd better join the party," Celestina said, "before the Jeproks drink all the booze."

Almost as soon as they emerged from the kitchen, Verg got swept away by a group of young photographers eager to hear about his job in the wealthy emirate. Celestina stopped to talk to the owner of the Bravo Café, who came with a friend from Singapore. The two women were flying to a yoga retreat the next day and wanted to have proper night out before their long weekend of silence and meditation. After a while, Lille joined them. With a mischievous twinkle, she sidled up to Celestina and said, "Someone wants to say hello to you."

Celestina saw him coming in, looking effortlessly elegant in a silk linen polo and slim cognac-hued chinos. She could barely hear Lille's next words through the beating of her heart. Then he was beside her, whispering in her ear. "I got tired of waiting for your call."

"How did you get yourself invited?" she asked.

"Lille approached me to propose new uniform designs for my staff. I noticed her business card had your address, so I dropped your name. I hope you don't mind."

"You don't miss a thing, do you?"

"Not when I want something."

His hand rested on the small of her back. This is mine, it seemed to say, my secret cove.

The music stopped, but neither of them noticed. Scattered claps and cheers erupted on the other side of the living room, before giving way to sensuous Romani guitars. They turned to see what the guests were cheering about. Lille and Rojo had taken to the dance floor. Celestina watched as they executed a flirtatious and playful "Bossamba" for the guests. Seeing her two friends on the dance floor gave her some hope that happily-ever-after did sometimes happen.

Josémaria watched as Celestina followed the older couple with her eyes.

"You look like you can dance," he purred in her ear. "Shall we give them some competition?"

"Why not?" she replied as she slipped off the intricately carved wooden sandals she was wearing with her flea market silk pantaloons and homemade tank top with lace insets.

He led her to the dance floor as a new song started, and they circled each other to the opening strums of the Gipsy Kings' "Quiero Saber." With a roguish smile, he swivelled his hips to the lush vocals, causing whoops of delight from the other guests. Celestina stifled a giggle as she sashayed closer to her partner. Confidently, he reached out for the delicious curve of her waist, lifting her into a spin, as if she weighed no more than a bottle of champagne. He gently set her down, and they moved together to the rise and fall of notes until she playfully spun away. As they came to the end of the song, he lowered her, holding her gracefully arched back until the tips of her fingers almost touched the floor. His heart was pounding, not from the exertion of the dance, but for her — her body, that ginger-and-honey voice. For the fire in her soul.

They paused to catch their breaths as the guests applauded wildly. Voices called for a repeat performance. Josémaria laughingly acknowledged the applause before turning to Celestina.

"We'll have to sit this one out," she said. She desperately needed to cool down, lest she vaporize from the heat of desire.

"Let's go someplace quiet where we can talk," he said as they walked away from the crowd.

They quickly grabbed some food and slipped away to the elevator. Somewhere in the huddle of people, Verg was watching and thinking, *Be careful, Celestina. There's a darkness in your golden prince like a black spot on the sun.*

✳

A rush of voluptuous scents welcomed Josémaria as they entered Celestina's apartment. Coming from a long line of gourmands, he could tell a lot about her from this sensory information, the lingering herbs and spices in the air. A man had lived here, not so long ago, and that man enjoyed smoking weed. Josémaria could smell the incense she burned for her ancestors, the paper and leather of her old books, and the native green oranges she had been eating to help curb her desire for alcohol.

The overture of scents was quickly followed by a visual feast. Josémaria's eyes were drawn to the high-ceilinged great room and its unusual puddle-shaped windows, which remained strikingly avant-garde several decades after they were installed. He liked how she filled her space with furniture in polished black bamboo, colours like cinnabar and jade, well-worn books with handsome bindings, and lacquered cabinets holding interesting tableaux and pictures. But what he liked most was the wildly eclectic art collection she had amassed. There were fine art prints, paintings, and a copper Sarimanok sculpture ennobled by the metal's aged green patina. Some of the artworks were unsigned, but Josémaria recognized familiar styles from his father's and uncle's well-curated collections.

"You've got quite a place. And a great art collection," Josémaria said. "You didn't tell me you were rich."

"Rich? Sure, that's why I live in this charming district with the street people, stray dogs, and ladies of the evening. Being rich would have made my life simpler."

She explained that most of the artworks were gifts, and many of the prints were trial impressions. He watched her trace the incomplete images, misregistrations, and off-colours with her finger, gently as one would touch scars. They could not be sold because they were imperfect, she explained. But that was the way she liked them.

He stood fascinated by this piquant little kingdom that hinted at fascinating meals and lives. In comparison, Ysabel's luxury penthouse seemed sterile.

"How did you come to own this place?" he asked.

"It's a gift from my grandfather. He owns the Twin Dragons MegaPlaza. You probably know him."

"Of course. Sebastien Sytanco. My parents know him well. He must love you very much."

"I wouldn't go that far," she replied without emotion.

"What do you mean?"

"He didn't approve of my father, so he cut off my mother's *mana*," she said. "He gave me a bit of money and this property as a consolation prize. I suspect nobody else wanted it. It's considered *malas*. My great-aunt was killed here during the war."

"I'm sorry to hear that. My family has its own little dramas. Every family is dysfunctional in its way," he said.

"I've made peace with it. I have a place to call my own, such as it is."

"It's enchanting. And your presence makes it even more so," he said without flattery.

"Thank you. Shall we sit out on the veranda?"

"Let's talk in the kitchen," he said.

He followed her to the green-and-black kitchen, where bunches of braided garlic and exotic baskets with shapes he had never seen before hung from the ceiling. Her cookware was basic but well-picked, he thought. She had a clay pot and a heavy kawali, which was the Southeast Asian cousin of the Chinese wok. She also had a well-seasoned cast-iron skillet, and a vintage Staub coq au vin co-cotte with the emblematic rooster proudly perched on the handle. A bamboo shelf held a collection of teapots and colourful tins of Assam, oolong, and green tea.

"I like your kitchen," he said wistfully as they laid out their little feast on the old wooden table.

As a baby, he spent a lot of time in the kitchen being breastfed by a wet nurse, who was their cook's niece. Every day, the cook would prepare a traditional nursing mother's soup of clams, malunggay leaves, and ginger so her niece could make enough milk for little Jo-ma and her own son. For little Jo-ma, this warm, gingery milk was his own ambrosia. He continued to suckle at his wet nurse's breasts until he was four, when his horrified grandmother finally put a stop to the practice. But his grandmother's intervention came too late. By then, he had already formed deep attachments to the fragrant world of the kitchen and the people who dwelt in it.

Celestina watched him wolf down his food like some famished farmhand.

"Worked up an appetite, did you?" she laughed.

"I have you to blame. You're quite the dancer."

"So are you, sir."

"I aim to please."

Celestina felt herself blushing at the naughty undertone in his voice.

"Stop. You're embarrassing me," she said.

"I'm sorry. I'll behave now. How've you been, Celestina?"

"Oh, I've been busy with work. And yourself?"

"In a word? Tormented."

"I'm sorry to hear that. What's tormenting you?"

"You," he replied.

"Please don't say any more, Josémaria."

"I have to say it or I'll go crazy. Since we met, I can't stop thinking about you. I hear your voice in my head, like a phantom. I hear it at parties, in my restaurant, everywhere. You appear in my dreams. And I wake up … wanting to see you next to me."

After a long pause, she confessed, "I've been thinking about you too. About that night at the opera. I almost wish you were that arrogant playboy I thought you were."

"I knew it wasn't just me. So, what do we do now?"

"I don't know, Josémaria. Should we really pursue this?"

"I fear we may miss our chance at happiness if we don't," he replied.

"Are you not happy with your life?"

"Mostly, I am. But something's missing. It feels flat. Like a dish thrown together with no thought or inspiration."

His pager buzzed just as he finished saying his piece. He tried to ignore it, but it beeped again minutes later.

"I think you're being summoned, Josémaria," Celestina said.

"Yes," he said, glancing at the text messages his girlfriend had sent him. "Ysabel and I seem to have less, not more, in common as time goes by."

"Why not take a break? It might do your relationship good."

"It seems that all we do is break up and make up," he said with a weary laugh. "Neither of us has had the courage to call it quits for good. But that was before I met you."

"I'm terrified," she said after a moment.

"Of what?"

"Of how you make me feel."

"We'll go slow," he said. "Please. Have dinner with me. Let me show you how good we are together."

"Very well," she said with some hesitation. "I'll have dinner with you. But I make no promises beyond that."

"I'm a great cook. You won't regret it," he replied as they prepared to say goodbye for the evening.

She did not think she would ever love again after Johnny. It hurt too much. Perhaps this beautiful man's attention was exactly what her heart needed to heal.

*

Ysabel's penthouse was still dark when Josémaria arrived. Knowing her, it would take another hour before she could disengage from the festivities at her Black and White Gala. He let himself in and put his ostrich-skin wallet and keys on the marble-and-bronze entryway table before heading upstairs to her bedroom. She had recently redecorated it with Art Deco–style furniture in light hues, pearlescent cream wallpaper, and mirrored accents. The new decor worked very well with her old bed, a dramatic statement piece with a fan-shaped headboard.

Josémaria decided to take a shower to wash away lingering scents that might arouse suspicion. The cool water felt sobering after that intoxicating dance with Celestina. He needed to get back to reality. Ysabel was still his girlfriend, and she was not exactly low maintenance. She had many needs, and he tried — as a good man should — to meet them all. As he finished his shower, he heard the tap-tap-tap of Ysabel's high heels walking through the front door. He wrapped a towel around his waist and turned on some music as her heels clicked up the stairs. Her perfume filled the room as she entered the door. It was Fracas by Robert Piguet, the scent she wore in the evenings. She smelled like a hothouse full of voluptuous flowers, with just a touch of crème brûlée.

"Hi there Big Boy, when did you get in?" she cooed.

"Oh, about an hour ago. How was your party, Bella?"

"It went very well. You missed out on a great gala."

"Oh, that's okay. I much prefer this little private party here," he said. "Is that the Valentino Couture dress?"

"No, I decided to go with the Chanel. Do you like it?" Ysabel replied as she struck a pose to show off her outfit — a mini dress with a bustier bodice in white duchess satin and a sculptural bell-shaped skirt in black satin. With a flirtatious smile, she gestured gracefully to her dress's intricately detailed corset waistline, then to her veiled fascinator decorated with a black camellia and feathers. She wore no jewellery other than the teardrop-diamond earrings he had given her for her twenty-fifth birthday, but she finished her gala look with opera-length gloves in patent leather and satin pumps with Lucite heels.

Only a woman as glamourous, sleek, and long-stemmed as Ysabel could pull off a look like this, thought Josémaria. For an encore, she flirtatiously peeled off one opera glove and twirled it in the air before playfully tossing it to him. As he caught the glove, he decided that she looked like a sexier tropical version of the super-model Linda Evangelista.

He walked over to her and kissed her hungrily. "You look spec-tacular, Bella," he whispered. "Now hurry up and get out of those clothes."

They chatted while she undressed, took off her makeup, and started her beauty rituals. She was in a good mood, as she usually was after organizing a successful party. He listened attentively as she described the ladies' attire, the special black tulips she had ordered, the cassis and champagne cocktails, the caviar, and the Black Swan pavlova made with merengue, blackberries, and black-currant coulis. There was a draw for a necklace of black and white Tahitian pearls. Josémaria was professionally interested in the sta-ging aspect of the party. Ysabel could certainly throw a memor-able bash. He tuned out when she started talking about the latest couplings and uncouplings, feuds, and the fight that had erupted in the ladies' room.

"And how was the designer's party?" she asked as she applied an elixir from a faceted amethyst-coloured jar.

"It was really fun," Josémaria said as he described the colourful town fiesta the residents had recreated at the Twin Dragons Tower. "There was a real dirty ice cream cart, complete with a sorbetero, and kiosks with pancit habhab and bibingka."

"Dirty ice cream? Seriously? I hope no one gets food poisoning," she quipped as she finished applying the elixir with a lifting facial massage.

"I guess we'll find out tomorrow," he laughed. "Come to bed. I know a better way to give you a glow."

"Just a minute," she said as she went into her large walk-in closet.

Ysabel came out wearing a pearl-decorated thong and a top that looked like two chiffon hankies held together with a bit of ribbon.

"I'm glad you had fun slumming," she said. "Were there any pretty girls at the party?"

"Well, it wouldn't be a good party without them, would it?"

"Did you ..." she began.

"I danced with one," he admitted, hoping to nip the questioning in the bud. "I'm allowed to dance, am I not?"

"Yes," she said through gritted teeth. "As long as it remains vertical."

"That goes without saying," he said, pulling her into bed with him. "I saved the horizontal for you."

He had been feeling rather lusty all evening, and the sight of Ysabel dressed in naughty lingerie was enough to give him an impressive erection, which he proudly unveiled for her. Ysabel's chiffon hanky top and tiny, exquisitely sewn panty came off quickly. They did not need much in the way of foreplay, as they each knew what turned on the other. She liked being the rider, and that was fine with him. He enjoyed seeing his women get their pleasure, and the sight of a woman climaxing was all it took to keep him going strong.

Ysabel climbed off after they finished, quite satisfied and ready to call it a night. Josémaria had other ideas as he hungrily devoured her perfect, cosmetically enhanced breasts. Truth be told, he'd much preferred the feel of her natural ones. But why complain?

"Easy there, Big Boy," Ysabel said.

"Not a chance," he shot back, as he pushed her down roughly with one hand.

Without so much as a caress, he drove himself into her, pounding harder until they both collapsed in a heap of sighs. Still quaking, Ysabel shoved him off.

"Sorry, Bella. Was I too rough?"

Realizing that he had behaved rather selfishly, he moved to make amends. Gently kissing her neck and shoulders, he whispered, "Forgive me, baby. I lost my head."

His peace offering was met with a stinging slap to the side of his jawbone.

"You weren't doing me. You were doing *her*. Your vertical partner. Do you think I don't know what's going on in your head?"

"Don't start! I drove all the way here for you, you know."

"You can drive all the way back to her. I don't care!" she snapped as she turned her back to him.

He took his punishment in stride and decided to let Ysabel sleep off her anger. Bristling with guilt, he closed his eyes and waited for sleep to come and end the night. Instead, he fell into a restless dream state in which he got up and walked toward the door. As he passed the mirror, he noticed two large appendages growing from either side of his spine. They looked like they might be wings, but for now they were just clumps of feathers, moist and crumpled in the manner of newly hatched chicks. The appendages flapped clumsily when he tried to move them. He walked out the bedroom, down the stairs, and out the French doors that opened to Ysabel's expansive rooftop patio.

The intense perfume of sampaguita flowers greeted him as he walked onto the patio. Ysabel despised these flowers and would never tolerate them near her penthouse. To her, they were common flowers who lent their overly frank perfume to everything from ribbon cuttings to funerals.

Josémaria followed his nose to the far end of the patio where, to his surprise, he found a ring of shrubs all in full bloom. Around them were dozens of moths — some in flight, and many others drinking the heady nectar. He watched with wonder as an elegant golden moth approached an iridescent black one feeding on a white blossom. The two flew off and commenced an extended mating dance before vanishing midflight. When he looked around, the shrubs were nowhere to be found.

He woke up back in Ysabel's bed, covered in sweat, with the scent of the white flowers still in his nose. He tried to go back to sleep, but his shoulders and back hurt, as if they had been bearing an unaccustomed weight. After tossing and turning for a long time, he got up to look for his clothes. Ysabel had already put them in the hamper, but there was a pair of pressed Bermuda shorts, a polo shirt, and some underwear in the drawer where he kept his spare clothes. After getting dressed, he went down to her kitchen for a cool drink, grabbed his wallet and keys, and headed out. It was already morning — though still dark — he was restless, and there was nothing like a long drive to clear one's mind.

25

Moon Dance and Dragon Pearls

The Maserati Coupé drove down a familiar road leading to San Pedro, Laguna. It soon passed the welcome monument featuring two psychedelically painted concrete roosters. Long ago, this was a town of duck farms, fishing boats, and orchards. Today, it was practically a city, with factories for Holland Milk Products and Cosmos Bottling Coporation. Tahu vendors, neighbourhood bakers, and other early risers waved as the familiar sports car sailed by, past the city hall, to the church, and then the market. Inside the car, Josémaria smiled and waved back. Past the market were housing projects built for office workers and teachers. Beyond this rather undistinguished residential area lay the pastoral town he had loved as a child, the home of his favourite uncle who still owned the largest sampaguita plantation in the country.

Josémaria slowed down as he approached his uncle's estate. The uniformed guard recognized the silver sports car and opened the gates. The long driveway was lined with old flowering narra trees, which formed a gentle canopy. The ground was carpeted with the trees' fallen yellow blossoms. At the end of the long driveway was his uncle's house, with its weathered but still graceful white pillars standing guard around the wraparound porch. Josémaria parked his car in his favourite spot by the laurel bushes. He got out and stopped to touch one of the aromatic leaves. He and his uncle shared a love for the world of scents and flavours. Josémaria walked up the stone steps and made his way to the back porch, where his uncle would be enjoying his Sunday breakfast.

His uncle was with the apprentice kitchen helper, demonstrating the art of whisking the thick tsokolate drink with a wooden batidor. Behind them were fields of shrubs laden with fragrant white flowers destined for altars across the region.

"Good morning, Tiyo Rico," Josémaria said, his smile warm and gentle as the morning sun.

The older man gave him a long, affectionate hug. Rico San Miguel had three daughters and Josémaria was the son who was mistakenly delivered to his brother's house, as he liked to put it.

"Have you eaten?" his uncle asked. "There's an excellent beef tapa and duck eggs in the kitchen."

"You know my appetite doesn't kick in until lunchtime. I'd love a cup of that hot chocolate, though."

The kitchen helper poured the drink into a demitasse for Josémaria. The two men chatted as the sun warmed the fields of fragrant white flowers. Finally, the older man spoke from his heart.

"I can tell something's bothering you, son. What's on your mind?"

"I've met someone, Tiyo Rico ... and I haven't been myself since."

"Oh my," Rico said as he looked at the wild, almost desperate look in his nephew's eyes.

"Tell me about this lady, hijo. How did you meet? Is she hermosa? Does she drive you to the brink of madness? Give me all the juicy details."

"Where do I begin? Her name is Celestina. I watched her read poetry at a café. Something about her and her words just shook me to the core."

"I hope that's not the end of it," Rico said.

"I saw her again at the opera. I managed to convince her to watch the show with me, but I didn't hear from her after that. I thought I'd never see her again. Until last night ..."

"Yes? Don't keep me in suspense."

"Last night, I got invited to a party. She was there and we danced. I told her how I felt about her. She feels the same about me, but she's afraid to take the next step."

"Hmm ... is she a good dancer?"

"Yes. I fear I'll be in a state of torment until I've ... you know —"

"Loved her all night long?"

Josémaria felt himself blushing at his immodest thoughts. "Yes, that's a good way to say it."

"Is she going to give me beautiful grandkids?"

"I'm certain of it, Tiyo. The girls will have faces like Chinese princesses and bodies like Spanish guitars. They'll drive men crazy."

"I'm intrigued. Do I know this young lady?"

"Not likely. She's the granddaughter of Sebastién Sytanco, but she lives in her own world."

"I think that's refreshing. Go on."

"Her heart carries sad secrets, but she bears it all with grace. I know I can make her happy, Tiyo Rico."

"If you love Celestina, do what it takes to make her yours. You've known for a long time that you and Ysabel are no longer good for each other. If you're going to call it off, better now than after you've tied the knot."

Josémaria's expression grew sombre as he contemplated the unpleasant task ahead of him. Then a soft breeze brought a familiar scent to his nose. He looked to the fields of fragrant white blossoms stretched out before him and remembered the night at the opera and the woman who adored sampaguitas.

*

Early Monday morning, Josémaria and his uncle drove to La Sulipeña's grounds with a landscaper in tow. The landscaper took Polaroid photographs, made measurements, and sketched out plant beds on the lawn with white spray paint. By Monday evening, the landscaper returned with an electrician and a team of other workers. Some came to dig and prepare the plant beds, while others installed garden lights on the grounds and among the trees. By Tuesday afternoon, a large shipment of sampaguita shrubs and other plants were delivered to La Sulipeña.

In another part of the city, a messenger dropped off two items at the reception desk at *Coup*'s office — a letter and a satin-finished box topped with a gold bow. Minutes after hearing from the receptionist, Celestina came to carry away the letter and the gift to avoid having to explain them to nosy officemates. Once in the relative privacy of her office, she opened the envelope. Inside was a letter handwritten on heavy ivory-coloured paper with the distinctive angel wings crest on the letterhead. It said, *I hope you haven't changed your mind about seeing me again. I'd be very honoured to have you dine with me at La Sulipeña this Saturday. My chauffeur will come for you at seven o'clock. I'll be waiting for your call. With love, Josémaria.* In the postscript, he also wrote, *It's going to be a full moon, so dress for moonlight.*

Celestina's heart filled with joy as she read Josémaria's invitation. She closed the blinds and locked the door, trying to calm herself. The last thing she wanted was to sound like a blithering idiot when she called him back. Wait another hour, she told herself. Don't look too eager. But after half an hour of pacing and trying to focus on work, she finally picked up the phone to accept his invitation.

"I was afraid you'd change your mind," he said.

"You sold yourself as a great cook. Don't disappoint me," she teased.

She did not know what the future held for them. But she was young, and she wanted to experience romance with this extraordinary man, even if just for a spell.

*

Early in the evening, in the mezzanine apartment of the Twin Dragons Tower, Lille heard a knock. It was Celestina, still in her office clothes, carrying her purse, her briefcase, and a large gift box.

"May I talk to you, Lille?"

"Of course," Lille said with surprise. Celestina rarely opened her heart to anyone, except Verg. Lille had tried to gain Celestina's confidence for as long as she had known her. Lille still remembered when Celestina first turned up with Verg at one of Rojo's exhibits. She seemed like a sheltered pet who had been cruelly cast out into a world where she could trust no one.

Lille fetched her guest a glass of water, while Celestina sat down. She drank the whole glass before blurting out, "I've been invited to dinner. How does one 'dress for moonlight'?"

Lille needed no further explanation for the question. She could see it in Celestina's glow and in the lilt of her voice.

"That's easy. One wears white. Why do you think night-blooming plants have white flowers? So that moths and other nocturnal pollinators can find them in the moonlight."

"White is a bit presumptuous. Don't you think?" Celestina asked. "Like I'm hoping to end up at the altar."

"He set the dress code," Lille shrugged. "Besides, it doesn't hurt to give him the idea ..."

"The last time I wore a white dress was for my confirmation. I just don't have the time or patience to go hunting for one. I will have to go with one of my little black dresses."

"Please, not the black dresses. They make you look too mature."

"I'm open to suggestions," Celestina said, trying to contain her growing panic.

Lille went into the room at the back, which had been converted into a walk-in closet for her collection of clothes and accessories for photo shoots and films. "I knew there was a reason I took this out of storage," she said, walking out with a large white box. She put the box on her work table, carefully took out a long, fluid ivory dress and put it on her dressmaker's mannequin. On top, she added a stiff pineapple silk cape, which had been painted with bold floral motifs in lieu of the more traditional embroidery.

"It's your wedding dress!" a surprised Celestina said, remembering it from the pictures she had seen in the couple's country home.

"Try it on," Lille invited.

Celestina went into the closet and quickly changed into the proffered dress and cape. The dress was made of silk charmeuse, cut on the bias, so it clung, just so, to her curves before falling gracefully to the floor. She liked the watery quality of the material and the way it caught the light. And she loved the slight sepia tone the silk had acquired with age. She took off the translucent cape, so she could see the dress better. It was a deceptively simple cut, almost like a slip, except for the inch-wide straps and the neckline, which was edged with silk ribbon to give it more structure.

Lille looked fondly at the young woman in front of her. Once upon a time, Lille had had a body like Celestina's. Now in her forties, Lille's body had decided to become fashionably thin. She missed her old figure, but Rojo assured her he liked her French tomboy look better than the bloated sausage figures of some matrons.

"The dress is perfect, Lille. May I borrow it for Saturday?"

"It's yours, hija," Lille said. "Let's face it, I'm never going to get my old body back."

Celestina picked up on the term of endearment Lille had used, which meant "daughter." Though they had known each other for a few years now, Celestina had never quite let this motherly woman into her heart. It was time to change that. She hugged Lille joyfully before running back to her apartment.

Now alone, Lille shed a tear as she recalled all the young people she had welcomed into her home and nurtured over the years. Sometimes, they even remembered to write.

✳

Celestina carefully unwrapped Josémaria's present as soon as she arrived at her apartment. It was a glass teapot and a small pine chest. Inside the chest were extravagantly perfumed orbs, roughly the size of large pearls. Tucked in the corner was this short note: *I noticed you were a tea drinker. These are dragon pearls. My uncle makes them for his Chinese clients. They're the finest quality green tea, tumbled seven times with jasmine petals, then hand-tied with silk mesh. Think of me when you have your cup tonight.*

After a light dinner, she made herself a pot of tea to settle the butterflies in her stomach. The tightly budded dragon pearl began to blossom as the water permeated its layers. Inside the pearl was a tiny, perfectly formed jasmine. She used only one, but it was fragrant as a night garden.

A soft, cool breeze blew through the house and brushed against her hand. It was her great-aunt, and she wanted to stay for tea.

✳

It was Saturday night at the mezzanine apartment in the Twin Dragons Tower. Lille was helping an anxious Celestina get ready for her dinner date. Lille removed the last of the large curl clips from Celestina's hair and carefully loosened the finger waves for a soft but polished look.

On Lille's advice, Celestina chose a rosy nude lipstick, instead of her usual red, and brushed the merest hint of mascara on the tips of her lashes.

"You have your mother's porcelana skin. Don't hide it with too much makeup," Lille said. "I want you to look radiant and touchable."

Celestina slipped off her robe, so she could see the dress with her hair and makeup done. She then put on a diamante body chain she had created from a long necklace bought in the vintage market in Divisoria. It was a dramatic piece that crisscrossed her shapely torso, with her mother's sunburst brooch as the centrepiece.

Lille caught a whiff of jasmine as she brushed luminous powder on Celestina's shoulders and décolleté. "Is that a new perfume?" she asked.

"Uh-huh," Celestina replied. She had been picking up the scent everywhere, all week. She initially thought Palmolive had changed the fragrance of her shampoo. But now, she realized it was the scent of dragon pearls tea rising from her skin.

"I think the two of you have a magical chemistry," Lille said.

"It's a little frightening. When he touches me, I feel I might just burst into flames," Celestina confessed.

"Have you two been intimate?"

Lille was aware she might be overstepping her boundaries. It was one thing to give fashion and cosmetic tips to Stella Sytanco's daughter, quite another to give bedroom advice. Still, the question had to be raised because neither Celestina nor her beau were known for their restraint in matters of love.

"No, we haven't been intimate. He's still in a relationship," Celestina replied.

"That's good. If I may ... give you some advice?"

"Please do."

"It's too easy for men like him to have everything — a trophy wife, a hot mistress here, some flings there. Don't squander your youth being someone's querida. I've seen how they end up. You're better than that. Let him get to know the real Celestina. Let him fall in love with you."

Celestina smiled and nodded but said nothing at first. She put on a pair of delicate silver sandals and examined her reflection one last time.

"What do you think, Lille?"

"I think Ysabel Duarte should be very worried."

Celestina picked up her mother-of-pearl evening bag and headed for the elevator. She paused for a few seconds before coming back to thank her friend.

"I'll try to remember everything you said. Wish me luck, Lille."

Inside the dragon gates, a gleaming Rolls-Royce Silver Spirit was waiting to take her to her prince.

✳

Celestina sat back as the Rolls-Royce glided through the boulevard's stop-and-go traffic, seemingly floating above the city's pockmarked streets. It was so different from her humble Honda Civic, which rattled with every pothole and speed bump. Soon, they entered the gates of Intramuros. In front of them, a horse-drawn kalesa traipsed along, oblivious to the pace of the twentieth century. The chauffeur patiently waited until the road widened enough for him to pass the kalesa. Up ahead, the full moon shone gloriously above the restored mansion that housed La Sulipeña.

On the grounds of the restaurant, uniformed valets stood by, waiting to park cars for customers. The chauffeur drove past them and pulled into the private driveway reserved for Josémaria and the executive chef. The chauffeur helped Celestina out of the car and led her to the long walkway leading to the garden.

"Thank you, Fidel, for the Rolls-Royce experience," she said cheerfully. "That was smoother than most plane rides I've been on."

"You're welcome, Miss Errantes. Enjoy your dinner."

The path was lined with candles nestled inside capiz lamps. The sultry air carried the distinct olfactory signature of Intramuros — a curious mix of sea breeze, horses, and diesel. It was the Old World colliding with the teeming metropolis. Cutting through the mélange of aromas, she detected the scent of her favourite flowers. The scent grew stronger as she followed the candlelit path. Somewhere in the garden, a cello was playing.

At the end of the path was a garden room, paved with white limestone and lined with sampaguita shrubs, about three and a half feet tall. Traveller's palms, moss-covered rocks, and birds of paradise provided colour and texture. Sheltering the garden room was a graceful, old tamarind tree, which she remembered from the last time she'd dined at La Sulipeña. Tonight, it was a luminous beauty dripping with globes of light. Under the tree, a sumptuous table was set with faceted crystal, polished silverware, and gold-rimmed porcelain on an immaculate damask tablecloth. Casually draped over one of the chairs was Josémaria's dinner jacket. Dazzled by the scene and intoxicated by the scent of night-blooming flowers, she did not sense the footsteps behind her.

"White suits you," said a familiar man's voice.

It was Josémaria, still wearing his apron, but otherwise impeccably dressed in ivory linen-silk trousers and a broadcloth shirt in azure.

"Hello," she said, momentarily at a loss for words.

"Hi. Just stand there for a moment so I can look at you," he said, eyes caressing her siren's body.

Slowly, he walked up to her and kissed her cheek, pausing to breathe in her skin's perfume. Jasmine and green tea with a hint of green oranges. The scent of a dream he never wants to wake from.

"Let me help you with that," she said as she flirtatiously undid his apron strings.

He laughed softly, savouring the delicious electricity from her fingertips. As much as he wanted to tear off his clothes and hers, he put on his jacket and resolved to go slowly, as he had promised her.

He led her to her seat and grabbed the bottle of Louis Roederer champagne, which had been chilling in an antique silver bucket. He deftly uncorked it, then filled their flutes in two smooth moves.

Raising his glass, he said, "To all things that blossom under the moon."

"Hear, hear!" she replied in approval. "And to happiness. May it forget its wandering ways and forever stay," she said.

Celestina took a tiny sip of her champagne while he looked on. She had never seen eyes like his — golden brown rays melting into a pool of green. Even at night, they seemed to carry all the heat of the tropical sun.

His eyes smiled as the waiter arrived with the first of many delectable courses. "Try my scallops ceviche. They really open up the palate," Josémaria said.

The scallops were cooked in the "liquid fire" of lightly fermented coconut water and served on oyster shells, large as plates.

With her appetizer fork, Celestina picked up a scallop and ate it slowly. It was meltingly tender and sweet, with a strong breath of clean brine. The bracing sourness of the marinade was spiked with minced green onions, grated ginger, sea salt, and a hint of fiery bird's-eye chili. It left her tongue with a gentle glow. Now she was ready for the rest of his feast.

Inside the restaurant, the sparkling chatter was replaced by a delighted, vaguely scandalized murmur as the beautiful people huddled by the windows to watch Josémaria romance his mystery date. Wild speculation on her identity ensued. Former Miss Hawaii, Hong Kong movie star, and Fil-American news anchor were among the guesses passed around the room. Amidst the murmuring were two people who knew exactly who the mystery woman was. Gidget and Mikee Sytanco had not seen their cousin since they'd graduated from university. Nevertheless, they would recognize her anywhere as the three of them had grown up like sisters. The fact that Celestina had drifted away did not change that one bit. Forgetting about their clueless boyfriends, they watched their formerly shy cousin flirting vivaciously with the notorious playboy.

"We should go out there and say hello," Gidget said brightly.

"Do they look like they want company?" Mikee asked.

"I guess not. Looks like Celle is not going to die an old maid after all," Gidget quipped.

In the garden, a server arrived with a paellera bearing the first course — Paella Negra, made with plump Bomba rice from Valencia, blackened with squid ink, and cooked with coconut crab from Batanes island, prawns, and sweet summer peas. Josémaria had taken care to add the aromatic stock only when the rice was al punto. He wanted every grain fully infused with the stock, so the dish would be flavourful and properly moist but not creamy and wet like risotto. Celestina smiled while Josémaria ladled a good helping onto her plate. The paella had the elusive tutong — the thin layer of crispy, caramelized rice at the bottom. This was the real thing.

"I thought I'd live my life without ever having a proper paella," she swooned as she took her first bite.

"Some things are worth doing right," he replied, taking her hand.

Back in the restaurant, Josémaria's business partner, Venicius, stood fuming. Josémaria told him he would be dining with a magazine editor that evening. Venicius did not think too much of it, as entertainment and promotion were not his department. Of course, that duplicitous son-of-a-bitch failed to say the editor was a C-cup in a Jean Harlow dress.

All evening long, the kitchen staff were distracted by gossip from the waiters, while the waiters were preoccupied with the action in the garden. In the restaurant, the fish was overcooked, dishes were served out of order or delivered to the wrong tables, and wine glasses were not refilled. Not that it mattered, because the guests did not seem too concerned with eating. The Pescado à la Provenzal and lemongrass lechon cassoulet simply could not compete with the spectacularly staged indiscretion taking place outside.

Feeling himself on the brink of a panic attack, Venicius gulped down a shot of vodka from the bottle he kept strategically placed for emergencies. His tightly run ship was being run aground while the bloody owner was out there cavorting. Venicius wondered if his childhood friend had taken leave of his senses. Josémaria had always been a lover — he enjoyed the good life, loved good food, and adored beautiful women. He flirted, had flings, and embarked on the occasional casual affair. But in consideration for Ysabel's pride, he did so with a level of discretion that made it possible for her to look the other way. In all the years Venicius had known his friend, he had never seen him display this level of recklessness. The crazy S.O.B. was daring people to talk. Venicius did not want to think what would happen if Ysabel should decide to drop by the restaurant. He had put the staff on high alert in case her car pulled into the parking lot. He took another long swig of vodka and prayed for his agony to end, and soon.

In the garden, Josémaria acknowledged the onlookers with a mischievous wave. He stood up and moved his chair closer to Celestina. "That's better. Why be formal?" he mused.

"I think we're making a spectacle of ourselves," Celestina said.

"Might as well. Love should be lived in the open, don't you think?"

His face took on an amused, devil-may-care look as he surveyed the scene he had created. There was no denying this was his heart shouting from the rooftops — to the upper class and bourgeoisie who flocked to his restaurant, in the megacity that gossiped like a small town.

The waiter came to clear away the remains of the first course and to tell Josémaria that the main course was ready for the next step.

"Come," he said to her. "I'll show you my private kitchen."

They walked together to the coach house, located across from the main building. The old structure had been updated with a security camera, a rolling door, and other modern features. The door slid open as Josémaria pressed the buttons on a keypad. Inside was a cavernous kitchen with a marble slab island large enough to prepare a calf for dinner. The room had every kind of shiny stainless-steel appliance, but it was the horno, a beehive-shaped, wood-burning brick oven that caught her eye.

"I hope you like duck," he said.

"I do. Perhaps a little too much."

Duck meat had always been a challenge for him. He found it overly fatty and rich, but strangely uninteresting. Matters were not improved by traditional sauces, which were often too sweet. The legs and breast required different cooking times, so that by the time the legs were tender, the breast was overdone and devoid of pinkness. Furthermore, marinades worked against the crisping of the skin, so he could not rely on them to make things interesting. He had to start with a naturally flavourful duck.

Instead of going to Pateros, the duck-raising capital, he went to an old rice farmer in Pampanga. This farmer had been raising ducks in his rice fields long before organic farming had become trendy. The ducks were a hybrid of wild and domestic ducks, left to forage in the rice paddies as a form of natural pest control. They were leaner than commercial breeds and their meat had a more complex taste due to their free-range diet. Josémaria bought four of them and had them fattened with nutritious rice bran, water spinach, clams, and shrimp.

After some experimentation in the kitchen, he opted to use only the duck breasts, saving the legs for a confit he planned on making later. Two days before the planned dinner, he deboned the duck and scored its skin in a crosshatch pattern to help it render fat during cooking. The duck was then given a dry rub of smoked sea salt and lemongrass-infused cracked pepper and left in a special cooler. This step was necessary to thoroughly dry out the duck skin and ensure a crackling-like result.

Josémaria and Celestina approached the horno where a kitchen assistant was checking on the progress of the duck breasts. "These are ready for searing, sir," the assistant said.

With a long wooden paddle, Josémaria took out the ducks and put them on a carving board to rest while the assistant warmed up a cast-iron pan on the stove. While the ducks were resting, Josémaria put his apron back on, rolled up his sleeves, and tested the temperature of the pan. He needed it to be just hot enough to render the fat but not too hot as to wreck the ducks' skin.

Celestina watched as he deftly and patiently cooked the skin side of the duck breasts at a nice sizzle, pressing down with his tongs to ensure even browning, and being careful to pour out the excess fat so the duck did not poach in it. He did not use a timer or even look at his watch. Instead, he listened until the energetic sizzle died down to a low hiss. Only then did he turn over the breasts to check the skin. They were glistening and golden brown, and the skin made a nice, crisp sound when scraped with the side of the tongs. Celestina felt her mouth watering in anticipation.

"How do you like it done?" Josémaria asked as the meaty side of the ducks was cooking.

"Rosy," she said. "Just past rare."

"That's how I like it too," he smiled.

After a few minutes, he tested the meat with his fingertip and determined it was done. With the duck breasts now resting on the carving board, he then turned his attention to the side dish — fresh spring rolls with a colourful twist. He had wanted the wrappers to complement the golden-brown colour of the duck. In a flash of inspiration, he had added purple yam flour to the batter. His experiment resulted in paper-thin crepes in a delicate lilac hue.

"May I?" Celestina asked as she saw the familiar assemblage. "I've been trained for this."

Celestina lined up some crepes and filled them with water chestnuts, pea shoots, pieces of braised pork belly, and slivers of young garlic bulbs. She skillfully rolled them into tight bundles, with a little frill of curly green lettuce peeking out of the lilac sleeves.

"Beautiful," he whispered into her ear.

With the side dish in good hands, he turned back to the duck. It yielded gracefully under his sharpened Ginsu knife. The skin was delicately crispy, as he hoped it would be, and the meat was moist with the colour of fine Bordeaux wine. He plated the duck and spring rolls on leaf-shaped platters and decorated them with a lashing of baby crab fat, ochre-hued and full of umami.

After taking off his apron, Josémaria and Celestina happily walked back to their table with their platters. The waiter had already laid out a selection of condiments in little bowls hewn from polished horn. There was a gremolata of minced chives and ginger, a sour-salty lime and shrimp paste dip, and Josémaria's own mostarda of almost-ripe mango.

"You'll have to tell me which condiment goes with what dish. I don't want to ruin perfection," she said.

"I leave that up to you. I don't believe in culinary dictatorship. That's not the Filipino way."

Celestina ate with undisguised enjoyment, trying all the sauces and condiments until she settled on Josémaria's mango mostarda for the duck, and the chive and ginger gremolata for the spring rolls. This duck was quite unlike the predictable Peking Duck dishes she had eaten during countless Sytanco family gatherings. It was crisp and succulent with a hint of wildness. With every bite, she could taste his deep love for the land's bounty. When she was done, she sighed contentedly and whispered, "Bravo. That was the finest meal I've ever had."

It had been a while since he had cooked for a woman. He had given up on pleasing Ysabel's palate, since she only ever ate steamed vegetables, salads with a spritz of lemon, and roast fish or chicken. Celestina's compliment was thunderous applause in his ears.

"It's not over yet. There's still dessert."

He was about to refill her champagne flute so she could cleanse her palate. Then he noticed it was still almost full.

"Your drink's gone flat. May I offer you another one?"

"No, thank you. I don't want to drink anymore," she said pointedly. "I want to experience this lovely night with all my senses."

"I understand perfectly."

By the time they settled down to have their Crema Sulipeña flavoured with sea salt flakes on darkly caramelized syrup, Josémaria had found a new purpose in life.

"I know there's been sadness in your life. I want to make you blissfully, mindlessly happy."

"I'm not sure I can take it," she said honestly. "I'm not accustomed to happiness. It feels like a luxury."

"Give me time. I'll spoil you until you're used to it."

She laughed helplessly at the determined man before her. How could he possibly top this night? "You're a madman!" she said fondly.

"In matters of food and love, yes. Guilty as charged. C'mon, dance with me. Let's be mad together."

The moon illuminated the grounds in silver light so radiant she could feel its heat. She followed his lead as they enjoyed a slow, melting dance. For days, he had longed to hold her curvaceous body. Now here she was, dressed in ivory silk and bathed in moonlight. He rested his hand where the small of her back met the fullness of her derrière, and they danced. Oh, the delicious agony of holding but not having her. When that became unbearable, he pulled her close and kissed her — tenderly at first, then hungrily, with his tongue.

Celestina responded without shame, her tongue meeting his in a serpentine dance. She wanted this giant of a man, with his magnificent gestures and great passions. In the restaurant, diners continued to watch. The song was over. The lovers were still dancing.

"Come, be alone with me," he said, his breath full of desire.

"You know I want to," she replied. "But perhaps we should put our houses in order first."

As much as he wanted her, he agreed and said, "How'd you get so wise, my princess?"

"Life made me so. I only wish the wisdom had come sooner."

He naughtily slid down her dress strap and planted a kiss on her shoulder. Quickly, she righted her strap and said, "I should go. Before I lose my head."

He nodded, though he wanted her to stay. Together they walked the candlelit path, savouring the last moments of their evening.

"I'll see you again soon," he said.

"Yes. Thank you for this unforgettable night," she replied as she got into the Silver Spirit.

"It won't be the last," he promised.

He looked on as the car left the grounds of La Sulipeña. He was going to have an agonizing night. But he also knew he was done wandering. It was time for his heart to make a home. With her.

26

Beautiful Serpents

The next day, gossip columns and society pages dripped with innuendo about a dashing and very much attached restaurateur, a mysterious beauty, and their wildly romantic dinner in the garden of a popular restaurant. Eyewitnesses gave detailed accounts of the dinner to their friends and families, who in turn passed on the gossip to their friends with a few extra embellishments for dramatic effect.

Josémaria's attempt to break up with Ysabel was foiled by her outright refusal to meet with him. She was used to his putas. They were little more than selections on a tasting menu to him. Just a tikim, a taste, to spice up their monogamy. But Ysabel did not know what to make of this latest infidelity. It hurt because it was so brazen and utterly lacking any attempt to spare her dignity. Humiliated and enraged, Ysabel boarded a plane and took refuge on her friend's island in El Nido, Palawan. She was going to meet Josémaria when she was good and ready, and not a minute before.

At the restaurant, requests steadily came in for reservations at "the garden table." They came from couples who wanted to celebrate their anniversaries, and from men planning marriage proposals. Then people began asking about holding engagement parties "in the garden." Venicius the chef requested a meeting with Josémaria in his office to discuss these developments.

"You know, I was ready to beat you up and quarter you after last Saturday," Venicius started. "But reservations are up 25 percent, so I'm giving you a reprieve. I can't think of a better publicity stunt than Saturday night's show."

"Really?" Josémaria said with obvious amusement.

"People want the garden table for their romantic fantasies. What should we tell them?"

"Tell them, yes. Why not? It might give me *swerte*," he shrugged with a wistful smile.

"Are you going to tell me what's going on?"

"What's to tell? You've seen it. It is what it looks like."

"Dear Lord … you're in love with the girl in the garden. Does Ysabel know?"

Josémaria's silence spoke volumes. Venicius could see this was going to be a messy battle. He had known this man since they'd been in short pants. Apart from their business relationship, they were like brothers, and Josémaria was the godfather of Venicius's only daughter. The man was a prize, even with his weakness for women and occasional flashes of immaturity. Life had given his friend an unfair number of blessings. The guy was endowed like a stud and had the exquisitely modelled features of Bernini sculptures in Rome. It would have been easy to hate him, but as it happened, Josémaria was also one of the most decent guys one could ever know — loyal, deeply intelligent, and generous of heart and pocketbook. Ysabel Duarte would not relinquish her prize just like that.

"What are you going to do now?" Venicius asked.

"The right thing. God help me."

Venicius left Josémaria's office knowing this was no ordinary affair. That woman, whoever she was, seemed to have touched his friend's wandering heart in ways the others never did. Venicius had a feeling he was going to be seeing a very different Josémaria from that point on.

*

Celestina's blissful Sunday gave way to a less-than-auspicious Monday. It started with a dream about her kiss with Josémaria. A wonderful heat enveloped her body as their lips met. She was liquid moonlight. "Be alone with me," he'd whispered. But when she opened her eyes, she was in another place, with another man. Her thoughts were foggy, and there was no moon. Just a large mirror ball spinning round and round as the familiar man of her nightmares had his way with her. Her screams were lost in monstrous heartbeats as she struggled against his great, devouring hunger.

A loud crash pierced the veil of sleep and pulled her from the clutches of the monster. In seconds, she was sitting bolt upright, wishing she had died instead of living to face the shame. Across the room, she found her reading lamp fallen and dented, its lightbulb broken into pieces. She had a feeling Manang was watching and had tried to wake her from her nightmare.

Somewhere in the city, a carelessly addressed letter was making its way to its destination. It bore nothing more than the name of the building and the district, but thanks to the memory of the postman and the notoriety of the property, it managed to reach the superintendent's hands. By the time Celestina was done with her tea that morning, the letter was waiting on her doorstep. Her hand began to tremble as she saw the flamboyant strokes on the yellowed envelope. Inside was a brief letter:

> *My dear, it's been too long since we've last spoken. I am*
> *sorry for everything. I understand if you can't forgive*

me, but I do hope you can let me back into your life, even a little. I miss having a family. It would be nice to see you again someday.

With Love, Papang

P.S. Well played with your handsome Mestiso. He's a young man after my own heart, much better than that gutless Pintado and the pretty castrato you cried over.

She could not remember what else happened after that. She woke up on the floor, with Lille cradling her head.

"Thank goodness I came up. Something told me I was needed here," Lille said.

Without a word, Celestina handed her the letter.

"But you haven't spoken to him in years," Lille asked after she read the letter. "How would he know all this?"

"That's the question, isn't it?" Celestina replied. In truth, she already knew. She had known since that day she'd walked into his darkened office and heard him speaking from the depths of time.

*

There were no clouds or fog that Tuesday morning, nothing to obscure the view of Lake Taal and the small but active volcano at the centre of it. The red Jeep Wrangler drove up Tagaytay's winding hillside roads. Inside the Jeep, Celestina watched as a small plume of smoke rose from Taal Volcano's crater.

The vehicle slowed down as it approached a heavily wooded area marked by a single trail. It pulled over by a roadside store that sold bottled water, coconut pie, and seasonal produce. Rojo and Lille got out and waited for Celestina to gather her things. Over the past decade, they had brought many young people like her to this very spot. After a few minutes, Celestina joined them, back-pack strapped on and ready for her hike.

"The retreat centre is at the top of the hill, at the end of the trail. About four miles," Rojo said as he and Lille walked Celestina to the small wooden sign marking the beginning of the route.

"Thank you again for arranging this," Celestina said.

"We'll walk with you," Lille said.

"No, you don't have to. You've done so much for me already."

"If for some reason you don't feel up to it, you can use the phone in the store to call us," Rojo said. "We'll be at our house, so we're not far."

"I can handle this. Don't worry," Celestina said as she set off for her hike.

"One last thing, Celestina ..." Rojo called out as she was walking away.

"Yes?"

"Whatever it is you think you've done, remember there's always forgiveness. You just have to ask. Promise me you'll go to confession. Trust me, you'll feel better," Rojo said.

She nodded and gave him a hug. "I must get going now. Thanks again."

Rojo and Lille got back in the Jeep as Celestina made her way up the trail. The tires crunched gravel as the Jeep slowly drove away. "Bye, Mom and Dad," she said to herself. "See you soon." They were not her parents, of course, but somehow the words sounded right.

*

After close to an hour of uphill walking, the wide path began to narrow. Celestina could see a clearing beyond the dense cover of trees and wild banana plants. A single wooden sign with an arrow announced that the retreat centre was not far. She sat down under a tree to catch her breath and to eat the last two chocolates sent to her by Josémaria. Sweets and alcohol were not allowed at the centre, Rojo had told her. Many of the people who stayed there had problems with alcohol dependency and other addictions. The nuns were aware that addicts frequently used sugar as a crutch when they could not get their drug of choice. It struck her as a touch severe on top of the spartan program of guided prayers, housework, and simple meals awaiting her. Her mouth tingled with pleasure as she took a bite of the first chocolate. This one was extra dark, and its heart was filled with Scotch whisky. It was her first taste of alcohol in more than a week, and it made her crave another. She quickly rinsed her mouth with water to get rid of the taste of whisky. After a moment's hesitation, she dropped the last chocolate on the ground and crushed it under her boot. It was filled with cherry kirsch, and the ants were already swarming it.

She got up to continue the last leg of her journey. Up ahead were the gates of the retreat centre and a cross on top of the centre's chapel. The forest trail gave way to a path paved with cobblestones, bleached white by the sun. It had been swept clean, save for a thick blade of wild grass that lay across the path. As she drew closer, she saw a flicker on the stone path. A glint of sunlight, perhaps, she told herself, or the reflection of some crystalline mineral in the stones. But something in the ancient part of her brain told her to stop. She saw another flicker coming from the fat end of the blade of wild grass. All at once, things came into focus, and she saw the object as it really was — with its tongue, eyes, and markings. It was a small snake commonly known as dahumpalay, named for its lovely green colour reminiscent of young rice stalks. Its venom was known to send people to the hospital with severe swelling and delirium. She stomped her boot on the ground to drive it away. The snake took this as a challenge and assumed a ready-to-strike position.

She backed away slowly, hoping the serpent would stand down and let her through. Several minutes passed and it became clear that it had no intention of retreating. Desperate for a solution, she found a fallen branch and used it to push the snake away from the path. It hissed menacingly and advanced a good six inches toward her. Once again, she looked at the gates of the retreat centre and, just beyond them, the cross on top of the chapel. It was too late to turn back; she had come this far. She decided she had enough of this animal's games. Crouching down, she picked up a rock, then marched toward the snake and crushed its head.

"Die, serpent! Die!"

The air echoed with her battle cry as life twitched out of the snake. Once she was certain it was dead, she wiped the sweat off her brow, drank some water, and sprinted toward the gates of the centre. The good Sisters were waiting.

*

Josémaria looked out his window as the pilot announced their location. The sheer beauty of the Sulu Sea hit him like a full-body punch. The water glistened like molten emeralds. He sat there in a kind of shock, momentarily forgetting his unpleasant mission. He told Celestina he was flying to Palawan to take care of unfinished business. He was not lying, but he did not want to say any more than he needed to. This was his problem to sort out.

When the pilot announced they were going to be landing soon, Josémaria clicked on his seat belt. Even on that clear, sun-drenched Wednesday, every air pocket felt like a speed bump in the unpressurized cabin of the small plane. None of the regular travellers to the island seemed disturbed by the turbulence. The plane landed with a thud and skidded, flinging mud on the runway before gradually coming to a stop.

The local airport was little more than an airstrip and a hut. Local drivers and boatmen were waiting to offer their services to the travellers. Josémaria got off the plane with only a small carry-on. That was all he needed as he was not planning to stay. A young man was there to meet him as soon as he disembarked. He declined the guy's offer to take his carry-on and quietly followed him to the nearby dock where a motorized banca was waiting. After a few sputtering tries, the motor roared to life and set off for the private island where Ysabel was staying.

This was the first time Josémaria had seen this side of Palawan. Cliffs and rock formations soared like Gothic cathedrals as the boat sliced through the water. He sat, unblinking, not wanting to miss a second of the operatically stunning landscape.

"You should see the view underwater, sir," the boatman said. "Those cliffs go hundreds of feet down."

Half an hour later, the boat slowed as they approached the island's pier. Sleek overwater villas on stilts ringed the island. It was all so picturesque, but he sensed he was walking into a perfumed trap. The engine shut down as the boat coasted into one of the designated spots. He thanked the young man with a generous tip and set off for Ysabel's bungalow.

He walked up a short flight of stairs, taking note of the tastefully detailed exteriors finished with weathered wood and volcanic stone. If he knew Ysabel, she would be by the pool. He walked in just as an attendant was finishing with her massage. Ysabel was naked but for a hot pink bikini bottom.

"I'm glad you could make it," she said nonchalantly. "Would you like to take a dip?"

"If you don't mind," he said after a moment's hesitation. The sky was the most celestial of blues, the breeze was sultry, and they were surrounded by tropical blossoms in riotous hues.

He followed her as she walked to the diving board of the infinity pool. She smiled at him with her long-lashed eyes before gracefully plunging in.

"C'mon!" she said. "No need to change. There's nobody around."

The infinity pool seemed to flow right into the emerald-green sea. He shed his clothes and jumped into the pool with her. They swam together quietly, both waiting for the right moment to address the inevitable. Finally, she spoke.

"You think you're in love with her, don't you?"

"I didn't mean for it to happen. Ysabel, I'm sorry, but —"

"What if I told you that you can *keep* her?"

"Are you saying what I think you're saying?"

"Yes. Every married man I know has a querida on the side. I suppose you need one too. So long as she stays in her corner and out of my face, we won't have a problem. And when you're tired of her, it'll be just the two of us once again."

Perhaps the beauty and isolation of the island was playing with his head, but he found himself seriously considering Ysabel's proposition. *Why not?* he thought. It was past time for him to get married. He could afford to have a wife and keep a mistress. And he had more than enough in him to satisfy both women.

"Think about it," Ysabel smiled as she got out of the pool. "I'll see you at lunch."

After a few minutes, Josémaria got out and walked to the viewing deck. His last proper vacation was two and a half years ago. He could stick around for a few days, he thought. It would be criminal to let paradise go to waste.

✳

Celestina inhaled deeply as she waited her turn at the confessional. The air in the chapel smelled of warm candle wax, floor soap, and freshly picked flowers. In her mind, this was the scent of everything that was sacred and pure. Of everything she was not.

She had not been to confession since high school. Her fingers gripped the edge of the hard wooden bench as she contemplated fleeing. Only a young woman bearing scars on her wrists stood between Celestina and her escape route.

"Best not to fight it," said the young woman. "It's like throwing up. Nobody likes it. But you'll feel better after it's done."

Celestina swallowed hard, knowing what she had to do. "May I go first?" she heard herself say.

The young woman smiled as she stood up and stepped aside for Celestina.

"Good luck," the young woman said as the door of the confessional opened.

A young man in a faded Kurt Cobain T-shirt stepped out and headed for the altar of St. Joseph to do his penance. In a moment, the light above the confessional turned green. It was Celestina's turn, and she entered the enclosed compartment. She glanced nervously at the silhouette of the priest on the other side of the screen.

Her breath filled the space as she blurted out the words that had been drilled into her by the nuns at the Colegio de la Inmaculada Concepcion. "Bless me Father for I have sinned. It's been ten years since my last confession." She was thankful for the script, as mechanical as her delivery was. Otherwise, she would not have known how to begin.

"Slow down, take your time. The Lord is patient," the priest said from the other side of the screen. The Lord may have been patient, but Celestina was not. She wanted to get this over with as soon as possible.

"I met a wonderful man and for the first time in my life I think I have a chance at happiness. He doesn't know I had an abortion when I was fifteen. I knew it was a grave sin. But I just couldn't have the child knowing the father … was my own father."

A tense silence, followed by an exhalation of breath came from the other side of the screen. "I see," the priest finally said after clearing his throat. "I have no doubt it was a shattering experience and a difficult decision for you."

"Yes, it was. I nearly died. Sometimes I wish I did."

"Abortion exacts a heavy physical and emotional toll," he replied. "Especially if the pregnancy is the result of abuse. Now, you were very young when it happened. Still very much a child yourself. How do you feel about your actions now?"

"I thought I had no choice. I thought I would hate the child every day of its life. But now ... I don't know ..."

"Go on."

"I dream of her often. The child. She's playing in my mother's garden. Then a giant bayawak snatches her. I can see her broken body in the lizard's mouth. The monster runs and disappears into its lair. Then I wake up and I cry like a part of me has been ripped out."

Celestina's sobs filled the confessional. The priest directed her to the box of tissues on her side of the screen, but otherwise gave her time to weep.

"You grieve as a mother would for a child," he said after she calmed down. "Every child is a child of God and a member of the human family. Even one conceived under terrible circumstances. You must tell your young man the truth. A relationship must be built on a foundation of trust and honesty, or it will not stand."

"Yes, Father," she said.

"Tell me, have you spoken with your father about this?"

"No, I have not spoken with him. Nor do I ever want to," she replied. "He wrote me a letter recently. He offered his apology ... but I can tell he wasn't truly sorry. He just wanted to remind me that he's watching ... I'm sorry, but I hate him, and I hope he burns in hell."

"I understand. You have every reason to be angry," he said after a thoughtful silence. "God made fathers to provide for, protect, and love their children. Your father betrayed those sacred duties and committed great violence to your body and spirit. He shall answer to God for his sins."

Celestina nodded as she let the priest's words sink in. After years of bearing the burden of shame, she needed to hear this simple statement, to be reminded that there is justice for her, somewhere.

"I know you will find forgiveness difficult, even impossible, particularly if there is no remorse on the other end," the priest continued. "But if you could let go of anger and hate, and pray for him, it would help heal the wound that's been inflicted on your soul."

Celestina wanted to say something, but she held her tongue. Forgiving her tormentor was not something she was prepared to do.

"The road to healing is long and difficult," the priest said. "You've done the right thing by coming here. Don't be afraid to seek further help. Listen for God's voice in the noise of the world, and put your heart, mind, and spirit into his hands."

Celestina bowed her head and listened as the priest gave her penance.

"Say one Our Father and one Hail Mary," he said. "Before going to bed tonight, pray the rosary. Ask the Blessed Mother to guide you on your journey back to God's kingdom. Now, recite the Act of Contrition with me."

It had been a long time since the words had crossed her lips, but she heard herself asking for forgiveness, for serenity in her heart, and a renewal of her spirit.

As she came to the end of her time in the confessional, she heard the priest say, "I absolve you of all your sins, in the name of the Father and of the Son and of the Holy Spirit."

Her eyes narrowed as she emerged from the shadowy womb of the confessional to the brightness of the chapel. She was drawn to the altar of the Holy Family as she set out to make her penance. She prayed for guidance and asked Jesus to help heal her and her family.

After saying her penance, she lingered at the altar and looked at the serene faces of the Virgin Mary, St. Joseph, and Baby Jesus.

She dared think that, maybe, she could have her own family too, with Josémaria.

Celestina desperately wished she could check her EasyCall pager for his messages, but electronic devices were not allowed at the retreat. She would have to wait until Saturday to reconnect with him. Until then, all she could do was learn to pray again and surrender her unholy mess of a life to a higher power.

*

That night, Celestina lay awake in her small iron bed in the retreat house, which was simply dressed in sun-bleached cotton sheets washed with Perla soap. She had spent much of the evening praying the rosary and thinking about how to put her house in order. She sat up and clicked on the bedside lamp. Perhaps God, in his great mercy, had forgiven her. But had she forgiven herself and could she ever forgive the man who continued to torment her? There was too much rage in her heart, still.

In the silence of the night, her conscience spoke clearly. She realized that one of these days, she needed to have a good talk with her mother. Maybe there was a chance to repair their bond and have a semblance of family. She did not know if she could ever make peace with her father. But she knew she would continue to be haunted by her nightmares if she did not at least try.

Her thoughts soon turned to Josémaria and that unforgettable night. She was standing on the cusp of a life-changing love. It was time to come clean about her past, about everything. Even at the risk of losing that love.

*

A winged figure stood on top of a dark cliff. Closer and closer, he walked to the edge until he was looking down at the glistening green waters below. The air around him stirred as he spread his massive wings. He could feel the muscles in his back cramping as he moved the limbs of feathers and bone. He had forgotten what he meant to do or why, until he caught the faint scent of sampaguitas in the breeze. Then he remembered the moonlit dinner and the woman he wanted to make a home with. He flapped his wings again and stepped off the cliff's edge, falling until he somehow found the strength to make his feathery limbs do his bidding.

The dream ended and Josémaria opened his eyes to the stylishly exposed beams of the guest bungalow. His memory was foggy, but he knew he had done something stupid. A glance at the nightstand reminded him. Beside the lamp were two wine glasses, one marked with pink lipstick. Beside him was Ysabel. Stumbling out of bed, he picked up his discarded clothes and quickly splashed his face with water. He then tossed his personal effects into his overnight bag and prepared to leave.

Ysabel opened her eyes just as he was stepping out of the bedroom.

"Are you skipping out on me?"

"I think we already said our goodbyes," he replied simply. "Let's not prolong this."

"You were never faithful to me. What makes her so special?"

"I wish I knew, Ysabel. Love's a mystery, even to me."

He walked away without looking back because her tears would melt his resolve and he would be right back where he started.

27

Firestorm

Josémaria's plane touched down in Manila just before sunset. Mechanical trouble had delayed him at the El Nido Airport for most of the day. Celestina was expected to come back from her retreat. He checked his EasyCall messages as soon as he disembarked from the plane. There was a message from her, sent two hours earlier: *I'll be on the seven o'clock bus from Tagaytay. There's no need to pick me up. We'll talk tomorrow. Praying for your safe journey.*

He sensed a certain detachment in her words. Perhaps she had a change of heart, he thought. He could not let that happen. Not now. A quick glance at his watch told him he had about half an hour to get to the bus terminal. He had just enough time to make it. He breezed past provincial travellers, Israeli backpackers, and officials looking for bribes and contraband. Outside the building, he hailed a taxi.

"Do you need a hotel, sir?" the driver asked. "I know a clean one in Mabini. Close to the bars."

"Sa Pasay Bus Terminal tayo, paré," Josémaria replied in Tagalog.

"Sorry, sir. I thought you were a turista."

"No problem," Josémaria smiled.

Josémaria tried to sit back as the driver wove his way through the tangle of pedestrians and taxis. It had been almost a week since he'd last seen Celestina. To his heart, it felt like the last stretch of a long voyage back home. He took out his wallet and handed the driver a five-hundred-peso bill.

"Find a shortcut," he said. He had no more time to lose.

*

Heads turned as the bus from Tagaytay lurched into the station bearing some unusual cargo on its roof. Amongst the luggage and the baskets of produce was a striking young woman flanked by two scruffy modern-day Vikings in tie-dyed T-shirts. The trio were flushed with the adrenalin of their unconventional mode of transport.

Even from the far end of the waiting area, Josémaria immediately spotted her. Standing on her rooftop perch, with a bandana tied buccaneer-style around her head, she looked like a very alluring windblown pirate to whom he would gladly surrender. *Dear Lord. I'm in love with this crazy girl.*

He followed the bus toward its designated pickup area, wading through the veritable river of people that, day after day, flowed through Manila. Keeping her firmly in his sight, he pushed through the crowd of hawkers waving tabloids and bags of rambutan fruit in his face. As Josémaria inched toward Celestina, wide-eyed newcomers from the provinces brushed against him. The more fortunate ones were met by friends and relatives waiting at the station. Others would drift inevitably to the slums or to the streets. On the platform, Josémaria stood his ground while dodging disembarking passengers bearing flapping chickens and enormous baskets of muskmelons.

Celestina saw him standing steadfastly in the crowd. Laughing, he touched his brow in a playful salute. His smile was like the sun breaking through the darkest midnight. She said her goodbyes to the admiring Vikings with whom she shared the rooftop ride. Both had flaxen hair and imposing physiques, though neither possessed Josémaria's elegance or blazing spirit.

Celestina made her way down the rooftop ladder, knowing that she might have to say both hello and goodbye to Josémaria in short order. On the platform, she found herself in his arms, a cradle of heartbeats and kisses.

"What were you doing up there?" Josémaria asked. "I could have lost you."

"Don't worry. I'm a little windburned, but I have all my limbs," Celestina said with a soft laugh. "I felt claustrophobic inside the bus with all the chickens and pungent fruit."

As they settled into a meaningful pause, his hand once again found the curve of her hip. She closed her eyes and savoured his touch. Perhaps for the last time, she told herself. She started to speak, keenly aware of her weakening resolve.

"Josémaria, we have to talk."

"Yes, I suppose we do. You'll be glad to know I've put my house in order. Starting now, I'm yours and yours alone."

Celestina remained silent after Josémaria uttered these fateful words. She wanted to say that he had made a mistake. That he should forget about her and make it right with Ysabel. But here was love offering itself. A chance at happiness in a new house with no ghosts.

Josémaria could see the conflicting emotions casting shadows on her luminous face. "Celestina, I'm trying to tell you that I love you. Without you, my days have no flavour, no fragrance."

Somewhere inside her, Celestina felt a spark, then a flame. She replied to Josémaria without words. Just lips, breath, and fire. The flame grew into a firestorm, engulfing her in intense, joyful heat.

Delicate white smoke, fragrant as incense, rose from her skin, and then his.

The smoke filled the chaotic bazaar that was the bus station. People and produce alike were saturated with the perfume of night-blooming sampaguitas. Days later, in the city's markets, butchers would stare, puzzled, at flapping chickens with scented feathers. And fruit sellers would discover muskmelons filled with a mysterious flowery honey.

✳

The taxi driver stopped at the house with the dragon gates. For a split second, he thought he saw a flicker of movement, a slight blink from one of the creatures' glass eyes. Maybe it was the fumes. The lovers had been smoking something that smelled like sampaguitas and incense, and they'd brought the residual vapours into his cab. Probably some kind of shabu the rich people were into. He did not care what drugs his passengers were on, so long as they paid.

"We're here, sir," he said, watching the lovers from his rearview mirror. They were barely going to make it to the front door, by the looks of it.

The Mestiso handed the driver two purple hundred-peso bills without so much as a glance back. It was one bill and a big chunk of change too much. The driver wanted to give back the other hundred, but the Mestiso's hands were otherwise occupied. Giggling, the lovers fumbled out of the taxi in a cloud of fragrant smoke and quickly disappeared into the pedestrian gate.

The driver suddenly remembered the first time he'd taken his wife to a love motel, twenty years ago, when they could hardly keep their hands off each other. It had been so long since he'd felt that delicious heat. Watching the lovers awakened a feeling in him he thought was long dead. He ran a comb through his hair, then took out a small mirror to inspect the result. He was not a bad-looking guy. He thought about his wife as he splashed on some cologne. She still had her figure, even though she was too harried to dress up and put on makeup these days. Rummaging through the glove compartment, he found a coupon for a popular love motel offering a 15 percent discount and complimentary soup for rejuvenation.

He put the coupon in his shirt pocket and turned off his taxi's top light. The Saturday night revellers would have to find other ways to get around and throw away their money. Tonight, he was going to give his wife some good loving.

❊

The lovers stumbled into the bedroom, electric, inarticulate with desire. With another deep kiss, Josémaria scooped up Celestina and carried her toward the bed.

"I have to take a shower," she teased, knowing she was prolonging his agony.

"No, you don't. You made me wait long enough."

Laughing, they fell into bed in a tangle of kisses and clothing. His mouth quickly found the breasts he had lusted over on many, many nights. They were full and insolently pointed, and she tasted like citrus, salt, and heady wine. Her back arched as his tongue made delicious swirls around her nipples.

She invited his hands to explore, letting skin whisper to skin. His fingers found the hollow that ran like a riverbed down her taut belly. They followed the path, past her deep navel, stopping to caress that special erogenous zone — the singit, the cleft where the thigh joined the pubis. No other culture he knew of had a name for that secret place. Her legs parted ever so slightly as he lingered on that spot. The skin between her thighs was moist, glistening with her honey. He slid off her panties and went down to the source of that tempting sweetness.

She cried out as his tongue found her pleasure spot. Again and again, he teased her, bringing her to the brink until she begged for release.

He quickly pulled down his boxers and showed himself, proud and fully armed. He wanted her to see how much he desired her and how much pleasure he could give her. Her eyes widened as she admired his sandata, the subject of much lascivious gossip among the society beauties he had bedded.

Without another word, he parted her thighs and plunged into her. No longer the bon vivant or the golden prince, he was hunger, pure and timeless. Gone, too, was the proud princess of the Dragon Gates house. In her bed was a beautiful, wanton animal riding wave upon wave of pleasure. He kept going until her gingery voice turned hoarse, and her sighs turned into song. Hearing this, he gave one last thrust before falling, with a cry, into la petite mort.

On the rumpled sheets, they lay, their bodies limp as they washed up on love's shore. The air was heavy with the heat from their bodies, and the mirrors were covered with droplets of water. Echoes of their sighs rose to the ceiling where the ghost of Selena Sytanco watched, unseen.

28

Sweet Honeymoon House

For a time, life was sweet in Celestina's house. Josémaria's silver Maserati found a permanent spot between her little black Honda and the ancient white Lincoln Continental they called Moby Dick. Over the next few months, his vintage cookware, antique furniture, and music collection followed his heart and took their places in her apartment and in Selena's Sytanco's former conservatory.

Once settled, he started making plans. Looking around the grounds, he said to Celestina, "This place will be glorious again. You'll see." True to his word, the driveway with the lightning bolt crack was repaved. The swimming pool, long dry and boarded, was revived and refilled with salt water, no less. Stainless steel stoves and refrigerators were delivered to replace the pre-war models that still clunked away in the kitchens.

Inside Celestina's apartment, the air was filled with the happy noise of pots and pans, and conversations that poured from their hearts into the wee hours. The otherworldly spirits were quiet, except for occasional creaks from Manang Rio's chair.

The most profound changes happened in the hearts of the two lovers. No longer did Josémaria tumble into bed with forgettable women or roam the city in search of novel experiences. Now he looked forward to the end of the day when he could go home to Celestina, have a simple late meal, then lay his head beside hers. During their talks, she would look deep into his eyes and say, "You built a place where life is beautiful. And you make it look effortless, like a dance." Hearing this, the weariness of his day would vanish, and he would, once again, feel like a prince of the world. The night would pass, not in hours, but in the overtures and crescendos of love. No other body felt so right, so perfect for his. And he thought, at long last his restless, wandering spirit has found its home and harbour.

As for Celestina, she would drift to sleep in his arms, body and spirit swollen with bliss. Neither the giant bayawak nor the man of her nightmares disturbed her during that blessed time. The tragic events that had marked her life seemed so very far away now. And she told herself, *malas* could no longer touch her in this fortress of his love.

29

Haunted

Celestina and Josémaria's unwedded bliss continued into the season of purple mangosteens and lychees, toward the end of the rainy season. It was during this time that Josémaria encountered one of the house's ghosts. He met Selena Sytanco upon waking one morning, at that moment before his rational mind could take control of his faculties. She was standing by his side, drawn to the warm glow of his body.

Looking at her grandniece's handsome lover, Selena felt the stirring of a very human longing she'd never quite forgotten. How splendidly virile and full of fire he was, even at rest. She reached out to caress his rippling chest as he hovered between the world of sleep and waking life.

For several drowsy seconds, Josémaria thought he was looking at Celestina, until he remembered she had left early for an out-of-town assignment. It was then that he noticed the bloody slash across Selena's throat. He could see her ghostly mouth moving, but the only thing he heard was the sound of a piano, broken and out of tune — a fragment of something she used to play for another man.

Josémaria sprang out of bed and mumbled an involuntary prayer. With that, the spectre vanished, the way many vivid dreams fade in the day's light. In minutes, he was dressed and raring to get out of the apartment. He would have to shower and shave at work. There was no way he was going to stick around for an encore. Just as he was ready to run to the elevator, the phone rang. He hesitated then decided to answer in case it was something important. There was some crackle and static on the other end, typical of overseas phone calls, then a man's voice.

"Hello, Rojo?" the man said.

"No, this is Josémaria," he replied with a hint of annoyance. "Rojo lives downstairs. This is Celestina's place."

"Oh, good. I thought I'd dialed the wrong number. Are you a new tenant?" the man asked.

"You could say that," Josémaria responded with growing irritation.

"I tried to call Celestina at work, but she wasn't in. May I speak to her?"

"She's out of town. She won't be back until later this evening. May I take a message?"

"Yes. It's Johnny. I'm in Amsterdam … no, sorry, Rotterdam … It's hard to keep track. I'll be flying to North America in two weeks. The band will be in Toronto for a few days. Tell her I can send her a plane ticket. Anyway, I'll call her again tomorrow."

"I'll let her know you called," Josémaria said as he hung up.

Downstairs, he greeted Rocky without their usual exchange about sports and current events. By the time the dragon gates opened, Josémaria had almost forgotten about his ghostly encounter, as he now had something more tangible to worry about. It was obvious Celestina was still in touch with Johnny, and Johnny had not given up on her. Josémaria drove away wondering if she still felt love for her old flame. Something primal and territorial surged within him as he weaved in and out of Manila's traffic.

Sorry, Mr. Rock Star. She's mine now. You're going to have a hell of a fight if you want her. I'm going to hit you with everything I've got. Trust me, there's no chance you'll win. As he made his way to the restaurant, he decided to call his real estate broker. Perhaps it was time he and Celestina made a home, in their own house, away from the lingering ghosts of the past.

*

It was impossible not to love her. A chubby-cheeked flower girl slumped on the steps of the Sytanco mansion. It was a picture of four-year-old Celestina at a relative's wedding party, looking like a charmingly dishevelled blossom in her tiered organza dress. She was irresistible with her plumpness and her halo of curls, but she was clearly not having fun.

Josémaria had other photographs of Celestina in his office, but it was the rumpled flower girl who turned his blood to syrup. He wanted to smother her cheeks with kisses and feel her chubby arms around his neck. Most of all, he wanted to tell her not to be sad, that he would make everything all right.

You and I will make the most adorable babies, Josémaria thought as he looked at little Celestina. He picked up his phone and called his real estate broker, Vickie Santana. The flower girl looked back at Josémaria with her wide, mournful eyes as he spoke to his broker. "No, I'm not looking for another old villa to turn into a restaurant," he said. "I'm looking to start a family ... No, this is not a prank ... No, it's not Ysabel ... Yes, it's Celestina ... No, I haven't told anyone yet. It's a surprise ... Oh, I'm sure my secret is safe with you and your dozen or so confidantes ... So, am I doing an interview for the society page or are we doing business, Vickie?"

Still surprised, but sufficiently convinced that her client was serious, Vickie told Josémaria that three stunning houses had just come on the market, and she could arrange viewings that very afternoon. One of the houses had been designed by Lionel Laxa, an architect Celestina admired.

For the next few hours, Josémaria's thoughts were happily occupied with daydreams of little Celestinas running around the lovely, gracious home they would make as Mr. and Mrs. San Miguel.

✻

It was pure instinct that had led Josémaria to buy the property that afternoon. It was an earthy, elemental house that some people would deem too modest for a man of his background. The architect had used reclaimed hardwood and roughly cut rocks of volcanic origin for the bones. Ferns grew from the spaces where the rocks kissed. And every surface had been smoothed and mellowed by sun, wind, and rain. Two mango trees provided shade from the intense tropical heat, while hibiscus and calla lilies lent colour.

The interiors were sensual, touchable, with richly grained mahogany wood and a sinuous wrought-iron staircase. More elegant than the marble-columned ostentations of his gated world, it was the style and spirit of his beloved captured in wood and stone. It was the first house he viewed, after which he declared he would see no other.

"It might be a good idea to show her the place first," Vickie said, shocked at how fast she had made the sale. "I mean, she's going to live in it too."

"Trust me, she'll like it," he replied as he wrote out a cheque for the down payment right there and then.

"I'll send you the paperwork tomorrow," Vickie said.

He nodded and thanked her, but his mind was already planning his next stop. The secret showroom of the jeweller at Cameron's Court. The one reserved for their most special clients. He needed a ring like no other. A spectacular piece for the woman who made his life fragrant.

✻

The blackout rolled into the district just as Josémaria's car approached the dragon gates. Flashlight in hand, Rocky came to open the gates. The silver Maserati took its place beside Moby Dick, but Celestina's spot was still empty.

"How long is this blackout supposed to last?" Josémaria asked as he got out of the car.

"The radio said two hours, sir."

Josémaria shook his head and laughed. In Manila, two hours meant four hours, so they would be without power until midnight if they were lucky.

"Might as well start up the generator," he said. It was noisy and emitted diesel fumes, but it was better than walking around a ghost-infested house with candles in hand.

On the way inside, Rocky handed him the day's mail. Up the stairs he went, his blood humming with anticipation. First, he would make a simple pasta with her favourite crab fat sauce, lemon, and lots of golden-brown garlic. After she got home, he would throw some of the dry-aged porterhouse steaks on the grill and make them "just past rare," the way she liked them. It would have been nice to have some champagne to toast the occasion, but she did not wish to have any alcohol in the house. Sparkling water would have to do. She was fond of cheese, so he would plate some buffalo milk cheese, slightly warmed with roasted pili nuts and mangosteen preserves for dessert. Then, he would serve up the ring with the coffee, where the sugar cube would usually go. It would be so, so sweet to see her melt. Yes, clinch the prize and send Johnny a wedding invitation, as an FYI.

He unlocked the door and put the mail on the table. Among the magazines and white envelopes from various investment firms was a red one. He recognized the name on the return address, Antonio Errantes. Celestina's father, spinner of Filipino nightmares. He had not been seen in public for years. By all accounts, he was now a recluse, but he never seemed to have gone away. Every few years, moviemakers and telenovela producers would adapt his stories with the latest starlets, and the nightmares would begin all over again.

The only time she'd ever spoken of him was during that night at the opera. "Regrettably, he was not a good father," was how she put it. Clearly, the rift still troubled her. He wished she would talk to him about her daddy issues, instead of keeping them locked inside. The envelope was unsealed. He thought for a moment, then decided, *What's the harm?* She would never even know, and maybe he would understand her problems better.

He slipped out the letter and unfolded the yellowed paper. For several seconds, he pondered the large loops of the handwriting, the extra curls at the ends of the letters, and the smudges and strikeouts. It all seemed so personal. *This is not mine to read*, his inner voice told him. This is wrong. In the end, he convinced himself that if he was going to marry her, then he had the right to know about her family. And so, he read the letter Antonio had written to his daughter.

> *Dear Celestina,*
> *What happened between us cannot be undone. I regret*
> *it, but I was not in my right mind. I'm still your father.*
> *I created and nurtured you, and I know you better*
> *than anyone. You cannot run away from me because*
> *I'm inside you, and I always will be. Once again, I ask*
> *you to let me back into your life.*
> *Love, Papang*

*P.S. Send my regards to your handsome Mestiso. He
and I have a lot in common.*

Josémaria felt the blood rushing to his head as he finished reading the letter. What happened between father and daughter? What
was it that could not be undone? Why did he sense a threat underneath the plea for reconciliation? And what of that knowing sneer
beneath the formality of the postscript? A wave of dizziness followed by nausea swept over Josémaria. He loosened his tie, walked
upstairs to the bedroom, and fell into bed without turning on the
light. He had picked a hell of a night to propose.

*

It was almost ten o'clock when Celestina walked into her apartment. She was fully expecting Josémaria to be puttering around
the kitchen, but the pots and pans were quiet that evening. Perhaps
he was tired and had dozed off. She went upstairs, eager for the
sound of his voice and his delicious touch. There was music playing
in the bedroom. Carefully, she opened the door so as not to startle
him. The room was dark, and the King was singing "Suspicious
Minds." She could make out Josémaria's silhouette as her eyes adjusted to the darkness. His head moved, glanced her way, before
sinking back into the pillow.

"Elvis ballads? Must have been a bad day."

"Yeah," he said flatly.

She slipped off her jacket and pants, turned on one of the lamps
at the far end of the room, and joined him in bed.

"Sorry I'm late. It was raining in Laguna, so traffic was an ab-
solute mess," she said as she stroked his arm soothingly. "I missed
you, Jo-ma. Want to cuddle?"

"Sure," he replied as he put his arm around her stiffly.

"Talk to me, darling."

"Tell me again how your Great-Aunt Selena died."

"Her groundskeeper murdered her. Slit her throat."

"Sounds about right," he said. "That was her then. She visited me this morning."

"Really? I sense her presence. I feel what she feels, but she only ever appears to me in dreams."

"Should I feel lucky I was chosen for a face-to-face?" he asked.

"I think she likes you. Did she ... do anything?"

"I didn't stick around to find out."

"I'm sorry she freaked you out. If it's any consolation, she didn't throw a bottle of patis at you like she did with Johnny."

"Speaking of Johnny, he called from Rotterdam. Said he was going to be in North America in a couple of weeks. He wants to send you a ticket."

"Oh, Johnny ..." she said with a weary sigh.

"I didn't realize you were still in touch."

Celestina held her head in her hands. She had not told Josémaria about the pining letters and the other phone calls. "Is that what this is about? Are you jealous?"

"Wouldn't you be?"

"Short of outright cruelty, I've told him a dozen different ways that it's over," she replied. "What else would you have me do?"

"Tell him to go fuck some groupies and leave you alone."

"You think I haven't told him that? Look, I'm here, and I'm yours. All yours. Why be jealous?"

Josémaria closed his eyes as he felt Celestina's hand sliding up and down his leg. "Everything I need is right here," she whispered softly. On any other night, her electric touch would have been all it took to end this bad day and turn it into a good one. But he could still hear Antonio's mocking words playing in his head. *Send my regards to your handsome Mestiso. He and I have a lot in common.*

"Your father wrote to you," he heard himself saying.

"What?" she said with an audible tremor in her voice.

"Here. Read it yourself," he said, handing her the unfolded letter.

"You shouldn't have done that, Jo-ma."

"You have no idea how sorry I am," he replied.

Celestina's tremulous breathing filled the dimness of the room. She read it quickly before tossing it aside. The bed, the room, and her lover seemed to vanish as she fell into a void. There was no light, nothing to tell her how far she had fallen or if there was a bottom to this pit. After a long, painful silence, Josémaria's voice brought her back to face her shame.

"Let's talk about the letter. What happened that could not be undone?"

"Everything. Imagine the worst and multiply it by ten," she replied.

In an instant, she felt Josémaria's hand clutching her arm. There was a menace in his eyes that she had not seen before. "Listen. I've had a long, shitty day. Be straight with me. *For once*," he said pointedly.

"Are you sure you want it straight?" she laughed desperately. "Like your mezcal? This is a different kind of poison."

"Dígame la verdad!" he said, his voice roaring in the shadows.

"Very well. You asked for it," she said, trying to steady her voice. "It was the summer I turned fifteen. My father got me a job at New Legends Comics. I was thrilled to be working with him. He treated me like a grown-up and took me dancing and to other fun places. He would tell people I was his date. It was our little game. Looking back, perhaps it twisted our relationship in ways I did not foresee ..."

She started trembling as her mind pulled her to that dark time and place.

"Go on."

"I think you already know," she replied.

"Spell it out for me, baby. I'm slow," he said in a low growl.

"I can't!"

"You better, Princesita, or we'll be doing this all night!"

"There was a movie based on one of his novellas. I was his date at the premiere. We had a VIP room at the club. He let me drink and we smoked joints. I think he laced the drink with something. I remember dancing with him, like a slow dance, even though the music was fast. And then ..."

"And then what?"

"My head was foggy, and my limbs felt like rubber. Before I knew it, I was on my back, and he was having his way with me."

"Oh God, oh God ... please let this be a bad dream."

"I tried to push back, to scream but he was on me like a man possessed. Something inside me just gave up. That was the first time. The other times, I don't know. I suppose I let him."

"You let him?! You should have fought back," Josémaria said. "Why didn't you?"

"He told me he loved me, and he didn't care if he went to hell for it. He would crawl into my bed at night and beg for my love. 'A small mercy for a wretched monster,' he would say. I thought about running away or killing myself. I should have, but I didn't have the guts."

Josémaria fell silent as he struggled to comprehend the foulness she had just laid bare for him.

"Did you tell anyone?" he asked after a long while.

"No. I was ashamed. Hated myself for letting it happen. Manang Rio found out when I got pregnant."

"Pregnant? This just keeps getting better. Where is the child now?"

"In heaven, I hope," she said as she choked back the tears. "Manang helped me end the pregnancy. I nearly died. It would have been better if I had."

For a long while, Josémaria sat clenching his fists until his fingernails drew blood from his palms. "It wasn't the child who needed killing," he finally said.

"Not a day passes that I don't think of that child. I've asked God to forgive me. I was hoping you could, too."

"Are you ... still able to have children?" he asked, dreading the answer.

"I don't know," she replied, thinking about the times she had been neither good nor careful. "There's a strong chance that I can't." Celestina stopped fighting it and let the tears come.

Shaken to his core, Josémaria nevertheless held her until she fell asleep from exhaustion. Then he laid her on the pillow — his damaged princess and the wreckage of his dreams. *I need a drink*, he thought as he got up to go to the mini-fridge he had installed in their bedroom. The shelves were stocked with coconut juice and sparkling water. Not a drop of alcohol in the whole house. Cursing, he slammed the door of the fridge and angrily sent a Tiffany lamp sailing across the credenza. Then he grabbed his car keys and ran downstairs. Outside, the city was still dark, and the air thick with sirens and the howls of feral dogs. He could smell the rain in the air. He called for Rocky to open the gates. The world might have been ending, and demons might already be walking the earth, but he did not give a damn. He needed a drink strong enough to erase this day from his brain. And he needed it now.

30

Broken

Things were never the same with the lovers in the days that followed. Conversations no longer flowed like music. In the house, the air felt heavy with unspoken anger. They tried, desperately, to make love the way they had before. But this joyful, lusty man who used to give her so much pleasure could no longer perform for her.

"Just hold me," Celestina told him one night. "It doesn't matter."

"Don't kid yourself," Josémaria snapped. "It absolutely matters."

He got dressed and stormed out, leaving Celestina alone in her house of ghosts.

From her window, she watched Rocky open the gates for Josémaria as he sped off into the neon lights of Remedios Circle. It hurt, but she had far too much pride to run after a man who was running away from her.

As she put her head down on the pillow, she felt something wedged between the mattress and the headboard. After some effort, she managed to pull it out. It was a small velvet box holding an exquisitely crafted ring. A night-blooming flower seemingly fashioned from moonlight and stars. At the centre was a perfect, round diamond surrounded by a halo of petals, made of white gold. Each petal was paved with smaller diamonds. She slipped it out of its cushion and put it on her ring finger. The white-gold band twined around her finger like tendrils of a vine. A tear fell from her eye as she realized what it was. She returned the ring to its resting place, closed the box, and put it on his dresser, next to the engraved cufflinks she had given him. The ring would have to go back to the shop. It was made for an epic romance, a love for the ages. This would-be bride simply could not measure up.

As she tried to find sleep that night, Celestina could sense she was being watched. Not by her great-aunt or Manang Rio, but by a malevolent presence. With her spirit at its lowest, darkest point, an ancient *malas* now had Celestina in its sights. Looking up, she could swear there were two spectral eyes staring down at her. She knew it was the Bangungot that took Manang Rio's life.

"Don't show her your weakness," Manang Rio whispered in Celestina's ear.

Summoning her strength, Celestina spoke to the presence, "No, you're not getting me. This is my house, not my tomb." And then she went to sleep knowing she had a bigger nightmare to face in her waking life.

*

The morning sun rose over the city by the bay. Outside the Manila Yacht Club, the silver Maserati glowed under the gentle sunlight. At the marina, Josémaria emerged from the cabin of *The Archangel*, where he had spent the night. He sat on the deck and looked out to the bay. Closing his eyes, he felt wings lifting him high above the city and beyond the marina.

To the east, he could see the great squatter colonies with shanties built out of old billboards, galvanized iron sheets, and truck tires. Many of the shanties had television antennas sticking out of their rusty roofs. To the west, he spotted a billboard advertising the future site of one of his father's developments — a gated community of mega-mansions equipped with their own boat docks, so residents could sidestep the city's epic traffic jams. Somewhere near the Baywalk, on the other side of Roxas Boulevard, he recognized the roof of an old low-rise building. It was the office of *Coup* publishing, where Celestina worked. His body felt a surge of longing, then anger, as he thought about her. *Oh, what a poisoned banquet you have served me.* His wings started faltering. Looking over his shoulder, he saw the pure white feathers turning into black, powdery mould. In an instant, he was plunging back to earth.

The sun was higher and hotter when Josémaria opened his eyes. He looked at his watch. It seemed improbable that more than an hour had passed. He was certain he had only closed his eyes for a few minutes. In any case, he should be getting ready for work. He went back to the cabin and looked for something suitable to wear. There was a navy-blue jacket and a striped pullover, which he recognized as his brother's. The jacket was a little tight, as Rafael had the streamlined physique of a swimmer, but it would have to do. He got dressed, splashed on some of his brother's cologne, and brushed his hair. Beside the hairbrush, he noticed a tray full of matchbooks and business cards left by various visitors and maintenance staff.

He picked up a matchbook bearing the image of a lithe Chinese girl done in spare, calligraphic black ink. Inside was an ad for The Pink Pearl Spa. "A Touch of Class. For Gentlemen Only," it proclaimed. He looked at the matchbook longer than he wanted to before putting it back. He had never paid for sex, never needed to, and he was not about to start now. The image on the matchbook looked back at him with an inviting smile. *Think of it as stress relief with a woman's touch*, it whispered. He picked up the matchbook again and looked for an address. It was in Binondo, Manila's original Chinese Quarter. He could use a quick massage before his long day, he told himself. His shoulders had been feeling quite sore lately.

*

As he drove toward the Chinese Quarter, Josémaria's mind was a blur, steering his car by instinct as if he had been to that particular spa a hundred times before. Perhaps it was the image of the girl on the matchbook, which was perched on his dashboard, directing him with her siren song. Once he was in Binondo, it was not long before he saw the sign for the spa and the flashing green light directing him to the underground parking lot.

He found parking near the elevator and was soon on his way to his relaxing massage. The elevator door slid open to the reception area, where the ambient sound of lapping waves on the stereo system underscored the permanent twilight of the establishment.

Josémaria liked the aesthetics of the place — especially the gold-tiled pond with the red koi. The spa looked like the love nest of a nobleman and his favourite concubine. A young man, dressed too sharply for his age and the time of day, greeted and presented him with a list of services.

"Just the steam room and a massage," Josémaria said.

"Very well, sir. We'll get you started by choosing your attendant."

The young man whisked him off to a room decorated with pastel drawings in the style of Toulouse-Lautrec. The main wall was dominated by what Josémaria knew to be a two-way mirror to protect his anonymity. At the young man's prompting, a parade of women in short rayon bathrobes filled the room on the other side of the mirror. The women were better looking than he'd expected. Toned bodies, tastefully made-up faces with good complexions. A few of the bolder ones struck beauty queen poses to show their assets. None of them piqued his interest, except for the waifish girl in a streetwise shredded bob. She was not posing or smiling. In fact, she seemed lost in her own thoughts, tapping her high heels to some unheard music.

"That girl," he said. "The punkish one."

"Yes, Nikki. Excellent choice, sir. I'll show you to your locker so you can get ready."

*

Half-sprawled on the bench, Josémaria let the room's fragrant steam dissolve his troubles. He smiled in anticipation of the promised stress relief with the masseuse he had chosen. The gentle hiss of the steam was punctuated by an odd electrical crackle. He looked around for the source, but it was hard to see anything through the haze.

"Mind if I sit here, son?" a man's voice asked.

"No, go ahead," Josémaria replied after a pause. He had not heard anyone come into the sauna. He was slightly annoyed at the intrusion, but politely made room for the man.

"Thanks, son. Come here often?"

"Nope," Josémaria replied without looking. "First time."

"You'll like this place. Colegialas and lonely housewives with talented hands. Very upscale. No whores."

Josémaria turned to say, "I don't mean to be rude, but ..."

Just then, the man's profile emerged from the steam. It was unmistakably the visage of Antonio Errantes, sharp as a satirist's pen — the iconic face on the serialized novellas that used to litter the servants' quarters of their home. But this was not the deranged, old storyteller he was rumoured to be. This was a man in his prime, not much older than Josémaria himself.

"I can see why my daughter picked you," Antonio said with an appraising look. "You're so much like me."

"I am nothing like you," Josémaria snapped.

"Oh? We're both restless, searching spirits, unafraid to write our own story. To find our own bliss. Maybe that's why we're both here. Looking for a *happy ending*."

Antonio's words lingered and filled the room, growing louder, not fading as they should. Josémaria's mind went back to the night of the blackout, with Celestina's harrowing confession. He remembered his last night with her when he could not perform his most basic function as a man. He saw the disappointment on her face when she said, "It doesn't matter ..." *The hell it doesn't!*

In an instant, Josémaria had Antonio by the neck and pinned to the bench. His hand balled into a fist and landed on Antonio's smirking face. Again and again, his fist found its target. He would pound that smirk down to blood and meat, pound it to oblivion. Antonio sneered through the blows, the cut lip, and bloodied nose. Then the room went blurry as the vent released another blast of steam. Antonio vanished, the same way he had appeared, leaving Josémaria crouching over an empty bench, his knuckles torn, a raging bull deprived of its kill.

A creak and a swoosh of cold air called Josémaria out of his head.

"Sir," the masseuse said through the partially opened door. "It's time for your massage."

"I'll be right out," he said after catching his breath.

"Very well. I'll be in the room across the hall."

The floor felt soft like quicksand as he stumbled out of the steam room, into a tiled hall, and then into a room lit with votive candles. The walls were decorated with erotic woodblock prints.

"Hello, there," Nikki the masseuse said as she relished the sight of the wildly attractive Mestiso. She noted his broad chest and thick muscles and glanced at his knuckles, which were red and chafed.

With a polite nod, Josémaria whipped off his towel and quickly arranged himself face down on the massage table.

"What brings you here?" she asked.

"Just a bit of relief from the madness."

"I can help you with that," she said as she started to untie her robe. She had seen nothing but potbellied businessmen and politicians since she arrived in Manila from Dumaguete. Perhaps her *swerte* was finally changing.

"You can keep that on," he stammered. The strange episode in the steam room had taken the edge off his desire. "I just want a straight massage. You know, a regular massage, without the extra *service*."

"You wouldn't be here if you just wanted a boring massage," she said, letting her robe fall open.

Deeply ashamed but desperate for a woman's touch on his skin, he surrendered himself to her hands. Occasionally, he opened his eyes to enjoy the girl's naked body, but her defiant gaze brought his thoughts right back to the one he was trying to forget. He avoided looking at her face and focused on the delicious strokes she delivered to his well-muscled legs and buttocks. He drifted off for a few minutes until he felt a gentle slap on his right butt cheek. "Time to turn over," she said.

He turned at her bidding and let her hands slither over his knotted muscles, bliss mingling with shame. Soon enough, her hands found their way between his thighs. With a catlike smile, she said, "A guy like you deserves a happy ending."

A familiar voice whispered in his ear. "I told you. You and I have so much in common."

*

It was two hours after noon at Celestina's office in *Coup*, and she had yet to take a lunch break. The sun was still in its full heat, but she decided to go up to the roof to get away from her desk for a while. Her midday escape, however, was interrupted by a call from the Twin Dragons Tower. It was Rocky.

"Miss, you'd better come home. There are some men here looking for Josémaria. They say he's been missing. Lille is with them right now."

Celestina spoke to her colleagues and quickly drove home to Malate. The traffic was light, and she did not have far to go. Outside the gates were three vehicles: a black Jeep, a grey late-model BMW, and a chauffeur-driven white Mercedes from the previous decade. She recognized the black Jeep owned by La Sulipeña's chef. Inside, Rocky was waiting for her.

"They're in your apartment with Lille," Rocky said as Celestina's car entered the gates.

She quickly parked her car and ran toward the building into the elevator, barely glancing at the students in the entrance hall where Lille held workshops. As the door slid closed, she said a prayer for Josémaria to turn up safely. The elevator soon opened to the great room where Lille was sitting with three men: Venicius the chef, a tall mestiso she recognized as Rafael San Miguel, and Josémaria's Tiyo Rico. Lille rose to her feet and introduced her to the visitors.

"Celestina, this is Josémaria's brother, Rafael. I believe you've already met his uncle, Rico San Miguel."

"Good to see you again, Celestina," Rico San Miguel said as he hugged her. "I only wish it were under happier circumstances."

Rafael smiled politely and held her hand briefly, saying little else. Josémaria's romance had caused considerable disruption in their social circles. He had assumed his younger brother had fallen for a gold digger. Seeing that Celestina was wearing a suit and appeared professional assured him she had a real job and was not just a mujer de cama. He looked around the apartment with his developer's eye and wondered how such a young woman had come to own this fine Peacetime-era property.

As Lille excused herself to get back to her students. Celestina thanked her friend, then turned to the chef to get the full story. "What's going on, Veni?"

"Josémaria is usually in by ten, but he did not even turn up for the lunch shift. He's not returning my EasyCall messages. I had a bad feeling, so I tried to call you at home. I spoke with Lille, who confirmed that he was not here."

"I got Veni's call around one o'clock," Rafael interjected. "I checked all the usual places he might be. The Polo Club, Tiyo Rico's place. The Yacht Club confirmed that he'd slept on our yacht last night. The security guard said Josémaria took off at around nine this morning. Do you have any idea where he might have gone?"

"I thought he might have gone home to Cameron's Court. I don't know where else he could be. We've been having some problems," Celestina confessed. "We had a fight last night, and he stormed off."

"You're having a rough patch. Every couple goes through it," Rico said kindly. "Whatever it is, I hope you two work it out."

Celestina smiled at the older man, touched that somebody was still supportive of their love.

"Do you think he's with Ysabel?" Rafael asked Celestina.

"I don't know. Do you?"

Rafael was already on his phone dialing Ysabel's number. After a brief exchange, Rafael handed the phone to Celestina. "She wants to talk to you."

Celestina braced herself for the pain that was coming.

"I honestly thought you'd last longer than the others," Ysabel said. "No, he's not with me. He's probably off with some new girl he found who knows where. Enjoy your karma."

"You have a good life, Ysabel. Thanks for your concern," Celestina said as she hung up.

"That went well," Rafael shrugged. "What now?"

"I'm going to call a private investigator," Rico San Miguel said in a sombre tone. "Someone we know. No police. We don't want this getting out."

"Do you think he's been kidnapped?" Celestina asked, alarmed.

"It's possible," Rafael replied. "One of our cousins was kidnapped when we were young. Thankfully, he escaped, unharmed. The kidnappers are more organized now, and they have more guns."

"In the meantime, let's all stay calm and keep in touch," Rico said. "Celestina, please call me if you hear anything."

Rafael handed Celestina his business card and smiled, this time more warmly. He did not think it proper to discuss business during a family crisis, but it would not hurt to plant the seed. "Thank you for your hospitality and your candour. This is an impressive property, by the way. Truly, one of a kind. I'm an architecture buff. Maybe we can sit down sometime, and you can tell me all about this place."

"I'd be happy to, Rafael," she said politely. "Please let me know if you hear from him."

"I'll show them out, Celestina," Venicius said. "Stay here in case he calls."

With the visitors gone, Celestina was left alone with her increasingly paranoid thoughts. Was Josémaria being tortured in some seedy warehouse? Had he been dumped in an estero and left for dead? She instinctively walked to the spot where the mini-bar used to be. It was now the designated spot for their growing collection of music. She put on a CD to quiet her fearful thoughts. Outside, dark clouds were gathering, and the wind blew fallen leaves into a circle dance. In a matter of minutes, the sky went from an almost unnatural blue to smoky grey. A mighty electrical crackle announced the storm, and the rain fell as if the sky had ripped open.

*

Forty-eight hours after he went missing, Josémaria quietly walked through the pedestrian gate of the Twin Dragons Tower. Nobody heard him come in — not Rocky, who was replacing some light-bulbs on the mezzanine, nor his girlfriend, Lucy, who was in the entrance hall vacuuming the rugs.

Celestina was in the kitchen, dressed for the office but still lingering, hoping her phone or pager would deliver some good news. As she turned around, he appeared in the doorway, unshaven and dressed in beach shorts and a T-shirt from an Ermita bar called the Wanchai Wench.

After a momentary shock, she rushed to him and welcomed him with her arms and lips. There were strange perfumes on him, scents that were not hers. She did not care. He was home safe, and that was all that mattered.

"Your family has been searching for you," she said. "We've all been worried to death. Where've you been?"

"I've been around. Just around ..." he said as he brushed away her caressing hands. His eyes were cold and dark, and his mouth was a hard, angry line.

"Listen, let's start again," Celestina implored. "We were so good together. It's not too late."

Her entreaty was met with a sneer as he pinned her against the wall.

"Oh, your sweet, lying tongue," he said. "We can't go back. Do you understand or should I demonstrate it for you?"

He reached beneath her dress and yanked her underpants down to her thighs. Then he pulled down his shorts to give her the pain and punishment he thought she deserved. Tugging and cursing, he attempted to push himself in.

"Go ahead," she taunted. "Prove yourself a bigger monster than my father."

Burning with shame, he pulled up his shorts and fled, feeling her eyes looking at him with contempt.

Still trembling, Celestina went upstairs, threw out her clothes in the garbage bin, and turned on her shower. There, she had a good, long cry, for herself and for Josémaria. When she was done, she dried herself and went back to the bedroom to call Venicius. She was grateful she got his answering machine, as she was in no shape to talk to anyone. After leaving a brief message about Josémaria's reappearance, she put on a clean dress and went downstairs to gather her things. She needed to tie up loose ends at the office. They were going to have to do without her for a few days.

31

From the Hearth

Following an unusually cold September was the second consecutive week of warmth in October, what Canadians called an Indian Summer. Stella Sytanco Errantes was settling into her new home in Markham, purchased with a loan from her mother. She went out to the patio to clean the ashes from the potbellied stove. It was late in the afternoon and evening was coming soon. She wanted to be ready for when the sun was no longer around to warm the air.

The patio, which came with the antique stove, was her favourite part of her house, and she was determined to sit outside until the cold winds and snow forced her indoors. This was her first autumn in Canada. Her cousins had already warned her about the Canadian winters, when the temperature goes down to minus twenty Celsius or worse. The wind chill alone, they said, will make you call out to all the martyrs and saints. Regardless, Stella had diligently read books, taken courses, and interviewed people about her new country. She felt prepared for anything.

With the ash drawer emptied and cleaned, she was ready to start another fire — her sixth. She had taken lessons from a local handyman, and she now felt like an old hand. Confidently, she opened the flue on the chimney pipe so the smoke would vent away from her patio. Then she put some balled up newspapers on the floor of the stove and made a teepee of dried twigs. With a long match, she lit the papers and let them burn until they ignited the kindling. She added a few small logs she had gotten from the local hardware store, closed the door, and adjusted the vents to make sure the fire got plenty of oxygen. She loved the crackling sound of burning pine and its warmth on her skin. With the fire going low and slow, she sat down with her tea and *Wilderness Tips*, the collection of short stories by Canadian author Margaret Atwood.

It was a Sunday, and tomorrow Stella would start working at her cousin Ernesto's real estate brokerage so she could get some Canadian job experience. With hard work and a bit of *swerte*, she could eventually move on to other opportunities. She had thoroughly enjoyed the hospitality of Ernesto's family during the summer, when he'd offered her the use of a spacious in-law suite on their property. It had been a long time since she'd felt like part of a family, but she did not want to impose on them any longer. Thankfully, she found this house with Ernesto's help — a two-bedroom bungalow with a large lot. It had been owned by a widow who recently passed away. It had decent bones and was well maintained, if a bit dated. And it was south-facing, which was very auspicious. For now, this house and the land it was built on suited her.

As the pine firewood scented the air, Stella thought to herself that Canada seemed like a good place to rekindle the modest hopes and dreams she once had. It was a decent country, even if it was a bit dull. The suburbs were recently built, orderly, and clean. Motorists obeyed the rules of the road, and cops did not expect bribes. It was so unlike the creeping decay and unrelenting chaos of the Philippines. In Canada, cleaning ladies drove nice cars, and everyone seemed middle class, even those who were not. By the same token, people were not so obsessed with wealth, family names, and social status. She could build a life of her own choosing here in Canada, where nobody aside from her cousins would know of the heiress who lost her *mana* for defying the great Sebastien Sytanco.

The rustling wind dance of fallen leaves called Stella back from her thoughts. As she turned to the patio table to pour herself another cup of tea, she saw a familiar creature standing on the edge of her patio. It was a feral cat that lived in the ravine behind her backyard. It had a ruddy brown coat and sad, expressive eyes that reminded her of her daughter. She had tried to pet it many times, but it was skittish and always ran back to the ravine. Still, it kept coming to visit, perhaps attracted by the warmth of the stove. Was it possible to tame it again? Stella wondered. To teach it to sit by the fireplace in a house they could both call home? She took the saucer of her Wedgwood teacup, poured a bit of cream in it, and set it down by the stove.

The feline's ears seemed to perk up when it heard the sound of bone china against the patio tile. Stella stood back as the cat slowly approached her proffered treat. After lapping up most of the cream, it meowed softly and finally sat down by the stove. Stella fought the urge to pet it for fear of scaring it away. Instead, she sat down and quietly went back to her book.

The sun had descended by the time Stella finished reading, and her feline guest was gone. But she had a feeling it would be back soon. She opened the door of the stove and put another log on the fire. Sparks flew out of the chamber and into the early evening breeze, and she felt the tiniest of embers glowing within her heart, which for so long had been cold and dark.

32

Where the Monster Lives

Celestina drove past faded billboards and grassy fields on the road to Tayabas. It was the same route the pilgrims and climbers had taken to Mount Banahaw. She got off the highway and drove down the skinny country road she once swore she would never take. She remembered the recent long-distance telephone conversation in which her mother had said, "Are you sure you're up to this? I can talk to him. You don't have to do this."

I'm ready, Mama. It's time to put this nightmare to rest. One way or another.

The rains came just as she approached the last leg of her journey: the steep, narrow road aptly called Calvario. She felt her wheels spinning as the dirt road quickly turned into mud. She let the car slide back before trying again, left foot on the clutch, right foot on the gas pedal, releasing the clutch pedal slowly as she stepped on the gas. In a moment of mercenary regret, she chided herself for refusing Josémaria's offer to buy her the latest Mazda. She would be the only San Miguel girlfriend who did not come away with shiny wheels or a diamond bauble. *Good job, Celestina. That's what you get for thinking with your heart.*

She managed to get up the slippery incline and continued through the small village lined with small vegetable farms and old wooden houses built on stilts. She spotted the colonial-style stone house with crumbling, vine-covered walls, as her mother had described to her. A faded wooden sign above the gate confirmed that she had arrived at Villa Errantes. Umbrella in hand, Celestina pushed the gate open and walked into an unkempt garden, barely dodging chickens who pecked at garden insects with deadly precision. Farther in, the sound of a TV soap opera mingled with the raindrops on her umbrella. She walked to the front door and rang the old iron bell. An old woman in a leaf-print housedress answered the door. She was nearly as tall as Celestina, solidly built, and had a high, slightly wide nose. Although it had been years since they'd last seen each other, Celestina immediately recognized the aunt who looked most like her father.

"Tiya Marta, it's me, Celestina. It's been a long time."

An old, familiar anger stirred in Marta's belly as she stared at the unmistakable features of a Sytanco spawn. Chinese blood, she often said, was like a mantsa on a garment. It turned up, wash after wash, generation after generation, like a stubborn stain that won't come out. She had warned her brother about getting mixed up with that woman and her family. Of course, there was no reasoning with young men in heat.

"Of course, I remember you," Marta smiled through gritted teeth. "Your mother called from Canada to tell me you wanted to visit us. Come in."

Marta snapped her fingers to rouse the maid from her soap opera. "Oy, Kulasa! Time to work. Iced soft drink and merienda for my famous niece here. Fix her a Hardinera sandwich. She's going to be a San Miguel soon, you know."

As her aunt complained about the quality of housemaids these days, Celestina laughed uneasily. "They're all Bisaya, not very hardworking," her aunt sneered.

Celestina had always been put off by her aunt. Marta talked before thinking and was prone to remarks that had long been banished by polite society.

"So, when is the wedding?" Marta asked eagerly. "Not good to wait too long. Got to seal the deal."

"You're a little late with your tsismis, Tiya," Celestina said as she sipped her cold drink. "Jo-ma and I broke up."

"Aye, por que? Why you break up?! You could have given us real mestiso children. You find a prize like that, you grab it and don't let go!"

"I don't want to talk about it. I came here to talk to Papang. How is he?"

With a deep sigh and a sign of the cross, Marta began her litany of complaints. "You know your mama had placed him in a first-class institution in Antipolo. It was very nice, just like a hotel. But he terrified the other patients with his nightly talks with espíritus, and the orderlies said garapons and other things would start moving and falling off shelves. So, they kicked out your father even when your mother offered to pay extra. Now of course, I get stuck taking care of him because I'm a matandang dalaga."

Celestina remembered her long-ago talk with her mother about old maids. Her mother was of the view that it was the biggest *malas* a woman could suffer. The nuns at school taught Celestina a more charitable perspective. Long before the advent of political correctness, the nuns reminded their students that "single blessedness" was a vocation, a call to holiness and service, just like religious life and married life. It was obvious that Tiya Marta did not share the nuns' view, but Celestina was suddenly grateful that she did not have to care for her own tormentor.

"How is his health these days, Tiya?"

"He's not as strong as he used to be. He gets dizzy and sleeps a lot. He refuses to see a doctor. His mind comes and goes. Sometimes, he's just like his old self. Other times, he doesn't know what year it is and mumbles about witches and demons stalking him. He asks for you a lot. 'Where's my wife, Celestina?' he says. I think he confuses you with your mother."

"May I see him?"

"He's in the guest house at the back. He likes to be alone. Finish your Hardinera sandwich, then we'll go visit him."

After she finished eating, Celestina followed her aunt to the back of Villa Errantes, past the old java plum tree and swarms of flies getting drunk on the fallen fruit. They could hear the television blaring from the guest house. A talent show contestant was in the middle of butchering "I Will Always Love You." Peeking through the window, Marta said, "He's napping." She gently opened the door into a simply furnished room with a bookshelf, a stool, and a bamboo daybed where the sleeping Antonio was curled up, draped in a light blanket. Celestina's nose picked up the faint scent of kerosene.

Marta turned off the television and walked to the daybed to wake her brother. Celestina's eyes were drawn to the coffee cans on the feet of the daybed. The coffee cans were filled with water with an oily film floating on top. Upon closer inspection, she saw carcasses of ants perished in the coffee can moats.

"Wake up, Antonio," Marta nudged. "You have a bisita."

The napping man stirred, groaned, then rolled onto his back before opening his eyes. He looked at the young woman accompanying his sister, and after a moment of confusion, smiled and said, "It's you. I've been waiting."

Celestina saw a flicker of the erstwhile gothic Maestro in his now-cloudy eyes. She was shocked to see how much he had aged. His thick reddish-brown hair was now a dirty grey mop. The broad shoulders, where she used to lay her head and cry, were now loose skin and sharp bones. A scraggly beard grew where his impeccably groomed goatee used to be. His lip was split, and there was a shadow of a gash on his cheekbone. She wondered if he had taken a fall. She almost felt sorry for him. Turning to her aunt, she said, "I would like to speak to him alone, please."

Marta looked to her brother and said something in Chavacano. Antonio sat up, whispered something in response, and promptly waved her away. Turning to Celestina, he said, "Sit down," as he tapped the edge of his daybed. "It's so nice of you to finally visit."

Celestina ignored his proffered seat and opted for the stool.

"Why do you harass me with your letters?" she asked. "Aren't you done ruining my life? What do you want from me?"

"If you can't forgive me, at least acknowledge me. Let me back into your life. Even a little bit," he said sadly. "I'm still your father."

"I acknowledge that I am, unfortunately, very much my father's daughter. But as much as I want to move forward, some things can't be forgiven. You deserve everything you got. And whatever you have coming."

"You're hard, like ice and steel. Like your mother. I can certainly pick them," he laughed bitterly before falling into a fit of coughing.

Celestina poured him a drink of water but fought the urge to touch his knotted hands. He drank the water gratefully, as if it were fine wine, before handing the glass back to her. The effort seemed to tire him, and he put his head back on one of the pillows.

"Thank you, my dear," he said, reaching out to stroke her knee.

Her whole being recoiled from his touch. It brought her back to the night of the movie premiere and to all the other nights when he would crawl into her bed to beg for her love.

In a fit of white rage, Celestina grabbed one of his pillows and began to shove it in his face. "You filthy, filthy old pig," she hissed. "You orphaned me that night. Do you understand? You deprived me of a father, and you broke our family. Now you want to ruin the rest of my life. Tell me why you don't deserve to die."

His arm flailed helplessly as he struggled against her. Once, he could hold her down while having his way with her. Today, he was the prey, and she was his monster.

She pressed down harder until she heard his muffled cries under the pillow. She then came to her senses and loosened her grip, thankful she had not succeeded in smothering him.

Laughing, he flung off the pillow and said, "You've got fire. I like that in a girl."

"Papang?!" she said in shock. He was no longer the frail old man who spent his days staring at the TV screen. He was once again the gothic Maestro, the king of young Celestina's world.

"Hi, baby! You're looking good."

Terrified, Celestina bolted for the door and pulled with all her strength. The door, which the elderly Marta had opened with no effort, was now as immovable as a steel vault.

Antonio calmly threw off his blanket, got up, and moved toward Celestina with an amused expression. "The humidity here makes the wood swell," he smirked.

She ran to the window and pulled the curtain open, only to realize the window had steel bars outside. She slammed her fist on the windowsill, cursing herself. *Damn it. Damn me. Damn this hellmouth of a house. I shouldn't have come.*

"No need to run. I won't hurt you," he said. "I'm just a father who wants to talk to his daughter."

And instantly, Antonio was the frail old man again, begging for a shred of acknowledgement from his estranged child.

He's messing with your mind, Celestina told herself. *Getting you to crack. Hell, you're already cracked. Just face it. You'll never, ever be whole. You'll always be broken.*

"Come, hija," the old man asked. "Let's have a drink together in the kitchen."

He parted the curtain that separated the main room from the rest of the guesthouse. To the side was the bedroom, and at the back was a small kitchen.

Celestina followed him in a daze as he walked with slow, shuffling steps, his tsinelas scraping the floor as he made his way to the back. The kitchen was reasonably tidy, and it had a window that looked out into a garden with a large banana plant. Beside the window was an old narra dining table fitted with a glass tabletop.

Celestina sat numbly down on one of the mismatched chairs while he rummaged in the refrigerator, like a troll looking for his treasure.

"Here it is," he said, as he hobbled over to the table with a slim, burgundy-coloured wine bottle and two small drinking glasses. "Your mother sent this from Canada for my birthday. Sparkling ice wine made from Vidal grapes, harvested frozen on the vine during those bone-chilling Canadian winters. All the sweetness of the noble grape wrapped in champagne effervescence. Quite expensive, I'm told."

He handed her the bottle saying, "You know your way around fine wines. Would you mind popping this open for me? These hands aren't what they used to be."

She took the bottle and removed the wire cage that held the cork in place. She then twisted the base of the bottle while holding the cork. A slight hiss, then a soft pop filled the kitchen as she uncorked the bottle.

"Very good, my dear," he said, inhaling the aroma of dark cherries, honey, and toffee. "Ah, my lovely daughter and the nectar of the gods. I can't think of a more perfect despedida."

"Despedida?" Celestina asked, confused. "Are you leaving? Moving to another place?"

"No. I'm just tired of living in this decrepit body. I'm ready to meet my Maker, as they say. Maybe this will be my last drink on earth."

"You used to put away half a bottle of Scotch like it was nothing but soda," Celestina said with a skeptical smile. "It would take a lot more than a little glass of wine to kill you."

"Those days of Scotch drinking are long gone. My liver is wrecked, and I'm severely diabetic now. I don't need a doctor to tell me. I know it, and the ants in this place know it. They're all lining up for the buffet."

Celestina felt a chill as she slowly realized what her father was saying.

"There's probably more sugar in this little glass than in a bottle of Coke. It should do the job," he said, as he pushed his glass toward her to be filled.

Celestina took the glass and placed it next to the wine bottle.

"Do it," he urged. "I'll drift off into the big sleep. Your aunt will be relieved of her burden. Your mother will be free … no more guilt over a sick husband she can't divorce. And you, you'll get your vengeance or justice, whatever you want to call it. Everybody wins."

"That's a big thing to ask," she said as her fingers touched the frosty bottle.

"I know," he replied. "But think of the relief you'll feel when I'm gone."

"May I try the wine?" Celestina asked after some thought.

"Be my guest."

She poured herself a glass and inhaled deeply. She had not touched alcohol in months. She drank slowly, sipping the rose-coloured liquid while tiny bubbles danced on her tongue. As it went down in an intoxicating velvety finish, she said, "You're right. This *is* ambrosia."

She touched the bottle and looked him in the eye.

"Go on," he said. "Let's have a toast."

Trembling, she poured out two glasses and set the bottle down.

"Are you sure about this, Papang?" she asked as she braced herself on the glass tabletop.

"I am," he said.

As she glanced at the glasses in front of her, she sensed the words *into your hands*. No more than a low whisper, they were spoken to her from within, bypassing her ears, but resonating like thunder in every fibre of her body. As the words rose to her lips, she knew what they meant and she knew what she had to do.

With one swift motion, her arm swept across the tabletop, sending both glasses and bottle flying across the room, to the other side of the kitchen, smashing on the stone floor. She closed her eyes and listened to the music of shattering glass. It sounded like tiny bells with razor edges.

"You crafty little minx!" Antonio said as he surveyed the wreckage of his planned final moments. His eyes were blazing, but there was a hint of amusement in his tone.

"Sorry, Papang," Celestina said. "You'll have to catch another ride to your destination. I'm not going that way."

With that, Celestina bade him goodbye and walked out the back door, thinking, *I leave your fate in God's hands. Bahala na ang Diyos sa iyo.* For the first time in years, she felt the leaden darkness lift from her spirit.

*

Two days after Celestina's visit to her father, a package arrived at the Twin Dragons Tower. Rocky handed it to Celestina, saying, "There's no stamp or address, miss. Just your name."

Carefully, she unwrapped the package. Inside was the original manuscript of *The Book of Whys*, written and illustrated in her father's own hand and bound in goatskin leather. She had almost forgotten he'd once penned a book inspired by one child's boundless curiosity. She looked for her favourite, "The Sea in Me (Why Tears are Salty)."

In the dedication page, he had written, "To Celestina, a little piece of heaven who graced my life's purgatory."

She wept and said a prayer for the father she had once loved more than anyone in the world. And at bedtime, she took the book with her and fell asleep to the storyteller's voice, the way she had when she was a child.

She dreamed of Manang Rio that night. In the dream, Celestina was at the bus terminal waving goodbye to Manang and a little girl. "I'm going home to my probinsiya now," the old housekeeper said. "Don't worry, I'll take good care of her. Pray for our safe trip."

After that, the old woman's chair never again creaked, nor did the lamps turn on by themselves. One less ghost in Celestina's house.

✷

The sampaguita garden swirled with frothy dresses, chaperones, and girlish laughter. It was many full moons ago when Josémaria had planted that garden for Celestina. He'd worn a sauce-stained apron and a lovestruck grin, and she had been draped in white silk. Tonight, the garden was blooming for another girl — his goddaughter Katrina, the daughter of Venicius. She had just turned fourteen.

The birthday party was a good idea, Josémaria thought as he followed the evening's festivities from the gazebo. This was his chance to re-christen the place with a memory that was not attached to pain and heartbreak. He watched Katrina and her group of friends dancing to a British pop group called the Spice Girls. Dressed in tulle and bursting with exuberance, they were pure sweetness. Why not? Life was good for them, and it would only get better.

Katrina watched him standing there on his perch, casually elegant in his white suit, looking very much like a movie star from a bygone era. Her heart beat a little faster, and she pushed an errant lock of hair back in place.

"Tell your hot ninong he can babysit me anytime," whispered Katrina's precocious friend.

She slapped her friend on the arm, even as she felt her own face flushing as crimson as a macopa fruit. "Shut up! You're so gross," she said.

Katrina flashed her godfather a smile and waved him over. "Come and dance with us," she called out over the music.

He shook his head and threw up his hands to protest. "Not my music," he said with a laugh.

"Oh, don't be a killjoy," a familiar voice said from behind. "Go dance with the girls."

Josémaria turned around, but he already knew who it was. "This is a private function. By invitation only," he replied.

"Sorry, I didn't mean to intrude," Antonio Errantes said. "I just wanted to see how you were doing. Things got a bit too heated in the bathhouse."

"I have nothing to say to you."

"Well, can I just say that your goddaughter is lovely?"

"Do you have a point or are you simply rambling?"

"The young princess has eyes for you. Don't bother to tell me you haven't noticed. I know you have."

"Don't be disgusting. It's just a schoolgirl crush."

"Sometimes, son, you must get them while they're fresh from heaven. Before life taints them."

"This conversation ends right now. Show yourself out or I'm calling security."

"No need for that. I'm just saying … in that garden lies the salve for all that ails your soul … and body. Think about it."

With that, Antonio disappeared into the night breeze.

Just then, Josémaria saw Katrina walking toward the gazebo with her graceful, athletic strides. Almost a woman, but still a tomboy at heart, clearly more comfortable in riding clothes than formal dress.

"You look so lonesome up here all alone," she said. "Come dance with us."

"Well, okay, Catty. As long as it's not to the Spice Girls."

"Don't call me Catty anymore. You and Papa embarrass me."

"Sorry, force of habit. You were in diapers when we first met," he teased.

"Say that to my friends, and I'll never talk to you again," she said.

Katrina marched back to the dance floor with Josémaria in tow. The delighted girls surrounded him as the DJ put on a Bon Jovi song. For the first time since his breakup with Celestina, he forgot about his troubles and surrendered to the sheer joy of dancing. After several rock and dance tunes, the DJ put on a slow saxophone piece so the guests could catch their breath.

"Thanks, Katrina. That was so much fun," Josémaria said as he attempted to leave the dance floor.

"Wait. I love Kenny G. Would you dance this one with me?"

As a gentleman, he could not very well refuse the young lady's invitation, so he took her in his arms for a proper slow dance. His eyes delighted in her youthful radiance, noting her dewy olive skin, long-lashed eyes, and cameo profile. The braces on her teeth added a final, charming touch to the whole picture. She looked a lot like a young Ysabel, he thought. With a hint of Celestina's fire. God help men when she really learns to wield her charms. As they danced, he noticed that her gangly child's body was starting to round out with little breasts and a hint of curves at the hips.

"I saw you dance once," Katrina said. "It was the coming-out party of Cousin Inez. You were with Ysabel."

"Oh, that makes me feel ancient," he said with a sad laugh.

"You looked like a prince," she said without embarrassment. "I promised myself I would dance with you someday."

"I'm very flattered," he said as he felt her head resting on his chest. He prayed for the music to come to an end, but Kenny G showed no signs of tiring.

"I think it's time I brought you back to your parents inside," he finally said. "You've had a long night, birthday girl."

"No, not yet!"

"Okay. A walk around the grounds, and then back to your parents."

"Fine," she pouted.

He offered the girl his arm and they walked until they reached the great dancing fountain in front of the restaurant. "Here," he said reaching into his pocket for a coin. "Make a wish."

She closed her eyes then tossed the coin in the water.

"What did you wish for?" he asked.

Silent and trembling, she moved closer to him, her lips quivering ever so slightly. He fought the urge to hold her because he knew he would not stop there.

"I'll be an old man soon enough, Katrina," he spoke. "You don't want to be stuck with me when you're twenty and just starting to live."

"You'll never be old. You'll always be golden. I know it."

A tear fell from her eye as she finished speaking. He gave her his handkerchief and said, "Goodnight, Katrina. Happy Birthday. Tell your parents I had to go."

Josémaria walked away quickly then sprinted the rest of the way to his car. As he started the engine, he could hear Antonio Errantes laughing at him. Josémaria stepped on the gas and drove — away from the restaurant, the garden, the girl, and his own restive demons. Antonio's voice stayed with him even as the car exited the walls of the old city. *She was giving you the keys to the kingdom,* Antonio said. *What kind of man turns that down?*

Go to hell, Antonio! A real man knows how to control his monsters.

33

The Flame

Celestina emerged from the 11:30 mass and into the crowded, sun-drenched plaza of Our Lady of Remedies Church. Rojo and Lille came out soon after.

"C'mon, we're treating you to lunch at Guernica," Rojo said. "It'll be your despedida."

"I won't say no to that. I'm dying for a proper paella," Celestina said. "I'll catch up with you. I just want to buy some candles."

She walked to the crone's stall and picked three candles shaped like the Virgin Mary: a green one for her great-aunt, a sky blue one for Manang, and a rose one for the little girl in her dreams. She prayed silently as the old woman lit the candles.

"I'm glad I found you," a familiar voice said as she finished with the sign of the cross. "Rocky told me you'd be here."

It was the voice of past caresses, soft kisses, and other delicious things she should not be thinking about after prayer. She turned and offered Josémaria a shy smile. "How are you, Jo-ma?" she said. He looked a little older, and there was deeply etched pain in his eyes.

"I've been better," he shrugged. "I came by to pick up some things. You're looking well. How are you keeping, Celestina?"

"I've been taking care of a few things I've neglected for a very long time."

"I need to do that too."

"Are you back at Cameron's Court?"

"No, it was way past time for me to leave the family nest. I set up a loft on the upper floor of La Sulipeña. I'm staying there for now, but I'll be leaving the city soon."

"Oh? That's certainly unexpected news," she said as she felt her heart wilt.

"I sold my share of the business to Veni. I also sold the cars and some properties I owned. I bought a small island, by Palawan. I'm just going to disappear there for a while. Put myself together again. Find a new dream."

"I see … I'm leaving too," she said.

"So, I heard."

"I'll be in Canada for a while. Trying to make things right with my mother."

"I'm glad you're doing that. Family is a blessing. It doesn't always seem that way, but even an imperfect one is better than none," he said.

"I just hope it's not too late."

"When are you coming back?"

"I don't know. I may stay if I like it," she replied. "Maybe it's time for a change."

"What about our … I mean, *your* house?"

"Rojo will look after it while I'm gone. Your brother said he'd make me a very good offer if I ever want to sell."

"Sell it to my brother?" Josémaria blurted out. "No! Sell it to me."

"Why would you buy the house you ran away from, Jo-ma?"

"Because …" Josémaria paused while trying to figure out why he had made such a rash offer. "Because it was ours. Our meals, our dreams for the future. Our life together. I can't stand the thought of anyone else having it."

They stood silent amidst the echo of these words, wondering if they could somehow pull love out of this bonfire.

"Damn you!" she finally spoke. "If you feel that way, why don't you come back?"

"You think I don't want to? You think I don't burn for you every night? Trust me, I'll be no good to you like this."

Passersby and lingering churchgoers slowed their strides to gawk at the lovers' spat. They looked away uneasily when they saw the man's tears. Now the woman was crying too.

Seeing her tears, Josémaria composed himself and took her in his arms, saying, "I'm sorry, Celestina. You know we both have work to do. You and I must put our houses in order."

"I hate it," she sobbed. "I hate it …"

After a silent moment, he took her hand and led her to the stone bench in the far corner of the church plaza. There, they sat until they had both calmed themselves and strengthened their will to face the inevitable.

"Forgive me," he began, "for the way I acted last time. That was no way for a man to treat his woman."

"I forgive you. I'm sorry too," she said. "I should have told you the truth. I didn't want to lose you."

"It was a harsh truth for me to swallow," he replied. "But that's nothing compared to what you had to live through."

"I've already let go of that. Right now, I just need you hold me. I want to remember how good that feels … before I go," she said softly.

He wrapped his arm around her and whispered back, "I love you, Celestina. Despite everything." With that, he slipped a small, velvety object into her cupped hand. It was the ring box she had discovered the night he left the house. Inside was the glorious night blossom ring, its diamonds sparkling like fallen stars under the midday sun. "Remember us when you wear this ring."

Then he kissed her for all the rainy days they would spend alone. A kiss to heat her long winters in a foreign land. A kiss for the nights they would burn. And she kissed him back for the time they would be apart.

Celestina said goodbye to her tragic Mestiso, but the memory of their blazing love would live on, like a fire inside her, as she made a new life for herself under the northern sky.

Across the plaza, in her stall, the crone picked up two red candles and twisted their wicks together. She lit them and said a prayer for the princess of the dragon gates house and for her tarnished golden prince. To this day, people in the Malate district sometimes see mysterious flickering lights — appearing briefly in glass windows, tabletops, and even in puddles left by seasonal rains. Somewhere, somehow, those two candles are still burning as one flame, holding out hope that the lovers for whom the flame was ignited will once again be together in their undying love.

Acknowledgements

Writing a novel is, for the most part, a solitary journey that's lonely even for natural introverts. I want to acknowledge the amazing people who graced my life, inspired me, cheered me on, and accompanied me on this trip.

A million thanks to Paul Chetcuti, my spouse, my first and best reader, and my Canadian Shield of common sense in this increasingly mad world. To Sofia, my beautiful daughter, thank you for being my cheerleader.

To Socorro and Nestor Gonzalez, my late parents, thank you for giving me your love and support and for passing on such fantastic stories. I hope I did justice to them. To my siblings, Bob and Cynthia Gonzalez, thank you for the moral and material support you provided during this trip. Special thanks to Ate Cynthia for reading my manuscript before it was a book.

Thank you to Kim Echlin and Helen Humphreys, my writing teachers at the University of Toronto Creative Writing program, for helping me develop my characters and hone my craft. I also want to acknowledge my advertising mentors, the late Antonio

Santos, Vince Pozon, and Rowena Velasquez, who showed me how to write, with purpose and style, for the real world.

To my early readers — Malu Marella, Carla Moreira, Glynis Tao, Aga Maksimowska, Doris Muise, Tracey McGillivray, and Zvi Gilbert — thank you for your feedback, encouragement, and friendship. To Carol Tansingco, Ali Dy, and Ethel Panlilio, thanks for answering my out-of-the-blue questions and for being my BFFs. I also want to thank Patty Rivera and Thom Ernst for their invaluable support on the last leg of this journey.

I want to acknowledge Gene Gonzalez, whose books and restaurants greatly expanded my knowledge and appreciation of Filipino food. To my friends, the late Jover Layno and Celeste Bueno, thanks for the inspiration and friendship, and to Red Mansueto, thanks for the lessons in art, advertising, and life.

I want to say a very special thank-you to my editor, Julia Kim, who found my manuscript in the slush pile and fought for it on my behalf. You rock! I also want to acknowledge Kwame Scott Fraser, who helped Julia acquire this story, as well as Erin Pinksen, my project editor, my copy editor, Jen Hale, and the rest of the Dundurn team. Thank you for your support.

Finally, I give thanks to God for the gift of writing and story-telling, and for all the angels he sent my way during this journey.

About the Author

Clarissa Trinidad Gonzalez was born and raised in Manila, where she grew up steeped in her family's colourful personalities and stranger-than-fiction stories. She developed a love for philosophy, modern classics, and drama in university. She then worked in the advertising industry, honing her craft as a copywriter, and later became associate creative director. She spent a good part of her twenties trekking around the Philippines, sampling regional food, and experiencing the joie de vivre and hospitality of her fellow Filipinos from Batanes to Mindanao.

She moved to Canada in the mid-nineties and worked as a technical designer for a Canadian retailer. She now works as a communications professional.

She studied creative writing at the University of Toronto and has published poetry in *Variety Crossing* journal, as well as online publications. She also received a Toronto Arts Council grant for an early version of *Celestina's House*, her debut novel.

When she's not writing, she likes to keep the memories of Philippine kitchens alive in her home in South Etobicoke, where she cocoons with her spouse and daughter as they plot their next family adventure.